Anne Borrowdale has spent many years working for the church in theological education, and is well-known as a speaker, writer, and occasional broadcaster. She lives in Oxford with her family, and is currently working on the final novel in her Leathwell trilogy.

Other books by Anne Borrowdale

PUBLISHED BY SPCK.
A Woman's Work
Distorted Images (Short listed for the Winifred Mary Stanford prize)
Reconstructing Family Values

PUBLISHED BY ASHTON PICKERING PUBLICATIONS
Messiahs Don't Fly (David Thomas Fiction-writing Award Winner, 2000)

An Inspector Falls

Anne Borrowdale

Ashton Pickering Publications

First published in Great Britain in 2000 by
Ashton Pickering Publications
44 Hollow Way Cowley OX4 2NH UK

Reprinted 2001
Reprinted 2002
Reprinted 2004

British Library Cataloguing-in-Publication Data
A catalogue record for this book is available from the British Library

ISBN 0-9534755-1-4

Cover Design: Claire Beadle 2000

The moral right of the author has been asserted

Printed by *Manuscript ReSearch Printing*
PO Box 33 Bicester Oxon OX26 4ZZ, U.K.
Tel: 01869 323447/322552   Fax: 01869 324096

Author's Note

I would like to extend my thanks to my sister and brother-in-law, for sharing their experience of schools and inspections with me; to the Revd David Barton for his comments on the manuscript; and to students and staff on the St Albans and Oxford Ministry Course for their patient answering of my sometimes obscure questions about church life. Any errors are, of course, my responsibility, and not theirs. My thanks are also due to my editor, Sonia Ribeiro, for her encouragement and helpful suggestions.

All characters in this publication are fictitious, and any resemblance to existing institutions, or to real persons, living or dead, is purely coincidental.

Anne Borrowdale,
Oxford 2000

One

Iain Sutherland inched his car down the school driveway behind an oblivious boy, whose why-hurry walk displayed complete disregard for the fact that afternoon lessons were already ten minutes old. The boy disappeared through the entrance. The Inspector smiled wryly as he directed his car between the pristine lines of a space designated VISITORS. The car park had been freshly whitewashed in anticipation of his visit; pupils were much less easily refurbished.

He switched off his engine. Indeterminate faces behind the glass of the long ground floor window in front of him eyed the slide of the silver Rover into the gap, then turned abruptly away, their attention demanded by the dimly visible teacher perched on the table at the front of the class. Iain checked himself briefly in the driving mirror, ensuring that the pasty he'd consumed during his journey had left no traces on his chin. He removed a speck from the left lens of his glasses, before drawing his briefcase across from the passenger seat.

Another school. Any school. A school like any other. Wellesley High this time: bright blue metal railings spiked to deter marauders, robust grass bordered by beds of straggling rose bushes, double-storeyed grey buildings housing some seven hundred pupils from eleven to sixteen and a staff of sixty-four, and every one of them surely rapturous at the thought of his arrival!

A car glided behind him and swung into a space a little further on. Someone else arriving for the meeting. Time he emerged. He got out, shuddering as the outside chill penetrated his suit. As he shut his door, a car alarm screamed abruptly across the car park, so loud he thought for a moment it was his own. The classroom window sprang to life once more, filled with faces gleeful at the disruption on this otherwise ordinary Tuesday afternoon. The white hatchback which had just arrived was flashing its lights, blaring for attention. He locked his car and approached it.

A woman in a black coat straightened up from scrabbling on the ground for fallen keys, the red of her gloves a gleam of colour against the

9

tarmac. 'Bloody thing! I hate you!' he heard her mutter, as she aimed the fob vindictively at the car to silence the screeching.

'Good afternoon,' Iain said politely.

She turned, startled, staring at him while colour rose in her face. An attractive woman, a fraction taller than him in her heels, with dark hair drawn back loosely from an oval face, discreet make-up, and animated blue eyes that dispelled formality. Embarrassment lent her youth, though fine lines discernible on her skin suggested maturity.

'Sorry. I didn't realise there was someone there. I will keep setting it off.' She opened a pocket on the side of a bulging leather handbag, and dropped the keys inside.

'Perhaps it's oversensitive,' he said. 'You should get it checked.'

She looked at him more closely. 'You wouldn't be our Reggie by any chance? Alex Cowley mentioned someone Scottish, and I can't help noticing ...'

He smiled. 'You're obsairvant as well as up on the jargon. Iain Sutherland. How do you do?'

He held out his hand, and she pulled off a glove to grasp it with thin fingers.

'By, you've got cold hands!' he said.

'I know. My next car's going to have a heated steering wheel. And a silent alarm.'

'Does that not reduce the effectiveness somewhat?'

She laughed. 'Probably. I'm Alison Thompson, by the way. I'm a parent governor, come to hear you reassure us that inspections are for the good of the school, and no one should feel threatened. Fat chance of that. I was a teacher until last summer, and we went through it eighteen months ago, so I know what it feels like.'

'Where was that? Not one of mine, was it?' he asked, following her along the front of the school towards the entrance.

'No. Nottling. Near Leathwell. I wasn't intending to have anything to do with schools once I left, but they've had trouble recruiting governors, and I've got two boys here - it seemed important with the inspection coming up. It's quite a lot of extra work, but I convinced myself I'd be able to fit it in.' She looked round at him and shook her head, smiling. 'I shouldn't listen to myself. I have a tremendous capacity for self-deception.'

He couldn't help returning the smile. 'Don't we all?'

'Do come and sit down, Danny. You're late enough as it is. You must have

10

heard a car alarm go off before. Or was it you set it off? Is that what kept you - a spot of larceny?'

'I never did! I'm in 'ere, aren't I? I couldn't 'ave!' Danny, a small, pale youth rumoured to be able to circumvent most car alarms blindfold, made his way self-righteously to his seat, and plonked himself down.

Terry Howells suppressed the desire to continue peering through the window himself, and prepared to restore calm to his Year Nine History class.

Gemma, fortuitously placed beside the window, turned round to the boy three rows behind her. 'Here, James, wasn't that your mum?'

James Thompson, who had been studiously concentrating on his book ever since the cacophonous hatchback hove into view, shrank further down behind his table. A good-looking lad, with his mother's dark hair and blue eyes, crucified by embarrassment not only at having her come to the school, but at her drawing attention to herself in so clumsy a fashion.

'What you done now?' Matthew called from the other side of the room.

'Thank you, Gemma. Sit down, Matthew,' Terry said firmly. 'She's presumably here for the governors' meeting with the Inspector. In fact,' he added, realising the significance of the white-haired man with the grey suit and large briefcase, 'that was probably him, so I'd appreciate it if you were to at least *look* as if you were here to learn.'

'What ...?'

'Enough, Danny. Excitement over.'

'But ...'

'I said, enough! James, you must have read that page a good half dozen times. Are you going to share your brilliant conclusions with us?'

Terry's thoughts wandered as James stumbled through a surprisingly intelligent reply. So that was Sutherland. He was supposed to be fair, but they'd said that about the Registered Inspector last time Wellesley High had gone through this rigmarole, and look at how ineptly that had been carried out. Dear Alison was hardly improving matters. Pull your finger out and give a good impression, woman, he admonished her. We need all the help we can get.

Iain followed Alison through the front door, heavy on its automatic closer, and waited as she stopped at the school office to sign in, and organise visitors' badges. He wrote his name, noting that the colleague who would attend this meeting with him was, as expected, not yet here. When he turned, he found Alison had removed her coat, revealing a navy suit with a straight knee-length skirt and loose-fitting jacket over a pale blue blouse with an oddly narrow collar. He wondered idly what she did now. Another disillusioned teacher swapping the frustrations of low morale and scant reward for the lure of business, perhaps? Probably making a packet selling insurance.

'Ready?' she asked.

He nodded, and she set off through another set of doors into the long corridor that led to the Head's office.

'You've been here before, haven't you?' she said.

'Aye. Once. I met Mr Cowley and he gave me a brief tour.'

This second visit was bringing back a kaleidoscope of recollection. The new technology block, networked and sponsored by local business, designed to impress. The bare brickwork of the cavernous sports hall in the far corner of the playing field. The maze of corridors in the original nineteen twenties school building, with bright artwork adorning the walls and lightening the otherwise drab off-white paint and grey stone floors. The classrooms clustered around two inner courtyards, one of which was visible now through the windows to his right, a small area paved with khaki slabs, and a series of small conifers in terracotta tubs.

Iain smiled to himself, imagining the hasty transfer of the shrubs from someone's garden in order to impress the Inspector. They'd surely not been there three weeks ago when he'd passed this way to spend an hour with the Head and an ailing Chair of Governors who, his mind concentrated by the forthcoming inspection, was finally offering a long overdue resignation.

'We're in here.' Alison stopped outside a small lobby, and ushered him in through one of the two doors that opened off it. Sitting on low, sagging chairs randomly arranged in the Head's large office were two women and four men.

'This is Mr Sutherland,' Alison said. 'Is Alex not about?'

'Gone to Year Ten. Again.' The woman who spoke filled her chair so completely it was hard to imagine her extracting herself. 'I don't know what it is about Year Tens, they're always causing trouble. I remember a few years ago ...'

'Let me introduce the governors to you,' Alison interrupted. 'We're a select group, as you can see. There's a couple who couldn't make it today, and you'll meet the teacher governors later, but we haven't got our full complement anyway. We like to think we make up for it in quality.'

There was a twitch at her lip that suggested she had her own views of the membership. 'Denise Linnet is our Vice-Chair ...'

'Nice to meet you.' The garrulous woman stretched a chubby hand towards him, beaming brightly. 'I hope you didn't get held up in the roadworks. I got stuck the other day when ...'

'... And possibly the next Chair,' Alison continued. 'We're sorting it out at our meeting in a few weeks.'

Iain maintained his polite smile, while registering the puff of tension her words had created: a discord, it seemed, in the governing body. He observed the remaining governors with increased attention.

'Have a seat,' Alison said, completing the circle of introductions, and lowering herself gracefully into a chair.

He sat down next to her. 'What do you do, now you've left teaching?'

'Oh!' She stood up abruptly, 'No one's offered you a drink. Hasn't anyone organised coffee?'

'The machine's on,' Denise said, nodding at the shelf behind the Head's desk. 'I was about to dish it out, but I got so comfy sitting here, I hadn't the energy. Besides, these shoes have been killing me all day ...'

'Don't get up. I'll do it.'

The Headteacher swept into the room as Alison distributed the last of the coffee. He bent to shake Iain's hand. 'Terribly sorry not to be here to meet you.'

Iain juggled with his coffee cup and stood up. 'No problem. I've been well looked after by er ... Mrs ... er ... Miss ... er ... Thompson ...' He glanced down, noting the bareness of her left hand, which told him nothing.

'Stick with Alison, it's easier,' she responded.

'Well, why not be informal?' he said. 'Alison has introduced me to everybody, and my colleague may be a wee bit late, so why don't we make a start?'

The meeting followed its familiar course. Between them Iain, and later, his colleague, explained their role and fielded questions. Intelligent ones from most of them, and incomprehensible ones from Denise Linnet. Iain more than once caught Alison's eye, and sensed her amusement as he tried to frame a polite response. Perhaps she was more capable when exercising a role, but the Linnet woman's woolly meanderings during the meeting had tried even Iain's patience. How she could have got to be Vice-Chair, let alone be on the verge of becoming Chair, was beyond him, though he had met some dubiously qualified members of the breed in his time.

Had he been Alex Cowley, he would have been doing some frantic arm-twisting behind the scenes to try to persuade an alternative candidate to stand. Someone like Alison Thompson, for example, who, from his brief acquaintance with her, seemed eminently capable. He would not, of course, allow himself to hint at that preference - why, it would practically be a violation of his prime directive - but the idea loitered in his mind as Denise Linnet cornered him after the meeting, and began one of her interminable anecdotes. He disentangled himself, and approached the Head, who was in discussion with Alison by the coffee machine.

'Ah, Mr Sutherland.' Cowley stepped back to include him. 'I'm trying to persuade Alison to help us out.'

'To stand as Chair of Governors, you mean?'

'Good heavens, no!' Alison interjected. 'I've only just arrived.'

'Outsiders can be the best people,' Iain said. 'They bring a fresh approach.'

'That's what I've told her,' Alex laughed, 'but I'm afraid her mind's made up on this one. Would you excuse me a moment? I'd better check whether the staff are ready for you yet.'

'I am happy to be a governor,' Alison told Iain as the Head left the room. 'I don't want to be Chair, that's all.'

'Well, that's no matter. You have a pairfectly capable person lined up for the job,' he said evenly, trying to be fair.

Alison looked at him, her head tipped to one side, assessing his words. She opened her mouth to speak, and shut it again.

Realising that she understood him far more than he had intended, Iain rushed to move the conversation on. 'How do you find the school, as a parent?'

'I think it's going in the right direction. I admire Alex, and everyone's tried hard to settle my boys in, though it was an upheaval coming to a new area, what with their dad staying behind.'

'Could he not find a job around here?'

'He didn't want to,' she said, a trace of bitterness flitting across her face. 'We're separated.'

'I'm sorry, I didn't mean to be insensitive.'

She shrugged. 'One of those things.'

'Hardly. I've been through divorce myself, and I know how painful it is.'

She met his eyes guardedly, and he wondered whether his attempt at sympathy had sounded like a calculated declaration about his marital status:

we're both free, so how about it?

He could have disabused her, but Alex was at the door again, and he was needed.

The staff greeted the inspectors' arrival with hostile silence. Rows of uneasy people in easy chairs sitting tensely folded in on themselves, hands shielding their mouths, dreading exposure, while Iain and his colleague offered another well-rehearsed input and received the anxious questioning, or questioned them and assimilated their defensive replies. The staffroom clown creaked a few jokes on cue, unconvincingly nonchalant in the face of the inspection. The odd cynic tried to ask highly original and clever questions that Iain had answered countless times before. A chap called Howells decided to be the awkward bugger; there was always one. A round-shouldered man, with a heavy moustache weighing down a mouth moulded by mistrust, and a gleaming bald head surrounded by a thatch of grey-flecked hair. He slouched back in his chair, hands in pockets, challenging the rationale of inspections, complaining about the waste of time, the undermining of morale, and the disruption of lessons, by people who didn't know one end of a blackboard from another.

'I was a teacher for many years, and I've been a Head,' Iain told him. 'I do know what it's like.'

'Yeah, back in the sixties,' Howells muttered.

Iain smiled and touched his hair. 'Don't let this deceive you. I'm only thairty-two.' The staff looked at one another before deciding this was a joke at which it might be politic to laugh. 'No, I did leave my headship a few years ago, but I was seconded to run a school for two terms last year, so I do have some recent experience.'

He doubted the reassurances helped, and the suspicions of the Wellesley High staff were especially understandable, given the weaknesses identified at the school's previous inspection. The Head at the time had been a disaster, unable to appreciate that the frequent absences he took in the name of his back complaint created unacceptable pressures for the rest of the school. The Chairman of Governors had been little better: autocratic, unimaginative, and inclined to shield the Head in the face of their OFSTED report. Eventually, however, with staff leaving and results plummeting, even the Chairman had seen the point in negotiating the Head's departure. So Alex Cowley had arrived eighteen months ago to begin the task of turning things around, but with so much still remaining to be done, this school was more apprehensive than most ahead of its inspection.

Some interesting undercurrents there, Iain mused, as he began his drive home. The Head was impressive, but he had his work cut out, especially with the governing body struggling as it was. And if they appointed that appalling Linnet woman to be their new Chair, they really would be in trouble. He found himself hoping that Alison would reconsider standing for the post. Not that he anticipated building on the element of flirtation that had surfaced in his interactions with her today - inspections allowed no time for indulgences of that kind. But it would undoubtedly be better for the school; and given a choice between liaising with an attractive, competent, intelligent woman with legs, or a vague, overweight one with a seventies perm and bunions, it was no contest. He laughed at himself. He did not make a habit of such ways of thinking, and should not be giving way to them now. The fact that Alison was the most fascinating woman he'd met in years, and he couldn't help wondering what she was like in bed, was incidental. Definitely incidental.

Two

'I've been flirted with,' Alison announced to her nanny when she got home that evening. 'That hasn't happened to me for ages. No, Lukey, it hasn't,' she added to her twenty-one month old son who had abandoned his clattering caterpillar mid-expedition to stairs or stars, and rushed through from the hall to attach himself to her leg. Alison picked him up and hugged him as she sat down at the kitchen table next to Lisa, embracing his sturdy body as best she might without transferring the remains of his tea to her clean suit. 'Nobody dares when I'm wearing my clerical collar, more's the pity. Good thing I'd left it off.'

'Tha's your lucky day, then, in't it? Who was it? Anyone nice?' Lisa put the copy of *Woman's Own* she had been reading to one side, and got up. 'I'll stick your supper in the microwave. D'you want coffee with it?'

'Oh, bless you. Yes, please.'

It wasn't Lisa's job to wait on her employer, but six months into an exacting first curacy at St Peter's Wellesley, Alison had given up remonstrating; she needed all the help she could get.

'It was our Registered Inspector, no less. He's Scottish, and he's got the most gorgeous voice I've ever heard, all soft, rolling vowels and whiths and Whellesleys. I could have listened to him all day.'

Lisa put a plate in front of her, and Alison began to pick away at chicken and potatoes, popping pieces of food into Luke's mouth every so often, to keep him happy.

'How old is 'e?'

'I don't know. His hair's white, but I'd guess forties. Not too bad looking either, for a mature man.' She laughed. 'Listen to me, you'd think I was desperate! One "och aye" and a twinkle in a fella's eye, and I'm anybody's.' She rested her cheek against Luke's soft, brown hair. 'So how's my family today?'

'Luke's fine. We 'ad a little walk into town, and then 'e went to Catherine's while I 'ad my driving lesson. James and Josh are watching telly.'

Alison looked at her watch. 'I'd better go through and say hello before I disappear again. Thanks, Lisa,' she added, as a mug of coffee arrived. 'I don't know what I'd do without you.'

'Tha's alright. No sweat.' Lisa leant back against the sink, with her own mug clasped in her hands. Devoid of make-up, and bulky in jeans and sweatshirt, with her artificially ash-blonde hair tied back from a heavy face, Lisa had lost much of the brash sexiness she'd cultivated as a teenager at Alison's school a couple of years before; before she'd found religion and the studiously pious boyfriend who was the third love of her life, though she'd scarcely turned nineteen. But then, Lisa was always wholehearted in her enthusiasms.

It took five minutes for Alison to disentangle herself from Luke, satisfying him only with the promise of an extra cuddle after Lisa had given him his bath. In the meantime, her two elder sons deserved attention.

In the living room, the nearly fourteen year old James and eleven year old Josh were sprawled variously on the floor and the sofa, watching television. Two dark heads, two thin bodies, with James already beginning his treacherous spurt towards manhood. Alison reached across the large green sofa that sat in front of the patio doors during the winter months, and drew the heavy striped curtains behind it. The nineteen-seventies house came with her job; four bedrooms, an attic conversion and a study, as well as living and dining rooms, and a large garden that Luke would revel in when the warmer weather came.

Josh shuffled next to her as she sat down, resting his head against her shoulder, and grunting with pleasure when she put an arm round him. James managed to convey his disdain at his brother's soppiness without turning round.

'I got my cycling proficiency badge today,' Josh announced. 'Can I ring dad and tell him?'

'What makes you think he'd be interested in anything you do?' James sneered. 'Anyway, they pass everyone who takes that test, however crap they are. It doesn't mean anything.'

'Yes it does! I had to practice and practice, didn't I, Mum? And dad asked me about it last time we were there, so he *does* care.' A trembling distorted his voice.

'Ah, he's going to cry now. You are a baby.'

'Do shut up, James,' Alison broke in. 'Stop being so mean. I'm sure dad will like to know, Josh. You can try later. If he's in.'

'I wish he'd get a job here and live with us,' Josh said. He'd made a variant of the same point almost every day since they'd arrived in Wellesley six months previously, and her evasive answers never satisfied him. He and James had both hated moving away from Nottling, leaving their father with his excuses about it being too far to commute to his workplace, and not worth finding something nearer if she was only going to be in Wellesley for three years.

'I don't see why we couldn't have stayed on with him.' James made his complaint less often these days, but it still rankled with him that he'd not been able to remain in Nottling with his dad - incomprehensibly to Alison, since she couldn't see that Steve had ever had any more time for his sons than he had for her. A slow puncture had been deflating her marriage for years. It had had little chance of surviving once she'd met Michael Turner during her ordination training, and begun to realise how much she was missing, how flattened she'd become by her husband's constant carping and sullen withdrawals. In public she and Steve had continued with the pretence that it was circumstances rather than intention that kept them apart, though after their encounter at Christmas, she doubted it could last.

'You know perfectly well,' she said to James. 'There's no way dad could look after you with the hours he works and the business trips he has to make.'

'I could look after myself. *I'm* not a baby.'

'There's no question of us leaving a thirteen year old on his own for days on end, so do stop going on about it. You're getting boring.' Guilt at the disruption and distress she'd caused her family sharpened the edges of her voice.

James got up, muttering something under his breath which she chose not to decipher, and stalked out.

'We'll be arranging for you to go to dad's for the weekend again soon, anyway,' Alison said to Josh. 'You can have a good talk to him then.'

'Why don't you come too? I want us all to be together.'

'I have to work at weekends, you know that.'

'I wish you weren't a curate,' Josh said, picking at the small smear Luke had contrived to leave on her skirt.

Alison took his hand in hers to stop him making things worse. 'I know it's difficult, but you're settling down really well now, aren't you? You've got lots of friends.' Relentless cheerfulness might not be what he needed, but she couldn't manufacture patient sympathy after a long day, and with an evening's work ahead of her. 'Come on, Josh, let go of me, I've got to go out again.'

'I don't want you to go.'

'I have to, I've got a service to do up at church.'

'I hate church!'

'It's what I do now, Josh,' she said, wresting herself free of him. 'It's what I really want to do. You'll get used to it.'

Forty minutes after arriving home full of maternal affection, she was shouting a long-range goodbye and rushing out, almost relieved to be separating from them all again. She jumped into her car for the short journey to the church half a mile away, remembering only as the square Norman tower came into view, her promised extra cuddle for Luke. Damn herself as she might, there was nothing she could do about it now. She drew the car to an abrupt halt on the gravel beyond the churchyard, and got out.

'Alison!' called a hesitant voice behind her.

She turned round, and stopped as she saw the middle-aged woman who'd hailed her. 'Hello, Maggie. I hoped I'd see you. Have your test results come through? I tried ringing at lunchtime, but I couldn't get you.'

'I've had the all-clear,' Maggie said, eyes moist behind her glasses.

'Oh, I *am* glad,' Alison responded, hugging her. 'What a relief for you.'

'Thanks for coming round yesterday. I'd got in a state with the worry.'

'That's alright. When did you hear?' She could hardly hurry Maggie's report; it took some time for them to pass through the gate into the churchyard, a further two minutes before Alison could veer off down the path that rounded the church, and head for the vestry.

As she put out her hand to the iron ring of the old wooden door, it turned on its own, and swung away from her. A grey, permed head poked round the door. Ella Mitchell, loyal sidesman, ('Sidesperson's such an ugly term, don't you think?') nodded at her, and said mildly, 'Ah, good, you're here. I was going to have a look for you. It's difficult getting to things at this time of the evening when you've got children, isn't it?'

Unfair to blame Maggie for delaying her, so although Alison hated anyone to think she could not manage the boundaries of her job, she merely smiled and said, 'Well, I'm here now,' and followed Ella into the vestry.

Brian Lyle, head server, and on the St Peter's Parochial Church Council for so long she suspected he'd had his name put down for it at birth, was bending over a small bureau in the corner of the crowded vestry, busy with papers. He straightened up as Alison called good evening; a stout Christmas card monk in his cream-coloured alb with its silken tie, though he would have balked at sacrificing a circle of his thickly waving grey hair for such a vocation.

He looked at his watch. 'You made it, then,' he said, with what was presumably intended to be a jolly smile. 'We weren't worried.'

Ella made a sympathetic face, and passed through into the church.

'It's been one of those days. I've never stopped,' Alison said, pulling off her coat and diving into her robes. 'Besides, it's only ten to seven. Plenty of time.'

'These are the papers for the PCC meeting tonight. Father Nigel meant to have them done on Monday, but the photocopier packed up. He says you're to introduce the item about the Wellesley Churches Together Summer Festival. That's the file for it, on top.'

'But I can't! I don't know anything about it.'

'You will when you've read the papers,' laughed Brian, holding out the sheets he'd been leafing through.

Alison stared in alarm at the pile: a good half-inch of paperwork that she had no hope of mastering in the time available. 'Why can't Father Nigel do it?'

'He doesn't know anything about it, either. Father Mark used to deal with all that. He was on the committee. They did a very good Songs of Praise in the Baptist Church.' He pressed the papers into her hands. 'You'll be alright, wonderwoman. Miss out half the service, and you'll have time to read it before the meeting.'

Alison did not smile. There were times when she felt distinctly a-pastoral when she looked on Brian's cherubic, bespectacled face. Fine, so she'd accidentally omitted the psalm the first time she'd led evensong back in September, but he didn't have to keep reminding her of it. 'Well, he'll have to ...' She broke off as the vicar came in. 'Oh, Nigel, this Wellesley Festival ...'

'Hello, Alison. You were cutting it fine. Everything OK?' Nigel Sanderson reached past her to place a book on the table: a burly, cheerful, outgoing man in his fifties, with thinning hair and a red face, whose main claim to fame was taking four Oxford wickets for thirteen runs in the Church Times Cup some years before. Alison had been here six months, and had already heard the story three times. 'Did you hear Maggie's got the all-clear?' he added in a low voice, before she could reply. 'Thanks for sitting with her yesterday, she did appreciate it. Sorry about the short notice with the festival papers. You're a quick reader, you can cope, can't you?'

Alison had never in her life said 'no' to such a question; she would manage somehow. She put the papers down on the table, and turned to the tarnished mirror high on the wall beside the racks of choir robes. Methodically, she smoothed her hair afresh into its clip at the base of her neck. Her image gazed back, reassuringly authoritative and capable in robes and collar. The events of the day receded as she began to focus on the service ahead of her. This is what I do now, she reminded herself. What I really want to do.

Nigel caught her eye. 'Ready to start?'

'I am.' She smiled cheerfully at him, and took her place in the procession.

The Parochial Church Council began at eight o'clock. The theory was that members would attend the service and come on to the meeting, so full of Christian charity that dissent would vanish, and they'd be back home with their collective feet up well before ten. Tonight, however, they seemed unaccountably voluble. While Alison grabbed a cup of tea, and tried to discover what the Wellesley Festival was about, various PCC members rushed to bend her ear about other ecclesial matters.

Bunty Ranger, brusque with outrage: 'Why isn't the drama group on the agenda?'

'Is it meant to be?'

'Father Nigel said he'd put it on. We have to get it up and running again; nothing's happened since Father Mark left.'

Alison suppressed a sigh. It seemed to be the general view of the parish that nothing worthwhile had happened since her predecessor had left, nor was likely to. Tall, good-looking, popular, a gifted musician with a gentle sense of humour, an energetic wife, and two perfect children, he had left an impossible legacy when he had been plucked from his curacy after only two years, to take up a high-flying job in another diocese.

'Oh, well, raise it under any other business, if there's time.' She turned back to her papers.

... It is hoped that the Wellesley Festival will draw together all the churches for fellowship and learning. A weekend of interesting talks will culminate in ...

'My dad's operation went very well.' Annie Hyde, with the tone of one grown fed up with waiting to be asked.

'Did it? That's good. I'll call in at the hospital tomorrow.'

'He won't have the bandages off for a while, they ...'

'Could I catch up with you later, Annie? I need to read this before the meeting.'

... culminate in an ecumenical Songs of Praise. Every church in the town is asked to appoint a representative to ...

'What did you make of the Inspector?'

Terry Howells this time, peering at her from below a shiny forehead, shabby in the dusty grey suit he'd worn all day at school.

'What did I make of the Inspector?' she repeated, trying to make the switch between ecumenical praise and educational proceedings. Iain Sutherland. She'd forgotten about him for the last few hours, but he'd been an interesting person. She'd admired his professionalism, and enjoyed the conspiratorial way in which he caught her eye when he'd essayed a little humour, as if he was relying on her to appreciate the joke. 'He seemed very pleasant - if inspectors can be pleasant. Approachable, professional. I think he'll be OK. He's got a reputation for being fair.'

'In so far as inspections can be fair. As if anyone can tell from half an hour in a classroom what someone's really like as a teacher. They only have to catch you on a bad day, and it can wreck your whole career.'

'Oh, I know. When I last got inspected, one of my little horrors farted practically in the chap's face, and several of the kids staged a protest saying they couldn't possibly study with germ warfare going on. It took me ten minutes to restore order.'

'Exactly. And then they put you down as a failing teacher.'

Terry had not smiled as people usually did when she told the story. Should she have used the word 'fart'? Perhaps clergy were not allowed to show acquaintance with flatulence. But the Lord was not in the wind ... Get a grip, Alison.

'Actually, they complimented me on how well I handled it. You'll be alright, anyway, Terry. Could you excuse me, I'm trying to get through this paper before we start.'

... to appoint a representative to ...

A half empty coffee cup appeared on the table beside her left elbow; a heavy hand landed on her shoulder. 'You don't mind being in charge for a few minutes?' Nigel asked. 'I'll kick things off with a prayer, but then I need to make a phone call to the hospital. Sandy's rung to say old Mrs Stubbings was rushed in at teatime, and I ought to check how she is.'

'Fine.'

Damn, she thought, putting down the papers about the festival in order to look at the PCC agenda. There went her chance of using the first part of the meeting to catch up with her reading. She took a deep breath as Nigel called the meeting to order, preparing for more prolonged concentration than she had anticipated. She ought to watch Nigel, she mustn't let him get away with dumping on her too often. She ought really to watch herself, in case she was acquiescing too easily - but then, whoever achieved anything by saying no?

Three

Colin Blatherwycke parked his mother's car at the side of the modern building that housed St Martin's, Greathampton, and approached the entrance. A couple of girls from the impoverished estate that surrounded the church sat on the low wall outside, talking loudly. They watched without interest as he mounted the four steps up to the heavy double glass doors. Tall, skinny, with unstyled wavy brown hair drifting around a face still scarred by the chronic acne of his teenage years, and a thin mouth that made him look repressed and judgemental when most of the time he was simply scared. What had he to do with them, with their precisely casual clothes, the oceans of cheap scent with which they'd doused themselves, their self-conscious cigarettes and their unforgiving language? Apart from the fact that they were exactly like Lisa five years ago.

In the window behind them, a large poster, white on red and black, blazoned publicity for the show Colin had come to put on: **Pure Power hits St Martin's Greathampton! Be there!** His idea, this series of sketches and spoof game show interspersed with numbers from the band from St John's, Leathwell. A group of about a dozen of them took it round local churches and schools, with Colin acting as producer, director, manager and roadie. The one worthwhile thing he'd done in his life.

He pushed open the door and passed through the lobby into the building that transformed itself from community hall into church and back again by means of the folding doors that stretched across it to conceal or expose the area around the altar. Away to his right, in front of vast picture windows, a series of stage blocks had been erected. Sitting on the edge was a slightly-built dark-haired man in jeans and a black tee-shirt, with a thick red check shirt open over the top, watching tolerantly as a small child raced up and down between the rows of chairs that faced the platform, shrieking her excitement. Michael Turner, an old acquaintance, though never a friend. In his early thirties but looking twenty-one, living off the earnings of a GP wife, and lacking all ambition. Colin had never quite approved of Michael's laid-back attitude; it offended his conformist nature.

Michael unhitched himself from the stage, and came towards Colin. 'Hi. This set-up look OK?'

'Yep,' Colin said, looking around. 'The van should be here soon, and then we can get set up. Do you think there'll be many coming?'

'I hope so. I told 'em it was a good show. Lots of sex and bad jokes, decent music, and not too much religion.'

'I hope you don't think we compromised our message,' Colin said, cursing himself as soon as the words were out because yet again he was sounding pretentious.

'Better to die than to have sex unless you're married? I think you make the point. I'm not sure I agree with being so absolute about it, but it'll get them thinking. Oh, Lyddy, what *have* you got there?' He broke off to remove a deliquescing boiled sweet from the palm of his daughter's hand before it could find its way to her mouth. 'We'll have to wash our hands now, won't we? Tell you what, let's see if we can find some biscuits. Do you want a coffee or anything, Colin?'

'Can do.' Colin followed him over to the kitchen that opened off a corner of the hall.

Michael sat Lyddy on the edge of the worktop and filled the kettle. 'Lisa seemed to be settling down well, last I heard.'

Colin shrugged. 'S'pose so. Haven't really spoken to her lately.'

'You don't sound very enthusiastic. All over, is it?'

'We've both been busy, that's all.' Colin began to open cupboards in search of cups.

'You've been very good for her. I don't know what she'd have ended up getting into, if you hadn't adopted her.'

'She adopted me, more like.'

The memory flared afresh in Colin's mind: Lisa, bursting out from the nave of St John's into the lobby where he was sorting out some books; a well-developed young woman with ash blonde hair, eyes of furious green and a round face made harsh by the heavy application of make-up. Colin learned later that she'd been giving the Sunday evening congregation a rather too graphic account of her past sins. His father had restrained her, much to everyone's amusement, and she had stormed off.

'Soddin' bastards!' she'd yelled at Colin, trying unsuccessfully to fasten a recalcitrant zip on her jacket with indignant fingers. 'How dare they bloody well laugh at me? I'm never coming 'ere again. Christians! Bloody hypocrites! Fuck the lot of 'em.'

Hardly the sort of language Colin was used to, but he hadn't been able to let her leave with that impression of the church embittering her. As she made for the street outside, a lost soul heading for outer darkness, he followed her, absorbed her anger all the way to the pub, where he bought her a drink. That was when he discovered she remembered him from the humiliating visit he'd made to Michael's youth group years before, conscripted to help his parents preach the virtues of chastity to a bunch of streetwise kids, who jeered at his appearance and laughed at his faltering words. But Lisa had been the one who hadn't jeered, he'd realised, managing to place her. From then on, he regarded her as his very own lost sheep, whom he must somehow restore to the fold. He took inordinate pride in getting her back to St John's, and when she had cornered him a year ago, to explain that she'd fallen in love with him, he'd been proud to start going out with her. What naivety!

'Is there something wrong?' Michael asked, observing his shudder. 'Can I help?' He bent down as he spoke, and unearthed a plastic container of biscuits from under the sink.

Colin almost succumbed to a desire to pour it all out, but how could he confide in Michael, or anyone, when he was so confused, and so ashamed of his confusions? Easier, as always, to tuck it all away, and to hope for some miraculous resolution before he had to see Lisa again.

'No, there's nothing wrong,' he said, when Michael straightened up.

Lyddy took a bite from the biscuit her father had thrust into her hand, and beamed at him. Michael's limpid brown eyes gleamed in her face beneath tousled dark curls.

Colin did not smile back. Despite being the eldest of five, he always felt clumsy in the presence of small children. 'So how old is Lyddy?' he asked.

'Nearly two,' Michael said.

'Same age as Alison's youngest.'

Michael began spooning coffee granules into mugs. 'Two weeks younger. Have you ever met Allie?' he asked Colin.

'No. She left her husband, didn't she? I don't think that's right, specially not when you've got kids, and clergy ought to set an example. I don't think people try hard enough. Marriage isn't just for the easy times.' And there he went again, pontificating in front of Michael, of all people, who'd stuck in a difficult marriage for years, if Lisa's gossip was to be believed. He felt himself redden.

Michael laughed and clapped him on the shoulder. 'Thanks for your ministry, brother. Any time I can return the favour, let me know.' He poured steaming water onto the coffee, slopped in milk from a carton, and handed a mug to Colin. 'I mean that,' he added. 'If you fancy a pint one night, if you want to talk about Lisa, give me a call.'

A bustle on the other side of the hall announced the arrival of the tour van bringing the sound system and lighting equipment over from Leathwell. Colin, thus excused from having to respond, muttered something about having to give instructions to his team, and escaped.

The PCC always seemed to spawn further meetings: sub-committees, working parties, action teams, and of course, the standing committee at which Alison now strove to keep her mind on the task. The trouble was James, who had not come home after school, and while he probably had told her he was doing something else, she couldn't for the life of her remember. Appalling mother that she was, she filed the events of her children's lives in her mind, but they always slipped underneath the bottom drawer. Who knew, perhaps he'd fallen off his bike and was even now in hospital, abandoned and dying?

'Are you with us, Alison, or on some other planet?' Nigel's voice recalled her from anxiety about James to the shabby confines of the church hall with its unvarnished wooden floor and Blutack infested plasterboard walls, an uninspiring backdrop for an uninspiring meeting.

'Wonderwoman's gone to the planet Krypton,' Brian laughed, boldly nudging Bunty Ranger on his left.

'That was Superman,' Alison said, and mentally kicked herself. The committee followed the red herring, and she had missed her chance to register her objection to the soubriquet.

'I was saying I've put your name forward for the Wellesley Churches' Festival committee, Alison,' Nigel said, drawing the meeting back to order. 'Father Rod said they were looking for new blood, and of course Father Mark was on it for a couple of years.'

'I thought I was only supposed to be our link with it. I didn't realise it meant going on the committee as well.'

'It'll be a good way for you to get to know people in other churches,' Nigel said.

'Is it likely to be a big involvement? I'm not sure I could fit it in if it means lots more meetings. I don't think I had a single evening in last week.'

'Neither did I, and nobody gives me a nice salary and a free house for *my* work for the church,' Bunty said loudly.

'It's important that Alison has some time with her family,' Louise said. 'We won't achieve anything by forcing her to overdo things.'

Alison looked at her gratefully. Louise Bates and her husband Dave were the churchwardens at St Peter's, and reliable allies when it came to reminding Nigel she might not be able to manage a seventy-hour week as regularly as he did. On the other hand, she already had some ideas about how the festival might be better organised. Starting the planning a year rather than six months beforehand would be a start.

'I could go to the first meeting, and see what's required,' Alison said. 'Then if it does look too much, perhaps someone else could ...?'

She looked round. Brian seemed mesmerized by the pattern of the formica on the table around which they sat. Bunty was whispering importantly to Annie.

'We'd offer, but I'm afraid we're not going to be around in July,' Dave said. 'I was going to mention it to Nigel first, but you might as well know. My firm's relocating to Manchester, and we're going to be moving after Easter.'

'Oh, no!' Alison cried. 'You can't go!'

'We're really sorry,' Louise said to her. 'We've fought so hard to get a woman appointed, and now we have to leave.'

'James will really miss Ellis ...' The Bates's youngest was the one real friend James had made among his classmates at Wellesley High ... Of course, that's where he'd gone after school.

'We'll have to start canvassing for new churchwardens.' Nigel pursed his lips. The Bateses would be hard to replace. 'Fancy doing it again, Brian?'

'I've got too much on with work.'

'Perhaps it's something I ought to consider.' Bunty's statement was greeted with a few seconds' silence.

'Ooh, that would be nice,' Annie said, stoutly.

'Excellent,' Nigel said. 'No shortage of candidates. Now, the roof ...'

'What do you think of me being Churchwarden?' Bunty said to Alison, collaring her as the meeting ended, and leading her to a confidential corner of the hall.

Alison tried to think of a tactful way of diverting her. Bunty, a slight, short-haired, sharp-faced woman in her mid-fifties, had arrived at St Peter's four years before, though she contrived to give the impression that she had run the parish single-handedly for decades. Her eldest daughter, Veronica, was married to Terry Howells, and when her husband retired from his job in the City, Bunty had decided a move to Wellesley was in order. Bunty believed unreservedly in her own abilities, and had plenty of time on her hands to demonstrate it. Nigel groaned whenever her name was mentioned, and had developed an uncharitable habit of passing her on to his curates.

'Haven't you just volunteered to get the drama group going again?' Alison replied. 'You can't do everything.'

'You're going to give me a hand, though, aren't you? Father Mark's wife was wonderful on the production side. No, I'm not one to push myself forward,' she continued, as Alison tried to break in to dispute her assumption, 'but I have been a churchwarden before, and I think I might have a contribution to make. I shall have a word with Toto tonight.'

Observing an irritable pekinese in the back of Bunty's Range Rover early on in their acquaintance, Alison had drawn the not unnatural conclusion that the Toto who periodically cropped up in her conversation was her dog. She had only realised seconds before committing an embarrassing solecism that Toto was Bunty's husband - Tony to his less intimate friends.

'Perhaps you could have a word with Dave and Louise, see exactly what's involved,' Alison said, hoping she could rely on them to make it sound as off-putting as possible. The thought of Bunty having the official authority of a churchwarden was daunting.

'I'll do that. We'll have to have a meeting of the drama group committee fairly shortly. Which evening would be best for you?'

'I'm not going to be involved. I don't have time.'

'Nonsense! What do you do with yourself all day?'

'I'm preaching every other Sunday, that takes time.'

'It can't take that long to do a ten-minute sermon.'

Alison regularly felt the same thing, but still frequently found she'd used up half a week by the time she'd researched and polished what she wanted to say. She did not dare confess as much to Nigel, and was certainly not going to admit it to Bunty. 'I've also got this festival committee now, and there's extra work at Wellesley High with the inspection coming up.'

'The parish comes first, though, surely? It's all very well for you to swan around town going to meetings, and dabbling in education, but the parish is your job. That's what we pay you for. Excuse me if I speak my mind, but that's the way I am.'

'Father Nigel sees the school as part of the parish,' Alison said. 'Would you excuse me, I need to catch him for a word before he goes.'

She moved rapidly away, reminding herself as she crossed the hall of the importance of zeal in one's parishioners, and regretting that she had not taken the opportunity to remind Bunty that a) their parish share barely paid for their vicar, let alone a curate, and b) - thinking in a's and b's seemed to be an unavoidable legacy from teaching - that Nigel had encouraged her to make involvement with the school her priority this term.

'Bunty seems to think she'd make a wonderful churchwarden,' she said, catching up with Nigel as he fastened his briefcase.

'Lord preserve us,' Nigel muttered. 'There must be someone else who'd stand. What about suggesting it to Patrick, or Lionel?'

'Patrick's just started a new job, and Lionel's away half the year. You could try them, I suppose. What about Ella? She'd say she couldn't, but she'd be good.'

'Possibly, possibly. Why don't you have a word with her? You could talk anyone into anything.'

Alison laughed. 'I'll see what I can do.'

She waited for him while he locked the hall, and he accompanied her over the gravel to her car. Across from the hall, the church loomed behind its hedge. The glow from the street light at the end of the car park caught the gold lettering on the notice board between the lychgate and the corner of the churchyard. Alison's name had been roughly inscribed in place of Father Mark's, whose name had in turn been painted in over his predecessor. Both were faintly visible despite Brian's attempts to expunge them.

'That'll need redoing with the new churchwardens,' Alison said, nodding towards it as she fished her car keys out of the pocket of her handbag. 'Mind you, I'd have thought it could do with a complete revamp, or even a new board. It's very cluttered, and it is rather the worse for wear.'

Nigel was prevented from replying by the screeching of Alison's car alarm as she aimed the keys at it.

'Damn! I hate this car!' She silenced the alarm with impatience. 'I really must get it checked, it's too sensitive.'

Nigel threw an arm round her shoulder. 'You've seemed on edge tonight. Is everything OK?'

'I'm tired, that's all.'

Nigel dropped his arm away from her. 'I'm probably not supposed to do that - don't the diocesan guidelines forbid all physical contact? Come to think of it, we're not even supposed to be alone together after sunset in case I change into a wolf.'

She laughed. 'I don't mind. I need all the hugs I can get.'

'No developments with Steve, then?'

She hadn't relished telling Nigel that her husband wasn't moving with her, but he'd been very understanding. Perhaps that was the influence of his wife Sandy, who was a counsellor. In conversation with the congregation, she'd explained that it was Steve's job that was the problem, and for some months, intercessors had dutifully prayed for 'Alison, Steve and the children at this difficult time', but despite his brief appearance at Christmas, it was apparent to everyone that she had very little contact with him.

'No. Not likely to be either,' she replied. Bitterness against her husband rose to her throat when she spoke of him. For all she tried to pretend the break had already been made and she cared nothing for him, the years of marriage clawed her back. He engaged her emotions despite herself. 'I need to talk to you about that sometime.'

Nigel nodded earnestly. 'When you're ready. I haven't wanted to intrude.'

'You've been wonderful. I've appreciated you not prying.' She turned back to her car. 'I'll see you in the morning.'

She drove home cheered by Nigel's kindliness. She had always enjoyed male friendships, and there'd been a gap in her life since she'd lost touch with Michael. Cut herself off from him, rather, because she couldn't trust herself. As she stopped the car, engine idling, prior to opening up her garage, she was visited by an acute memory of him ... the spring and summer of their first year on the Leathwell Programme for Ministerial Training, giving him lifts home and stopping outside his house, her body longing for him, waiting for the moment when he'd lean across to kiss her with carefully controlled passion before disappearing out of the car and back to his gloomy wife. As always when the memory resurfaced, shame washed over her. She had been so staggeringly wrong about Michael, so ludicrously irresponsible in her pursuit of him.

Well, she'd learned her lesson now, or hoped she had. She would only really be tested if some gorgeous married man looked into her eyes the way Michael had done, and, as she'd observed to Lisa, that wasn't normally the way men regarded women priests. Not that she wanted them to, of course. She'd had her fill of all that, she had her calling to pursue. It was just that there were occasional times when the road ahead looked unbearably lonely.

Four

A week after accepting her nomination to the festival committee, Alison was making a late entrance into the sun-starved back room of Wellesley's Baptist Church, ten minutes after the start of the festival planning meeting. Lateness, it turned out, was a crime punishable by hard labour.

Roderick Little, the rural dean, smiled warmly at her. 'Ah, it's Father Alison! Glad you're here. We've volunteered you to take the minutes. Eileen's been doing her best, but she's got an arthritic hand. I said the C of E would come to the rescue.'

Like many in the Wellesley Deanery, he had no love for women priests, but it was probably too much to suspect him of deliberate malice in landing her with the burden.

Alison sat down. 'I don't feel I know who people are ...' she said, tentative where she should have refused outright, but too flustered to assert herself properly, after the rush she'd had to get here from visiting Mrs Stubbings in hospital.

'No problem,' Little said. 'We'll pause and introduce ourselves. You'll soon get the hang of things. That's the advantage of having a young mind.'

She was about to protest that having turned thirty-six two days ago, she was scarcely juvenile, but, looking around the room at the collection of elderly clergy and lay people being primed to spearhead the revival of Wellesley, decided it was all relative. She got a pen and notepad out of her bag, and began to record everybody's name.

Little rattled through the agenda as if he felt the whole exercise was a waste of time. Alison, struggling to keep up with his uninterrupted flow of decision-making, was disinclined to force herself to get involved until a single comment caught her attention:

'I think we should do something for the young people,' said the Baptist minister.

'I hardly think the young people of Wellesley are going to stir themselves to come along to something the churches put on,' Little said.

'That depends what it is, surely?' Alison objected. 'I know a church in Leathwell that puts on a really good show for church youth clubs and schools, and lots of young people come to that. Why don't I see if they could come to Wellesley? I know it's fairly short notice, but it'd be worth a try. And why not base the festival at Wellesley High instead of here, so they'd be more likely to come?'

'Let's not get carried away,' Little said. 'We've been lucky to get fifty people the last couple of years, we'd look ridiculous hiring a large school hall at great cost and having it a quarter full.'

'It wouldn't cost much. I'm a governor there, and I'm sure I could negotiate something reasonable. And if we've got a good programme, and publicise it properly, I don't see why we shouldn't have hundreds coming along.'

Alison's enthusiasm was infectious. The rural dean's festival plans were thrust aside as the committee grew more ambitious. Taking notes, and confirming with the group members what they'd agreed to do, Alison at first failed to register that Roderick Little was sitting back in his chair, grim-faced.

'We'll need another meeting fairly soon,' she concluded.

'You'd better tell us when you're free, as you seem to be being Chairman as well as secretary,' Little said. 'I don't know, women! Give 'em an inch ...!'

He laughed as he spoke, but it was clear that she'd offended him.

'I do apologise,' she said, trying to make amends. 'I got carried away.'

The woman from the Evangelical Free Church winked at her. 'You're doin' jus' fine. Don't let him bully you.'

Within forty-eight hours, Alison had obtained Colin's agreement to bring his Pure Power show over to Wellesley for the festival, and had fixed a date for him to visit to discuss the arrangements on site. Site was going to mean Wellesley High, for Alex had agreed to let the churches use the school at a specially low rate. His generosity came with strings attached, however; Alison had felt obliged to say she would reconsider standing as Chair of Governors. It should have been out of the question, but Denise Linnet was clearly not up to the job, and who else was there? The Inspector had been polite and fair, but Alison had known what he was thinking. A governing body with Denise at the helm would be absolutely slated.

'I don't see why you shouldn't take it on yourself, you know,' Nigel said thoughtfully, when Alison shared her dilemma with him. 'I was Chair of Governors in my first parish, and I thoroughly enjoyed it. I know this isn't a church school, but it is part of the parish. Mark used to do assemblies there regularly, and you haven't wanted to do that because of your boys, so it's good that you're involved in the governing body. How much more work would it involve?'

She tried to convey the size of the task; he offered to reduce her preaching to once a month. She voiced concern about how the parish would feel, and Bunty in particular; he spoke with fervour about St Peter's mission in this benighted community. He left her to mull it over in her prayers, but her mind was almost made up. She missed school more than she expected, missed the satisfaction of being in a world where everything came naturally, and she felt professionally competent, rather than a novice. She would grow into her ministry, and would cheerfully persevere until she did, but in the meantime, having a bigger role at Wellesley High would fulfil some of her own needs. If Nigel could see it as part of her vocation, why should it not be right?

The fact that, as Chair of Governors, she would be working more closely with Iain Sutherland, was not uppermost in her thoughts as she prepared for the meeting of Wellesley High parents with the Registered Inspector. She dressed no more carefully than she would normally: tailored black trousers, long-sleeved white body and a loose-fitting black jacket, with a delicate strand of patterned silk around her neck, and dangling gold earrings. Formal enough to be Chair, informal enough to be parent. She never attended school functions wearing her collar, to avoid embarrassing James and Josh.

Despite what she had said to Lisa, Alison had attached no significance to the Inspector's friendliness. It had been his job to put them at their ease on that first occasion, and she recognised that his clumsy statement about his marital status had not been a calculated advance. Indeed, judging by the speed with which he'd changed the subject, it had embarrassed him, too. She was expecting to find him much more officious on this occasion, and the evident pleasure with which he came across the hall to greet her on his arrival surprised her.

'Welcome,' she said, holding out her hand. 'Did you have a good journey?'

'Yes, thank you. Congratulations on your appointment.' He smiled as he returned her handshake, and the little spark that had hopped between them at their first meeting flickered again. Odd, for he couldn't be called conventionally attractive. A stocky man of middle height with a hint of a paunch; hair practically white, though thick, and cut long enough to touch his collar and to brush across brown eyebrows. A square face with a short nose, full mouth, and tiny bags under the amused blue-grey eyes that regarded the world through silver-framed glasses. He dressed well, too. His suit had an expensive cut to it, and you didn't pick up shoes like that in the sales at Shoe Express.

Having introduced Iain and the fellow inspector who'd arrived to record proceedings, Alison took a seat at the back of the forty or so parents who'd turned up. She studied Iain as he spoke, admiring the authoritative way he handled the criticisms flowing uncensored from the floor. That rolling voice was a help. It spoke of trustworthiness and integrity, of economic prudence and Calvinistic values. Would you buy a used school from this man? Quite definitely. An entire education authority.

'That was all fairly negative,' she said to him later, claiming his attention as the last stragglers left the hall. 'I don't think that group in the corner were representative. I know a lot of what they said used to be true, but they didn't seem to realise we've begun to change things.'

'We're used to evaluating parents' meetings. We know they don't give the whole picture. It must have been difficult for you to sit through without wanting to pop up and defend the school. It's not often that Chairs of Governors are at these meetings. I thought you restrained yourself admirably.'

'It wasn't too bad. I'm too new to feel defensive about what's happened before my time. I mean, I realise I am responsible, but I see it more in terms of meeting the challenges of the future than justifying what's gone on in the past.' She laughed. 'Don't I sound pretentious!'

'Not if you mean it.'

'Oh, I do. I'm looking forward to your report to give us something concrete to work with.'

'It's a pleasure to meet someone who's so positive about inspections. You don't work for OFSTED yourself, do you?'

Alison smiled. 'No.' The natural response was to tell him what she did do, but she held back. Once people knew, they tended to start questioning her membership of the human race.

Iain persisted. 'What is it you do, exactly? I'm sure you did tell me, but I've forgotten.'

She took a deep breath. The spark between them was about to be extinguished by an oceanful of water. 'I'm a curate at the parish church.'

His face remained still, but a shadow of disapproval or disappointment had passed across it. 'Are you! That's not what I expected, somehow.'

'Is that because I swear too much, or you think female clergy have to be fifty and ugly as sin?' She grimaced. 'I shouldn't have said that - you probably do think I'm fifty and ugly as sin.' Good grief, Alison, talk about fishing for compliments.

His mouth twitched. 'Cairtainly not that. No, you seem rather too normal and intelligent to belong to a church. I'm afraid I don't have a terribly high opinion of religion.'

It was Alison's turn to feel disappointment, though she attempted to hide it with a smile. 'I expect we could have a long discussion about that.'

'I'm sure we could. But not tonight, preferably. I've a long drive back.'

'I ought to get home, too,' she said, though neither of them made a move.

'Did you get your car alarm sorted?' he asked.

'Yes. You were right, there was something wrong with it.'

'Glad to be of assistance.'

'Well, I'll see you again in a few weeks.'

Iain held out his hand. 'I shall look forward to that.'

His hand closed warm and square about her own, and she drove home pleased that her revelation did not seem to have diminished his friendliness, once the first shock had passed. She was Chair of Governors, after all. She could not afford to alienate him.

Back home, Alison found Lisa in the living room watching television. Lisa had her own room, but both she and Alison liked to gossip and unwind in company at the end of the day, and she had increasingly become a member of the family.

'Josh wants to see you,' she said as Alison went to sit down. 'He says if 'e's asleep, you're to wake 'im up. And then can you ring your mum?'

'Right.' Alison went upstairs, praying Josh's crisis would be minor. Her days were extended interminably by such items of Any Other Business. Listen to Josh's tale of fraternal persecution; struggle up the narrow set of steep stairs to the attic where James slept, to touch base with him and get his side of the story; then twenty minutes of her mother asking after the children and Steve, and were they getting divorced, and hadn't she met anyone nice in Wellesley, after all she'd been there a while now?

'You must be joking, Mum, when do I have time for socialising?'

It was eleven by the time she could collapse with a drink in the living room. Lisa was curled in an armchair with a catalogue, dreaming of her summer wardrobe, while on the television in the corner an intense drama unfolded unnoticed. Alison knocked the sound off and sighed.

Lisa looked up. 'Was there many there tonight?'

'About forty. I admired the way Iain Sutherland handled them. He'd got a nice way of being slightly rude about inspections, which defused the situation when it got overheated.'

'An' was he flirting with you again?'

Alison laughed. 'Oh definitely! He said he was looking forward to working with me, even after I told him I was ordained.' The sound of the telephone intruded itself. 'Damn.'

'D'you want me to get it? Say you're still out?'

'No, I'll go.' Alison heaved herself out of her chair and went through to her study.

'Ah, Alison, I hope you don't mind me bothering you at this hour ...' said a male voice.

Unsure to whom she was speaking, and the nature of his possible crisis, Alison did not feel able to say 'yes', and settled for 'not at all'.

'I wondered how the parents' meeting went, down at the school.'

'With the Inspector? OK I think.'

'Nobody gunning for me?'

That all depends on who you are, she wanted to say. 'They weren't gunning for anyone in particular, more general things about discipline and results.'

'But not History?'

At last she placed him; it had been the uncertainty in his voice that had fooled her. With his Head of Department going off on maternity leave at the end of the summer term, and no one quite knowing if she'd come back, Terry needed a good inspection to make sure of his appointment as acting, and possibly one day actual, Head of History himself. Alison could understand him being anxious, but he surely did not have to leave it till practically midnight till he rang? 'I'm sure you've not got anything to worry about, Terry.'

'I'm not worried, I just know what inspectors are like. They seize on anything they can, but they don't check out whether the person complaining is a pathological liar or parent of the worst kid in the school.'

'I'm sure they know what they're doing. Iain Sutherland said to me afterwards they go by what they see much more than what parents tell them.'

'When you've been in this business as long as I have, you learn not to take what people like that say at face value. They have their own agenda. I've seen it all before.'

'And so have I, and it all seemed perfectly fair to me.'

She heard him grunt, and spoke quickly, before he could warm too much to his theme. 'Look, could we talk about it tomorrow? It's after eleven, and I've been on the go since before breakfast.'

'Sorry, I'm accustomed to Father Nigel and Father Mark being available whenever we needed. I forgot you need your beauty sleep.'

'I am available if it's an emergency, but not if it can wait. I'll be up at school tomorrow, I'll talk to you then.'

She replaced the phone, and went back into the living room. 'Now why did Terry Howells have to phone me at this hour to tell me he's not remotely worried about the inspection?' she complained to Lisa.

'You should get an answerphone,' Lisa said. 'That'd stop 'em bothering you.'

'Ah, but Father Nigel doesn't approve. He thinks we should be available twenty-four hours a day, otherwise what if someone really desperate wanted us, and couldn't get us?'

'I wouldn't 'ave thought you could help 'em much when you're knackered.'

'The Lord provides, Lisa, with the gift of energy.' Alison sank down onto the sofa and put her feet up. 'I don't think.'

Lisa smiled, and returned to her perusal of the catalogue. 'This'd suit you,' she said a few minutes later, holding up a picture of a dusky-red, sleeveless dress. 'Dead sexy on its own, or you could wear something under it. Bit pricey, though.'

Alison reached across to take the catalogue. She had too little time and too little income for clothes shopping these days, though it had been one of the chief pleasures in her life before her ordination - and one of Steve's many complaints. Lisa was turning out to be a bad influence on her.

'I don't get much call to look sexy,' Alison said, visualizing the way she could do her hair, and the jewellery she might put with it.

'Wear it for the inspection next month, and that nice Inspector bloke you fancy.'

'I don't fancy him. I hardly know him. You don't think it's too short?'

'Nah, you got good legs. Not like me. Col won't let me wear short skirts no more. He don't think tha's decent.' She pulled a face. 'There's a lot 'e don't think's decent. D'you know, I bin goin' out with him a year, and 'e's never tried to get me clothes off once? Weird!'

'I thought you'd both taken that pledge.'

'Oh, yeah, we 'ave. "No matter what the urge to screw, I'll be married 'fore I do".'

Alison laughed. 'That's not how it goes, surely?'

'Naah. Tha's one me an' Wayne made up. I did a good one. "I'm a Christian, what bad luck, now I in't allowed to f ..."' She stopped, as if she was not quite sure whether bad language might still earn detention, and giggled instead. 'I mean, I do agree with it, I'd never do nothing, 'cos Col wouldn't like it, but tha's still weird. When you bin goin' out with someone that long.'

'It's quite nice, though, don't you think? It shows he likes you for yourself, not just for sex.'

'Yeah.' Lisa grinned. 'He don't know what 'e's missing, though.'

Alison looked down at the catalogue again. 'It's ages since I splashed out. Perhaps I ought to get something new for the inspection. Give myself confidence for when it's my turn to be grilled by Mr Sutherland.'

He would probably become an ogre once the inspection began in six weeks' time, but for now, she had to admit that she rather liked him. She must surely be the only person connected with Wellesley High who was actually looking forward to it.

Five

Colin had not felt able to refuse Alison's invitation to bring the Pure Power show to Wellesley, though the thought of meeting Lisa filled him with trepidation. What to say? How to respond when she threw herself at him, expecting him to embrace her as lovingly as before? He needed to talk to someone, but his usual circle of friends at St John's were out of the question in the circumstances. It came to him one night, as he brooded in the darkness, that he ought to take up Michael's offer. He might not agree with all of Michael's views, but this was someone with a wide experience of life, a prior knowledge of Lisa's turbulent past, and a reputation as a sympathetic listener. And if not Michael, who? So the next morning, Colin gathered his courage and rang Michael's number, and a few days later, was on his way to Greathampton.

He parked his mother's car on the road in front of the small, semi-detached house where the Turners lived, and swallowed nervously as he walked down the short drive.

'Hi, come in!' Michael said, greeting him at the door. 'You don't mind having a beer here instead, do you? Jenny's got to go out to a meeting.'

Michael's wife appeared as he spoke, a rather dumpy woman with clear grey eyes that scrutinised him from a sensible, broad face framed by mid-brown curls. Nothing like the glamorous soap-opera medic he'd always imagined Michael would have in tow.

'Nice to meet you,' she said, extending a hand to Colin. She reached for a jacket from the rack by the front door. Michael took it from her and began to help her on with it. As Jenny bent her arms back, her jumper tightened across her stomach, suggesting that some of the dumpiness might be attributable to pregnancy.

Michael, standing behind his wife, with his arms loosely about her shoulders, bent and kissed her neck affectionately. 'You're right, she is,' he observed, reading Colin's thoughts. 'August it's due.' His hands lingered over Jenny's stomach.

She pulled away from him. 'Michael ...!' For a few seconds they met each other's eyes.

She's going to shout at him, Colin thought with alarm, mentally measuring his distance to the front door.

Then Jenny relaxed, put a hand on Michael's shoulder and kissed him, saying, 'I hope I won't be long,' and left the house.

'She loves me really,' Michael said wryly as he led Colin through to the living room. 'I expect Lisa told you about last summer.'

'Not really, only that Jenny had a kind of breakdown while Lisa was visiting.'

'She's a lot better now, fortunately. Have a seat and I'll get you a drink.' He passed through a frosted glass door in the corner of the room and went into the kitchen, whistling.

Colin removed a child's board book from the armchair just inside the door, and sat down on the edge of the seat. Evidence of Lyddy was everywhere, from the pictures on the mantlepiece above the gas fire, to the boxes loosely piled with toys in the corner by the bookshelves, and the odd finger stain on the pale cream walls.

'So you're off to Wellesley,' Michael said, returning to toss a can of lager in Colin's direction. He flopped down onto the sofa. 'You must give my love to Allie, I haven't seen her for months.'

'It's easy to lose touch,' Colin said politely.

'I wouldn't have done, only Allie decided I wasn't safe to know.' Michael stretched out his legs in their black jeans, and settled back comfortably against the cushions. 'So, you want to talk about Lisa.'

'It's what I say when I see her ... I'm confused ... I don't want to hurt her, only I don't know if I can carry on ...' He paused to open his can, careful lest he make a mess.

'You're having second thoughts?'

It was still difficult to admit, but this was what he had come for. Colin took a deep breath. 'I ... I'm ashamed of her. I know I shouldn't be. I hate myself for it. But I am.'

'When did this come on?'

'A few weeks ago. I overheard some people talking.' He stopped, chewing at his thumbnail while he tried to find the words to explain. 'You know what she was like - the way she dressed, and swore all the time. I wouldn't have said I'd anything in common with her. But she seemed to like me, she looked up to me. I knew she'd done lots of awful stuff when she was younger, and I explained if she was sorry, God would forgive her, and then it would be like it had never happened. I was really proud when she decided she wanted to be baptised. It was like she was a whole new person, and I'd helped make her like that. When she told me she fancied me, and we started going out, I couldn't believe my luck. You know, *her,* to want *me!* I thought the other lads at church'd be jealous. Then I heard some of them talking about her, after she'd been back for the weekend.' He halted, feeling his colour rise as memory invoked their words.

Michael took a swig from his can and belched discreetly. 'What did they say?'

'That she was a stupid, fat slag, and always would be. They thought it was hilarious, her going out with me. They were being crude about her, and you could see they despised her. And me, for being naive enough to be taken in by her. It was horrible. I'm one of their leaders, I thought they respected me!'

'You know how lads talk. They probably are jealous. And you know what she's really like, you shouldn't take any notice.'

'I know. I know I should have challenged them and stood up for her, but I didn't, I more or less disowned her. They realised I was listening, and said had Lisa gone, in a sneering way, and I made out I couldn't care less. I'd seen her off that afternoon, telling her I loved her, and couldn't wait to see her again, and there I was saying she meant nothing to me, and I'd only gone out with her to humour her. I know you must despise me for it, I despise myself, but I couldn't stand being laughed at behind my back like that. I never wanted to be seen with her again, if that's how people saw us.'

'I don't despise you,' Michael said. 'We all sometimes let down people we love.'

'I don't know if I do love her.' He bit at his thumbnail again. 'Lisa seems to think we're made for each other, and we'll get married and everything. I've even gone along with it sometimes. But I can't love her, can I? Not if I behave like that.'

'If you don't care about her, why don't you simply finish with her?'

'I can't. I feel responsible for her. She might go off the rails without me. She might lose her faith and start messing around with men again.'

Michael laughed. 'You can hardly stick with her for life, just in case. Not if you don't care about her. Besides, don't forget she's living in a vicarage. She's not going to go that far wrong with Allie looking out for her. I know you don't rate poor old Allie that highly, but she's very caring, and she's known Lisa a long time.'

'But maybe I don't want to finish with her, that's the trouble. I'd hate it if I never saw her again.' He put his hands to his face. 'Oh, I don't know what I want!'

Michael ran a finger thoughtfully around the rim of his can. 'How old are you? Twenty-one?'

'Twenty-two.'

'Still, that's quite young to be talking about getting married. Why should you know what you want?'

'Lisa knows, and she's younger than me.'

'You know what Lisa's like. She gets these enthusiasms. I remember talking to her after you'd been with your mum and dad to do your talk to the youth club, and she was all set to become a nun. I mean, she might be right to be enthusiastic about you, and maybe you will get married, but I'm sure she'd understand if you said you weren't ready for that yet. As long as you tell her sensitively, and she knows you still care about her. She's had enough of being dumped by men who treat her like shit.' He hesitated. 'You're not sleeping with her, are you?'

'Of course not!' Colin replied, indignant.

'Just checking. That would complicate matters somewhat.'

'I wouldn't dream of it.'

Michael laughed. 'How very disciplined of you. When I was twenty-two, I dreamt about it all the time.'

'I've got other things to think about,' Colin said. If he was being a little disingenuous, there was only himself to know it.

The promise of April evaporated. May remained cool, and overcast skies reflected the gloom at Wellesley High as it waited in trepidation for the inspection. Alison had claimed special dispensation from morning prayer with Nigel, in order to be in school before eight o'clock to meet the team. Much as she valued these early daily services, today she was left feeling heretically liberated. She rose, showered, put on a deep-blue summer dress with chaotic patterns that reflected her mood, made up her face and managed a snatched breakfast before leaving the house with a dissident lift to her step.

As she turned into the car park, she recognised Iain Sutherland's Rover gathering drizzle on this disappointing May morning. The staff had told her to pray for sunshine, but the Almighty hadn't seen fit to listen, so bang went her credibility there. Within the small room which had been allocated to the inspection team, the tables were already piled high with papers.

Iain stood by the window talking to a blonde, middle-aged woman with a file under her arm. The movement of Alison's entrance caught his attention; he excused himself from his companion immediately and came over to her.

'Good morning, Mrs Thompson. Good to see the Chair of Governors here bright and airly. How are you? Still propping up the Church of England?'

He smiled as he shook her hand, and she found herself beaming back. 'I'm fine. Have you been here long? Where are you staying?'

'Half an hour or so. We're at the Hawkshill, a little way out of town on the road to Leathwell.'

'I've heard of it. I've not been there.'

'Well, I don't advise popping in this week. It would never do for you to see the wild parties we have once we've finished here.'

'I don't believe that for a moment. It's working till three a.m. most nights, isn't it?'

'No fooling you, is there? Come along, let me introduce you to my colleagues.'

The inspection team swung into action; every corner of the school liable to be scrutinized by some earnest stranger with a clipboard and a schedule graded from one to seven: excellent, good and very poor. In and out of lessons, prowling the corridors, searching out a semi-private space in which to talk to pupils or staff or governors, harvesting evidences with automotive efficiency. The tension in the staffroom was palpable; the silence of the unsocial more pronounced, the laughter of the extrovert more forced.

Though it was far easier viewing an inspection from the relatively safe position of a newly-installed Chair of Governors than living through it as a teacher, Alison still found the process draining. While several staff deliberately avoided her when she dropped in, resenting anyone from outside, others found her a useful outlet for their complaints and anxieties. Alex spoke to her frequently, appreciative that she could hold his hand - literally at one point - during a disastrous day:

'Don't tell anyone I said it, but thank God I've got you instead of Denise. I'd have gone spare!'

Or there was Megan, the new young French teacher, needing to be

45

put back together sufficiently well to take her lesson after a breaktime spent throwing up in the toilets:

'You can do it! You're good, Megan, you're a brilliant teacher. No one's going to fail you. Come on, I'll walk to the class with you.'

'Aren't you in the way, wandering round the school when they've got all these other people in as well?' Bunty asked as they gathered in the vestry after Tuesday's evensong. Despite subtle lobbying by Nigel and Alison, and a plethora of jokes about St Peter's being taken over by women, Bunty had managed to get herself elected churchwarden alongside Ella, and her contributions to parish life had become even more tiresome.

'Certainly not,' Alison could say with feeling. 'The Head's asked me to come in as much as I can. He needs someone to talk to, and so do lots of the other staff. And I have to be at meetings with the inspection team myself.'

Bunty looked doubtful. 'I don't see why that should take precedence over the parish. Poor Father Nigel's having to do a great deal of extra work, no wonder he looks tired.'

'I thought he seemed very cheerful,' Alison said. 'Besides, I am learning things. I'm working on a sermon that makes a parallel between the Registered Inspector and the Holy Spirit. They both examine your life and convict you of sin, but the Inspector leaves it at that, whereas the Spirit gives you the resources to rectify what's wrong. What do you think?'

'I hardly think it's helpful to trivialise the Holy Spirit,' Bunty stated.

'And our Inspector's Scottish, but I'm not sure whether that's the most appropriate nationality for the Spirit. It's an interesting theological conundrum.' Alison caught Ella's eye as she spoke; working with Bunty, they readily admitted to each other, occasionally rendered them juvenile.

'Well, there's no time to stand here chatting,' Bunty said. 'One of us had better get on with tidying things up for tomorrow.'

'We weren't in very good voice this evening,' Ella remarked as Bunty left.

'It didn't sound too good, did it? What a dismal pair of hymns,' Alison said. Terry's method of relieving his feelings about the inspection was obviously to force some half dozen people to sing 'Lead, kindly, light amid the encircling gloom', amid the genuinely encircling gloom of St Peter's on a damp May evening. 'And what *was* he doing with the organ? Crash, bang, wallop, he sounded like he was playing with boxing gloves on. God, I sometimes think he must be tone deaf ...'

'Glad to hear you appreciate my playing,' said a voice behind her. Damn. Trust Terry to sneak in at the wrong moment.

'I was joking. I didn't mean it.'

Terry smiled. 'The way you sing the responses, Alison, I don't think I need to worry about your judgement. Not your fault, you can't help being off-key. It's only a shame you had to come to a parish where the music is so important. But we love you all the same.' He patted her shoulder.

Alison blushed. She had practised for hours before this first public attempt at singing evensong, and had not thought she'd done too badly. 'I'm sorry, Terry. I do appreciate your playing, it was only that I was feeling like something more cheerful tonight.'

'Why not? You're having a very easy week, aren't you? Nothing to do but sit in our staffroom drinking coffee and pretending you're busy. Well, some of us have work to do. Goodnight!' Terry picked up the case he'd left in the corner of the vestry, and walked back into the church.

'I wasn't off-key, was I?' Alison protested to Ella. 'I know I'm not up to Father Mark's standard, but he'd sung professionally.'

'You don't want to mind Terry. He was very fond of Father Mark, and he'd hoped our new curate would be interested in the musical side as well. Ooh, he did have a lovely voice, Father Mark. Sent shivers up your spine to hear him do the Collects.'

Bunty reappeared bearing the large red plastic file that was becoming her badge of office. 'What's this I hear about you being rude about Terry's playing?' Bunty said, fixing Alison with a concerned gaze. 'He's very sensitive.'

Alison frowned. 'I didn't mean to upset him ...'

Nigel strode in as she spoke, fresh back from the meeting in London that had caused him to miss the service. 'Causing trouble again, are we?' he asked, clapping her on the back.

'Terry overheard me saying I thought the hymns were gloomy.'

'Haven't I told you the second cardinal rule of parish life? Never upset an organist!'

'I know. I'm sorry.'

'What's the first rule?' Ella asked.

'Always obey your churchwardens, especially if they're women!' Nigel roared his amusement. 'Perhaps I'd better see if I can catch him, soothe him down. You're not going yet, are you? I want to hear how your inspection's going.'

Alison shook her head, and he rushed from the vestry.

'*Is* it going well?' Ella asked.

'We won't get a glowing report, but we should get by. I have to be interviewed by the Registered Inspector myself tomorrow. I hope he's not too hard on me.'

At nine the next morning, Alison arrived at the inspection team's room. Through the glass of the door, she observed Iain engaged in earnest conversation with one of his already dwindling team. She'd seen him many times as he rushed around from class to meeting to hotel, in school from seven thirty to seven thirty, fuelled by adrenaline and whatever refreshment the school threw at him. He had barely acknowledged her, which wasn't surprising. She was intrigued to know whether it would be different when she sat down alone with him, however; for while she dismissed as ridiculous Lisa's view that she went into the school more than she needed because she fancied the Inspector, she had donned the new dress her nanny had persuaded her to buy.

Iain signalled to her to come in, and she hovered uncertainly by the door while he completed his discussion. Eventually the two men drew apart.

'See what you can do, and have it with me by twelve if you can, Phil,' Iain said.

His colleague nodded assent and left the room.

'Sorry to keep you waiting, Mrs Thompson.' Iain held out his hand for Alison to shake. 'Come and sit down. We should be safe here for half an hour.' He indicated one of two low chairs set at angles opposite each other. 'Are you ready for coffee? Your Head's been very kind and let us borrow his machine for the week. I wouldn't survive without a drip-feed of caffeine.'

'I know the feeling. Yes, black, no sugar. Thank you.'

She sat down, crossing her legs with care so that her dusky red dress would not ride too far up her thigh. She noticed Iain's eyes resting for an infinitesimal moment on her legs; thereafter he looked only at her face or the charts and artwork decorating the walls of what was usually the home of Mrs Tarbuck, the Year Ten tutor.

He handed her a cup, and produced a half-empty packet of chocolate biscuits from his briefcase. 'My secret store. Go on, it's a long while since breakfast.'

'I shouldn't,' she smiled, taking one.

'I wouldn't have thought you needed to worry.' He sat down on the chair near her, drew his clipboard of papers onto his knee, and pulled the top from a gold-nibbed fountain pen. 'This has to be rather formal, I'm afraid,' he began. 'I've a series of points I need to raise with you.'

'I understand. I'll do my best to answer, but I've only been a governor since October.'

'I realise that. Now, what do you see as the main role of the governing body ...?'

It was a curious conversation. At one moment a formal grilling which left Alison feeling hopelessly inadequate as her inexperience was exposed, at another, descending into a friendly exchange of personal information from which Iain would hastily retrieve them.

'... I'm interested in that area of the curriculum because I taught History,' she said.

'Really? So did I. That and politics.'

'Do you miss it?'

'Not greatly. Cairtainly not the marking and preparation. The school trips to Rome, mebbe yes.'

'I only ever got as far as the Isle of Wight myself.'

A smile. 'You were saying how you monitor curriculum development.'

'So I was. Sorry ...'

'... I'm very conscious of how new I am to this role ...' Alison ventured, guilty at her ignorance of the Governors' Annual Report.

'There's a lot to get to grips with, I appreciate that.'

'It's all the other bits of my life that make it difficult. There's no such thing as free time when you work for the church, and if I do get some, I can't simply pick up governors' things, I have to give some time to my children, especially with their dad not being around, though he does have them for weekends once a month ... you're making me nervous, I'm rambling.'

'It's all part of the picture. I think what I was actually getting at was how the governors communicate with the school and the local community ...?'

'... That's an impossible question. You've forgotten what governors' meetings are like - when were you last at one?'

'Last month. I'm a governor at my local primary school, so I do understand.'

'Have you ever been OFSTEDed?'

He looked amused. 'Yes, but much as I'd like to compare notes with you, I do have a lot to get through this morning. Can we continue?'

A few minutes later, he completed writing his latest note, and looked up. 'Good.'

'Is that it?' Alison asked.

'Yes.' He laid his pen and clipboard down on his chair and stood up. 'Thank you for that, Alison.' He extended a hand to her as she rose. 'I notice some of the staff call you Allie, which do you prefer?'

'I don't mind. People I work with usually call me Alison; most of my friends call me Allie. You can choose.'

Iain nodded slowly. 'Thank you.'

Considering herself dismissed, Alison made for the door, the colour high in her face. God, what had possessed her to say that? Sounding every bit as if she were coming on to the Registered Inspector of all people! He'd probably draw attention in his report to the improper range of methods used by the Chair of Governors to influence the outcome of the inspection. OFSTED probably had a euphemism for that, as for everything else.

She stole a glance at him through the glass as she closed the door. He had returned to his seat, and picked up his clipboard, but he was watching her exit with an abstracted air, and did not return the nervous smile she gave before she hurried away.

Six

'Now, we all know we've got the Inspector sitting at the back of the class, but I want you to ignore him and get on with your work. Let's show him the benefit of your brilliant minds, shall we?'

Terry was not anticipating much help from the little bastards. Just his luck to be revisited by an inspector on a Thursday, when he was stuck with 9M. Just his luck to have Sutherland, whose judgement Terry trusted not an inch, for all his cultured politeness. He sat there now at the back of the class with his clipboard, pen poised, while Terry prepared to address point one on the detailed lesson plan he had produced for the occasion. It was not something he normally bothered with, but it had seemed politic to play the game and do exactly what the inspectors expected. Sticking to his plan was another matter. He'd intended to speak for only part of the lesson, and then get them working on their own. Nerves made him ramble, however. He was aware of the class getting restless, damn them, and he was only halfway through his input.

A sudden movement from the side of the class caught his attention. 'What *do* you think you're doing?'

The rubber Danny had chucked across the room arched back towards him with added velocity as Matthew, its inadvertent target, took revenge.

'James is asleep. I was tryin' to wake 'im up for yer. Sir. In case 'e missed something important. An' 'e would've done, wouldn't 'e,' he added, with a sidelong glance at the Inspector, 'cos everything in your lessons is brilliant, sir. We learn ever such a lot.'

'I am indebted to you for your confidence in me, Danny.'

The Inspector had a finger to his lips. Terry hoped it was to conceal a smile, but it might equally indicate judgement.

James continued to sit, his head propped on his hand, his eyes shut.

'James!' The boy jerked awake, and stared at him with the bewilderment of one woken from a dream. 'I should prefer it if you paid attention. Watching telly all night, were we?'

James rubbed his eyes. 'The phone went at three. I couldn't get back to sleep.'

'One of your numerous girlfriends, huh? Assignations in the music cupboard don't suffice, they can't last a night without hearing your voice?'

Terry had caught him snogging Emma Baker in the music cupboard one lunchbreak, and had given him a week's detention. Perhaps unfairly, since Emma had snogged most of the boys in the class in some cupboard or other at some point, and when caught, they usually got off more lightly.

'It was for my mum,' James said flatly.

'Your mother. Works all night as well as all day to keep you provided for.' Laughter tumbled round a class ever alert to innuendo. Terry cursed himself. He should have chosen his words more carefully, but the tension produced by the Inspector's presence was getting to him. 'I should have thought you'd be ashamed of yourself,' he continued, 'falling asleep in class. I expect a lot more from the son of the Chair of Governors.'

'Hey, look 'e's gone all red,' Emma called, standing up at her table and leaning towards James.

The boy sat with his head bowed and his hands clasped behind his neck, muttering, 'Piss off, can't you?'

Terry strove to be heard. 'Quiet! QUIET! Sit down, Emma. I fail to see what's so amusing. I hope I didn't hear what I thought I heard, James. That will be one detention for swearing, and another for falling asleep. I will not tolerate this kind of behaviour in my lessons, do you understand?'

James glowered at him, but said nothing.

'Did I hear a "Yes, Mr Howells, I'm sorry, Mr Howells?" ... I'm waiting.'

James continued to sit with a mulish expression on his face.

Towards the back of the class, the murmurings intensified. Danny had turned round in his chair to address the Inspector. 'Are you a teacher?'

'Not currently, no.'

'You got a funny voice. Are you Irish? Hey, you in't brought a bomb in, have yer?'

'Danny!' Terry kicked himself for allowing himself to be distracted by James and rushed to deal with the impending disaster at the back of the class. 'Turn round at once! You and James, see me after the lesson. I'm not prepared to waste everybody's time with you now. Be quiet everyone. Face the front. Emma, you can do your hair later. Now, where were we?'

There was little point in asking the class if he didn't know himself. What a catastrophe this morning was turning out to be. He struggled to reconnect with his lesson plan, but his students had already picked up the fragility of his control, and their attention, once lost, was hard to regain. The sound of the bell brought only minimal relief; he still had James and Danny to deal with, to say nothing of the grim Inspector, jotting his condemnations on his clipboard.

Danny swaggered up to Terry's desk. 'I never done nothing. I was bein' friendly to the inspectors, tha's all. You said we had to.'

Terry could no longer remember why he'd felt it necessary to keep Danny behind. He simplified matters. 'Right. Off you go.'

James was sidling towards the door.

'James! Here!'

The boy turned back, heavy-shouldered.

'I believe I'm waiting for an apology from you.'

James stared at the floor and muttered a grudging 'Sorry.' Then he looked up, his eyes showing not the expected defiance, but distress. 'That call last night - it was about Ben and Tanya Brundall. They got killed in a road accident, both of them. Their mum wanted my mum to go to the hospital. I couldn't sleep ... I couldn't stop thinking about it.'

'Oh, no.' Shock rocked Terry for a moment. He'd taught both the Brundall children, and their mother went to St Peter's. 'How awful!' Poor Maggie ... to lose both her children. 'I hadn't heard. What happened?'

'A lorry smashed into their car. They were on their way back from a concert. There were two others in the car, and they're in intensive care.'

'That's terrible.' Terry took a deep breath, fending the tragedy away. He couldn't allow it to get to him with the rest of the day to get through. 'It's not as if you knew them, though.' Out of the corner of his eye, he could see the Inspector making his way to the front of the class. 'And I can't have students falling asleep in my lessons or swearing. It doesn't give a very good impression, does it? I know your mother's work will impinge on you on occasions, James, but if you don't want all your classmates to know exactly what her job entails, you'll have to stop using it as an excuse. I'm afraid I'll have to give you detention for the rest of the week.'

'But I've got football tomorrow.'

'Then you'll have to miss it. You should have thought of that before you decided to opt out of my lesson.'

'It's not fair. I couldn't help it.'

'I think you could. And you certainly won't do it again, will you? As I say, you don't want everyone to get to know your mum's a priest.' The boy looked away. 'So I'm going to see some improvement, am I?'

'Yes, Mr Howells.'

James turned and left the classroom, shoulders bowed under the strap of his bag.

Terry glanced round to where Iain Sutherland was leaning against a table a couple of feet behind him.

'He's a boy who needs firm handling,' Terry said. 'I often find that with boys from broken homes. Alison does her best, of course, but boys of this age need their fathers.'

The Inspector was observing him coldly, as if Sutherland, too, had walked out on his family, and was mortally offended. 'I'd understood he had a good deal of contact with his father. Still, that's by the by. I wonder if I might ask you a couple of questions about your lesson. Shall we sit down?'

Terry leaned back against his desk and folded his arms. He had no time to reflect on the singularity of the Inspector having knowledge of James' home situation; he had a damage limitation exercise to pursue.

'Fire away,' he said.

'I understand you were in trouble with Mr Howells today,' Alison said to James at tea.

He shrugged, non-committal.

'What happened?'

'He fell asleep in the lesson,' Josh chipped in, 'and Howells went for him, 'cos the Inspector was there.'

'You pick your times well, James. Which Inspector was it?'

'White-haired git with glasses,' James said.

'There's no need to be rude about him.'

'Wasn't my fault. I didn't sleep last night, after the phone went.'

'Neither did I,' said Alison, remembering yet again those endless, appalling hours with Maggie in the hospital. She threw out yet another prayer for her, and carried on. 'Did you get a detention?'

'Yeah. It's not fair, he's always picking on me. He made me stay in last week, 'cos my homework fell out of my bag and got muddy, but Sarah Day comes in and says her dog chewed hers, and he just laughs and says, copy it out again for tomorrow. And he gets at me for saying "piss off", but Danny says much worse, and he gets away with it. It isn't fair. I reckon he takes it out on me 'cos he doesn't like you.'

'Oh, nonsense. He and I get on fine. Apart from when I'm disrespectful about his organ.'

Lisa started to giggle.

'Why are you laughing?' Luke asked her.

Alison decided it might be politic to carry on. 'But that was his own fault for creeping up on me in the vestry, and Nigel's sorted it out anyway. You don't want to draw conclusions from how teachers are this week - they're all worried stiff about the inspection.'

'He's always doing it. However hard I try, nothing's good enough.'

'You're exaggerating.'

He scowled at his plate. She turned her attention to Josh.

Friday afternoon, and school had ended for the students. Only one or two loitered, busy with their activities after lessons were over. The car park remained scattered with the cars of staff staying on to sort out classrooms and lessons for the following week, but most had headed home, anxious to escape now that the inspection was over.

Alison had come to the school to be on hand once Iain had delivered his verbal report to the senior staff. She had expected them all to be gathered for the meeting, and was taken aback when she came face-to-face with him outside Alex's office. It took her a few seconds to compose herself.

'I thought you were giving the senior management team your report. Have you finished already?'

'No, no. Alex is pacifying an irate parent, so we've put it back half an hour. I'm just about to grab a breath of fresh air, it's been a hectic day.' He hesitated. 'I thought I might take a look at your student garden. My team were very impressed by it. You wouldn't like to give me a tour, would you?'

'Yes, of course. You definitely ought to see that. It's one of our achievements.'

She led him back through the school and out through a rear entrance, explaining how Terry Howells had supervised the pupils in designing the area, and digging and planting it out. By the time she had finished, they had crossed the playing field and arrived at the entrance to the garden which had been created between the rear of the sports hall and the fence at the edge of the school grounds.

She stopped and ushered him through an arched trellis set among spreading bushes in extravagant bloom. 'After you.'

Iain ducked under the trailing shoot of a briar rose, pursuing the gravelled path into the interior. Alison followed, feeling again the lifting of spirit she always had when she came here, soothed by the plants clambering wildly about her, the small pond, dotted with life, dark and green between the rushes.

'I come here sometimes when I've got a few minutes, to read papers, or to sit.'

Iain stopped and turned back to face her. 'How long's it been established?'

'Three or four years, I think. It's highly commendable that it survives undisturbed with some of the pupils we've got. I hope you're impressed.' She smiled at him.

A restful silence fell, interrupted only by the arguing of birds and the occasional pluck of a frog scared into the water. Somewhere in the distance, a plane hummed.

'It's charming. Thank you for bringing me ... Allie.' His eyes remained on her long enough for her to become self-conscious, and when he spoke again, there was an unusual degree of hesitancy in his voice. 'I wonder ...' he began, then stopped, looking away through the shrubs towards the school buildings. 'I'm going to be doing an inspection up the road in September, and that'll mean visiting in July. Supposing I was to ring you ...' He looked directly at her again, nervous without his role to sustain him. 'Do you think you might be willing to come for a drink with me or something? I'd like to get to know you a little outwith all of this.' He waved his hand in the direction of the school.

She could not quite believe what she thought she had heard, and hardly dared reply.

'I've not offended you, have I?' Iain asked, misunderstanding her silence. 'I'd thought there'd been a lot we could have talked about, I thought it would be nice to have a chance to ... You can say no, it won't make any difference to my report ... I wasn't going to say anything, then bumping into you, I thought I'd risk it. I apologise profusely if I've misread ...'

Alison let her pleasure take over her face. 'You haven't, I'd love to. As long as we're allowed to.'

'Once my report's in, there's no problem.'

'In that case, yes. I'd like to get to know you, too, away from it all.'

His face relaxed at last, and they stood beaming inanely at one another, unsure what to say next, until the sound of footsteps on the gravel gave warning of another visitor.

'Ah, Terry,' Alison said self-consciously. 'I've been showing Iain the garden.'

'I thought you'd already seen it,' he said, looking between the two of them with some surprise.

Alison met Iain's eyes, amused to find him embarrassed. 'It bears a second trip,' she said, helping him out.

Terry looked unconvinced. 'Alex said to find Mr Sutherland to say he's free now, if you'd like to come.'

'I'll be right along,' Iain said. 'See you again in a week or two,' he added to Alison as he took a step to squeeze past her along the path.

'Yes. OK.' He brushed against her as he went, unsettling her emotions, and bringing a flush to her cheeks. Terry must think her guilty as hell.

'Glad to see you're taking your job seriously,' he said as Iain disappeared out of earshot. 'Dragging our Reggie off for assignations in the rose bushes. Do you think he's falling for it? Is he going to give us top marks?'

'Don't be silly. As if I'd do something like that. What do you think I am?'

'Alright, keep your hair on. I was only joking.'

'It's my job to be friendly. I was trying to give him a good impression of the school.'

'Methinks the lady doth protest too much ...' Terry said, leading the way back out through the arch.

Alison said nothing, afraid he might be right.

'What were you talking about, to be so flustered at me coming along? Not about me, was it?'

'You? No, of course not. Other than about how you set up the garden.'

'He wasn't exactly complimentary at the end of my lesson. Your lad didn't help matters.'

'It wasn't his fault,' she said as she led the way out of the garden and back across the field. 'He was upset about the Brundalls. We all are. I'm sorry, Terry, but I'm sure Mr Sutherland knows enough about teaching not to judge everything by one incident in one lesson.'

'I wish I had your confidence. I find him rather too smooth and plausible. He'll be pleasant enough while he's here, then hammer us in the report.'

'I don't think so. He's talked enough to us through the week for us to know the kind of things that'll be in it. Anyway, we'll soon know, won't we?'

Ahead of them, Iain's back in its respectable light-grey jacket disappeared inside the school. He'd practically asked her out; the enormity of it hadn't sunk in yet. Parting from Terry in the corridor, she sought the staff toilets to allow herself a moment alone to digest the implications.

Oh, maybe she shouldn't have agreed, maybe it wasn't wise or proper behaviour for curates burdened by as yet undissolved marriages, with an inspection aftermath to endure, and oh God, Ben and Tanya's funeral to take on Monday, at Maggie's particular request ... But for this moment, just this, she could not stop herself smiling.

Seven

Colin arrived in Wellesley on a mid-May Saturday morning after an early drive from Leathwell, trundling along the country roads in vibrant sunshine behind a decrepit van. In the adjacent fields, adolescent lambs started at imaginary perils while their mothers grazed; trees and shrubs exploded into whites, pinks, yellows and greens. Colin observed them serenely, his mind at ease. Like the student who has gone beyond the point for last minute revision, he had ceased to rehearse the words he planned to say to Lisa: I like you a lot, but I'm not ready for a long-term relationship, not yet. I'd like us just to be friends for a while, and maybe in the future, we could try again. If he said it carefully, and sensitively, as Michael had suggested, she'd understand, and not get too upset.

He followed the signs that directed the adventurous through the outskirts of Wellesley towards the Norman architecture of St Peter's; negotiated the lefts and rights into the small close on the modern housing estate where Alison's map indicated she lived.

Colin parked carefully on the gravelled sweep of the driveway in front of a detached, red-brick house; a wooden pergola entwined with scrubby foliage ran along its length, mitigating the severity of its lines. He stepped under it to approach the patterned glass of the front door.

Lisa herself answered his confident ring, smart in a navy dress with white buttons down the front, and Luke sitting on her hip. Whether it was the presence of the toddler, or the slight changes she'd made to her appearance, he wasn't sure, but she seemed older. Her hair was several shades darker, tucked back behind an ear on one side, and falling across her cheek below her chin on the other. A little make-up highlighted her eyes, though her skin was uncharacteristically bare.

Her face lit up when she saw him. 'Hiya!'

She hugged him as best she could without squashing Luke, and began telling him about her plans for the morning. 'Allie's going to take you round the school now, and then drop you back. I gotta show you my car. Allie give me an interest-free loan for it after I passed my test last week, so's I can take the boys around. Bright green, it is. I thought we could use it to go off on 'oliday some time.'

'I'm not sure ...' he began.

She met his eyes. The brightness drained from her face as she read his expression.

An elegant figure in flowing trousers and a long jacket appeared behind her.

'We'll talk later,' Colin said, tearing his attention from her in order to focus on her employer.

Alison finished slipping a sandal onto a bare foot anointed with a deep-red nail varnish, and held out her hand to him with a disarmingly friendly smile. 'Sorry to be in a rush, but I've got a wedding to get to. I'll be back after lunch, though, so if you think of any more questions, you can ask me then.' She was walking to her garage as she spoke, opening up the car and ushering him into a seat.

'Michael Turner said I should give you his love,' he essayed as Alison drove out onto the road.

'Did he?' Alison snatched a glance at him, her face momentarily vulnerable. 'How is he?'

A number of things fell into place for Colin as he contemplated the contrast between Jenny's sturdy plainness and Alison's glamour, and he thought he understood why she might have felt it safer not to stay in touch with Michael. He began to warm towards her, his disapproval of her abandoned marriage and Catholic leanings suddenly irrelevant.

'Seems happy with life,' he told her. 'Did you know they're expecting another baby in August?'

'No, I didn't. That's nice. I always thought Michael should have reams of children. He was wonderful with Luke. Well, give him my regards if you see him again.'

Ten minutes later, Colin was being whisked around Wellesley High to the accompaniment of a stream of explanation and questions as Alison showed him the hall, and grilled him about the practical requirements involved in staging the show. He tried to sound professional about it as he followed her through the echoing emptiness of the corridors, and tested the stage lighting in the high-ceilinged hall. Occasional noises suggested others were present in the buildings, though the only person he encountered was the Headteacher, discovered frowning at the computer on his desk, trying to catch up on all the work he claimed he would have got done had they not had the inspection.

Alison commiserated with him before introducing her visitor, then it was off to a deserted staffroom to make Colin coffee, his first chance to draw breath.

With the details hammered out, she led him back to her car, and delivered him once more to her house. He left her in the car, inserting the clerical collar she had just extracted from her handbag, and rang the bell again.

'Is she always like that?' he asked Lisa as the front door closed behind him. 'I'm exhausted.'

'Not always. Only when she's dead keen on something, an' she wants to make sure it goes right. Mind you, she's been like that ever since the inspection, rushing round like she's on something. Says she likes a challenge.'

She stopped speaking. Silence fell between them.

Colin thought of his carefully rehearsed opening sentence. He could hardly launch in standing here in the gloom of the hall. 'Can we sit down?' he asked.

'You'd better come up to my room.' She set off up the stairs, and on down the landing to a room at the far end.

There was little floor space available, with one wall taken up with fitted units, a bed against another wall, and the capacious armchair by the window that spread across the breadth of the room. On the bedside table stood the small television Lisa had bought out of her first and second pay packets.

She turned to face him.

'Where's Luke?' Colin asked to break the awkwardness.

'He's gone over to 'is friend's. Their dad's taking them to the park. James an' Josh have gone swimming.' She regarded him steadily through large eyes, waiting.

He was going to have to say it. He cleared his throat. 'Lisa ...'

She folded her arms. 'I know what you're gonna say. You don't wanna go out with me no more. I in't really your sort. No hard feelings.' Her eyes became wet. She blinked rapidly. 'Tha's OK. I should've known better than to think someone like me'd end up with a decent bloke for a change. You don't want me, an' tha's that.' She attempted to smile. 'Let's forget it, Col. We don't want things to be awkward with you coming 'ere for the show.'

She'd said it all for him, but he couldn't ratify it, not with her gazing at him with that air of hopeless defeat. She was his, and he could not walk out on her. 'It's not like that,' he said, crossing the two steps between them to take her in his arms. Affection surged within him as he held her; he'd been a fool to let himself be swayed by the derision of the lads at St John's, what did they know? 'I do want you,' he whispered, 'Oh, Lise, I really do want you.'

She tightened her arms around his neck, and kissed him with a slow deliberation that turned his body to steel and his mind to water. 'About time,' she murmured. She tugged him gently towards her bed. 'Come on, let's get more comfortable.'

Up at St Peter's, Alison was looking fondly at the young couple who stood in front of Nigel, waiting to be joined in holy matrimony. The bridegroom, pale and preoccupied, sweating in his suit. The bride, bouffant in ivory, clenching her fingernails into her palms lest she fulfil the nightmare she'd confided to Alison the previous week, and faint before she could take her vows. Gina and Don, whose marriage preparation Nigel had entrusted to his curate because he had double-booked himself the evening they were supposed to see him. Alison's careful plans for her meeting with them had been exploded, first by Luke bursting in to howl on her lap, then by Lisa, come to recover him, and discovering Gina was her hairstylist. Difficult under those circumstances to stick with Nigel's rules about maintaining an appropriate professional distance. Alison had ended up sitting with Luke asleep in her arms, her list of questions abandoned, establishing a friendship with them. Which was why she was regarding them warmly now.

On the stall lectern in front of her lay the notes for the brief wedding address she would be delivering in a few minutes time. Gina and Don had been upset to find she wasn't yet allowed to take weddings herself, but had wanted her to do something for them. It had taken days to prepare. What on earth could she legitimately say, when she had screwed up her own marriage so badly? She liked to feel she had reached a stage of indifference towards Steve, having passed through distress at his loss of interest in her many years before, but it wasn't altogether true. Those weekends when she took the boys to stay with him reactivated the emotions she tried to suppress, leaving her alternately fuming with rage at him or tearfully sobbing her loneliness into her pillow. Marriage is an honourable estate? Hah! Well, please God, for them it would be. She caught Gina's eye, and smiled her encouragement.

Some half hour later, address given, rings exchanged and registers signed, Gina and Don were on their way down the aisle to the sound of Terry thumping out the traditional accompaniment.

'You're James's mum, aren't you?' said a voice.

Alison looked up from the lectern at which she was arranging the books for tomorrow's Eucharist. A skinny girl with long mousey hair and prominent teeth captured by a multi-coloured brace, was regarding her with interest. The smartness of her dress labelled her a guest at the wedding, which was currently at its photographs stage on the grass outside.

'Yes.'

'I seen you up at the school for the inspection. You're a governor, aren't you? I thought it looked like you up here, but then I thought it couldn't be. James never said you were a vicar.'

'No, he wouldn't. He doesn't want anyone to know.'

'I won't tell, promise.'

'Who are you? Are you in his class?'

'Yeah, I'm Sarah Day. I sit next to him in Biology.'

'Oh, yes. He's mentioned you.'

'Has he?' Sarah's face brightened, and Alison smiled sympathetically. Her son's moody good looks would make plenty of conquests as he grew older.

'Here, Sarah, you're needed!' came a voice from the back of the church.

'Gotta have my photo taken. Cousins of the bride,' Sarah said. 'See you.'

'Bye,' Alison called after her. She must remember to tell James that he had mentioned Sarah's name occasionally. She crossed herself before the distant altar, and headed for the vestry to remove her cassock.

Colin lay as someone will when, winded from a heavy fall, they monitor arms and legs, head and back, to gauge the extent of the damage, before hazarding movement. In Colin's case, it was not his arms, the one round Lisa's neck, the other crushed behind her back, that spoke of disaster. Not his head, resting cheek by cheek, face down on her pillow; nor even his legs, lying between her own. Rather, his consciousness was filled by the knowledge that a single pulsing part of him was connecting his body to hers in forbidden intimacy. He dared not move. To do so was to advance the frozen moment of time, to face the consequences of his unforgivable action.

'Col?' Lisa's voice, husky at his ear, expanded his awareness. Her hands were against his flesh under jeans that had lost their moorings. His shirt was undone, and her breasts were squashed against his chest. Her ribs moved under his own as they both struggled for breath.

'I'm sorry,' he managed to say.

'Tha's alright. Tha's OK if you love each other, an' we do, don't we?'

'No! It's not OK. I've broken my pledge. And I've made you break yours.'

At last he summoned the courage to withdraw from her, and got up, fastening his clothing back around him as he walked across to the window. The green lawn of Alison's garden stretched out below it, dotted with thin trees that rocked in the sharp breeze. Here and there, blooms added colour under a bright sun. He stared out, horrified at his lapse. How on earth had he come to travel so far beyond the pattern of their usual comfortable embraces? Him of all people to get carried away like that!

'I'm sorry,' he said again. 'It's my fault. I should have had more control. I'm older than you. I'm the man.'

'There's nothin' to apologise for. I wanted to.'

'You *wanted* to?' He turned round.

Lisa was lying on her bed, her navy dress falling away on each side where he'd undone the buttons, forcing the stubborn cloth with sweating fingers. Her breasts and thighs rose white and rounded and eminently desirable. This was what she'd been leading up to all along, he could see it now. She had no respect for his principles, and had none of her own; the lads were right, she'd never really changed. He would continue to pray for her, of course, but he could not possibly associate with her after this.

He went back over to the bed to sit beside her, and took her hand. The words were already there, meticulously rehearsed; he had only to recall them. 'I need to tell you that I'm not ready for a long-term relationship yet. I do hope we can still be friends, but ...'

'Are you tryin' to dump me?' she interrupted, sitting up.

'I think it would be better if we didn't see each other ...'

'Bloody Christ!' Lisa erupted upwards off the bed, pushing him aside. She stood, hands on hips, and let rip. 'You did this deliberately! You come here to dump me, but you thought you'd fuck me first, see what it was like. All that shit about wanting me - all you wanted was sex, wasn't it? 'Cos Lisa don't matter, do she? She's 'ad more pricks in 'er than a dartboard, what's one more? She don't 'ave feelings. She's just a fuckin' slag, so why not treat her like shit like all the bloody rest of 'em? Christ, I hate you! I don't never want to see you again. You can piss off ...'

Colin began to feel sick. He had not witnessed one of her explosions of passion since she had stormed out of the service at St John's, and he shook before her onslaught. All he could think of was how to escape from the shrieking, hysterical harridan before him.

'I have no intention of staying,' he said, with exaggerated calmness, edging backwards towards the door. 'I'm only glad I've found out what you're really like. I should have known you couldn't change.'

Lisa whirled round, picked up a pillow from her bed, and flung it at him. 'You fuckin' hypocrite!'

Colin dodged the pillow. He reached the relative safety of the door, and opened it. 'And I suggest you go down on your knees and pray for forgiveness after I've gone, because you're going to hell otherwise, and I can tell you now, nobody decent is ever going to want anything to do with a ... with a stupid fat slag like you!' He headed swiftly for the stairs.

Lisa lunged after him, crying, 'I'm not! I'm not! Don't go, Col! Please. I'm sorry. I love you. I didn't mean it. You can't go. Colin!'

He fought her off. Down the stairs, out of the front door, into the car. Start the engine, wrench the vehicle round on the gravel, past her dishevelled form clutching her dress around her on the doorstep, and away onto the road. Her outburst had left him shaking; he forgot the tenderness with which he had caressed her. He couldn't imagine how he had ever thought he loved her. He had to stop on the way home for some strong coffee to settle his trembling body, but nothing would ever eradicate his shame.

Eight

There was no escaping the training the Leathwell diocese put on for its new clergy, but Alison would have been happy to attend in any case. She welcomed anything that took her the seven miles to the tranquil village of Farnthorpe, and the Diocesan Retreat House that occupied a series of thatched and timbered buildings on its only street. Twenty-four hours here would always nourish her spirit, and this conference had the further advantage of reuniting her with some of the old friends she'd trained with on the Leathwell Programme for Ministerial Training. Like Jackie, with her ample proportions dignified by a black suit, clerical collar and bright pink shirt. Currently socking it to them in a group of rural parishes, by her own account, with hundreds of farmers falling at her feet and wanting her to baptise their cows. Or diminutive, soft-spoken Pam, made unusually belligerent by a new vicar who hardly let her do anything.

But not Michael, of course, who'd withdrawn from ordination barely weeks before the service, having decided, so he'd written to them all, that his vocation lay in as yet unknown fields elsewhere. When she arrived in the main meeting room for the second of their Saturday morning sessions and found Michael sitting casually on a chair chatting to one of her fellow curates, the shock mesmerized her.

'Are you OK?' said Jackie's voice behind her.

'It's Michael,' she whispered. 'What's he doing here?'

'Michael! Darling!' Jackie called, surging over to throw her arms around him.

Alison slipped into a seat at the back, and busied herself getting her notebook from her bag.

'Aren't you going to say hello?' Jackie asked, returning to slide into the seat next to her.

Alison was aware of Michael looking across at her, waiting for her to acknowledge him, but she needed to prepare herself first. 'Later,' she told Jackie. 'We're about to start.'

'I thought you two were buddies.'

'Were. We kind of lost touch.' Jackie was looking at her acutely.

'Jenny was getting jealous, so I kept out of the way. Sshh. I'll tell you later.'

Alison settled herself, hands folded over the notebook on her lap, eyes fixed on Nan Patten, who had come to address them. Nan had taught on the Programme before becoming Diocesan Director of Ordinands, and had been instrumental in persuading Alison to try for ordination. A small, wiry priest in her late forties, with short, dyed-gold hair and a fiercesome reputation that had only been enhanced by her marriage to Christopher Ridgefield, who was the strait-laced Principal of St Barnabas Theological College.

Alison usually enjoyed listening to Nan's lectures, but today, her attention kept switching to Michael. Nearly a year had passed since she had last met him, but he'd scarcely changed at all: a slim, brown-limbed figure, casual in shorts and tee-shirt, with his dark hair flopping over straight brows, deep brown eyes and that wide smile. Once, simply seeing him would have rendered her senseless. She'd pursued him desperately, manipulated him, if she were honest, into falling in love with her, and done all she could to ensnare him ... the passionate exchanges in her car, the rendezvous in the night-shrouded grounds of St Barnabas when the Programme held its residential courses, the creeping to his bed to hold him in an ecstasy of longing, overwhelming his senses with her need to be loved. She'd justified herself with a blinkered insistence that his recent marriage to Jenny was already doomed, whatever his repeated assertions to the contrary. In the end, though, she'd pushed him too far, taken him to the brink of consummation only to have him tear himself away and run back in horror to his wife. They'd all suffered from it. Her own marriage had been dealt a death-blow, despite the half-hearted attempt she'd made to rescue it by having Luke. Jenny had had a breakdown and put Michael through hell. Sacrificing her continued need of his friendship had been Alison's way of trying to make amends.

Conscious of her stare, Michael turned towards her. He grinned and mouthed 'hello', and she grinned back. No, the danger was past. She could look at him with equanimity now, cured by time and experience of the lonely longings that had haunted her for so long.

'Allie! I hoped you'd be here,' he said, coming to find her directly the session was over. He kissed her, not quite on her mouth, and laid an arm across her shoulder. 'How are you? I am glad to see you! You're looking wonderful. I like your hair like that.' He ran a finger along her head to the knot of hair clipped at the back. Michael had always touched and hugged practically everyone who came within reach. It hadn't made things easier.

'I'm fine,' she said. 'Let me buy you a drink, and we can catch up.'

They got drinks from the makeshift bar in what had once been the grand hall of the main building, and took their drinks out onto the patio by the dining room, while they waited for lunch.

'I hear you're having another baby,' she said.

'Yes, August. How did you know?'

'Colin Blatherwycke mentioned it when he came to Wellesley to see about doing his show at the festival.'

'Oh, yes. How did he get on with Lisa? He had a long talk with me about her before he went, but he hasn't been in touch since.'

'They had an almighty row, from what I can gather. She's unusually silent about the cause. I haven't quite worked out who dumped who, or whether she's heartbroken, or wanting to kill him. I don't think she's too sure either, but she's been getting through a lot of tissues.'

'I'll have to ring him and see how he is.'

'Give him my regards and say I'm looking forward to seeing him. Do you know, he had the cheek to try and pull out of doing the show? I gave him a rocket, and told him he had to come, and I'd send Lisa away for the weekend if that was what was worrying him. Stupid man! How's Jenny enjoying pregnancy this time round?'

'She's thriving on it - it was her idea to have another one. Things have improved no end since September, she's much more herself. She finally worked out why she'd been treating me like dirt practically since our honeymoon, and it makes a hell of a difference now she's stopped pushing me away all the time.' He dropped his voice and leant towards her, setting his drink rocking on the rickety wooden table. 'I'm sorry we didn't sort it out years ago, then I wouldn't have ended up messing you about.'

'Don't!' Alison felt herself colouring. She leant forward herself, cupping her cheek to conceal her face and her words from the small groups dotted around the shaded courtyard. 'It was my fault, and you know it was, throwing myself at you. I can't believe how selfish I was.'

'I encouraged you.'

'Not really. You were trying to be tactful about telling me what a fool I was making of myself.'

The sound of a handbell signalling lunch intruded on their inquest. Michael held her eyes a moment, and smiled. 'Fool or not, it is good to see you again.'

He stood up, picked up her drink for her, and led her inside. 'What's this festival Colin's coming for?' he asked as they took their seats at one of the six round tables in the low-beamed dining hall.

Alison explained while Jackie served them with quiche. 'I'm having nightmares about it. I've persuaded them to think big, and hire the school hall, but what if no one comes? The rural dean's annoyed enough at me taking over the organisation of the thing - as he sees it. If it's a failure, I don't know how I'll face everyone.'

'Why don't you ask Ty Nixon to come and cover it for his TV company?' Michael asked. 'That'd get you publicity.'

'Did I hear you mention my mate Tyrone?' Jackie asked. 'I've wondered how he was getting on.'

'He's doing pretty well now,' Michael replied. 'He's involved in this religious cable TV company based in London. His beloved mummy pulled some strings originally, but he's taken his chance. You should see his car. He drops in sometimes to impress Jenny, being her cousin. He says he's always on the lookout for ideas, so he could be interested doing something about your festival. He could film Pure Power - it'd come over well on the TV.'

'That's an idea,' Alison said. 'We'd get a lot more people if they think they're going to be on telly, even if it is a minority channel. I don't know what Lisa will think about that, though. She hasn't seen him since he walked out on her. Still, she won't be around. She's taking the boys to Steve so she can avoid Colin. It doesn't half complicate everything, having a nanny with a love life.' She took a mouthful of salad, and chewed it thoughtfully. 'It'd be a lot better if it was the BBC, or someone people had heard of.'

'Why don't you ask Becky Patten if she'd come along?' said Michael.

Alison considered the proposition. Nan's daughter was a television presenter who had graduated from fronting children's Saturday morning television programmes to doing shows for young people. She'd had a brief relationship with Michael before his marriage, and as was the way with Michael and his various girlfriends, they'd remained close.

'I don't know her well enough to ask,' she mused. 'Anyway, she wouldn't come to something as trivial as this, and she'd charge the earth. And it's far too short notice ...'

'Bet she'd do it for free if I asked her,' Michael said. 'If she's available. I'll tell her it's good for her image to do the odd spot of charity work. It's not as though you want her to do very much, just turn up and say "I declare this show open", so you can plaster her name across your posters. She doesn't even have to stay and watch. We could get Nan to ask her as well - a two-pronged attack. She won't dare refuse.'

Lunch ended. Michael and Alison took their coffee cups with them and strolled through the terraced gardens that tumbled down to a somnolent river, shaded by the exotic trees that had been planted by an adventurous householder a hundred years before. They settled themselves on the grassy bank above the water. The day was warm and sticky, Alison's long shorts and close-fitting vest clung to her skin, and she rubbed sweat from the back of her neck as Michael spread himself out beside her.

'How are things with Steve?' he asked.

'He's a slimy bastard and I hate him!'

Michael waited for her to continue, and when she remained silent, said, 'So shut up, Michael, nothing to do with you?'

'It's not that. I'm not sure whether it's right to tell you everything like I used to. Jenny might not approve.'

He laughed. 'Jenny doesn't mind. We're happier now than we've ever been. She knew you'd be here today, and she's expecting me to talk to you. I mean, I'm not pushing you into anything, but if you can't talk to me about what Steve's been up to, who can you tell?'

Alison hesitated. She'd been too embarrassed to talk to anyone about the distressing encounter with her husband that had, as far as she was concerned, finally ended any possibility of reconciliation. Only Michael, as he had pointed out, was not anyone.

'He stayed over Christmas,' she said. 'The boys pleaded with him to come, and we agreed he ought to, for their sake, though he'd have to sleep on the sofa. It wasn't too bad on Christmas Day. I had various services to do, so with that and Christmas dinner, and the telly, we survived pretty well. He was being quite good-tempered, for him.' She clasped her arms around her knees, staring at the ground as she picked her words. 'Then on Boxing Day evening, we stayed up watching a film, with a few drinks, you know. And Steve came and sat next to me on the sofa, leaned against me, put his hand on my leg.' She lifted her head and let herself meet Michael's eyes. 'I thought he was coming on to me, it seemed like it. And I hadn't had sex for months and months. I was lonely. I wanted it. And he was my only legitimate chance. So when the film ended I said why didn't he spend the night with me.'

'And did he?' Michael prompted, as she paused before reliving the memory.

'He laughed at me. Said I must be mad thinking he'd ever want to have sex with a flabby middle-aged wreck like me. I was boring and predictable in bed, and I hadn't turned him on in years. I was shocked - he's never said anything like that before, and it was such a turnaround after him being relatively nice all evening. I couldn't think what to say. I tried to hit back and say he'd never done anything for me either, but then he said he'd been with other women since I walked out, and they'd not made any complaints, so it must be my fault.'

'You shouldn't take it seriously - his pride's hurt, that's all.'

'That wasn't all. He said I hadn't even been able to have an affair with you when I tried, because you couldn't bring yourself to do it with me. And then he said he thought at first Luke wasn't his, but he realised he had to be, because there wasn't a man alive would want to fuck me.'

Michael laughed, and reached over to lay a hand on her arm. 'Oh, Allie, he's talking bollocks, you know he is.'

'But supposing he's right, and there isn't a man alive who's ever going to want me? I mean, you didn't, not really. I am getting on.'

'I don't like to remind you about it after what we were saying before lunch, but you know perfectly well what effect you had on me, and how difficult it was to stop. Boring and predictable are not the words that spring to mind.' A mischievous glint appeared in his eye. 'I still think you're drop-dead gorgeous, I merely try to keep it in the mind, rather than the groin. If you do divorce Steve, you'll have queues of men after you; they're probably forming already.'

His jollying tone was having its effect. In the sultry air of a summer afternoon, Steve's venom was losing its power. She smiled. 'I don't know about queues. Most men think I must be far too holy for sex to enter my head. Though I did meet a man a few months ago who seemed interested in me, and that cheered me up. Not that it came to anything.'

She'd heard nothing from Iain, and his conduct when he returned to the school with a colleague ten days after the inspection to present his report, suggested he had either forgotten - or wished to forget - his invitation in the garden. He had not been unfriendly, but neither had he singled her out in any way. He had shaken her hand and said goodbye with a carefully neutral smile, and then he was gone, back to his home somewhere in the Midlands and beyond her reach.

'And how are things with Steve now?'

'We've barely spoken. I paid for Lisa to have driving lessons, and now she's passed her test, she's ferrying the boys there for weekends, and

I don't have to see him.'

'Have you not discussed a divorce?'

'Not yet. I definitely want one, only I haven't been able to face the thought of raking it all over for lawyers. I thought I'd just wait till we've been separated for two years, that's the simplest thing.'

'Ring me if you need to talk. Ring me anyway, I want to keep in touch. I'll have to let you know what Becky says.'

'As long as you're sure Jenny doesn't mind.'

'Why should she?' He gave a satisfied, uxorious, little smile.

'Was she pleased about you backing out of being ordained?'

Michael considered her for a moment before replying. 'She wanted what was best for me. I realised it wasn't really right.'

'So what *are* you going to do?'

He shrugged. 'Nothing. What I do now. Look after Lyddy and the new one, and whatever comes along.' He grinned. 'It's a good life.'

'It'd drive me mad.' She looked at her watch. 'I ought to be getting back inside. Thanks for listening.'

'Any time, Allie.' He stood up, reached out a hand to help her to her feet, and together they slowly began to make their way up the bank.

The after-effects of the inspection lingered through the summer term, increasing the irascibility of the teaching staff and escalating their absences for ill-health. Alison met Megan outside school hours to help her recover from the trauma Iain's team had visited on her; perhaps one day she would ask him how he could possibly justify it. The conifers stayed in the courtyard, since Mrs Tarbuck lacked the energy to retrieve them, and Alex's office was strewn with extensive drafts of the action plan the school had to produce in response to their inspection report.

The report lay in Alison's lap now, as she sat with Alex discussing the plan. Thirty-plus formal, carefully worded pages, patched together by reporting Inspector Mr Iain Sutherland from the evidence collected by the various members of his team. A relentless recitation, to be studied and acted on within a specified time limit on pain of rude letters from OFSTED or a personal takeover by the Secretary of State for Education and his dog. It gave them more to work on than they'd expected, but the school had got through.

Alison stretched her arms behind her and yawned. 'I hadn't realised it would be forty nights as well as forty days producing this wretched action plan. It even had me awake for hours last night, worrying about how

I'm going to weld the governors together into an effective team. It was a shock to find I was in one of the key issues for action.'

'He was a little harsh, I thought, given you'd only just taken over. I did try to get the wording toned down, but he wouldn't buy it.'

'He turned out to be quite stubborn, didn't he?'

She'd had her first intimation of that side of Iain's character when he'd presented his report. He had handled the meeting with his usual good humour, responding politely to the questions and challenges she and the other governors posed to his critique, but he was clearly not prepared to concede anything bar the odd typographical error.

'I suppose they have to say what they find,' she continued. 'It's a challenge. I shall enjoy getting my teeth into it. Have you decided what to do about the History Department?'

'Ah, yes.' Alex made a steeple of his hands. 'Very awkward. They don't name names, but it's obvious to anyone who knows anything that it's Nina and Paul who are providing the good and very good teaching, and Terry who's unsatisfactory.'

'He did have a particularly difficult lesson when the Inspector was there - James being awkward didn't help.'

'It wasn't just that. I had a long talk to the Inspector about it, with History being one of our key issues. I know Terry's never going to be first class, but Nina and I had both been working with him, and I must admit, I would have expected his teaching to be sound. I wasn't expecting young Paul Croft to do so well, either. I thought it would take him a couple of years before he recovered from his experience at his last school, but he's been gaining in stature all year. Given that, and given the report, and given Terry's simply going to have to do some further training, I shall have to ask Paul to be acting Head of Department next term, rather than Terry. And that is not going to go down too well. You may get him complaining to you.'

Alison made a face. 'I'll try and be sympathetic.'

Colin arrived in Wellesley with the St John's van towards the end of the afternoon, just as the festival workshops were finishing. Alison welcomed him cheerfully, relieved that he had not had another of his infuriating fits of reluctance about bringing the show.

She showed him and his team to the school hall, and left them backstage to make their preparations, while she returned to the entrance lobby to await Becky Patten. It was something of a coup to have got her, and a tribute to Michael's powers of persuasion that she wasn't merely turning up, but was going to take part in the show as well. As soon as Becky appeared, Alison took her into the hall to introduce her to Colin.

'This is Becky Patten,' she said. 'As if you won't recognise her.'

Becky laughed, black hair swinging round her ears, lips wide with orange lipstick. 'Hello, Colin. Michael's told me lots about you.'

Colin shook hands awkwardly, as if he felt some consternation at having a young woman who had been through a number of high profile failed love affairs included in his show, especially if she were going to wear her current short, brown dress. The rest of the St John's team were enthusiastic, however; excited about the interest Becky's presence was generating, and about the fact that there were television cameras there to record it. They crowded round her, explaining about the cameo role they had written for her as a contestant in their dating game sketch.

While they took her off to rehearse, Alison went down into the body of the hall to see how Ty was getting on with setting up his equipment. At some point, there was going to be an interesting encounter between Becky and Ty, for he had been responsible for the scandal about Becky's mother that had enlivened the Diocese of Leathwell and much of the rest of the country three years before. Christopher Ridgefield had been a leading campaigner against women priests, and it had been a shock when the tabloids broke the news that he was romping in a Cretan love-nest with one of them. In fact, Nan and he had married some months previously, but that had not been allowed to spoil the story. The two of them were still understandably angry with Ty, and Becky would surely have her own views on the topic.

Ty these days was a stockily built man of around thirty, with a fleshy face, gold-rimmed glasses, short light hair receding from his forehead, and a neat beard around a full mouth. He was gesticulating as he talked to his cameraman.

'Any problems?' Alison asked him.

He looked up, frowning, as if he had forgotten who she was. 'I need to talk to the guy in charge of the show.'

'Come with me.'

They found Colin wedged in the narrow space under the stage, fiddling with a faulty cable.

'Having trouble?' Tyrone asked. 'What's the problem?' He removed an expensive black leather jacket which he handed to Alison, and crouched down to join the inspection.

Problems with the cable continued, delaying the start of the show, but eventually they got under way. Ten minutes after the scheduled starting time, Alison stood at the back of the audience of some two hundred young people, and watched Colin walk onto the stage to testify in the strongest possible terms to the advantages of virginity. Then, before anyone could get restless, he signalled for the lights to illuminate the band from St John's, male and female alike alluring in black leather, and allowed them to blast him from the stage.

Once she was satisfied that the show was well under way, Alison left the hall. She had been driving the festival all day, and needed a moment to catch up with herself. She fetched a plastic mug of coffee from the machine, and sat down on one of the low chairs that lined the entrance lobby. Fortunately, there'd been time to change out of her formal suit into loose trousers and a vest; she could slip off her shoes, and tuck her legs up under her. She was not the only one escaping. Outside the front doors, Ty and Becky stood on the step with cigarettes in their mouths. It had not taken them long to reach an understanding; the sound of their laughter floated inside above the noise of the music.

Colin appeared from the direction of the hall, looking as if he too needed escape. It took courage to speak as he had in front of that kind of audience; no wonder his face was haggard.

Alison indicated a seat. 'Do join me. I am going back in in a minute, but I needed a respite. I'm dead on my feet. It's going well, don't you think?'

'I'm praying they don't mess it up with the cameras here,' Colin said, sitting down on the edge of a chair.

'I expect Ty will cut out any serious cock-ups.'

'It's useful, you knowing him.'

'I don't know him that well. We coincided for a year when I was training.'

'How do you mean? He's not ordained, is he?'

'No, no, he got chucked out. You must know, he's the one who snooped after Nan Patten and Christopher Ridgefield and got them spread all over the *News of the World.*'

Colin stared at her. 'I didn't realise ... You mean he's the one who went out with Lisa?'

'Went out with? Bullied and exploited her, more like. She thought he was the love of her life, and he was an absolute bastard to her. Treated her like dirt, and then abandoned her one afternoon in the middle of

Leathwell without a word, and she's never seen or spoken to him since.'

What little colour Colin had left his face as she spoke.

'She must have told you,' Alison said.

'Yeah. I don't care. It's nothing to me. We've split up. She wanted to split up. So did I.'

'I can't say either of you seem terribly happy about it. I don't know what happened, but ...'

'It's none of your business,' he said, standing up. 'You're as bad as Michael, going on at me. I'm perfectly happy, just leave me alone.'

'But Lisa ... '

'Damn Lisa!' he hissed, and went back into the hall.

Nine

'Hello, is that Alison Thompson?'

The telephone rang just as she'd brought her morning coffee through to her study to finish composing letters of thanks after the festival - agreed by everyone to have been an astounding success, with Becky's contribution the highlight of the evening. The momentary irritation she felt at the sixth call of the morning vanished when she recognised the burr of the voice on the other end.

'Iain? Hello. I didn't expect to hear from you.' She checked herself, suddenly afraid her enthusiasm might be misplaced. 'Or is it something about the report?'

'No, no, that's all finished with as far as I'm concerned. I did say I'd ring you in July.'

'I know, but you didn't say anything last time we met, so I thought you'd given up on the idea.'

'I'm sorry. I was afraid mebbe I'd overstepped the mark by luring you to the garden, so I was making sure I wasn't appearing partial. I didn't mean to give the impression I regretted the offer. You've not had second thoughts, have you?'

'No. I'd like to meet you.'

'I'm coming your way the week after next. Name a day - the school's flexible.'

'Thursday's my day off.'

'I'll see what I can do. I'll want two or three hours at the school, but supposing I was free for one, how about making it lunch? We could go to the Hawkshill, have a bar meal or go in the restaurant, whatever you prefer.'

'A bar meal's enough for me.'

'Very well. You know where it is? I'll see you at one, Thursday week. I'll look forward to it.'

'So will I. Thank you. I am glad you rang.'

She put the phone down, smiling to herself as she scribbled in her diary. That done, she sat back in her chair with her coffee clasped in her hands, gazing out of the window at the shrubs that lined the tangled lawn she kept meaning to nag James into mowing. Very likely this foray would come to nothing. She'd discover exactly why Iain's ex-wife had got fed up with him, or he'd find her boring, predictable, and a severe disappointment. But maybe there was a chance ... she dreamed on.

Her reverie was disturbed by the sound of the doorbell.

Luke's feet pattered down the hall, pursued by the slow feet of Lisa, who was taking time to recover from a debilitating stomach bug that had mercifully missed the rest of the family. A minute later, Bunty was being shown into her study.

'So this is where all the work's done, is it?' Bunty asked, advancing to Alison's bookshelves and peering closely at the titles. 'You've not got that many, have you? Father Mark loved his books, he had them all down the hall as well as in here, and he used to give sermons about the latest ones he'd read. I don't suppose you got to do much theology, with your not being at theological college. Now, about the notice board,' Bunty continued, without drawing a breath that would have allowed Alison to defend her academic abilities. 'I've been talking to Father Nigel. It's a disgrace.'

'It is untidy, certainly,' Alison replied politely.

'We can't go on making alterations for ever. We need a new one.' She sat down in the chair opposite Alison's with her red file on her knee. 'A notice board should grab people's attention, tell them clearly what's going on in the church. We need to get rid of that archaic printing, have something new, and bigger, and modern. Father suggested I had a chat with you, because you were looking into it.'

Dear Nigel. He would. 'I wouldn't exactly say I was looking into it,' Alison said. 'I haven't had time.'

'Then why don't I do some research, get a few ideas of what might be possible, get some brochures?'

'That's a good idea.' Anything that kept Bunty occupied was probably a good idea, though it niggled a little to allow her to take over a job Alison had fully intended to do one day. 'You can bring your findings to the PCC in October, and we can all discuss it then.'

'Righty-ho.' Bunty's gaze strayed past Alison to the garden. 'Such a shame you've not managed to keep the garden up. Father Mark ...'

Father Mark no doubt bred prize roses and preached inspirational sermons on the ethics of slug-baiting, but Alison wasn't prepared to hear about it. 'Was there anything else?' she interrupted.

Bunty consulted her file with deliberation. 'Not at the moment,' she said.

Alison showed her to the door, wondering why their brief conversation could not have been conducted on the phone. It dawned on her, as she went back to her desk, that Bunty was simply being nosy, seizing her chance to see inside the house, and to check that the new curate was using the place as Father bloody Mark would have wanted. What a shame she'd been hard at work, formally dressed for a promised visit to the old people's luncheon club, instead of sprawled half-naked on her sun-lounger with papers in her lap and her eyes closed. Now that would have given Bunty something to choke on.

With a sense of snubbing Bunty, she decided to take the extra time to walk to the church. Folding her jacket over her bag, and with the bag slung over her shoulder, she set out with an insouciant air. The farmland that had once surrounded the church had long since been re-sown with the large housing estate where she lived, but in the distance, tall trees marked the edge of the fields where the countryside began again. The soil was still fertile; either side of the street, gardens shouted with colour. The neighbours she encountered responded to her smile with cheerful greetings. Her bare arms luxuriated in the soft caress of the sunshine. And in two weeks' time, she'd got a date ...

She paused by the lychgate to contemplate the notice board, a square metre or so of varnished wood set at an angle in the corner of the churchyard across from the car-park.

FR NIGEL SANDERSON, ST PETER'S VICARAGE ...
REVD ALISON THOMPSON, 45, KESTREL ROAD ...
CHURCHWARDENS: BUNTY RANGER ... ELLA STEADMAN ...
SUNDAY SERVICES 8 AM MASS 10 AM SUNG MASS ... ALL WELCOME

Hardly an inspiring design, but heaven knew what Bunty would prefer. A twelve-foot high board with Repent Ye spelt out in foot-high pink neon lights? Why not? The Church had to enter the modern age.

'Checking when to turn up on Sunday?' Nigel's voice was close enough to her ear to startle her.

'Oh, hello, Nigel. Thanks for sending me Bunty this morning. I told her to go off and do some research on a new notice board, and we'd discuss it at the PCC in October.'

'That sounds sensible. If in doubt, defer it, and hope everyone'll forget.'

'We do need to do something about it, though, and it saves me a job. Where are you off to?'

'The luncheon club. Annie Hyde asked me to drop in.'

'So was I. That's a waste of effort, isn't it? Shall I let you go, and I'll come another day?'

Annie appeared at the door of the hall on the other side of the car park, and waved a hand at them.

'Too late, we've been spotted,' Nigel said.

'Elderly lunches it is, then,' Alison murmured as they headed towards the hall. 'But don't forget we have our meeting at one-thirty, at your house.'

Nigel raised his eyebrows. 'What meeting's that ...? Ah, of course. Good thinking, wonderwoman, you're learning fast.'

'Do you have to ... oh, hello Mrs Stubbings, how are you?' She stopped to help the stout elderly lady out of the taxi that had pulled up at the edge of the car park, and her chance to reprimand Nigel was gone. Still, what did it matter on a day like today? She gave Mrs Stubbings her arm. 'How's your daughter? Did she get that job she went for?'

Together, they advanced towards the door.

Alison set out for the Hawkshill Hotel a little late, feeling decidedly nervous, because she hadn't been out on a date for decades. Not that this was a date, as she kept reminding herself firmly. A date might not be appropriate, but there could be nothing wrong in lunching with a friend and colleague; why only the other day she'd lunched with the new male curate in the nearby Tatsford team ministry, and thought nothing of it. Though that engagement had not given her the agonies over hair and face and dress that this one gave her. She left a trail of clothing across her bed as she discarded one outfit after another, before finally returning to a long button-through blue dress that echoed the colour of her eyes, if Iain thought to look closely.

He was sitting reading some paperwork at one of the three tables on the hotel's small forecourt when she arrived, his grey suit jacket over the back of a white cast iron chair. The cloud had parted to allow warmth through from the summer sun, and he had turned back the sleeves of his faintly striped shirt to expose arms on which the hair remained dark.

He stood when he saw her approach, and held out his hand, smiling broadly. 'How very good to see you again. I was beginning to think you'd got caught up with some parochial emairgency or other.'

Alison returned his handshake. 'Sorry. I always take Luke swimming on a Thursday morning, and I tried to fit Tesco in as well, but it took longer than I thought.'

'It always does, doesn't it? I always mean to be in and out in an hour, but it never works that way.'

'I wouldn't have thought you'd need to buy much, being on your own.'

'It still takes time. Shall we go through to the bar and order, then we can eat in the garden out the back if you like? I'm afraid I need to be away by half-two, I've a meeting to get back for.'

The bar was dark, its low ceilings and panelled walls doing nothing to compensate for the brightness excluded by its small windows. They had to fight their way through groups of workers striving on this fine day to make more of their lunch hour than sandwiches at a desk.

Iain found a menu, bought her a drink while she studied it, and managed to place their food orders almost immediately, despite the queue at the bar.

'How much do I owe you?' Alison asked as she carried her glass of wine out into the garden.

'Nothing. I'll pay.'

'I'm quite happy to pay for myself.'

They sat down at one end of a long wooden table already occupied by an elderly couple and an infant with the excited tone of an indulged grandchild.

'I invited you. I'd like to treat you.'

His voice was polite, but Alison was aware she had touched that stubborn strand in him. It took her aback for a moment, shattering some mythical expectation of instant rapport with the reminder that developing even this modest friendship would require endless adjustments. She observed Iain laying his jacket on the bench next to him, careful that his wallet didn't fall out, and wondered what she'd let herself in for.

'I expect you think I'm terribly chauvinistic,' he said in a low, apologetic voice, leaning forwards over the table. 'I expect to pick up the bill if I invite someone out to lunch - male or female. But I know I do sometimes come across as patriarchal and oppressive.' His lip twitched. 'You see, I know the jargon. My first wife was very heavily into that kind of thing.'

'Your first? How many have you had?'

Iain looked awkward. 'Ex-wife, I should have said. She was right, though I couldn't see it at the time. I insisted my career was the most important thing, and her place was to back me up. When she started questioning that, and trying to be more independent, it got very unpleasant. Yelling and plate-throwing from her. Quiet dignity from me.' He laughed sourly. 'I can see why it drove her up the wall. The odd thing is, after the divorce was through, I got involved in working on equal opportunities policies, and realised there was something in all the accusations Ros had been making.' He took a sip from his half pint of beer. 'Forgive me. That's not what I was intending to talk about.'

'I don't mind, I'm interested. It's not like listening to the fifth person that day telling you they'll leave the church if you mess with the notice board.'

Iain looked amused. 'Is that what they worry about?'

'Oh, that, and the misprints on the flowers rota, and whether the British Legion banner goes on the left or the right of the altar, or there's weeks of pique because you haven't visited the old people's luncheon club. I shouldn't say that. It must give you a very bad impression of the church.'

'I didn't have a terribly good one to start with. I'm afraid I'm an atheist. By conviction. As far as I'm concerned, the universe makes some sense without a god, and very little if you postulate one.'

'You mean the problem of evil? How can there be a loving God when there's so much suffering in the world?'

'Amongst other things. I sometimes think the Church itself is the ultimate proof of the non-existence of God.'

'Don't tell anyone, but so do I sometimes,' Alison said, propping her chin on her hands, knowing she was flirting when she should have been defending the faith, but what the hell - Henry the Eighth did the same thing.

He regarded her, his head on one side. 'You're not a bit like any clergy I've ever come across. Are you sure that's what you do? You're not having me on?'

'Perhaps I'm too new to have been clericalised.' She hesitated, not wanting to put him off with piety, but needing to be honest. 'I might not be complimentary about the church as an organisation, but I am passionately committed to my work. To God.' She grimaced. 'There, do I sound clerical now?'

'No. You sound like someone I'd like to get to know better.'

He spoke with a quiet seriousness that touched her. She wasn't sure what response to make, but was saved by the call of the young woman weaving through the garden, tray in hand. 'Chicken Salad and Steak Pie? Chicken and Steak?'

Iain beckoned her over.

'We've been up to our ears preparing our action plan,' Alison said, when they had finally settled into eating. 'The History department's ...'

'I'd rather not discuss anything to do with your inspection with you,' Iain broke in.

'Why on earth not? My old head used to say inspectors were a gossipy bunch. I've been looking forward to hearing some of the juicy snippets you didn't dare put in the report.'

'I prefer not to confuse my professional role with my pairsonal life.' He sawed carefully at his piece of steak.

Alison tried again: 'Do you do a lot of inspections and travelling about - can I ask that?'

'A fair amount. Three or four inspections a year, which means several visits per school on top of that. I quite like getting away, meeting new people. Then I do a lot of in-service training and consultancy around the place.'

'Do you think things are improving?'

Iain hesitated, his knife and fork poised above his plate. 'I'm not sure I want to discuss education in general with you either. Do you mind?'

'Oh.' Alison fought off a sense that her wrists had been slapped. 'I thought that was one of the things we had in common.'

'I'm sure we have a great deal in common, and we'll have some interesting discussions in the future, but I don't think it would be appropriate at this stage.'

'You make it sound as if we shouldn't be meeting.'

'No, we're not doing anything wrong, but I really don't want to talk about your inspection, and it would be difficult to talk about education generally without you, well both of us, thinking about Wellesley High. Once I'm involved somewhere else, we can chat about it all you like. That is, assuming you want to meet me again. You're mebbe thinking what a pompous and boring old sod I am ...' He was looking at her anxiously.

'Not at all, I realise you have to be careful.'

'I got myself in an awkward situation once, that's all. It's probably made me over-cautious. I'm not entirely sure how one manages these things when you live a hundred miles apart, but I would like to see you sometimes.'

She smiled. 'As long as we can find something to talk about.'

'Somehow, I don't think that's ever going to be a problem.'

He was right - by the time they parted an hour later, they'd barely started.

Two weeks to go now until the term ended. One and a half hours, one afternoon and ten more days. Terry had been ticking the time off in his mind since half-term. He sat now wearing his way through the sagging bottom of his regular chair in the staff room, hands in the pockets of shapeless brown tweed trousers, jangling change in one and a set of keys in the other. Occasionally he interjected remarks into the conversation going on on his right between Lil and Megan. With a few minutes to go before the end of morning break, the long narrow room was full of teachers finishing tea and coffee, gossiping, or sitting with their heads in papers, retrenching for the next lesson. The summer was always an exhausting round of marking and reports, and the turmoil of the inspection had left everybody on edge. He was one of the few who hadn't been off sick since. He hadn't dared. The way things were going, he'd have lost all his classes to the caretaker.

'Oh, here's Allie,' Megan said. 'Like the outfit!'

Terry looked up and sighed at the vision of his curate sauntering through the staff room in long blue shorts and a bright-green vest more fitted for the beach.

She paused to exchange a word with Megan, before sliding herself onto the edge of the low square coffee table in front of him.

Terry offered no greeting. Not content with ridiculing his music at church, she'd done bugger all to advance his position at the school - almost as if she was engaged in a personal vendetta against him.

'You here again?' he sneered. 'Anyone'd think you worked here!'

'Alex asked me to drop in, but he's with a pupil. It's supposed to be my day off, but never mind.' She leaned forward and dropped her voice. 'I gather you're not happy about Paul being your acting Head of Department.'

'Of course I'm not happy! It's always been understood I'd take over while Nina was away. I'm by far the more senior teacher.'

'Alex had to take the inspection report into account.'

'Hah! You know perfectly well OFSTED made me a scapegoat. Typical! Just because I don't fit with their trendy notions, they generalise from one difficult lesson. Fat lot of support you were, you should have got them to rewrite that part of the report.'

'He wouldn't alter anything. These Reggies are an intractable lot.'

'You should have insisted. You would if it had been anyone else, but no, no one at this school appreciates the work I put in!' Terry had raised his voice, and he sensed conversations elsewhere faltering as faces turned in his direction.

'That's simply not true,' Alison said calmly. 'I didn't come out of the report all that well either, and I'm not complaining. Come on, Terry, if you really believe you're not being treated fairly, you should go and talk to Alex again. It's not down to me.'

'You're the bloody Chair of Governors! You neglect all your other work at church because you say you've got to come here, and then you say you've got no influence.'

'I don't get involved in the day-to-day running of the school, that's Alex's area. I'd only come into it if you were to make a formal protest.'

'That's what I'm doing.'

'Then put it in writing, and we'll have a formal meeting about it - preferably not in the middle of a crowded staff room.'

Terry rose, his irritation increased by the reasonableness of her tone. 'You'll be hearing from me!'

He stomped from the room, deriving a certain satisfaction from leaving Alison embarrassed at the centre of the staff room's attention. Resentment at his treatment grumbled away inside him as he made his way to his next lesson. His temper required earthing, and he strode into his Year Nine History class ready to use anyone who stepped out of line as a conductor.

'... And where's *your* homework, James?' The boy was crouched over his table, warned of what he could expect by the way Terry had treated two other offenders.

'I left it at home. I have done it. I went up to the library and spent hours on it, only I took it out of my bag to finish off, and I forgot to put it in again.'

'Of course you did. It's amazing how many brilliant pieces of work get left at home, or accidentally eaten by the family dog.'

'It's true! I did do it.'

'You are *supposed* to have your homework to hand in *in* the lesson. I've had just about enough of excuses! You can stay in detention tomorrow, and write me an essay on a subject I'll set you.'

'That's not fair! You can't give me detention for that! You didn't give one to Danny and Gemma.'

'I can do what I like.' Conscious, nonetheless, that he ought to be seen to be fair, he attempted justification. 'Danny and Gemma did give me some work of sorts last week, whereas I seem to recall you had some other fanciful excuse from your repertoire.'

'What if I go home at lunchtime and get it? That'd prove I'd done it.'

'I'm not interested in whether you've done it or not, it's not here when it should be, you'll be in detention tomorrow, and there's an end to it.'

James subsided in his seat, glaring at him. The class as a whole, detecting that it was a bad day to try anything on, sat mute and relatively still.

'Right,' Terry said, pulling a bunch of leaflets from his briefcase, 'I don't suppose you care, but there's a new play about Martin Luther on at the Arts Centre next week. Special rates for school parties. Let me know if you're interested.' He looked around. 'You don't even know who he is, do you? Anyone volunteer a suggestion?'

Thirty faces dropped from sight, intent on their tables. 'Surely the name Martin Luther rings bells with someone?' More silence. 'Come on, James,' he added nastily, 'you must know, with your mother doing what she does.'

That hit the spot. James raised his head. His jaw sagged open, his skin increased its pallor. Ridiculous to think James and Josh could avoid being known as the local curate's sons for ever, but she'd made a big thing of it to staff in case the poor sensitive little dears got teased about it. The threat of revelation certainly stirred James up, but Terry wasn't vindictive.

'No?' he said more kindly. 'Obviously having a History teacher for a mum hasn't improved your knowledge of anything. Sarah, what about you?'

'Martin Luther was the leader of the American Civil Rights movement,' Sarah stated confidently. 'He did that speech about "I have a dream", and ...'

'That was Martin Luther King. You're only a few hundred years out. I was hoping someone might mention the word Reformation ...'

Sarah clapped a hand to her mouth, blushing.

Terry smiled, his temper improving now that he had established his supremacy. 'Right, enough of that. Now, last week ...'

As he got the lesson under way, he was aware of James, slumped back in his chair, sullenly unappreciative of the mercy that had been shown him. Of course, Terry himself would never treat a pupil unfairly simply because he had a tiresome mother, but with an attitude like that, the boy was asking for serious trouble. And if Alison thought that her position in the school would save her son from the retribution he deserved, she would bloody well have to think again.

Ten

August arrived, and Alison drove the boys over to Nottling for Steve to take them camping in France. It was part of the deal she'd made with him when they separated: you must have them for a weekend once a month, and a fortnight in the summer. Their usual campsite offered plenty of activities for him to do with James and Josh, and there was a children's club for Luke; they would, she insisted, be perfectly happy without her there to cater for them. Driving away, she was less convinced. As Luke waved goodbye stoically from Josh's arms, clutching his cuddly dragon and his bucket to his chest lest either be forgotten, she had to blink back tears. She hadn't been apart from him for longer than a weekend before this, and she hated entrusting him, or any of them, to Steve in his current foul mood. Typical Steve, of course, timing his tempers to make her feel bad. She'd been wise not to book a holiday for herself this fortnight, for he'd have been impossible had he thought she was dumping the boys on him while she went off to enjoy herself.

You know he's always a lot better with them when you're not around, she told herself. Josh will mother Luke, they'll be alright. It didn't seem to help much when she was back in an empty house, missing them. Even Lisa had departed, blowing her savings in Spain with a fellow nanny, going at peak time because it was the only time their employers could do without them. Alison had plans for a week away herself in the late autumn; for now, she was going to continue working, but at a more leisurely pace. With the school closed, and many of the parish's regular activities shut down for the holidays, there were fewer demands on her time. She could get to the bottom of her In-tray, organise her filing, take all the time she needed over her next sermon. She had time to study, and to pray, to visit another prospective - but ultimately unsuitable - spiritual director, because she'd not as yet replaced the one she'd given up when she moved to Wellesley. She could even spend the occasional hour sunbathing with an escapist romantic blockbuster, and pretend she too was on a Mediterranean beach.

There was also time to sit with Nigel in his study, making detailed plans with him for the year ahead, the year in which she would at last be a full-blown priest. Her diary was filling rapidly with meetings, and with the services at which she would, from October, be celebrating the Eucharist.

'You know,' she said to Nigel, 'I'm incredibly nervous about it, in case I get things wrong, but it still feels absolutely right. I love the work. I know it's what I'm meant to be doing, even though I do still have a lot to learn, as Bunty and Terry like to keep reminding me. I apparently have an awful long way to go before I'm half as good as Father Mark.'

'Oh, you don't want to take any notice of them,' Nigel responded. 'You're doing very well. Look at how successful the festival was. You sound a lot more confident when you're taking services, and people really appreciate your sermons. Last Sunday's was tremendous, you were much more relaxed.'

'Life's a whole lot less complicated with everyone away.'

'As long as you're not too lonely.'

'I'm alright. I'm catching up with a few people. I'm going to see my friend Jackie over on the other side of Leathwell tomorrow.'

This was a point at which she might have mentioned to Nigel that she was also meeting Iain for lunch later that week, but to say so would be to give the event more significance than it warranted. She did, however, mention it to Jackie as they sat in the garden of her friend's spreading bungalow, consuming unclerical quantities of gin.

'God, Jackie, he is so *nice*! I had lunch with him after the inspection was over, and we were so at ease with each other, like we'd been friends for years.'

'I suppose he's married? They usually are.'

'No, divorced. I'm not sure when, but I got the impression it wasn't that recent.'

'So if he's so nice, how come he's still single? Must be something wrong with him. Really nice men don't stay available. He's probably a wife-beater, or an alcoholic, or something.'

'I think he just works very hard.'

'A workaholic.' Jackie shook her head. 'Just as bad.'

'Well, he makes time for leisurely lunches with me, he can't have that much of a problem.'

Jackie's question stuck in Alison's mind, nonetheless. Perhaps Iain's professional competence and charm masked some less agreeable characteristics. After all, plenty of her teacher friends would say that only the morally and socially deviant ever became inspectors. Well, she could always ask him.

Once again, she found herself taking great care with her appearance before setting out for their rendezvous. She paused for a final time before the mirror in the hall, noting how well the dark turquoises and blues of her new strappy sundress brought out her tan and flattered her figure. Difficult to wear a bra under it, so she hadn't bothered - she'd always been small-breasted, and as long as it didn't look too risqué ... well, if you couldn't dress up for what was practically a date, what were clothes for? Her shoulder-length hair was drawn into a knot at the back of her head. Carefully she pulled a few strands loose to soften the effect, practised looking sexy, and laughed at herself. She gathered up her handbag, and went to get her car from its garage.

Another fine morning. Who needed Spain? Alison sang as she drove to the village on the main road some thirty miles north of Wellesley where they were due to meet, her voice competing with the drone of air from the opened sunroof. Forty-five minutes after setting out, a sign was warning her of good food two hundred yards ahead, and she was slowing down for the entrance. Grey stone buildings spread out beside the road, with a large car park half-occupied away to the right. As she headed for a space in the shade of an immense chestnut tree, she noticed Iain's car, with the outline of his figure in the front seat.

She locked up and approached him. He had tilted his seat back, removed his glasses and sat now with eyes closed. The two front windows were open, and the resultant breeze fingered the thick silver of his hair and tossed at the papers retained on his lap by the hand that held his glasses. He was wearing a lightly patterned short-sleeved blue shirt that revealed a smattering of dark hair at the neck, and khaki trousers, the first time she'd seen him out of a suit. On his wrist, a gold watch jerked the seconds around its face. She paused to study him unobserved for a moment before she disturbed him. What secrets were locked up within his peaceful dreaming? Nothing worse than her own history would show, surely? She would find him out one day, and she saw no reason to be afraid.

'Hello,' she said gently.

He opened his eyes and smiled at her. 'Sorry, I was snatching a few minutes' rest.' He raised his seat and settled his glasses back on his nose. 'I had something of a distairbed night last night.'

'Are you not well? You should have said. We could have done this another time.'

'Oh, no, I'm fine. And I've been looking forward to this. No, my, er, my neighbour's daughter, Hetty, was poorly with a tummy bug, so they were up and down all night with her, and I can hear the doors going, and the toilet and so on.'

'You must have thin walls!'

He pressed buttons to raise the windows as she spoke, replaced his papers in the case that lay next to him, and got out of the car.

'My nanny had the same thing the other week,' she said. 'There's a lot of it about.'

'Let's not dwell on it, it'll put us off our food.' He looked her up and down. 'I never knew vicars could look so sexy.'

'I'm not being a vicar today.'

He raised an eyebrow. 'That sounds promising.' He touched her arm lightly, and guided her into the pub.

Once they had ordered, they went to sit out in the garden. Here, the noise of traffic was a constant thrum, and children shrieked from the fenced-off play area fitted out in the corner of the pub gardens. A parasol hung over their table, evoking intimacy as they leaned forward under it to eat.

'Do things slow down for you in August?' he asked.

'Yes - though I've been helping Nigel with a few weddings. Fortunately everyone at school's gone on holiday now. I had to chair an appeals panel for Terry Howells just after term ended, where he ranted on about the inspection. Alex has made Paul Croft acting Head of Department, when Terry thought it should have been him. He's furious, and he blames it all on you because he thinks you marked him down over one difficult lesson. And he blames me too, to some extent, because it was James causing the problems. I've been defending you like mad.'

Iain communed silently with his food.

'I know,' she continued, 'you don't like me mentioning the inspection, but it's been preying on my mind.' She picked up her tonic water. 'Here's hoping he'll have calmed down by the end of the holidays.'

'It's unfortunate,' Iain said, looking up with a little frown. 'I'd rather not have someone in a position to think I might have been influenced because of you.'

'You know you weren't.'

'That's not the point. I have to be seen to be impartial.' He considered her for a moment, then smiled. 'Ah, well, I don't suppose it'll matter.

Let's talk about something else.'

'You could tell me what you get up to in the summer. Do you get school holidays off?'

'Afraid not. I go into the office some days, and I've been working at home on a conference paper for September.'

'Hetty doesn't distract you too much?'

He looked bemused for a moment. 'Oh, no. Then I'm away to Scotland for a couple of weeks. My sister lives near Dumbarton, and I usually go there, play some golf, do a few things with the children. My mother lives with them, so it's a chance to see her too.'

'Have you any other family?'

'No, just them. And I've a daughter, Claire. She's nineteen, just finished her first year at university. I don't see an awful lot of her. I wasn't a terribly good father, I'm afraid, and with the divorce being messy, she's never really forgiven me.'

Alison paused to take another sip of her drink. 'You haven't had the urge to remarry, in the last however many years it is?' She put the question casually, though she had been seeking a way of introducing it ever since they sat down.

'Since the divorce? Six years.' He chewed slowly on a mouthful of food, then said, 'It's a mistake to rush straight into marriage again. You need time to work out who you are, and what you're doing, and why it all went wrong the first time, otherwise you simply repeat the mistakes.'

'I know. That's why I tell myself not to rush into new relationships. I mean, I'm not even divorced from Steve yet. We haven't even instructed lawyers.'

'Is that because you think you might get back together?'

She shook her head. 'No way! Sometimes he literally didn't speak to me for days on end, and he never took any interest in anything I did. There's a limit to how long you can stay with someone who makes you feel a complete shit all the time.' She grimaced. 'Sorry. I don't want to think about him, it'll ruin my lunch. I want to know about you. I suppose you've had other relationships in all this time?'

'Oh aye, one or two. Three or four.'

'Serious? I know I'm being nosy, but for all I know you make a habit of chatting up a new woman for every inspection you do.'

'How would you know whether I was telling the truth?'

'I trust you. I think you've got too much integrity to lie.'

Iain looked at her in silence for a minute, then cleared his throat.

'Thank you. I'm not sure I always live up to it.' He wiped his bread across his plate, taking his time to finish up the scraps of mayonnaise that remained from his salad. 'There's been a few women I've fallen for over the years, but it's always seemed to fizzle out after a few months.'

'So there's not been anyone serious?'

He propped his chin on his hand. 'There was one, around the time of my divorce, a woman called Carol.' He paused.

'And? What happened?' She pushed her plate aside and smiled encouragingly at him. 'Come on, I want to know all about you.'

He sat back. 'She was a parent at my school. She'd married a Greek Cypriot lad after a holiday romance, and they came over here some years later to set up a restaurant. The two elder boys came to my school, and she had a baby girl as well. The business went bust, and the husband disappeared back to Cyprus leaving her responsible for massive debts. I seemed to be the only person around who was willing to help her sort things out. She was one of these pretty, blonde, somewhat helpless women, and she thought I was wonderful, which was exactly what I needed to soothe my ego after Ros. She sued for divorce, and they got into a pretty nasty battle over the children. Then the husband came and abducted them, took them back to Cyprus. Carol was devastated. I went over there with her to try and get them back, but we couldn't trace them. She tried using the courts, but that took time, and she had a breakdown, which meant no one wanted to award her custody in any case. In the meantime the wee girl was so upset and unsettled at being away from her mother, the ex-husband brought her back to England, but Carol never got the boys. She never saw them again. It was a pretty traumatic time, as you can imagine, and I suppose I got drawn into being a little more supportive and helpful than I should have been.'

'Did it last a long time?'

'I came to my senses within a few months. I couldn't believe I'd been that stupid. I was fond of her in many ways, I really did want to help her, but I must have been out of my mind to start an affair with her.'

'It's funny, you don't strike me as the kind of person who'd get carried away like that. You seem too sensible and down-to-earth.'

'I don't know about that. Mebbe I've mellowed. Or matured. Changed, anyway. I want different things from a relationship now.'

'Like what?'

He reached for her hand. 'You,' he said quietly.

Alison enclosed his hand between her own. The touch was as potent as a kiss, and it left her voice shaky. 'What was all that we were saying about not rushing into anything?'

'Holding your hand is hardly rushing into something. I'll be content so long as I can see you or speak to you from time to time.'

I don't believe you, she could have said. They might agree to a long time-scale, but they would certainly want more of each other than this chaste embrace of clasping palms.

When Iain eventually escorted her to her car for the drive home, they stood awkwardly, needing to say goodbye, but unsure what ritual of parting might be appropriate. In the end, he rested his hands gently on her waist, and touched her cheek with his lips.

Alison leaned against him for a few seconds, savouring the moment. 'Could I ring you sometimes?' she asked. 'I got your office number from some papers at school, but I wasn't sure if you'd want me calling you at work.'

'No, no, don't do that. Pairsonal calls are rather frowned on. I'll give you my mobile number, that's the best way to get me.' He scribbled on the back of a business card, and pressed it into her hand.

She drove home in a state of exaltation. He'd opened himself up to her, and there was absolutely nothing wrong with him except a commendable caution about rushing into a new relationship. That episode with Carol had been significant, Alison could tell from his awkwardness as he related it, but he'd clearly learnt from it. Learnt to want the kind of relationship between equals that he knew he could have with her. Though the weeks ahead would be dominated by preparations for her ordination to priesthood, the knowledge that this new friendship had the potential one day to become something infinitely more precious hovered at the back of her mind, and she felt uniquely blessed.

Autumn began with the mild inconvenience of Luke catching the chickenpox that was spreading with gleeful speed round the children in that part of Wellesley. That was swiftly followed by the much more significant disaster Lisa chose to reveal, with impeccable timing, the day before Alison's priesting.

She wandered into Alison's study on the Saturday morning and sat down on the edge of a chair. 'Luke's gone off again,' she said. 'I gave 'im some Calpol, and put more cream on. He's got a spot come up on 'is eyelid now - he can hardly see.'

Alison put her pen down and yawned. This was Luke's third day of erupting with spots, and she had been partially alleviating his restless misery by allowing him to sleep in her double bed, complete with an arkful of soft toys. 'I lost count of how many times he woke me up in the night,' she said. 'It was like having a new baby again.'

Lisa looked down at her hands, worrying silently away at her bottom lip with her teeth.

'Is there something else?' Alison asked, conscious of the letter she hoped to get in the post before lunch.

'I'm gonna have to hand in my notice.'

'Oh, Lisa! Why? I thought you were happy with us. Luke loves you, we all do. Please don't!'

Tears welled in Lisa's eyes. 'I don't want to, only you'll chuck me out when you know.' She sniffed loudly. 'I'm pregnant, in't I?'

'Pregnant?' Alison swivelled her chair round to face Lisa. 'But how? I mean, when?' Disbelief had sharpened her tone; she tried to soften it. 'I didn't know you were seeing anyone. Was it someone you met on holiday?'

'I went with Colin when he come over in May.'

'Colin? But you split up.'

'That's 'ow he does things. He came to dump me, but 'e thought 'e'd see what it was like screwing me first. Goes on about how much 'e wants me, then he turns round an' says I'm a slag, an' he never wants to see me again. Well, I didn't want to see him neither. Bloody good riddance, I thought.'

'But you were pregnant ... So you must be, what, four or five months? You've kept that pretty quiet - I had no idea. It doesn't show.'

'I thought you'd guess when I was off me food.'

Alison shook her head. 'I'd no reason to think of it. Have you told him?'

'Not bloody likely. I hate 'im.'

'But you have to tell him. It's his responsibility. Financially, if nothing else.'

'He's not havin' nothin' to do with it.'

Alison decided not to press the point. 'Where did you think you'd go?'

'I dunno. I'll find somewhere. You'll want me out before it shows, won't you?'

'I don't want you out at all. You're part of the family. We'll work something out.'

'But you can't 'ave me living here. Not when you're a priest.'

'It's hardly very priestly to kick someone out because they're in trouble. You've been a godsend to me this last year, I can't let you down now. Oh, Lisa, you're much more than a nanny, you're a friend, I wouldn't dream of getting rid of you.'

'Really? Oh, thank you ... you shouldn't ... I don't deserve it ...' Lisa tried to say more, but the words were overtaken by sobs.

Alison got up to pass her a box of tissues, and knelt by her chair to put an arm round Lisa as she wailed. Her brain was frantically computing how to manage the situation. Treat it as maternity leave, perhaps, but could she afford it? Steve was unlikely to stump up any more. She'd have to search for a childminder for Luke, though at least with Lisa living here, there would be cover if Alison had to be away overnight. James wasn't quite old enough to be in charge.

Her gaze wandered to her eldest son, working in the garden beyond the study window. His back was bent as he dug over the border, grimy tee-shirt flapping over jeans, earphones trailing from the stereo tucked in his back pocket. Stirred by Bunty's criticism of the state of the garden, Alison had bribed him to tackle the grass and flower beds. To her, and his, surprise, he'd taken to horticulture with enthusiasm, which was why he'd managed to negotiate a pay rise with her and was currently engaged in a complete revamp of the back garden. Eat your heart out, Father Mark!

Lisa's tears were subsiding. Alison returned to her seat.

'I've still got Luke's baby things in the attic. We'll have to go through them, see what you can use,' she said. 'I do think you should get Colin to take some responsibility, though.' A thought struck her. 'I suppose when he came for the festival, and went on about how he'd taken the pledge, and how cool it was to be a virgin like him, he was lying through his teeth.'

'Shows what a bloody hypocrite he is, don't it? God, I'd like to see his face if I turned up in the middle of one of his stupid shows and said 'e'd put me in the club!'

'He wouldn't look too good, would he? To be fair, he did try to get out of coming to the festival. I suppose that's why.'

Lisa blew her nose loudly; it sounded like a snort of utter contempt.

Eleven

Michael's grin was the first thing Alison saw as she processed into church on the Sunday after her priesting, to celebrate her first Eucharist at St Peter's. It radiated out from the front pew, until the solemn, priestly dignity with which she had intended to proceed down the aisle dissolved before it, and she was beaming helplessly back at him. He was a dear to come, when it meant leaving Jenny and their new baby, Rosie, back in Greathampton. He'd brought Lyddy with him, and put her in the crèche with Luke, and in her absence, was standing with a fatherly arm around Josh, keeping him calm. Lisa, on the other side of Michael, looked as if she were about to cry, presumably because this was a great occasion, and somebody had to. Next to Lisa was Alison's mother, alarmingly elegant for sixty, cheerfully putting up with this service, as well as last week's ordination.

Alison included them all in her smile, and composed her features again. Rainbows of light poured in through the saints in the windows, dappling the weighty green and gold of her vestments as she walked. The thurifer hurled incense around and about while the organ cascaded sound, and the congregation sang out its collective heart. In front of her, Nigel, followed by Nan - here as the preacher - and a full complement of acolytes to lead her to her appointed place.

The opening hymn died away. Alison turned to face the congregation. The nerves were still fluttering inside her, but thank God they did not show in her voice as she proclaimed the opening words.

The readings and prayers flowed by. Nan delivered one of her punchy sermons with her usual warmth and humour. The pace slackened as everyone turned to wish peace to their neighbours, and then to the strains of another hymn, Alison was swept up towards the altar. However often she had listened to the words of the service, however often she had watched Nigel, and rehearsed in her study, this first public celebration was still an ordeal. The first woman to perform this function in this church in all of its thousand year history, and imagine the shame if she got things wrong, or spilt something, or ... Nigel smiled encouragingly. With him beside her to hiss 'Proper Preface' when she looked like forgetting it, and to point to the right place in the service book when she temporarily lost her way, she got through without mishap. She was having to concentrate too hard to be able to feel the significance of the rite for herself, but she could sense the power it held for the congregation.

'Well done!' Nan said at the church door.

'I was nervous as hell. I could see my hands shaking.'

'It didn't show.'

'That was lovely!' Ella said, thrusting a single red rose into Alison's hand. 'You looked absolutely beautiful!'

'You're not supposed to be looking at me,' Alison protested.

'I couldn't help it. You looked radiant. Didn't she, Father?'

Nigel laughed. 'She always does.'

In ones and twos, the congregation emerged to press her hand, or kiss her cheek, or like Ella, to present her with a celebratory red rose: the regulars, the curious, old friends like Louise and Dave, returned for the occasion. Lisa came out with both Lyddy and Luke in her arms; by the time she passed on, Luke had somehow managed to transfer himself over to his mother. Alison sat him on her hip, and he pressed a tired head to her shoulder while she continued to greet people. For the first time since her arrival at St Peter's, she could feel wholeheartedly accepted, swamped by their affection. Even Bunty's dry cheek was offered an inch from her own, before the churchwarden disappeared back into the church to count the collection.

When Alison eventually got back inside, it was to be met with a glorious volley of sound as the organ launched into Handel's 'The Arrival of the Queen of Sheba'. So that was why Michael had not appeared; he had appropriated the organ to play his party piece while Terry went over to the hall for coffee. Well, why not? She had arrived. This was what all her preparation and training had been leading her towards. She set Luke down, and dragged Michael off the stool to throw her arms around him in a joyful embrace from which even Bunty's censorious stare could not detract.

'It was good of you to come!' she said. 'I hope Jenny didn't mind too much.'

'She knew how important it was to me.'

'You must thank her from me, for sparing you.'

Michael declared himself spared for lunch as well, a noisy meal, with

Luke and Lyddy tearfully tired, and Josh being silly. Afterwards, Lisa took the little ones for a lie-down, and Alison's mother ordered James and Josh to help her clear up:

'You and Michael go and put your feet up with your coffee,' she told Alison. 'It's probably the last chance either of you will have for a rest for months.'

Alison made a perfunctory objection, then gave in. She lay on the sofa, coffee in hand, while Michael produced photographs of Rosie, Jenny, Lyddy, and himself, in every imaginable combination.

'Oh, Michael, she's gorgeous! You're making me all broody!' She examined a snap of Jenny, beatifically cradling her new daughter in her arms. 'I've never seen Jenny look so happy. I'm so glad everything's alright with you both again.'

'So am I.' Michael began putting the photos back into their packet.

'Where's the clean tea towels?' James demanded, putting his head round the door.

'In the middle drawer,' Alison told him. 'That shows how often you help with the clearing up, doesn't it?'

'He was saying he's not too happy at school,' Michael said, when James had withdrawn. 'One of the teachers - Mr Howells, is it? - doesn't like you, for some reason, and so he picks on James?'

'Oh, James is always going on about that. It's not true. I had a run in with Terry over the summer, when he objected because he wasn't asked to be acting Head of Department. He complained to me as Chair of Governors, but he realised he wouldn't get anywhere with it, so in the end he let it drop. He's our organist, and we have the odd disagreement over hymns, but he's been polite enough the last few weeks, given that he's a miserable sod at the best of times.'

'He did well today, I thought.'

'Yes, he even congratulated me after the service. But even if he hated my guts, he wouldn't be unprofessional enough to take it out on James. Most of the time when you're teaching, you're not aware of the class as individuals anyway, you don't have time to think "ah, that's James, I must find something to tell him off about because his mother doesn't appreciate my music". Besides, when James has got into trouble with Terry, he's deserved every bit of it. He's forgotten his homework, or fallen asleep in a lesson, or answered back. He's so arrogant! Just like Steve. He can't believe anything he does could possibly be wrong. I reckon part of the trouble is that some of the other teachers let him get away with things because of me, but that won't happen much longer. We've had to tighten up on our discipline policy since the inspection, and James'll have to pull his socks up.'

'Lisa says you got off with the Inspector who led it,' Michael observed.

'Of course I didn't. We were all far too busy.'

'And yet he sends you flowers with friendly messages on them.'

Alison blushed, leaving Michael laughing at her discomfiture. The flowers had arrived the previous Saturday, and still stood on the shelf above the fire in the living room; a large bouquet that flung a riot of purples and pinks up the wall. Tucked in among them, the small card with its message: My very best wishes for your big day. I'm sorry I can't be there to support you. I hope I can do so in other ways in the future. With love, Iain.

'I've had lunch with him a couple of times, that's all. He lives miles away, I don't suppose anything'll come of it.'

'But you hope it does?'

'I'm not allowed to hope, not yet.'

'So you say. Why does that make me think you're more than half in love with him already?'

'I'm not.' She met Michael's eyes, remembering Iain's hand taking hers ... the shock of his lips on her cheek. Honesty compelled her to add, 'But you're right, I could be. Easily. That's why I've told him I'd like to see him, but not to rush into anything, and he's happy with that. He was divorced a few years ago, and he doesn't want to make any more mistakes, either. He's very kind and understanding, and even though he says he's an atheist, he's a lot more supportive and interested in what I do than Steve ever was.'

'Men always are when they're trying to get you into bed.'

'Don't be cynical. The most he's done is hold my hand. I wish you could meet him, I'm sure you'd get on. You do think it's alright to see him, though, don't you? I am separated, and as long as I'm sensible and don't get too involved too soon?'

'In theory. On the other hand, once you fall for him, you won't be sensible. Look at how you were with me.'

'I've changed,' Alison protested. 'I've learnt my lesson.'

'Perhaps you have, but it could be a hard test. He's not going to have my scruples.'

Lunchtime. James slung his bag over his shoulder and left the school buildings by one of the back entrances. Past the brats of Year Seven, being shepherded towards the hall for their dinners, out over the tarmac with its yellow, green and red lines skewed across it in geometrical disorder, over the grass, long and damp underfoot, until at last he had reached the wild garden. Where once an archway had opened into it, an old metal gate had been roped and padlocked into place, and there was no access. Howells said it was a temporary measure, but everyone knew he was sulking at not getting to be Head of Department, and was deliberately letting the garden go to ruin as a way of making his feelings known. James would never have let anyone see that he cared, but as he looked through the slats of timber at the triumphant weeds pushing up through the pathway, he was filled with anger. Much of the foliage would be dying back now it was October, and the first ground frosts were hinting at the winter to come, but without attention, it would be that much harder to tame next spring.

He sat down with his back to the red-brick of the sports hall's side wall, and pulled a crushed cheese roll out of his bag, lunching alone as usual. He missed Ellis, though he wouldn't have admitted it to anyone. Ellis had accepted him as he was. No need to apologise or explain about his mother, no need to live in dread of having her profession discovered. James occasionally hung around with the lads in his class, but he was far too embarrassed to have them come to his home. As he chewed his roll, he found himself wondering whether it was worth asking Howells if he might do some work in the garden sometimes, as Michael had suggested when they'd talked in the garden back home. 'Get you on the right side of him,' Michael had said. 'And if he says no, it makes you look keen, which can't hurt.'

Howells had been impossible this term, short-tempered and harsh with anyone who stepped out of line, but James had somehow managed to avoid any direct confrontations thus far. He could try asking; Howells could only say no.

'Yes?' Howells, summoned from the staff room in his lunch hour, did not look pleased.

'I was looking at the garden,' James said. 'I was wondering if you'd let me help out sometimes, at lunchtime or after school.'

'You're volunteering to *work*? Well, this is a turn-up. What's brought this on? You never showed any interest last year.'

'I've been doing a lot of gardening for my mum, and you ought to be preparing for winter. There's things should have been cut back, and you should clear the pond of leaves.'

'Should I? Well, your enthusiasm is most commendable, James, but I'm not letting you loose in there on your own, and I haven't got time to supervise you. Interest noted. If I start gardening club up again, I'll let you know.'

'I wouldn't do any damage. I know what I'm doing, you can ask my mum.' He didn't like to mention her twice in a minute, but it had become important to him to get his way. 'Please!'

'I'm sorry, James, I appreciate your interest, but I can't have you in there on your own. I'll go in if necessary, make sure it doesn't run to ruin.'

'But ...'

Howells raised a hand in dismissal, and went back into the staff room, leaving James standing in the corridor swearing at him bitterly under his breath. Typical Howells, treating him like some stupid kid. Grovelling to teachers did no bloody good whatsoever. James kicked the wall, and made his way back outside.

The tiniest of babies lay asleep on Alison's lap, its head resting in her hand. The child's mother, no more than seventeen herself, sat morosely in an armchair on the far side of the room, watching television. The grandmother, Susan, who had requested this baptism visit, sat alongside Alison on the sofa, explaining how she'd been brought up a Catholic, but had stopped going because she was divorced.

'He's got to be baptised, though. I'm not having my grandson go to hell.'

'I don't think God's like that,' Alison replied. Which was one reason she wasn't entirely convinced of the efficacy of infant baptism, but this wasn't the time to say so. What mattered was the opportunity to sit in this immaculately kept house, with her tea and cake in fine china on the polished table in front of her, waiting to discover why it all felt so wrong.

'Are you allowed to do baptisms? I'd quite like a woman to do it. Seems more natural, really.'

'I'd be happy to,' Alison said, stroking the baby's waxy skin with a gentle finger. He had been ten weeks premature, and was not long out of hospital, poor mite.

'His dad won't come, of course. That's my son. He's in the army, he's not interested. Danni hasn't got any family, so I said she could come here. It's time for his bottle, Danni. Why don't you go and get it ready?'

The girl made a face, and went sullenly out of the room.

Susan turned to Alison, and laid a thin hand on the baby's lacy, hand-knitted cardigan. She dropped her voice. 'I'm dying,' she said. 'Cancer. I've only got a couple of months. She doesn't know, neither does my son.'

Alison laid a hand over Susan's, and met her eyes. She might have read the diagnosis in the gaunt pallor of the woman's face. 'I'm so sorry.'

'I don't know what'll happen to them. I don't think she'll look after him properly on her own, and she won't be able to stay on here. How can I die leaving it like this?'

The television continued to burble inanely in the corner. Alison shut it from her mind, and tried to focus on Susan's agony, to gauge what, if anything, she could possibly say. There was little time to respond. Danni would be coming back from the kitchen.

'Is there a time when she's out?' Alison asked quickly. 'Would you like me to come back, so we can talk properly?'

Gratitude flared in Susan's eyes. 'Would you? Tonight?'

'So I've been making some discreet enquiries with social services to see who's the best person to help them, and I said I'd go back there this evening,' Alison explained to Nigel, ringing him that afternoon. 'You can do the Eucharist for me, can't you?'

'I don't think I can. I was about to ring you myself. I've gone and got shingles. I know it sounds funny, but it's damned painful. I was going to ask if you could do a funeral for me - twelve o'clock tomorrow at the crematorium.'

'Thursday's my day off.'

'I know. Do you mind? I could ask the duty person at the crem, but it's old Harry Stone, and his family will be upset if it's not one of us.'

'OK, I'll fit it in. How long are you likely to be out of action?'

'Oh, not more than a few days, I should think,' Nigel said breezily. 'You'll need to do all the services this Sunday, but with any luck I'll be fine for next week. I shouldn't think anyone would mind if you used an old sermon at evensong.'

'I haven't got any old sermons,' Alison pointed out.

'And there's a surveyor coming from Church House at ten tomorrow to look at the rotten joists in the bell tower - could you take him up? You're not scared of heights, are you?'

'No. Ten o'clock did you say?'

'Yes. And you'd better wear trousers for going up the ladder, rather than one of your short skirts, or you'll give poor old Bill a heart attack.'

'Thanks, Nigel. Good to know your mind's running on higher things.'

She put the phone down, and spent a few moments planning how to fit everything in. The surveyor, and the funeral ... which meant doing the talk as well, thank you very much, Nigel, so she'd have to call on Harry's family and get some more details. She'd already done some work on her Sunday morning sermon, but now she'd another to do for the evening. She didn't want to disappoint Luke, so she'd have to take him for his swim early, and get Lisa to forgo her day off to have him after that.

Alison frowned as she thought about Lisa. Meeting Susan had left Alison worrying about her nanny and her continued refusal to tell Colin about the baby. Surely the more family a child had, the better? What if something happened to Lisa, or she couldn't cope? Lisa had made her and Michael swear not to inform Colin, but maybe there was some way of engineering a meeting between the two of them. She felt she had to do something, and so she picked up the phone again, and deftly laid the problem in Michael's lap. One down, two hundred tasks to go.

When Alison called at the vicarage, she found Nigel lying on a sofa in the living room with his feet up, looking drained.

'How are you feeling?' she asked, sitting down on the chair nearest to him.

'Pretty rough. I'd no idea shingles could be so painful. I'm cramming myself with painkillers, but they don't seem to help much. How was Harry's funeral?'

'It went OK, I think, though I'd have liked more time to prepare my talk. I went to see his son yesterday afternoon, but then I had to go back and see Susan, so I didn't get the talk done till nearly midnight.'

Nigel had closed his eyes as she spoke. 'Good. Sorry, I'm not too good at concentrating. Could you have a look through my diary, and take over anything that looks urgent, do you think?'

Alison studied his duties, asked a few questions, and then stood up. 'As long as you're better for the PCC. I don't fancy dealing with that on my own.'

'I'll do my best.'

She left him to recuperate undisturbed, and went through to the kitchen to talk to his wife. She found Sandra sitting with a newspaper spread out on the large, worn kitchen table, while a pressure cooker hissed loudly behind her on the gas cooker. Her face was made up and her grey hair neatly waved, though she had discarded the smart clothes she normally wore for her counselling in favour of a faded green jogging suit.

'Hello, Allie. Pull up a chair. Have a cup of tea, the kettle's just boiled.' Sandra got up and swiftly produced a mug of tea, talking all the while. 'You did have a lovely service the other Sunday. I meant to grab you to say so, but I couldn't get at you. And who was that lovely young man hanging on your arm? Is this something I should know about?'

'He's an old friend. A married old friend, though his wife didn't come because they've just had another baby. He was on the Programme with me.' Alison pulled out a chair and sank into it. 'I was thrilled he came, but I almost wish he hadn't now. I've had Terry on at me because he thought I'd brought Michael along to audition as a replacement organist. Then when I explained Michael was simply amusing himself, he complained about me letting someone play his organ without permission.'

'It's not his organ, it's the church's.'

'That's what I said. And Michael's a professional organist, it's not as if he was going to constipate the pipes or eff up the f-stops, or whatever it is you can do to organs. And then Bunty's been getting in little digs about how friendly I seemed to be with Michael, until she was practically accusing me of having an affair with him. I could have hit her!'

'Oh, no one takes any notice of Bunty,' Sandra laughed. 'Nigel always recites psalms to himself while she's talking, that way he keeps his temper, and he's never missed anything important yet, so he says. You mustn't let her aggravate you.'

Alison clasped her mug with both hands, finding comfort in its heat. 'I guess it's too near the knuckle. I really was in love with Michael a few years back. To be honest, if he hadn't been so strong-minded, we might have ended up lovers. I know it sounds dreadful.'

'I can understand it. He seemed exceptionally nice when I talked to him. If things weren't going so well in your marriage ... Or was it him that caused the trouble?'

'He focused the trouble. Steve and I hadn't been getting on for years, so when Michael came along being his normal friendly self, I hadn't got a chance. It's only the last few months I've known I was properly cured, so hearing comments like that gets to me.'

'You might as well brace yourself. An attractive young woman like you, people will be pairing you off with every available man you so much as speak to.'

'I don't have to be young and attractive for them to do that, I only have to be unattached. But I will want to have new relationships sometime.'

'Of course you will, but you'll want to take your time. You're not

104

even divorced yet, after all, and even then, as far as the church is concerned, you'll be expected to wait a few years before you form any new attachments. I know some say that's harsh, but it makes a lot of sense. Mind you, I expect you'll find the parish keeps you far too busy to give you time for a social life.'

Alison smiled and agreed. She had intended to mention her cautious lunches with Iain, but she could hardly confess after what Sandra had said. Besides, her friendship with Iain was still very tentative, and at this moment, there were weightier issues on her mind.

She took another sip of tea. 'I made a really harrowing visit last night,' she said. 'Can I tell you about it?'

Soon after the weekend, Iain rang. He was due to spend a day working with a school some twenty miles away, and wanted her to meet him for supper in a pub between there and Wellesley. She could not really spare the time, not with two more sermons to produce for Sunday, and another long visit to Susan, and half a day at least in school, and all the parish business she'd inherited from Nigel. On the other hand, she'd lost her day off, and a break of a few hours spent seeing Iain would help her to manage all her responsibilities much better. She sent her apologies to the house group she would normally have attended, and set out.

She found Iain in the corner of a low-beamed lounge bar adorned with polished warming pans on the walls and dusty collections of dried flowers in jugs on every window sill. He rose and kissed her cheek, and Alison's stresses fell away.

'... And I don't know what I'm going to do about childcare once Lisa's out of action,' she told him. 'It's such a bind, having to interview childminders. I won't be able to ask her to take the boys to Steve's anymore, either, so that'll take up half my weekends. How could she have been so silly? I leave her alone for five minutes with a bloke who's sworn to forgo all sexual activity, and he manages to get her pregnant. I ask you!'

'There is such a thing as getting carried away,' he said, amusement creasing the lines around his eyes.

'There is such a thing as self-control!'

Two large oval plates descended onto their table: two jacket potatoes with salad garnish, the one piled with cheese, the other exotic with sauteed mushrooms in a red wine sauce. Iain rearranged their glasses to make room for them.

'So you'd never have that kind of lapse?' he continued, unwrapping his cutlery from its white paper napkin.

Alison held his eyes a moment, checking whether he was adding anything more to the question. Now was clearly the perfect time to explain her strict commitment to extra-marital chastity. Instead, she found herself temporizing. 'I'd never have a casual affair, no. I'd have to be in a serious relationship.'

'Same for me,' he said. 'I confess it's not always been the case, but it is now I've met you.'

Alison pushed a mushroom onto her fork. 'Would you say you were a moral person?'

'I'd like to think so. My mother's a staunch Presbyterian, so I was brought up with strict standards. I can't say I always live up to them.' He took a mouthful, and chewed it slowly. 'I suppose you could say being an inspector's about applying moral standards. Equality of opportunity, helping the disadvantaged, that kind of thing.'

'I'm interested to hear you say that,' Alison said, leaning forward and smiling into his face, 'because I'm looking for someone to be on a panel to discuss young people, education, morality, etcetera. I want someone from a non-religious moral perspective.'

'Why do I get the feeling I've been set up?'

'As if I'd do such a thing! Go on, Iain, next July, you can't be booked up for then. The churches in Wellesley put on a festival, and I'm the secretary for it. There's going to be an Any Questions Panel, chaired by Christopher Ridgefield, I hope, though he hasn't confirmed it yet, with Becky Patten - you know, she's on TV - and a couple of others. It is a church event, but you wouldn't mind that. You could be as controversial about religion as you like, get people going.'

'I'm not sure ...'

'And there'll be workshops, and I thought you could do one with me, then we'd have to meet a few times to plan it, and I wouldn't feel I was skiving off like I am tonight.'

A smile bent his lips. 'You make it irresistible.'

'I'm trying. Even if you've got fed up with me by then, we ought to be able to work together. Please?'

Iain narrowed his eyes, and got out his electronic organiser. She watched him type in the date, and tuck it back in his inside pocket. 'So that's the business out of the way,' he said. 'How else are things for you, apart from your nanny defaulting?'

'The boss has gone down with shingles and I'm being rushed off my feet covering for him. We had an awful PCC last night. At least I managed to head off Bunty - she's one of the churchwardens and she's been looking into redesigning a new notice board for us. God, you should have seen it, Iain, she'd really gone over the top. She wanted us to have this vast triptych, all glazed and lockable, with lighting. It was going to cost well over a thousand pounds. Trouble is, Bunty was chairing the meeting, and she has a way of putting things that makes disagreement seem like betrayal of the faith, and they're all terrified of her. Even the treasurer only raised a mild protest. They all said "very nice" and got ready to nod it through, until I pointed out we oughtn't to pass something that important until Nigel was back, so we've postponed it, and he can be the one to break the news it can't be done.'

'Couldn't you have told her?'

'Not politic. I have to keep in with the churchwardens while Nigel's ill. Anyway, I'm not sure what authority I have when I'm only the curate.' She paused. 'I can't believe you're interested in all this.'

'Och, I am, I am. It's a whole new world. Tell me more!'

Another hour of conversation, of seductive attention, while the winds of autumn rattled the windows beside them, mitigating the effect of the coal fire that blazed at their backs. When last orders were called, they stood with reluctance to drag on their coats ready for the long drive back to their respective homes.

The wind hit them as soon as the heavy pub door swung shut behind them, making them gasp as they teetered round the corner to the car park. Around them, other pub-goers called their goodnights, doors slammed, engines stuttered into life. Iain put his arm round her shoulder to shelter her as they walked towards the back where she had parked her car; her skin shivered beneath her coat with the contact.

'Here I am,' Alison said, stopping and turning towards him. 'Thanks for tonight.'

A spotlight illuminated the central rank of cars, but here, their faces were in shadow. He drew her closer, sliding his other arm around her waist. 'Am I allowed to kiss you?'

She barely hesitated. Each meeting had, like an advancing tide, been throwing her ever more steadily towards him. She slipped her hands under his jacket and, slowly, aware of the significance of what she was about to do, brought her lips to meet his. They kissed with a gentle restraint that spoke more of the intensity of their feelings than any more passionate onslaught might have done. Each time she recalled it in the weeks ahead, it was with a sense of disintegration, and she found herself recalling it a great many times.

Twelve

Terry hoisted his briefcase onto his desk and pulled out the set of exercise books he had marked over the previous weekend. Striding around the classroom between the tables, he casually distributed the books to his Year Ten students. His mood had not been improved by the memo he'd just got from Paul Croft, announcing the introduction of peer appraisal in the History department. As if someone as inexperienced as Croft could be his peer, or presume to tell him anything about how to teach! It was all the fault of Sutherland, and that inept and hopelessly distorted inspection report. He'd been made a laughing stock.

James Thompson's book appeared at the top of the pile; Terry returned it with irritation. 'What happened to you, James? I've never seen such a careless piece of work. I thought I was reading *1066 And All That.* Check your facts occasionally.'

'I did. I spent ages on it!' James complained.

'Then you must have a lot fewer brain cells than I thought. Get your act together. I don't want to see anything as shoddy as this again.'

Terry sat down at his desk and began the lesson. As he spoke, he delved into his briefcase for a newspaper article he wished to refer to. Not until it was in his hand did he realise he had instead recovered the July issue of the Leathwell diocesan newspaper, placed in his bag because it had details of a summer exhibition of medieval manuscripts in the Cathedral, and then forgotten. He was about to drop it into the bin behind him when his attention was caught by the picture on the front cover. In the absence of other news, the editor had enlivened the front page with a photograph of a curates' weekend at Farnthorpe - taken on the Sunday morning, as they all posed formally in their dog collars. Terry's mind was largely occupied with keeping the class's attention, and he acted without thinking to rise and toss the paper in James's direction.

'There's a nice picture of your mum for you to take home,' he said. 'Shame to throw it away.'

'Let's see,' Emma said, intercepting it before James could react.

'What're they all dressed like that for? Ugh. She's never a vicar. Hey, Bridget, look. That's James's mum, she's a vicar!'

James turned a look of such hatred on him that Terry flinched. He'd genuinely forgotten that Alison's cover had not yet been blown among her son's classmates. Though, really, the boy was making too much of it, it had been bound to come out, and was in any case a nine-minute wonder that would soon be forgotten.

Around them, James's fellow students were making the most of their teacher's temporary indiscipline.

'How come that's your mum? I thought priests weren't allowed to have it off,' Matt said.

'Perhaps 'e's a virgin birth,' said Danny.

'It's only Catholic priests can't marry, stupid,' Sarah told him. 'Don't you know anything?'

'No wonder 'e's such a creep,' Danny laughed.

'He snogs alright for a vicar's son,' Emma announced.

'His initials is J.C.,' Matt said with a sudden inspiration that would have gladdened the heart of any RE teacher. 'Jesus Christ Thompson!'

'Bow down to the son of God!' Danny called, raising and lowering his arms in mock homage.

'That's enough, Daniel,' Terry said, emerging from his preoccupation to take charge. 'And from you, Emma,' he added as she started to speak again. 'Quieten down. I'm sorry I drew attention to it. It doesn't make any difference what any of your mothers do, and being the son of a priest is hardly the same thing as being the son of God.' He located the article he'd been looking for. 'Let's get on, otherwise you'll be staying in after the bell.'

After the lesson ended, he beckoned James to stay behind, intending to apologise. James gave him no chance.

'You'd no right to do that! You did it deliberately, you've kept that ever since the inspection, waiting for me to do something so you could humiliate me. It's not fair!'

Terry laughed. 'Oh, absolutely. I've nothing better to do with my life than to plan revenge on fourteen year old boys! Run along, James, they'll have forgotten all about it by this afternoon. Go on, hop it.'

He shook his head as James stalked out. The newspaper lay on the floor under James's desk. Terry picked it up and dropped it into the bin and out of his mind.

Colin made his second visit to the Turner household late one Saturday afternoon at the far edge of November, summoned by a phone call from Michael:

'I can't get over to collect those music books I ordered, and we need them tomorrow. Could you possibly bring them over for me ...? Now, preferably, so I can get plastic covers put on them, and get them stamped before the morning.'

Having avoided Michael for the last few months, Colin had no wish to go to Greathampton. He had locked the 'incident' (as he named it to himself) with Lisa firmly away in his memory, and had taught himself never to revisit it. He had no intention of allowing Michael the opportunity of questioning him and dragging a reaction from him.

As he loaded the box of books into his mother's car, he determined that this call would be business only: Hi, how are you? Absolutely brilliant, here's the books, here's the invoice, must fly, see you around.

Michael put paid to that scenario by coming to the door with Lyddy in his arms. 'Could you take them through? I haven't got a hand free. Jen's in there, with our latest, I expect you want to say hello.'

Politeness took Colin and his package towards the glass door ajar at the end of the hall. He pushed it open with his foot, and took a step into the room. Jenny sat at one end of the sofa, lightly bouncing a grizzling baby in a fabric chair. She smiled tentatively at him.

He nodded at her, and looked round the room for somewhere to place the box; only at that point did he notice the third person in the room.

'Lisa!' he breathed, dismay giving way to anger as he realised the meeting had been engineered. He would have fled, but Michael and Lyddy blocked the doorway, and shock had rooted him to the carpet. Shock at seeing her at all, and shock at the changes in her as she stood awkwardly clutching a large handbag in front of her. Her hair had grown lank, her face rounder, and she'd put on weight ... no, the bulge of her stomach against the long shirt she wore was more significant than that.

'Lisa's been dropping Allie's boys off,' Michael said casually.

'I'm jus' going,' Lisa said, though her exit too was barred by Michael. 'I didn't know you were coming.'

Colin barely registered their words; he was absorbing the fact of her pregnancy with the outrage searing colour into his face. 'You didn't waste much time taking up with someone else.'

'There in't been anyone else.'

His first impulse was disbelief. May, said a voice in his head. May to

110

June, July, August, September, October, November ... one, two, three, four, five, six, nearly seven months ... The blood drained from his head as quickly as it had risen, and he swayed on his feet. The box tumbled from his grasp as the carpet lifted itself towards him.

'Here, mate, sit down, you'll be OK.' Michael grabbed him, and pushed him down in an armchair.

'Put your head between your knees,' Jenny said, getting up to put a hand on his shoulders and press him down. 'We shouldn't have sprung it on him like this, Michael,' she said quietly. 'Are you alright, Colin?'

He managed to nod, and lifted his head to sit with his elbows on his knees, hands clasped behind his neck, trying to breathe again. He was aware of whisperings, of rustling movements, and then of the door to the hall closing. When he eventually raised his head, he was alone with Lisa, who sat on the edge of the sofa, biting her lip.

'It can't be mine,' he whispered.

'There in't been anyone else, Col,' she said again, wearily. 'You're the only bloke I've slept with in the last two years, so unless tha's a bloody miracle, tha's yours, but don't worry about it. I'm not telling no one. I weren't goin' to tell you. Tha's only Michael, tryin' to play God as usual, thinking you oughter know. Go on, Col, you might as well go. I in't after you for money or nothing, an' you don't want people at church to know. Allie says I can stay on with her, so I'll manage.'

'I can't go, not now I know, not if it's my baby, if I'm its father.'

'If? You still think I went out an' did it with the first bleeding bloke I met?'

'No. I do believe you. It's my baby.' Repeating it didn't make it any more believable, but there she sat, her belly accusing him. 'But why didn't you tell me? I had no idea.'

'Why should I 'ave told you? You go on at me till I 'ave sex with you, an' then you say that means I'm a slag, an' you don't want nothin' to do with me no more. Christ, Col, I don't want my kid to 'ave a dad like that.'

'It wasn't like that. *You* were the one who made *me* ...'

'You said you wanted me.'

He stared at her. She had flushed as she spoke, as if the memory pained her as much as it did him. 'I didn't mean it like that,' he said. But if that was how she had taken it ... loving him, giving herself to him, only to have him throw it all back in her face ... And he had gone off, excising the incident from history as best he could, while she was left to face both his desertion and the shock of pregnancy by herself. He passed his hands over

111

his face. 'Oh, Lise, I'm sorry. I thought you were ...'

'A slag, yeah, I know.'

'No!' He couldn't let her think that. He got up and knelt in front of her, taking her in his arms. 'I was ashamed of myself, and I blamed you,' he said, his voice muffled by her hair. 'I should've got back in touch. I did think about you.' He took a deep breath. 'We'll have to get married.'

Lisa pushed him away gently. 'Tha's not right to marry someone if you don't love them. I don't need you comin' over with a conscience about me, Col. Allie's gonna help me manage. You can always visit, or send me money if you feel that strong about it, but I in't marryin' no one who couldn't care less about me.'

Colin took her hands. 'I do care about you. I want to look after you. Come on, Lise, we used to talk about it, we're just doing it earlier than we thought. Unless you really can't stand me any more.'

'You know bloody well I've loved you for years,' she said shakily.

He leaned forward and kissed her gently. 'How have you been?'

'Not so bad. Apart from sickin' me guts out at the start. How 'ave you been?'

'So-so. It wasn't easy doing the show. I felt awful.'

'I should think so, too. Bloody hypocrite!' She grinned.

He found himself smiling. Months of earnest agonizing dismissed in two words; that was his Lisa. 'I'm going to have to go, Lise,' he said, standing up. 'There's things to sort out at the shop, and then I need to tell them at home. I'll ring you tomorrow.'

As Colin opened the door into the hall, Michael appeared from an adjoining room, with Rosie comfortably asleep on his shoulder. That's going to be me in a few months, Colin thought, trying to quell the panic.

'We're going to get married,' he told Michael firmly.

'You decided that quick enough - are you both sure?'

'Of course. And thanks for fixing it up like this, you did the right thing.'

He reached the front door and made his escape before Michael could question him further. He needed space to come to terms with the somersault his life had performed in the last hour. His job would have to go - he could hardly stay on at the church bookshop after this. He'd have to leave home, find somewhere for them to live. He did care about Lisa, of course he did, and he had no option but to marry her, but he was no readier for it than he had been seven months ago. And a kid, as well! How could he have been so stupid? Not just to lose control and sleep with Lisa in the first place, but not even to think of what might have happened as a result? Already he could feel in his bones the seismic shock that would run around the church at the revelation. He'd be derided for hypocrisy. Pure Power would be made a laughing stock.

And, oh Jesus, from somewhere he had to find the courage to tell his parents.

Saturday nights for Alison were usually spent wrestling with a sermon. With the boys away at their father's, she'd finished the next day's sermon that afternoon, and was going to read a meditation out of a book in place of a sermon at evensong. Bunty would complain, but Bunty always complained. It would make a change for her to enlarge on some topic other than Alison's failure to safeguard her nanny's morals. What Bunty would say if she knew that Alison was neglecting her sermon-writing in order to meet a male friend, did not bear thinking about, but dear God, she hadn't seen Iain for weeks, and she couldn't get by on the occasional phone call. He'd felt the same. He'd had a preparatory meeting on Friday at the school fifteen miles up the road where he was due to do another inspection in January, and had stayed on an extra day at his hotel because Alison couldn't get away to see him until Saturday.

She made the journey in driving rain, following his directions until she could park in front of the red-brick facade of what looked like an old farmhouse. She scanned the other cars until she could identify Iain's Rover with its twin exhausts; yes, he was here. Tidy hair, reapply lipstick, kick off boots and exchange them for court shoes, button her coat to protect her from the rain, and she was ready to leave the car and make her way into the building.

'Hello.' Iain appeared behind her from an unexpected alcove. An ordinary man in a grey suit and bright tie, with his white hair and glasses, and yet he had only to smile at her, and she was winded. He embraced her formally, his hands touching her arms lightly as he kissed her cheek, and helped her off with her coat.

Intimate in the circle of light cast by the small oil lamp on their table, they talked of inconsequential matters.

'Any more problems with your manic organist?' he asked as they began their starters.

'No, he seems to have forgiven me for letting Michael play his organ. I stood up for him the other week when I got a complaint from a baptism family who'd wanted a pop song played during the service. I told them I didn't care whether it was the original or the Boyzone cover, Michael Jackson's "Ben" was about a rat, and not appropriate in a liturgy.'

Iain laughed. 'Very brave of you.'

'I'm not sure they were persuaded, but Terry was impressed. I think he's sorry for me having to cover for Nigel for so long.'

'That's dragged on a long time.'

'I know. It does sometimes, apparently. He's still in pain, and he's very tired. I only hope he's back for Christmas, I'd hate to be on my own. It's bad enough with all the church things, let alone all the carol services and Christmas lunches at the schools, and in the residential homes and day centres. I've had them all getting on to me: but we *always* have someone from the church to read the lesson, or say grace, or draw the raffle, or whatever it is.'

'You must be careful not to overdo things.'

'I don't feel I can let them down. And I enjoy a lot of it. It would just be a lot easier with Nigel around. I miss not having him to advise me, as much as anything.' She frowned. 'I've been seeing a lot of this woman and her family, Susan, she's called. It's a tragic situation. Could I talk to you about it?'

Iain nodded. He listened attentively as their meal progressed, the impartial outsider who gave her perspective, the friend whose partiality relieved her isolation. How could anyone think her meeting him a fault?

'Coffee?' asked the waitress.

'No, we won't, thank you,' Iain said, before Alison could accept. He waited until their dishes had been taken. 'I thought we could have coffee in my room.'

Coffee, she thought. And then? A locked door, a bed, the chance to carry on where they'd left off in October ...?

'I was simply thinking it would be nice to be able to say goodbye somewhere other than in a hotel car park,' Iain said, observing her confusion. 'Especially given the weather tonight.'

'If that's all it is.'

'It's whatever you want it to be.'

'Strong coffee, I think. I shouldn't have had that glass of wine, and I have to drive back tonight.'

Alison eased her chair back from the table and stood up. She talked aimlessly as they took the lift to the second floor, shutting off the possibility of questioning what she might be doing.

Iain's room was a square, utilitarian twin-bed-with-en-suite,

114

television, mini-bar, and little sign of occupation but the black case resting on the broad shelf just inside the door. She arranged herself in one of the low chairs by the beige-curtained window, and watched him as he set out cups, hung his jacket in the wardrobe, threw his tie over the trouser press, and loosened his shirt at the neck.

Observing the neat creases of his sleeves, Alison was struck by a thought. 'Do you do your own ironing?'

He looked a little embarrassed. 'Well, no. I use a kind of house-keeper.'

'Why not, if you can afford it? How many days does she do?'

'Er, it's not regular.' He prepared her coffee and handed it to her. 'Apologies for the quality, but at least we get to drink it without waiters asking if everything's satisfactory all the time.'

He sat down on the chair opposite her, balancing his saucer on the wooden arm of the chair. 'Don't look so worried.'

'I'm nervous. I'm not used to being alone with you. I'm not sure my mentors would approve of me having an assignation in a hotel bedroom, that's all.'

'Do you talk about me?'

'Not as much as I should. I just say I've had the occasional lunch with a man I like very much. I don't tell them how often I think about you.'

'Would they not approve?'

'They don't think I should rush into anything, not until I've ended my marriage properly. It's all very sensible.'

'And are you sensible?'

She shook her head. 'Not always. But I am going to try to be this time.'

He watched her, returning the little smile she gave. 'I'm leaving it up to you, Allie, it's for you to say what happens between us. As long as I can see you sometimes.'

Alison put her coffee cup down on the floor. 'When are you back here? Can we fix something up now?' she asked, taking refuge in practicalities.

A few minutes later, however, the clashes of their diaries meant they had to admit defeat. No time in December, and Iain away visiting his sister and mother for Hogmanay, and then involved with his inspection until the middle of January. It would be at least another six weeks before she could see him again.

She rose tiredly to her feet. 'I probably ought to get back, I've an eight o'clock service in the morning.'

Iain stood, hands by his sides, eyes fastened on her face, waiting, leaving it up to her to direct the manner of their parting.

She intended to kiss him with the same restraint he had shown in the car park, but her disappointment at the long weeks that would go by before they met again propelled her towards him, devoid of caution. Hands about his head, his neck, his back, clamping his body to hers, with her mouth sliding around his as if he had already been her lover, while his fingers found her breast, a button ...

She tore her lips away, letting her cheek fall against his shoulder while his rapid breathing warmed her hair. She had forgotten how overwhelming desire could be; her only defence was to stay perfectly still, her fine intentions shattered by the knowledge that all she really wanted was to fall back onto the bed with him, to make love over and over again, because she had been starved of loving intimacy for far too long.

'Too much?' he asked.

'Too soon,' she whispered back.

Iain's finger travelled around her neck and lifted her chin. 'You know I've fallen in love with you, don't you?' he said softly.

Alison swallowed and touched his cheek. 'I rather think I've fallen in love with you, too. I didn't mean to do that yet. I don't get to that in my relationship development plan until next year at the earliest.'

He laughed. 'Perhaps we could tweak the plan a little. There's no harm in being ahead of yourself.'

'I'm not so sure.'

'Ah, well. Next year's no so very far away.'

'It's an age,' she said. 'Especially when I'm not going to be able to see you.'

Their lips met again. This time the intensity didn't surprise her, but it still took all her self-control to bring it to an end. She found herself wishing away Advent one to four, Christmas and the Sunday next, entirely unrepentant at such shameless disordering of her priorities.

He really wants me, she thought, lying in bed that night. One hint that I was willing, and we would have been rolling on the bed ... He's had affairs before, after all. What he really wants is to have an affair with me. Her imagination watched those warm, capable fingers sliding over her skin, moved his mouth from her lips to her throat to her breast. A wave of desire crashed over her. No!

She got out of bed to kneel on the floor, with her head buried in the quilt, praying with naive desperation for the self-control she already knew deep-down was likely to elude her.

But Iain's imagination knew no such barriers. She was with him in his bed as he lay in the gloom of his hotel room, with the passage light a yellow rectangle around his bedroom door. Her clothes fell away and her skin burned beneath him as she urged him on, teasing him towards consummation. So easy to have made this reality; to have responded to the unambiguous passion of her embrace by pulling her down onto the bed, and overriding her tentative scruples. I'll wait, I'll leave it up to you, he had told her. I don't want a casual affair, I want something that will last. That much at least was honest. And the way things were going, they would be lovers, sooner rather than later. He would find in her the substance of the shadows he had pursued in his previous ungratifying relationships. She would, for a time, blossom in the warmth of his wholehearted adoration. Oh yes, he could give her that. Would give her that for as long as she would accept it.

And if he had an iota of integrity, an ounce of genuine love for her, he would ring her now and end it, before he destroyed her.

Thirteen

Colin and Lisa's wedding was booked at St Peter's for the first Saturday of the new year. The evening beforehand, Alison invited Colin's parents and all four of his siblings to supper. They were booked into the hotel in the centre of Wellesley where the reception was due to be held, and she felt she ought to be hospitable, given that Lisa's family weren't taking much interest in the alliance.

Alison had not met Midge and Bernie Blatherwycke before, and though Lisa assured her that the rest of the family was not nearly as shy and serious as Colin, she was not anticipating an enjoyable evening. Colin's brothers and sisters ranged in age from nineteen down to twelve; a well-mannered and fresh-faced tribe, who treated Lisa as an old friend and Josh as a new one. To Alison's surprise, James, too, made an effort. Perhaps he enjoyed meeting fellow clergy children whose street credibility was so demonstrably less than his own. After the meal, he led them all off to his attic to play computer games. The stairs shook under six pairs of feet.

'Don't wake Luke!' Alison called after them, too late.

'I'll check on 'im,' Lisa said, getting up slowly from the table. 'We're goin' up, any'ow, aren't we, Col? You oughter see what James 'as got.' She held out her hand to him.

'I don't play computer games.'

'Then tha's time you learnt. Anyway, I need someone to get me up that staircase, else I'll get wedged. You can come an' give me a shove up me ...' she looked at Midge and Bernie, and stopped.

'Arse,' Bernie supplied, chuckling.

Colin frowned at his father, but Lisa laughed at him, and seized his hand. 'Come on,' she said again. 'Tha's your last night of freedom. Do something wild.'

He hesitated a moment, then his face broke into a smile, and he followed her.

'I do hope they're doing the right thing,' Midge said, as the sounds from the hall died away. 'We did *say* to him, you don't have to marry her, not these days, but he said he wanted to.'

'I said the same thing,' said Alison. 'We had a couple of long sessions, and I've talked to Lisa a lot too. I do think they're rushing it, but that's what they both want, and I think they do love each other. I only wish they'd have more time to get used to being together, before the baby arrives.'

'It was such a shock, wasn't it, Bernie, darling? I mean, Colin, of all of them! He's always been so reliable, so full of faith. And there he was, going round all summer, preaching chastity ... such a shock.' Midge shook her head, loosening even more strands of greying blonde hair from the wooden slide at the back of her neck.

'I never guessed that was why he suddenly turned so reluctant to do the show,' Bernie said. 'Silly boy! You'd think by his age he'd have worked out that sex leads to babies. Heaven knows, we've made no secret of it.'

'We do like Lisa, of course we do,' Midge said. 'It's just that she's not the kind of wife we expected for him.'

Alison took a sip of coffee. 'She has got a lot of good qualities, you know. I've known her a long time, and when I think how rough her life's been, it's remarkable she's so level-headed and capable. I think they'll do well, as long as they've got people around to support them. I'll have to try and keep in touch, and obviously they'll have you. And if they're going to be living in Greathampton, they'll have Michael and Jenny Turner on the doorstep. It's a shame they won't have a phone, though.'

'We offered to get one put in for them, but Colin wouldn't have it,' said Bernie. 'He doesn't like to be helped. We only just got away with paying for them to have a couple of nights in a hotel for a honeymoon.'

'Well, perhaps that's one of the things Lisa will do for him. She can stop him taking himself too seriously.'

'Oh, I know,' Midge exclaimed. 'He is terribly serious, he always has been, even when he was a baby. I don't know where he gets it from, do you, darling? Our home's always been full of laughter.'

'Mostly at my dress sense, if the truth were known,' Bernie said. He touched a hand to the striped green and white clerical shirt that shouted from under his pale grey suit. 'I've noticed you tactfully averting your eyes and saying nothing,' he added to Alison.

'Well I do prefer black or plain colours myself ... ' She smiled. She and the Blatherwyckes were at opposite ends of the religious spectrum, and Midge's flowery prints and her husband's seventies' length hair and wispy goatee took some getting used to, but she found herself rather liking them. It was reassuring to know that Lisa would have them as family, as well as herself.

Alison would like to have been less nervous as she conducted the ceremony, but it was only the second marriage she had ever done, and the sense of responsibility lay heavy on her as Colin and Lisa stood before her: Colin in his new navy suit, as sombre as if a life sentence had already been passed on him; Lisa voluminous in pale cream satin, grinning excitedly. Alison tried to quell her slight sense of unease about them by recalling the obvious sincerity with which they'd discussed their marriage plans with her, but it did not quite disappear. There was little of the sense of enthusiastic celebration she had felt at other weddings; but then, this one was a compromise between Colin's desire for a quiet ceremony, low on whiteness and witnesses, and Lisa's belief that she deserved the full works, however far it reduced her bank balance. That was why there were so few guests from Colin's side of the family, while Lisa's ragtaggle relations and her friends from Wellesley half filled the pews across the aisle. Poor Michael, playing the organ with Terry's grudging permission, had struggled to find music that would appeal to both sides.

But none of that was Alison's concern now. She checked her place in her service book, smiled at Colin and Lisa, and got the marriage service under way.

It was over almost too quickly, but at least it all went smoothly. The newly married couple kissed, completed the registers, submitted to photographs, and then trekked across Wellesley with everyone else for the reception. Lisa and Colin's kith and kin separated themselves out on party lines around an overheated function room. Only Midge and Bernie, making a creditable if parsonical attempt to fraternize with Lisa's mother and stepfather on the top table, and James, pursuing Lisa's half-sister Kelly, showed signs of trying to cross the divide.

A faint haze of smoke began to hover above the tables, and wreathed itself around the Christmas decorations that looped about walls and ceilings. Alison gathered food from the buffet for herself and Luke and went to join Michael and Jenny, who sat in a corner near the door that led into the hotel lobby. Jenny had wedged herself by the wall with Rosie asleep on her lap, while Michael, next to her, tried vainly to keep Lyddy's only feminine frock free of finger food. While Michael had arrived in the church early in order to play, Jenny had been at the back of the church with the children, and Alison had not yet seen her to speak to. Conversation now was stilted, with Jenny obviously ill at ease; though given the way Lisa's stepdad had threatened her a few years ago, that was understandable. Whatever the excuse, Alison was conscious that she had never yet seen the companionableness, intelligence and sense of humour Michael swore he loved in his wife. Though Jenny had made an effort to dress up today, with a beige suit and ochre silk blouse, a trace of make-up around grey eyes, and her mid-brown curls recently styled by a hairdresser, she held her body tensely, and her face was wary. Alison's cheerful adulation of Rosie's mottled cheeks and gummy smile was met with formal politeness, and she sighed inwardly; the knowledge of what had happened between her and Michael was always going to hamper her attempts to get to know Jenny.

'I've seen Iain a couple more times,' she told Michael, hoping it might reassure Jenny to know she had another interest. 'I definitely think it could get serious.'

'As long as you take it slowly,' Michael replied.

'Oh, I am. We're being very careful. We only meet every couple of months, though he does phone occasionally.' If two or three times a week was occasional; if it was careful to lie back in her bed on the wrong side of midnight, her eyes shut, with Iain murmuring into her ear with that mellifluous voice, while she wished and envisaged him there. 'You'll be able to meet him in July, when you come to our festival. There'll be you, and Iain, and the Headteacher from the school, and Christopher Ridgefield's agreed to chair it. I'm hoping to get Becky along. She enjoyed it last year, and she did say she'd be willing to come back, but she hasn't confirmed it yet.'

'She'll be too busy bonking Ty,' Michael said.

'No!' exclaimed Alison. 'When did that start?'

'After you introduced them at your festival last summer,' Jenny said drily. 'He's fancied Becky for years. He used to video all her children's shows on Saturday mornings, to watch over and over again.'

'Very sad,' Michael said, as he helped Lyddy to wriggle down from his lap and out under the table to escape into the room beyond. 'He got in touch with her once they were back in London. They went out, they hit it off, they had it off, and there we are.'

Alison set Luke down to join Lyddy in racing slalom-fashion around the tables. 'What do Nan and Christopher say, or don't they know?'

'They don't know, but they might have to some time if it goes on at this rate. Jen and I have been saying nice things about Ty to soften the ground. Beck's best hope is for Christopher to get to be Bishop of Wellesley, like everyone says he will, then he can't go on resenting Ty for screwing up his chances.'

Alison made a face. 'I don't think I could stand having Christopher as my bishop. I do like him in a lot of ways, but he wouldn't be any kind of support at all, not with his views about women priests. I wish they'd hurry up and allow women bishops, and give Nan the job.'

'That sounds heartfelt,' Michael observed. 'You must have a lot on your plate with the festival, and being Chair of Governors, and running your parish, to say nothing of losing your nanny. Are you managing?'

She shrugged. 'Oh, you know, it gets done. I've got a couple of childminders covering for Luke, and Nigel helped with a few things over Christmas. Though that wasn't a good idea, because now he's collapsed again, and Sandy says it might be ME. Still, things won't be as hectic for while.' She found she was clenching her fists, and forced herself to relax. Christmas week had been a nightmare, with a dozen services, three sermons, and congregations stuffed in to the rafters; she'd never stopped.

Michael frowned. 'Isn't anyone helping you? I'd have thought your rural dean ...'

Alison gave a sour laugh. 'He's not going to do anything. I've mortally offended him by getting too involved with the festival. He regards it as his baby, and he resents how successful it was last year. He says Nigel will be back any day, so there's no point making complicated arrangements.'

'There's no knowing, if it is ME,' said Jenny. 'It can go on for years.'

'Oh, God, don't!'

Across the room, Colin's best man was endeavouring to produce a hush for the speeches. Conversation ceased.

Colin sat on the right hand side of his hotel bed and waited for Lisa to come out of the bathroom, desperately wishing he could be somewhere else. He'd survived the embarrassing hurdle of the wedding itself; now he faced the ordeal of this first night with his new wife. While he could kiss her with reasonable enthusiasm, the idea of actually making love to a woman on the verge of motherhood filled him with confusion, and he didn't know what to do about it. The trouble was, from the way Lisa had been all evening, he guessed she was looking forward to a wild night.

The bathroom door opened, and Lisa emerged wearing a shiny black negligée through which the domes of her breasts and stomach were clearly visible. She'd taken a shower, and a musky scent preceded her towards the bed. Her hair, brushed out of the floral arrangement into which it had been fastened for the ceremony, swung loosely on her shoulders.

'Hello,' she said, cheeks and eyes glowing as she pulled back the covers and heaved herself into bed. He switched off the light and lay down. Lisa pushed herself as close to him as her bulge would allow. She put her arms round his neck and kissed him, her tongue taking over his mouth. Her hand slipped inside his pyjamas. 'Nice thing is,' she whispered, 'we don't 'ave to bother with johnnies or nothing.'

Colin held her in his arms, waiting for hell to break loose.

'Wha's up?' she said. 'Or rather, wha's not up?'

'It doesn't feel right,' he said.

'Tell you what, tha's easier from behind. You snuggle up behind me.' She turned round, pressing her back to him.

Colin put an arm over her waist. His hand encountered her stomach and drew back. 'I'm sorry. I don't think I can,' he whispered. 'Not with you like this.'

'Don't be silly. Tha's not goin' to hurt it.'

'I would if I could ... I'm sorry,' he said again, head bowed wretchedly against the back of her neck.

They lay in silence for a few minutes.

'Tell me the truth, Col,' Lisa whispered. 'Is this really only 'cos I'm pregnant, or don't you fancy me no more?'

'I do. I will do. Oh, I don't know what I think or feel any more. Everything's happened too quickly.' His voice was too tremulous to be his own.

'Ah, well. Story of my life. I shouldn't expect things to work out right.' She took his hand, and drew it round her stomach. Something shifted under his fingers. 'D'you feel that? Tha's kicking you. Saves me doin' it.'

'I've talked to a lawyer,' Alison told Steve. 'About the easiest way for us to get divorced. You've admitted adultery, so that makes it simple.'

'No, I've not,' Steve said tersely, his expression impossible to read behind his beard and glasses.

'You said you had, the Christmas before last. You told me you'd had relationships.'

'I've done no such thing. I don't have any bloody time, Alison. I have to work all hours to earn enough to keep you lot.'

They were hissing at each other in the narrow hallway of their old home, keeping their voices down for the sake of the boys who hadn't yet been told that their mother had arrived to collect them from their new year visit. Alison could have done without the added pressures of having to drive to and from Nottling over a busy weekend, but Steve had exchanged his saloon car for an elderly two-seater sports model that didn't have room for children. If she wanted the boys to visit him, she had to transport them both ways herself.

'But you said ...' She stopped. She had no energy for a fight if he was going to deny it. 'I thought you *wanted* a divorce.'

'Not if you're going to make out it's all my fault, and try to sting me for more money.'

'I don't sting you for money. I hardly get anything off you. *I* can't afford to go skiing.'

'You go off out often enough, I hear. Managed to get yourself a man, have you? Is that why you're in such a hurry? Your bishop might be interested to know what you're up to.'

'I'm not up to anything. I just want to get everything sorted out. Being separated is neither one thing nor the other.' She bit her lip. 'Make this easy, Steve. It's not fair on the boys if we fight over every little thing.'

'Concerned for the boys now, are you? How motherly! You might make a start sorting James out. His report was a disgrace.'

'He was doing a lot better the last few weeks of term. He's not been in any trouble this term.'

'Yet!'

'Has it not crossed your mind that he's upset about us splitting up? Why not try giving him some attention?'

'Why should I give attention to a lout like that? He says he wants to come back here for Sixth Form, but I told him, why should I want him around when he shows no consideration for anyone else, and sits around on his arse all day, whingeing? It's your fault. You've always let them do as they want and walk all over you.'

'And you've ignored them most of their lives! You never even wanted them! What makes you think you've got a right to say anything when you can barely be bothered to see them, and you really let them down at Christmas, going off skiing when they thought they were going to see you. I mean, skiing! For God's sake, since when have you been interested in skiing? You'd never try it when I wanted to.'

Steve smiled nastily. 'One holiday a year with you was bad enough. I'll tell the boys you're here, shall I?' And he turned his back on her and disappeared into the living room.

James appeared at the turn of the stairs with his sports bag hanging by his side. He made his way down into the hall and leaned against the wall, head bowed, saying nothing.

'Have a good time?' Alison asked.

James grunted.

'Were you listening just now?' she asked, interpreting his sullen expression. She put a hand on his shoulder and he pulled away. 'Don't take any notice of what we say when we're arguing, it's not about you.'

His eyes remained glued to his trainers, a flawless demonstration of the Thompson gene for uncommunicativeness, handed down in perfect working order from father to son.

When Josh and Luke emerged, they went out to the car in the grey chill of a January afternoon beckoning already to dusk. She had to put her foot down to get back to Wellesley in time for evensong, and though the worshippers seemed inspired by the service, it did little to lift her own spirits.

Alison began her bedtime ritual early that evening. Sundays left her shattered in any case, with the pressure of services, and so many people to greet and listen to, their problems saved up all week for a thirty-second consultation at the church door, and hell to pay if she seemed inattentive or unsympathetic. Annie's intercessions that morning had been a final straw, with her passionate plea for the Almighty Father's blessing on all poor unhappy children from broken homes, which left Alison and half the congregation curling with embarrassment. She'd had insufficient reserves with which to face the journey to Nottling and the subsequent argument with Steve; by now she was way overdrawn.

She finished tidying up for the cleaner who'd arrive at nine the next morning, and dragged herself upstairs. Check on Luke, nothing but his hair visible and kissable under his covers, look in on Josh and shut his door, but leave James undisturbed in the room that had been Lisa's; he didn't like intrusion. Into a dressing gown and through to the bathroom: brush hair, clean teeth, fend off the wrinkles for another night with expensive cream ... Iain had stroked her face ... if only he'd ring tonight ...

The phone went, coterminous with her thoughts, and she rushed to her bedroom to snatch it to her ear.

'Hello? ... Oh, hello, Sandy.' She struggled to push the disappointment from her voice.

'Sorry it's late,' Sandra began, 'but I didn't manage to catch you after evensong, and then I had to go on to a meeting, and I've only just got in. I didn't think you seemed yourself. I hope Annie didn't upset you this morning. She wouldn't have meant it personally.'

'I know. No, I had to go and get the boys this afternoon, and Steve and I had a run-in over James. I was still thinking of all the things I wished I'd said to him.'

'I can imagine. I won't ask you about it now, but do let's meet up for lunch or coffee, or something. I've hardly seen you, what with Christmas, and looking after Nigel, and doing extra sessions at work because we're short-staffed. It's time we caught up, and with Nigel ill, you'll be needing someone to grumble to, won't you?'

Alison laughed non-committally. 'Yes, give me a ring.'

'I'll let you get off to bed. Nigel was always shattered by the end of Sunday, not that he'd admit it. Let me know if there's anything I can do. You mustn't let yourself get overworked.'

'I'm fine. All those years of surviving state education are standing me in good stead. Goodnight, Sandy, thanks for ringing.'

And just how truthful was all of that? Alison asked herself as she got into bed. You're not fine at all, you're buckling under the strain, and if it wasn't for Iain ... He must ring tonight. She'd ring him herself, but he didn't like to be disturbed when he was working, and he'd be spending the evening grappling with his latest inspection report. She tried instead to pray, seeking the words and patterns and silences that would nourish her spirit and bolster her vocation, but the inner stillness she sought eluded her. No peace, until at last came the sound for which she strained, and he was there. She could lie with the phone tucked underneath her ear, and the bedside light casting a dim shadow around the room, pouring out the vagaries of her life before him like prayer, for reassurance; flourishing under his attention as a dry garden opens to rain.

Outside the Head's office, James leaned nonchalantly against the wall, as if he had chosen to be there, rather than awaiting his mother prior to the disciplinary meeting with Cowley and Mrs Tarbuck that was to decide his fate. Smoking in the bike sheds. Worth a couple of days exclusion at least. He wasn't altogether sorry; if he was honest, he'd wanted it to happen. You got respect for things like that, and they could hardly call him Jesus if he was permanently in trouble. Mum would go ballistic, but that was her own fault for refusing to take any notice when he told her how everyone picked on him. Howells was still the worst. Practically the first thing he'd said in the first History lesson of the term had been to ask what it was like having a birthday on Christmas Day.

'My birthday's in March,' James had said.

Howells had smiled nastily. 'Really? Someone told me it was Christmas Day. I beg your pardon.' One of these days he'd get a fist in his face, and serve him right.

The clatter of heels on the grey stone corridor forewarned his mother's arrival. She was unbuttoning her coat as she swept unsmiling towards him, unwinding the red scarf from her neck to disclose the white collar around her neck.

'Take that off!' he hissed, stepping towards her, his hand outstretched as if he would snatch it from her by force.

'Surely everyone knows by now,' she said impatiently, as she tugged the collar loose and put it in her pocket.

'You don't have to rub it in.'

'What's this about you being caught smoking?'

He shrugged.

'How could you be so stupid? This is the worst possible time, you *know* how much I've got on at the moment, you might at least try and help instead of making me miss meetings because I've got to come here and be lectured at by Mr Cowley! Don't you realise how humiliating it is for me? The Chair of Governors to have a son who does nothing but get into trouble. You're bound to get excluded, you do realise that? It'll be on your record for ever, and dad's going to be furious.'

James glared his hatred at her. That was all she fucking well cared about, her reputation, her time, her bloody job. Serve her right, he didn't care. She stepped forward and knocked on Cowley's door, and James followed her inside, extending a single finger upwards behind her back, and drawing some satisfaction from his surreptitious defiance.

Bunty turned up on her doorstep halfway through Wednesday morning, while Alison tried to catch up with herself after the embarrassment of James's two-day exclusion.

'We don't seem to have got the agenda for the PCC,' Bunty said, advancing through into Alison's study without being asked. 'I know Father Nigel said he wanted you to look at it before it went out, but that shouldn't take a week. If we don't have it in the next twenty-four hours, it's barely worth having a meeting, and,' she added, picking up the lift of Alison's head, 'we can't *possibly* cancel the PCC.'

'I'm sorry. I simply haven't had time,' Alison said, sinking into her chair and running a hand over her hair. 'I had to be up at the hospital yesterday, and James has been in trouble at school, and everything's got behind.'

Bunty sat down firmly. 'You could have asked one of us to do the hospital visiting. I know people don't feel they've been seen unless it's someone with a dog collar, but you can't cover everyone, especially at a time like this. What we need is a proper team of visitors like we had in my last parish. We called it the Home Ministry Team, and if anyone's sick, or lonely, it gets passed to the team leader, and they arrange for a suitable visitor, or get one of the clergy to call if that's necessary. It works extremely well. It frees the clergy to do their job much more effectively. What do you say?'

Alison struggled, as she often did with Bunty, with her automatic inclination to dismiss the idea simply because of its provenance. 'That certainly sounds a good idea, though it wouldn't have worked yesterday, because this was a lady I'd got to know. I had to be there.' Susan, who'd survived a few more weeks than she'd expected. Long enough to see Danni and her baby taken into the home of foster-parents who were prepared to look after the girl as well as the child. A better ending for Susan than it might have been, and Alison was grateful that she had been able to play a part in easing her dying. She hesitated. She'd had nowhere to offload her feelings about Susan's death, and for a moment, she even contemplated telling Bunty. But no, Bunty would have no sympathy.

'Who'd organise a team like that, though?' she asked Bunty. 'You're too busy with all the other things ...'

'I'm sure I can find a volunteer, and I can make time to set it up properly. Then it's a matter of recruiting and training the visitors, and it more or less runs itself.'

'If you're sure ... perhaps we could add it to the PCC agenda. There might be someone there who'd like to take it on.'

'Good,' Bunty said. She opened her file, found the draft agenda, and wrote on the bottom. 'You could have a look at it now,' she said, passing the sheet across to Alison. 'Then I can take it straight to Janet to get it copied. You'll see we've got the notice board back on the agenda. We can't go on postponing it until Father Nigel's back, and it looks very untidy as it is. I've made a few amendments to the design I did for the last meeting, and I'll get Janet to make copies for everyone. It's time we made a decision. It won't take long.'

'Right, yes.' With Bunty keen, there wasn't much chance of keeping it at the bottom of the agenda in the hope of it falling off. Damn Bunty. 'That seems fine.' She handed the page back to Bunty.

'It would have helped if you could have spared ten seconds to do that last week.'

'I'm sorry,' said Alison, hating the way Bunty made her feel like an incompetent junior, when she knew herself to be perfectly able to fill Nigel's shoes and her own. 'I'll help you deliver it, if you let me know when it's ready.'

'That's hardly a sensible use of your time, Alison. I can easily deliver the agendas myself. I'm sure you've got other things to do today.'

'There's a chapter meeting this afternoon.' She checked her watch. 'I hadn't decided whether to go or not.'

'You ought to. Father Mark always used to go if Father Nigel couldn't. We need to be kept in touch with what's going on in the Deanery.'

'But I can't leave you to do the PCC agenda.'

'Of course you can.' Bunty leaned forward and patted Alison's knee. 'That's what I'm here for. And we can't have you going under like poor Father Nigel. We have to look after you.'

Alison resisted the urge to kick her. 'Well, if you're sure you don't mind, that'd be a great help. Thank you.'

She showed Bunty to the door, and went back into her study, her concentration gone. What now? Work at her desk? Go to the chapter meeting? A temporary paralysis gripped her: decide, act, I can't think. She retreated to the kitchen, and got her strongest coffee down from the shelf.

Fourteen

On the day of the PCC, Alison made the hour-long trip to Diocesan Church House in Leathwell for a training event. A chance to take time out and gain some sympathy from her fellow curates for the extra responsibilities she was having to carry. A chance to tell Jackie how she was faring with Iain, though she found herself playing it down: of course I'm being sensible. He knows I have to be. I'm a priest. The day reinforced the identity and sense of vocation that so frequently slipped away from her as she struggled with the complexities of parish life and her isolation within it. When she left Church House at four-thirty, she felt truly inspired, truly able to cope.

Reality did not take long to catch up with her. She had left plenty of time to get back to Wellesley and to have supper before going out again to take the service that preceded the PCC. The dual carriageway out of Leathwell was busy, but she was making good progress when a rash of red and flashing amber lights ahead warned of stationary traffic. She came to a halt behind a double-glazing van, with a juggernaut looming above her on her left. Two hours later, she was still behind the double-glazing van, although the lorry had moved nearly a car's length ahead of her. An accident a little further along the dual carriageway had blocked both lanes. With traffic stacked up for miles behind, there was nothing anyone could do but wait until the emergency services had freed a trapped driver, and cleared debris from the road.

Local radio conveyed news of the jam to Alison as she sat watching the minutes flick by. At this point, Josh ought to be collecting Luke from today's childminder, getting him home, feeding him. Fortunately the boys already had experience of her failing to get home as expected between meetings, and they knew what to do. And the service, too, she was going to be cutting that fine ... going to be late ... going to miss it altogether. If only she'd agreed to Bunty's suggestion that she get a mobile phone, instead of clinging on to her rare moments of inaccessibility in car or town centre. She contemplated walking among the cars until she discovered someone who would allow her to use their phone, but sleet had begun to drive onto the windscreen, and she shied away from exposing herself to it. Ella knew where she'd been today. Somebody would have heard about the delays on the road. They'd have to manage, that was all.

Alison arrived at the PCC nearly half an hour late. She rushed into the hall where Bunty sat next to Janet, chairing the meeting.

'I am sorry. There was an accident, I was stuck in a jam for two hours,' Alison said, sitting down in the vacant seat on Bunty's right, and extracting her papers from her bag.

Grunts of sympathy rumbled round the table.

'Where have you got to?'

Bunty scanned the ticks on her agenda. 'We've done minutes of the last meeting, matters arising, the request from the church hall for new chairs, and the flower festival and church fete. Annie and I have got the fete in hand, and Mrs Kershaw will organise the flower side of things, but you need to invite the Mayor and plan the service.'

'Oh.' Alison had forgotten that Nigel had spent several weeks being preoccupied with the flower festival the previous summer. With the Wellesley Festival consuming her attention, St Peter's parochial summer highlight, a riot of horticulture in the church and a scrapyard of stalls outside the church hall, had passed her by. 'Right.'

'And we've agreed the design for a new notice board,' Bunty continued. 'It seemed sensible to get that item out of the way, as it was a small one. I've got the costs down, and Benny says we can afford it.'

Damn the woman, seizing her chance to slip her pet scheme through. Alison's head had started to ache.

'Any chance of a coffee?' she inquired.

Ella got up to oblige, returning with the drink and a couple of plain biscuits which were a poor compensation for Alison's missed supper.

'I need to say what *I* think about the notice board,' she said testily. 'There should be some clergy input on it. Neither Father Nigel nor I have had a look.'

'I mentioned it to Father Nigel when he came for evensong.'

Alison's heart sank. 'Nigel did evensong? You shouldn't have got him out.'

'Well, you weren't here,' Bunty said pragmatically, 'and he was on the doorstep. One little service wasn't going to hurt. He seemed very pleased to be asked, and to see us all again.'

'That's the trouble,' Alison said. 'He can't say no, but it'll knock him out for weeks.'

'He shouldn't give in to it,' Bunty stated. 'ME! Pah! It's all in the mind, he needs to make an effort. Anyway, he seemed to think my notice board was eminently suitable, but of course, if you don't trust us, you can have a look for yourself. I don't see why you should have a problem, you agreed with the principle of the thing when I first raised it.'

'The principle, yes, but the design last time was ...' she could hear Iain's voice urging her to assert her authority, but the circumstances didn't make it easy. 'I realise my opinion doesn't count for much, but I would like to feel consulted,' she finished, feebly.

'Course we need you, wonderwoman,' Brian beamed.

'I'm extremely sorry if I've hurt your feelings,' Bunty said.

'Not at all.' Alison strove to sound confident. What on earth had possessed her to come over all pathetic at a PCC of all places, and with a hellishly long agenda still in front of them? It would be an upward battle to establish any authority now. 'I'm sure the new notice board will be fine, but I'll have a look after the meeting.'

Bunty sniffed. 'We will move on to the plans for Easter. Alison?'

'Father Nigel and I want to cut out some of the long anthems and hymns we've had in the past ...' She tried to speak brightly, to reproduce the enthusiasm with which she and Nigel had discussed it out in her garden last summer, but she could feel hackles rising as she spoke.

'Oh, but we can't lose those lovely anthems Terry produces. It's the highlight of the year. People are still talk about when Father Mark sang that piece.' Bunty was adamant, glaring round the table, daring others to disagree.

'Ooh, yes, and we must have "The strife is o'er, the battle done",' Annie chipped in.

Alison's headache worsened as the PCC squabbled noisily about its favourite hymns. 'Oh do shut up!' she heard herself screech.

They stopped as one and stared at her. She forced herself to meet their eyes levelly, pretending it was perfectly normal for a curate to succumb to momentary hysteria. 'It's getting late. Please could we move on, Bunty,' she continued in an ordinary voice. 'It's up to Terry to choose the hymns, in consultation with me, we don't need to discuss it here.'

'I think I'm capable of moving the meeting on when necessary,' Bunty said coolly. 'I was about to do so. The next item is for me to share my thoughts about a Home Ministry Team.'

The PCC members were subdued for the rest of the meeting, but it was still a quarter to eleven before Bunty finally brought the meeting to a close.

'You have had a day,' Ella said to Alison. 'A long meeting like that on top of everything else. I thought you did very well.'

They were the last two in the hall. Alison gathered her belongings together and fastened them in her case. 'I was a disaster, shrieking at everyone like that. I don't know what came over me. Oh, damn, I meant to check out Bunty's notice board design. What's it like?'

Ella screwed her face up, choosing her words carefully. 'Better than the last one. She's suggesting we only have two glazed panels instead of three, and lesser specifications. I expect it'll be very nice. I'd have preferred varnished wood and gold letters like we had before, but I'm old-fashioned. Everyone else seemed to like it.'

'I can't see glass lasting a week, it's too tempting a target. I'll have to ring her and get her to drop the design off for me to see. I can't go along with that kind of expenditure unless I approve of it. I can't believe Nigel meant to give the go-ahead, Sandy says he can't make any decisions these days, and anyway, I'm the one who's supposed to be dealing with it.' She gave a last look round the hall, and headed for the door. 'I do wish he'd get fit.'

Ella peered at her closely. 'You will say if it's getting too much for you? Bunty and I will do what we can.'

'I know. No, I'm fine. This Home Ministry Team of Bunty's will help, and things should be easier for a few weeks. Until Lent, anyway.' She smiled confidently. 'Let's get home.'

Gazing at her reflection in the mirrored cabinet in her downstairs cloak-room the following day, Alison was struck by how worn she appeared in the drab afternoon sunlight. Betrayed not only by the lines, unaffected by two decades of emollience, but by the expression in her eyes. I look desperate, she thought; and what's Iain going to make of that tonight? She frowned at herself, and went back to her study, where she picked up the phone and dialled Michael's number.

'Oh, hello, Jenny, it's Alison. I thought you'd be at work,' she said to the abrupt female voice at the other end.

'I've got the afternoon off.'

'Is Michael there?'

'No.'

Alison suppressed a sigh of irritation. I've said sorry, she wanted to shout. I don't want your husband, give me a break! 'When will he be back?'

'I don't know. Teatime?'

'Could you ask him to ring me when he gets in? I need to talk to him before I go out tonight.'

'I'll tell him.'

'Are you all well? How's Rosie?'

'Growing. Feeding. Crying. You know.'

Since Jenny clearly had no wish to prolong the conversation, Alison gave up and rang off.

Michael didn't ring back. She was on her own. Without his common sense to shore her up, to advise the safety of jeans and baggy jumper, she followed her instincts. Iain was staying at the relatively smart hotel where she'd met him the previous November, and that, she felt, entitled her to dress up. She donned a plain black knee-length dress that hugged her figure under a loose-fitting deep-purple jacket, and underneath, the expensive lingerie that had been her Christmas present to herself. Her sheer black stockings would ladder at a glance, but why not give them their day?

'If Michael rings, say I've gone, and it doesn't matter,' she told the boys as she stood in the doorway of the living room, trying to force her foot into a shoe that had seemed perfectly sized in the sales a week before.

'You're tarted up,' James sneered from the sofa where he lay watching television. 'Another "meeting", is it?'

'I've told you before, this is my work consultant, and we talk over dinner, so I have to dress up.'

'I think you look lovely,' Josh said loyally, getting up off the floor to envelop her in an enthusiastic bearhug. 'Mmmm, and you smell nice.'

'Thank you. I'm glad someone appreciates me.'

She detached herself from Josh, wrapped her coat around her, and went out to her car.

She saw Iain immediately she stepped inside the hotel door. He was standing perusing a notice board that told of tourist attractions in the vicinity, and there was a hint of weariness in his posture. Presenting his report at the school where he had just completed his inspection, after weeks of intense activity, had left a mark.

As soon as he saw her, his expression lightened. 'It is good to see you again,' he said, hugging her closely. 'You're looking lovely. But tired,' he added, fingering her cheek.

'One of those weeks. I'll be alright. You're looking pretty smart yourself.' She touched the lapel of his well-cut navy suit. 'And I like the tie.' What she had at first taken to be a random pattern revealed itself, on inspection, to be a series of undulating Nessies making their way across the dark waters of the loch. 'A Christmas present?'

'Ah, that's Hetty's sense of humour.' He hesitated. 'You remember, my neighbour's daughter? They invited me over for Christmas lunch, and she'd decided I needed a gift. I put it on this morning without thinking. I'm not sure it gave the right message for the meeting this evening.'

'I don't know. "I am not a monster, honest"?'

Iain laughed as he steered her towards the restaurant. They took their seats over in the corner and perused the menu. Alison let Iain pay for her these days; his own meals were on expenses, and she enjoyed feeling taken care of. He passed their orders to an attentive waiter and leant forward, his glasses reflecting the glow of the candle on the table between them.

'So how are you?'

'Cracking up. I got hysterical in the PCC, which isn't like me at all. James was caught smoking, and he's being excluded ...' She related the saga while Iain listened intently, elbows on the table, his chin resting on steepled fingers. 'He overheard me and Steve arguing, and I think that upset him. He won't admit it, of course. He doesn't talk to me. And Nigel's been signed off for another three months. He will keep trying to do things, and it sets him back for months. I want to strangle him sometimes.' She sighed. 'I can't cope.'

The waiter appeared with a half bottle of wine and filled their glasses.

'Do you not get some help if your boss is off sick?'

'Bring in a supply vicar, you mean? It doesn't work like that. There's one or two people I can call on, but you know how it is, it's more effort to organise help than to do it yourself. I thought I'd get a break after Christmas, but there were always people calling for something or other that couldn't wait, and then there was Lisa's wedding, and every week there's bloody sermons to do, and they seem to take me longer and longer instead of getting easier, and ...' Unexpected tears rose in her eyes. The exhaustion had crept up behind her and jumped her. 'I'm sorry,' she sniffed. 'I'm being boring. I don't mean to be this pathetic.'

'I'm not surprised you're worn out, the amount you've been doing.' He reached across and enclosed her hand in his own. 'You need a break. You need to get right away from everything for a while.'

'How can I? I can't leave the boys on their own, and Steve's not going to have them simply so I can have a holiday, and anyway, I can't be away for Sundays.'

Iain narrowed his lips and shook his head. 'It's not good enough,

Allie, you need a proper break,' he repeated. A tear dropped from her cheek to darken the white of the tablecloth. Iain let go of her, and fished a clean handkerchief from his pocket to pass to her. 'There must be someone who'd have them. What about your mother?'

'I couldn't, not with Nigel ill ...' Alison blew her nose, and put his handkerchief in her bag.

The waiter appeared, and she held herself still while he settled their plates in front of them.

'Look at it like this: either you make arrangements for the children and the church so you can have a break at a time that suits you, or somebody else has to cobble something together in an emaircency, because you've had a breakdown. I'm serious, Allie. I've seen it happen. You've got to take care of yourself.' He took a mouthful of food, and took his time savouring it. 'I'm going to Rome for a week soon, why don't you come with me?'

'That's out of the question. I couldn't possibly.'

'Couldn't what? Get the time off, or come away with me?'

'Both!' She dismissed the possibility abruptly, before she was tempted to focus on it, to imagine dropping everything and escaping with him, and all that it would mean ...

'No? That's a shame. I'd enjoy showing you around.'

Alison took refuge in eating, refusing to be drawn into discussion. When she judged that enough time had gone by for her to be able to change the subject, she asked, 'How are you, anyway? You must be pleased you've got another inspection out of the way.'

'Not quite, I'll still have to finalise my report ...'

She fed him questions as the meal unfolded. It was easier than paying attention to herself.

'Do you want to come to my room for coffee?' he asked her as they finished their desserts. 'Or is that out of the question too?' He frowned a little as he spoke, as if her hasty dismissal of his invitation had upset him.

She rushed in, stuttering through the words in her anxiety to convince him she cared. 'No, not at all. You mustn't think I don't want you ... to be with you. I've ... I've missed you. I need you. I need you to hold me.'

Iain's eyes rested on her face, vesting every phrase with a significance she had not realised she intended.

They stood and left the restaurant: along the richly carpeted corridors, into the lift; standing silent, a little apart, as desire, unmasked, deprived them of speech. Alison caught her reflection in the smoky mirrored glass in front of her. Her hair pulled back into a knot and fixed with a silver clasp; the jet black earrings that dropped from their silver clasps, matched by the silver chain of Celtic design that lay at the base of her throat, a present from Iain. He had phoned to listen to her delight as she opened it at one-thirty on Christmas morning, in the middle of filling the boys' stockings after midnight mass.

Behind her, Iain reached out to touch the delicately worked links. 'It suits you,' he said. 'I imagined it resting against your throat like this ...'

His closeness unsteadied her. She couldn't look at him. Coffee, she told herself. I am only going for coffee.

Along the passage, Iain taking his room key from his pocket to let her in; in front of her, the bed beckoning, double this time, dominating the room. A thick quilted bedspread in pale green stretched over it, with jagged pink lines across it, like the track of a hospital monitor. Light from the lamps on the wall at either side cast pools of light that left the rest of the room in shadow.

Iain shut the door behind them, and turned the key in the lock. He put a hand under her chin and kissed her once, very gently. 'I'll fill the kettle.' He picked it up from a small shelf and disappeared to the bathroom.

Alison put her handbag down on one of the bedside tables. The room was several degrees warmer than the restaurant; she removed her jacket and hung it over the back of the chair by the mirror. No welcoming armchairs here to retreat to; she slipped off her shoes, sat back against the end of the bed, and swung her feet up. Those shoes had been a mistake. Her toes complained as she rubbed them back into shape.

Iain came back, and plugged the kettle in. 'Sore feet?'

'A little.'

She watched him toss his jacket on top of hers, and pull his tie off, then he sat down on the edge of the bed and took her left foot into his lap to continue the massage with tender deliberation. His touch left her shaking; tiredness made her emotional, and her emotions were too bound up with Iain for her to think straight. She spoke to break the spell.

'I'm sorry I've not been very good company this evening.'

'I wouldn't say that.' He included her ankle in the delicate circular motion of his fingers. 'You're under pressure, you needed to unload some of it. I wish you would come away with me. I'd love to spend some time with you.' His hand crept up her calf. 'I'd love to take you to Rome.'

'I couldn't ...'

'You could have your own room, I'm not meaning to put any pressure on you. I know you're wanting to take things slowly.' As he spoke, his hand passed her knee, sliding over the sheer black smoothness of her thigh, insinuating itself under her dress. He had been watching her intently. She caught in the narrowing of his eyes the moment when his fingers discovered the top of her stocking. 'On the other hand I wouldn't be being honest if I didn't say that I've been wanting to go to bed with you practically since I first met you. You must know that.'

He let go of her and got up to seat himself beside her at the head of the bed. His right arm came round her, his left hand replaced itself on her thigh. Somewhere behind them, the kettle clicked itself off.

Alison put her arms round his neck, and kissed him, lips, mouth, tongue inviting him in.

Iain drew back. 'And I have to say,' he whispered, gazing at her, one finger beneath the rim of her stocking, 'that when you come dressed like this, and you kiss me like that, I can't help suspecting you want it quite as much as I do.'

'I ... I don't. Don't ask me. I mustn't. I'd get myself in such a mess ... You said you wouldn't pressurize me ... I'm not allowed to ...'

'Why not? Who are you hurting?'

Somewhere at the back of her mind was the set of words with which she could rebut such inappropriate advances. Touched by his hands and lips, unsteadied by the intentness of his gaze and his care for her, she could not now recall any of them. Her rejection of Iain's proposition carried no conviction, even to herself. All she wanted was to wrap her arms around his neck and let herself go.

Iain removed his glasses, and laid them down beside the bed. His eyes, unguarded, broke the last of her resolutions. She locked her mouth to his, letting herself fall back down with him against the pillows.

'Do not do this!' said a voice in her head, the fragile ghost of her self-control. It had no chance: she had lost her boundaries. Roused beyond resistance by the pressure of fingers denting skin, the faint damp excitement of a hand manipulating the flesh of her thigh, slipping inside her unresisting underwear. What did anything matter but to mould her body to his, to learn the contours of his mouth, the warmth of his skin as she unbuttoned his shirt and pressed her face to his chest? A groan escaped her. She shut her eyes and stopped caring.

'Do you want to stop me?'

The question was breathed into her ear while his hands continued to travel over her; there was only one answer she could make. She reached down to undo the button of his trousers, to draw his zip slowly down, to caress him with eager, knowledgeable hands.

'Have you got something you could use?' she whispered.

Presciently, he had.

'Are you alright?' said a voice in her ear.

Alison pressed her face more closely to Iain's neck, unable as yet to speak. She was lying on top of him, her dress reduced to a crumpled ruck around her waist, held so tightly she could scarcely tell where she began and he ended.

'You've no regrets? No twinges of conscience?'

'I expect I will have,' she said, when she had found her voice. 'It's not that I think it's all that wrong, not when we love each other so much, but I don't expect anyone in the church would see it that way.' She lifted her head. 'And I didn't mean to do it quite yet.'

Her hair had come loose, and fell across his face. Iain brought a hand up to gather it at the nape of her neck, and kissed her again. 'I can't see what can be so wrong with something that makes you look like this.'

Alison smiled at him. 'What's wrong with me?'

'Absolutely nothing. Apart from being somewhat pink. You're very beautiful, and incredibly sexy. I love you to distraction, and I should have seduced you months ago.'

She giggled. She'd have giggled at anything. 'Have you really wanted to go to bed with me right from the start?'

'Definitely. I drove away from the school thinking: I bet she's amazing in bed.'

'And?'

'You are.'

'I thought I might be out of practice.' She rested her head on his shoulder again. 'Or boring.'

Iain's snort of mirth tickled her ear, putting to flight all that had remained of Steve's barbed accusations. He ran his hand through her hair. 'You'll have to come away with me now.'

'Do we get to do this all day?'

'Absolutely. And all night.'

She wriggled against him, enjoying the security of his arms. 'I'll see what I can do.'

She shut her eyes and sighed contentedly. Regrets? Conscience? When she'd met the man she was going to spend the rest of her life with? As if God would be that small-minded.

Fifteen

Colin returned home from his job in the booksellers and stationers on Greathampton High Street to find the hall of the flat full of cardboard packaging, and the cot his mother had lent them leaning against the wall in several pieces. Through the open door of the boxroom that was due to serve as a nursery, he could see the new cot of light pine that had unaccountably taken its place. He frowned at it. A light under the bathroom door, and the intermittent sound of splashing, suggested that was where Lisa had taken herself after her exertions with the furniture. He knocked at the door.

'Hi, sweetie!' she called. 'Come in!'

He went inside, and sat down on the toilet, since there was nowhere else.

Lisa was lying in a tub full of milky water, her belly jutting out of the water like an upturned boat.

Colin, trying to keep his eyes on her face, rather than the disturbing curves of her swollen breasts, asked, 'Where's that cot come from?'

'I got it off my catalogue. Self-assembly. It weren't 'alf fiddly to put together.'

'I never said you could ... How much was it?'

'I can't remember exactly. A few quid a week.'

'Lise, you mustn't spend money without checking with me.'

Her belly heaved violently. 'There it goes, did you see that? Right in me ribs, that one.'

He watched, fascinated despite himself.

Lisa stroked her stomach gently. 'Your mum's one wasn't safe. The bars are too wide apart, a baby could get its head stuck.'

'My mum's had five children in it, and it never hurt us. You shouldn't have bought a new one, not without asking me.'

'We're not that skint, are we?'

'We will be. Looks like I won't have a job after this month.'

'Oh, Col!' She struggled to sit up. 'Wha's happened?'

'It's this takeover. They're closing the small stores down.'

'You'll get another job, won't you, though?' She unhooked the plug with her toe. 'Give us a hand.'

He helped her to her feet, passed her a towel, and supported her while she stepped out of the bath.

She began to dab herself dry. 'I could always get a bit of work with kids once the baby's bigger. There's a nursery over on the Rows ... Gawd, look at that, I got stretch marks already.'

'You don't need to get a job. I'll find something.'

'I'll want to get a job sometime. I in't sitting around all day doin' nothing.'

'You'll have the baby to look after, that's a full-time job. No, I'll go down to the job centre, see what there is.'

He saw the challenge taking shape in her eyes, and said quickly, 'What else have you been doing today?'

'I give Allie a ring. Thought I'd see 'ow they're all gettin' on without me. She seemed a bit off.' She unhooked a large white towelling robe from the back of the door, and wrapped it around herself.

'She was probably busy. You can't expect her to drop everything to talk to you, it's not as though you work for her any more.'

'She always said I was a friend.'

'You've got me now,' Colin said, rubbing her shoulder.

She looked at him. He could see her thinking: you're supposed to be a husband, not a friend. Any minute now, and she'd be asking when he was going to start acting like it.

'I'll make you a cup of tea,' he said quickly, and made his escape.

Alison went through her morning rituals in an abstracted manner: Luke to be fed and kitted out for his childminder, instructions for Josh when he delivered his brother there, the exchange of monosyllables with James who was still regarding her suspiciously after her late and preoccupied return the previous evening. Then off to say the morning office in church for herself and the three stalwarts who joined her. Her voice, confident and sincere, praying for mercy and forgiveness, though she could not bring herself to repent too strongly for the raptures of last night. Not when it felt so right, and who was possibly being hurt by it?

The service was followed by deliberations with Janet in the office, and then back home to catch up on parish business before a lunchtime meeting. Letters to answer, papers to study ... She was distractedly staring out of her window, when Michael's phone call came through.

'I'm sorry I didn't ring yesterday. Jen only told me over breakfast that you'd wanted to speak to me before you went out.'

'Is she OK? She sounded fed up.'

'She's got something on her mind, she'll be alright. What did you want?' He sounded uncharacteristically tense himself; living with Jenny in one of her moods no doubt accounted for it.

'I wanted you to bolster up my self-control before I met Iain for dinner last night.'

'Oh well, I daresay you managed without me.'

'No, I didn't. I slept with him.'

'Oh, Allie!'

'Don't sound like that. It was wonderful. He's amazing, he really is. I've never felt so happy.'

'Whatever happened to taking things slowly?'

'I love him. I need him. It's not as though we're hurting anybody.'

There was a silence at the other end of the phone. 'I suppose you know what you're doing,' Michael said eventually.

'Is that it? I thought you'd be telling me off.'

'It's not going to make any difference, you'll carry on whatever I say.'

'Yes, but ...' But what? I need to justify myself to you? I need you to be my conscience? It does make a difference, I listen to you? But he gave her no chance to say it.

'Look, Allie, I've got to go. You know the risks. For God's sake be discreet, that's all.' And he rang off.

Alison replaced the phone, irked by his uncharacteristic lack of concern. Perhaps he's jealous, she mused. He can't have me himself, but he still wants to feel I'm in love with him. Well, he'll have to get used to the idea that I've got someone else.

Nevertheless, she did ponder the wisdom of going away with Iain, the impact on her ministry, the deceptions that would be involved, the risks of encountering someone she knew in Rome. Pondered through the rest of that hour at her desk, as she followed up the list of tasks the PCC meeting had left her with, through the lunchtime festival committee meeting, and the afternoon visit to Wellesley High to shortlist for a temporary appointment for the summer term.

By the time she was back at her desk listening to the litany on the answerphone, however, her mind was virtually made up. *Bleep* I want to arrange a wedding *Bleep* We want our baby done *Bleep* I want to look round your church, why isn't it left unlocked? *Bleep* Can you come and speak at our Women's Guild? *Bleep* We've had to change the time of the premises committee. *Bleep* Bunty here! Don't forget you have to come to the drama club meeting. Oh God, she could not cope with all of this. Her sanity depended on escape.

'No, Bunty, I don't,' she said, ringing back. 'I can't. I'm going to be away.' The words, once said, filled her with an enormous sense of liberation.

'You can't go away,' Bunty said, 'not at this short notice! I thought you wanted to check the design of the new notice board before I ordered it.'

'You can drop that in to me any time. I need a break, Bunty. And an old friend's just given me a chance of a holiday, and I'd be mad not to take it. I'm going after the Sunday morning Eucharist, and I'll be back by the following Sunday, and I can arrange cover for the other services. There's not much I'll miss.'

Only the confirmation class and the luncheon club and the premises committee and thirty-seven people in mortal distress, but they'll bloody well have to survive. She put the phone down on Bunty, and rang her mother.

'Don't lose your head now, Lisa', said the midwife. 'Come on, settle down, it won't be long. One last big push.'

Lisa yelled again, thrashing against the hands that were trying to push her back down on the high, narrow delivery bed. 'Aaaaah! I wanna go home. I fuckin' wanna go home. Can't you cut the bloody thing out ...?'

She was panicking now, and in increasing pain, scarcely aware any more of Colin, pale and bewildered by her head. That one last push she kept being exhorted to make was required again and again, and nothing was happening. More anaesthetic. The pain mercifully dulled as forceps appeared. She couldn't feel the cut, the stretching, the increasingly urgent attempts to draw the baby from her.

Anxious attention to the monitors, Colin's hand sweating as it clasped hers ...

'There's something wrong. Oh, God, oh God, it's gonna die.'

Consultations, conversations around her, and a reassuring voice that penetrated her moans.

'We're going to do a Caesarian, Lisa. You and the baby are both getting tired. You won't feel anything ...'

A practised ritual: a screen across her stomach, a touch like a pencil drawn across her, a wrestling match within her belly, and then at last the baby being lifted free.

'It's a little girl,' said the midwife's voice. 'She's perfect.'

The repair work seemed to take hours, but she floated through the cleaning up, the stitching above and below, because all she cared about now was the plump red-faced bundle lying on Colin's knee, a tuft of black hair visible above the white of the hospital sheet, her eyes screwed shut.

'Can I hold 'er now?' Lisa asked.

He leaned over and placed the baby in her arms.

'Hello, Karli,' she said. 'I'm your mum. An' I'll tell you what - you're never havin' no brothers or sisters, I'm not goin' through that again whatever your dad says.'

She looked up at Colin and smiled. Gradually his mouth relaxed, and he smiled back.

'You'd better go an' ring your mum,' she said. 'And Allie, and Michael. And my mum. Bet they can't wait to hear!'

But even as Lisa spoke, Alison was standing on the gravel in front of her house, fluttering with last-minute instructions for her mother before leaving for a week with Iain in Rome. She'd told her mother the truth about her lover, figuring correctly that the admission of romance and intrigue would be sufficient to persuade her to help out at extremely short notice.

'I'll manage, Allie. Off you go. You don't want to miss your flight.'

Alison kissed her, and turned to let Josh fling his arms round her.

'If I don't let go, you can't go, can you? Why can't I come with you? I don't want you to go. What happens if there's a plane crash?'

'There won't be. I need a holiday, Josh, I need a break. You don't want me to end up having to lie in bed all day like Father Nigel.'

'At least you'd be home,' he said, clinging on until she forcibly detached him.

James hovered by the front door with his headphones on, treating the jamb as a keyboard, feigning indifference to her departure.

She waved to him. 'Bye. Be helpful.'

Luke decided to add to the tension by howling, halting Alison's progress to the car while she hugged him again.

'He'll be fine,' her mother said. 'Stop crying, Luke, Mummy'll be back soon, and we've got that nice video to watch that Granny brought, haven't we? And those nice chocolate biscuits.'

It had no immediate effect, but Alison told herself it would be alright. Even Luke couldn't cry solidly for six days and nights, and he normally liked his grandmother.

'Hell! Is that the time?' She got into the car and started it up. 'I'll see if I can get that Juventus shirt,' she called to Josh, hoping Iain knew the Italian for 'age twelve', and 'how can this be official merchandise at this price?'

'Enjoy yourself, dear.' Her mother winked indiscreetly.

'Thanks, Mum, I'll try. I'll phone when I can.'

The sense of freedom exhilarated her as she drove through the desperately slow Sunday afternoon traffic. An age passed before she saw Heathrow on the motorway signs at last, and glimpsed the huge planes, slow as barrage balloons, rising and falling across the skyline. She left her car, wondering how she would ever remember its location in a week's time, and took the bus to the terminal. Iain would be getting impatient, though she was only twenty minutes over time. It was alright for him, he had no family to complicate things.

He was at least easy to identify; his head of thick white hair standing out across the concourse, although the brown leather jacket, navy jumper and khaki trousers he wore were unfamiliar. He made no comment on her lateness, but formality marked his manner as he organised the checking in of their luggage. Her visions of a romantic interlude faltered; now they'd spend the first day not speaking to each other. She might as well have been with Steve.

But Iain was not Steve. He slipped his arm round her as he led her away. 'I'd started to worry you might have had second thoughts.'

'As if I would! It took longer than I thought saying goodbye to the children, and I kept thinking of things I had to tell my mum. Anyway, I'm here now.' She hugged him. 'I'm as excited as a ten year old. I couldn't sleep at all last night. A whole week with you. And in Rome!'

'I'm sure Rome won't let you down. I only hope I don't.'

'You could never do that. Come on, let me buy you a coffee, make up for keeping you waiting.'

Buying Iain coffee was Alison's only contribution during their journey. She had rarely flown, and not for many years; he had made this trip to Rome some half-dozen times, and three times to the same hotel in which they would be staying. She could leave everything to him. Follow him through the boarding procedures, rest beside him on the flight, let him steer her through the confusion of walkways and trains and traffic that lay between the airport and the hotel, while she wallowed in the luxury of not having to think, or decide, or cope.

'I didn't realise you were so fluent in Italian,' she said, as they followed the hotel proprietor and their bags back down the stairs from the first-floor reception desk.

'Not fluent. I get by so long as it's not complicated.' He held the door into the street open for her. 'I hope you don't mind having a room across the road, but it's quieter over that side. I hope this hotel's alright for you. I come here because it's friendly, and it's fairly central, but you're mebbe used to something a little more upmarket?'

'It'll be fine. I'm not fussy. Not when I'm with you.'

They crossed the road, a narrow side street, almost devoid of traffic. There were no gaps between the three and four-storey houses that rose from the pavement's edge, only a series of doors at irregular intervals, and a couple of dowdy signs advertising *Trattoria* and *Pizzeria*, to go with the *Pasticcerie* Alison had noticed earlier at the nearby crossroads. They passed through an unmarked door to enter a gloomy hall. An old-fashioned lift carried them up a floor, and the proprietor showed them into a small lobby, and flung open doors to either side. To their left, a long, narrow bathroom, basin, bath and toilet in order along one wall. To their right, a high-ceilinged bedroom with a tiled floor, and a window with a small balcony that jutted out over the street below. The bed that dominated the room was literally double, two single frames fixed together, with the bedding hiding the join between the mattresses. A television stood on the dressing table opposite it, dwarfed by the wardrobes on either side. Just inside the door, a couple of low chairs occupied an otherwise bare corner.

Alison stepped inside, gratefully dropping her coat and her flight bag onto one chair, and sitting down on the other, while the proprietor held a conversation with Iain in the doorway. She looked around her. So this was where they would spend a third or more of their hours in Rome. Sharing that bed, learning to be lovers. Blotting out the voices that whispered of the work she was neglecting, and the codes she was breaking. She caught Iain's eye, and, with a final '*Grazie*', he brought the conversation to an end, and closed the door.

Alison went over to put her arms around him, and for the first time that day they were at last able to kiss each other properly.

Iain stroked her hair. 'If you want to eat, we could find a restaurant.

146

Or if you're not that hungry, I could just get us some pizza, and bring it back here. Then we could have an early night.'

'An early night sounds good,' she said, running her hands down his back. If she ought not to be here, it was too late now.

Sixteen

The waters of the Tiber slipped through the bridge beneath them, a sluggish reptilian green. On either bank, the plane trees were beginning to unfold into leaf as the mild winter nodded to spring. Alison undid her coat, warm from walking so far in this beneficent weather, then leaned over the parapet again, trying to make sense of the juggle of buildings arrayed ahead of her.

'You must tell me what you like,' Iain said.

She glanced at him, uncertain at first of his meaning. For the hour since breakfast, he had been an assiduous guide, giving her a flavour of the city, and helping her to put the confused layers of history into context. Now, he gazed down at the river, refusing to meet her eyes.

'In bed, I mean,' he continued. 'I'm sorry about last night. I didn't mean it to be over so quickly.'

'That's alright.'

'I've not had a partner for so long, and I find I want you so much ... And then going straight to sleep, that's not what I intended. I promise not to be so selfish next time. That's why you must tell me what you like.'

Alison slid her arm through his. 'It's nice to find a man who's bothered. And who's prepared to talk about it.'

Iain moved closer, his head a breath from hers. 'We won't be together all that often, and I want it to be special for you when we are.'

'It is,' she said, kissing him. 'It will be. Don't worry.'

They moved from the parapet, and began walking again in the direction of their destination: the dome of St Peter's, dominating the skyline.

'I think I need a sit-down,' she said. 'My feet are starting to ache.'

'I suggest we get a bus to the Vatican, and we can get a coffee there.'

'My friend Michael says there's a suggestions box at the Vatican. He said when he was there, he put a note in, suggesting they ordain women. I wouldn't put it past him.'

'Perhaps you should be wearing your collar today, to make a point.'

'Oh, don't. I'm trying not to think about that, I need a break ... Look, there's a kiosk, I must get some postcards.' She began to scan the cards on the rickety rack, selecting one for her family back home, and one for Jackie. 'And I think I'll get this for Michael,' she said, fishing out a picture of the pope meeting a nun with an entourage of children and babies. 'With one small addition.'

She paid for her purchases, borrowed a pen from Iain, and drew a speech bubble from the Pontiff's smile, in which she wrote: Haven't you heard of contraception?

Iain laughed, and took her hand. 'I wouldn't post that in the Vatican. It'd never get through. Did you know it has its own postal service?'

And he was away again, drawing on his fund of knowledge; entertaining her, and driving away all her disquiet.

But Alison's disquiet could not aways be kept at bay. Religion was threaded too tightly through every aspect of the city's life and history. For a start, there were the black-suited priests round every corner: Italian, American, French, English, Irish of course. Touring the holy sights, hurriedly shepherding little parties of parishioners past lascivious marble, explaining Latin inscriptions to curious nuns standing in formation, robes and headscarves whipping around them. Reverential in the Vatican corridors: a lifetime's ambition fulfilled, 'We have seen His Holiness!'

Rome tore at Alison's sense of identity: I'm one of you, she wanted to proclaim as she stepped past the accusatory statues into the twilight of the churches they visited. This is my vocation, this is who I am. I belong at these dimly lit altars, in these towering pulpits. These are my possessions, my heritage. The candlelight falling into the shade of side-chapels, the echoing smell of incense, the saints shedding tears disguised by cracked varnish, or highlighted in luridly restored colours, appropriated her senses. They called to her soul: stay a while, worship, let us speak to you! But she could not allow it; could only cross herself, and turn away hurriedly before Iain could notice. Turn from the altar, past the rows of confessional boxes strung along the nave with their lights above, red for occupied, green for free. Confession invited in four different languages, and absolution in none, not for this: 'I am a priest, and I have come away with my lover.'

Iain's devotion was what kept her sane, overriding her anxieties by day, and helping her to survive the darkness each time she woke. Each afternoon, they returned to their hotel to rest, and grew to understand the responses of each other's bodies as they strained together on the wide expanse of the bed, with the noise of the city at bay beyond the windows.

They passed much of their fourth day out of the city, exploring the grassy paths of deserted Ostia. By the time they returned to the hotel, they were exhausted, with no energy to do anything other than sleep. Alison woke to find it was already early evening. She left Iain reading, and went to take a shower. When she emerged, towel indecorously swathed around her, she found him out on the balcony, speaking into his phone with barely suppressed impatience.

'Don't get yourself into a panic. Phone Jean,' he was saying. 'You should have got on to her first thing this morning, you know she doesn't mind.'

Alison put a hand on his shoulder. He spun round with a forbidding expression. 'Do you mind? It's a problem at work. I'll be in in a moment.'

Thus dismissed, she went back inside, pulling the glass-panelled balcony doors closed behind her. She stood in front of the wardrobe, selecting a long cream silk shirt to wear over her black trousers, and a thin russet-coloured scarf that would go with her amber earrings, then she sat down on the bed, wondering whether to get dressed.

Iain came inside a few minutes later.

'Do you want to join me?' she asked, patting the bed beside her.

He shook his head, his face grim and set. 'I'll have my shower and get changed.'

Alison hadn't seen him annoyed before, and hoped he wouldn't, like Steve, hold onto it for the rest of their holiday.

'Serves you right, bringing your mobile phone on holiday,' she tried, hoping to lighten his mood.

He frowned. 'I don't like to be completely incommunicado.'

'Would you mind if I used it to phone home again?'

'Go ahead.'

Though he was polite and attentive to her as they prepared to go out to eat, he was obviously still distracted by his phone call.

'Do you want to talk about it?' she asked, as they waited for the lift.

'No. Not now, anyway. How about your call? How's the family?'

'They seem to be doing alright. Josh is sleeping in Luke's room, because he was waking up in the night crying, and James is being remarkably helpful, for him. He hasn't sworn at mum once.'

'See? You could have taken a fortnight, and no one would have missed you.'

'There's church, I didn't dare ask about that ...'

The lift arrived, a tiny bright box that juddered apathetically towards the ground floor much slower than they could have walked. Iain guided her out of the building, and began to trace a tortuous route through a confusion of side streets made hazardous by the young scooterists she had already christened Vespal virgins. A quarter of an hour later, they reached the restaurant he had selected for them, and negotiated the steep staircase down into a windowless basement bright with candlelight.

'Not much atmosphere, but the food's good,' Iain said, accepting the menu.

She watched him, sensing his distance without understanding it. 'What's the matter, Iain?'

'Nothing. I've a headache, I'll be alright when I've had something to eat.'

They had just finished their antipasto when the flower seller approached them. More Asian than Italian in appearance, he moved between the tables with his bunch of roses, offering a bloom to any diners who looked as if they might succumb.

'For the lady,' he said, bowing as he held the single rose out to Alison. 'I will love you for ever, yes?'

Her hand began an automatic movement to take it, but Iain had already said something in Italian that caused the man to withdraw and take his wares onwards into the restaurant.

'What did you say?' she asked.

'I told him to take his overpriced tat somewhere else.'

'I thought you might have treated me.'

'Not at that price.'

'Not even to say you'll love me for ever?' She was fishing again, her anxieties about what she was doing here with him resurfacing to need reassurance.

'How can anyone say they'll love someone for ever?' he replied, cynicism hardening his voice. 'You can promise to be faithful, or to take care of someone for ever, but how can you promise to feel an emotion for any length of time? You don't know how you're going to change, or how they are.'

His words stabbed at Alison like the unguarded edge of an opened tin. The waiter, removing their dishes and bringing their main courses, gave her time to regroup.

'Some people might think it was romantic to say that kind of thing,' she said as she picked up her fork. Her *farfalle* looked less appetising than she'd hoped, even with the extra pepper she'd encouraged the waiter to grind over it.

'What?'

'I'll love you for ever.'

'Hmh. I've never been a romantic soul, I'm afraid. Or if I have, I've soon learnt my lesson.' He gave her a tight-lipped smile before turning his attention to the dissection of his meat.

They ate. Iain picked up his wine glass, drained it, and refilled hers and then his. They both jumped into the silence together.

'There's something I should tell you ...'

'I was in love with someone on my course ...'

'After you,' Iain said, picking up his glass again.

'I was going to say, I fell in love with someone on my course,' she repeated. 'With Michael, actually, and at the time I thought that was for ever. Then since I've met you, I've been able to see him again, and I still ... well, love him, I suppose, but it's a different kind of love. I care about him, I enjoy his company, but I'm not in love with him any more. I see his faults. Maybe what I'm trying to say is that things do last, if they're real, even if they have to change shape.'

'What went wrong?'

'Oh, he was married. So was I, of course. It was realising that there were men like Michael in the world that made me realise how dead my marriage was. But Michael wasn't going to leave his wife. They hadn't been married very long, and he insisted he loved her, only she always looked so grim I didn't believe him. I was incredibly stupid. I'll tell you, I'd run a marathon before I got involved with a married man again.'

'I've noticed you still talk about him a fair amount.'

'He's a good friend, there's nothing more to it than that. You don't need to look so worried. Anyway, what were you going to say?'

He took a minute to finish his mouthful. 'Oh, nothing. What do you think you'd like to do tomorrow?'

'I thought we were going to do the Forum and the Palatine hill.'

So, he wasn't interested in getting too personal tonight, she reflected, as their conversation drifted into itineraries. He didn't like the idea of friendships that lasted for ever, of relationships that had any hint of permanence, so what the hell was she doing here with him? She tried to respond with enthusiasm to his plans for the following day, but the fifteen-minute walk back to their hotel was made in virtual silence. When they arrived there, she claimed a stomach-ache, and lay down early to court sleep, longing for him to override her, and take her in his arms. Instead, he turned on the television to become absorbed in a dubbed film. Before it had finished, she was asleep.

It happened again. An hour or two of sleep followed by anxious wakefulness. Again it was the refuse lorries that woke Alison at two in the morning, as they negotiated the narrow street behind the nearby trattoria to pick up its rubbish. The engine straining, voices calling, a car impatient at the hold-up. Eventually the clatter died away, and her mind was open to all the apprehensions that daylight and activity kept at bay. Behind the shutters of their room, the darkness was solid. Next to her, Iain lay on his back, breathing heavily. It was alright for him, he had what he wanted. He'd decided he wanted to sleep with her, and she'd given way with hardly a murmur. He'd sent her flowers once, when it was a matter of luring her into bed; now he didn't need to any more. The more she remembered of their conversation in the restaurant, and the expressions on his face, the more depressed she became. Perhaps he'd become bored with her already. Despair, intensified in the low hours before dawn, had her in its grip, transforming Iain's caution into an avowal of dislike. After the holiday was over, he'd never want to speak to her again, and how then could she claim justification for what would have been merely a brief affair? She had compromised herself and betrayed her vocation for nothing.

Sobs rose to her throat. She'd disturb him if she gave way here, no doubt provoking some rough retort about women who got over-emotional. With a quietness born of practice, she eased herself out of bed, and headed for the bathroom. She sat on the toilet to relieve herself, and stayed there to give herself up to her misery. Above and to her right, the shadowy light cast by a lamp outside in the interior courtyard infiltrated the gloom, so that she could see the pale outline of her hands, and the sheen of her nightdress across her knees. With the door closed, she could howl uninterrupted into the soft, swiftly disintegrating sheets of toilet paper she clutched from the holder beside her.

'What's the matter? Are you ill?'

She had been too engrossed in her self-pity to hear the door open, and she started at Iain's voice.

'Just going to the loo,' she said, striving unsuccessfully to sound normal.

She felt him approach through the shadows, until he was a dark shape beside her.

'Are you crying?' He squatted down, and found her hands clenched about a soggy ball of tissue. 'What is it?'

'Nothing.' She grabbed more toilet paper and blew her nose loudly. She sensed his breath of amusement at her inapposite denial. 'You hate me,' she sniffed, knowing herself to be behaving pathetically, but past caring.

'Is this because I didn't buy you a rose?'

Alison sniffed again.

'Allie, I cannot carry out this kind of detective work on a freezing stone-tiled floor with you stuck on a toilet. Come back to bed, you silly woman, and tell me what the trouble is.' His hand slid up her arm, and he stood up, pulling her with him.

She could hardly stay put, so she let him propel her back past the bath towards the bedroom. Her own side of the bed had already grown chill, and she was grateful for Iain's warmth as he drew her to him.

'You're cold as marble,' he said, cupping her buttocks with his hands. 'What were you thinking of? How long had you been there?'

'I don't know. I couldn't sleep. I didn't want to disturb you. Oh, I should never have come away with you. You don't love me, there's no future for us. I'm so stupid.'

'Hey, come on. I'm sorry if I was being insensitive in the restaurant, I didn't mean to be.' He held her tightly, breathing the words into her ear. 'Just because it doesn't make sense to me to swear undying love doesn't mean I don't love you. You mean more to me than any woman ever has. I can't imagine ever not wanting to be with you.'

Alison slid an arm round him, warmth and sanity returning to her as she lay enclosed by his embrace.

'To be honest, Allie, I live in fear that you're going to want to be rid of me. It's far more likely. You'll mebbe find out things about me you don't like, and that'll be it.'

'Don't say that. Of course I won't.' She pressed herself against him more closely. 'I'm sorry for being silly. Everything's too difficult at the moment, and I can't stand it when you don't seem to care.'

He began to kiss her, dispelling, for the time being at least, the wraiths of insecurity that had wreathed themselves around her. Though their love-making was both gentle and swift, it was enough for her to fall asleep in his arms, and not to wake until morning was already well under way.

'I'm sorry for waking you up last night,' Alison said as she sat with Iain over breakfast next morning in the hotel's narrow first-floor breakfast room. She was feeling self-conscious about her infantile display now, and hardly dared to meet his eye.

'I really don't mind.' He paused to receive coffee from the waitress. 'You must tell me if you're unhappy about anything, not keep it to yourself.'

'It was one of those early morning things, I do get things out of proportion sometimes. Actually, I've been waking up and brooding a lot. Three o'clock's an old friend these days - all the parish things I've done badly, and all the things I haven't done, start jumping up and down in my brain, and it takes at least two hours before I get back to sleep.'

'That's happening even here? I hoped you'd be able to stop thinking about work for a few days.'

'So did I. It's only nights it comes back. Well, no, it isn't. Every time I see a bloody priest or go into a church, I'm reminded of what a lousy priest I am.'

Iain smiled. 'There do tend to be a lot of churches and priests in Rome.'

'I know. Why couldn't you have been going to Tenerife?'

'Do you think it would help if we tackled some of your worries head on? I'd happily go through some of them with you, help you plan a strategy to deal with them. I do that kind of exercise with Headteachers sometimes. Face up to things, and they don't look so bad. There's no such thing as a dragon.'

'I beg your pardon?'

'It's a children's story. A wee dragon comes to stay in a house, and it's befriended by a boy there, but the mother doesn't notice it. So each day it grows and grows until it fills the house, and eventually runs off with the house sat round it. Then the mother acknowledges it's there, and it shrinks back to a manageable size. I've always thought it a profound story.'

Alison laughed. 'I didn't know you were so familiar with children's stories.'

'I'm very vairsatile. You say, anyway. I'll talk about it whenever you want.'

'That's spoiling your holiday, making you work.'

'I doubt anything could spoil my holiday, as long as I'm with you.'

'That was almost romantic.'

'Make the most of it, it won't happen again.'

A dissonance. The sleeping stones red-brown under the arch of hazy cloud that hung over the city, their memories of opulence, lust, intrigue, death and harsh survival washed into history; and the knot of nightmare anxieties Alison brought to the fore. Trivialities from an inconsequential community in an unimportant town nine hundred miles away. Or maybe not so disparate, when Rome too had its St Peter's, the petty wranglings and ambitions, and the bruising interaction between the dictates of holiness and the grumblings of defected humanity. She sat with Iain on their jackets on the grass of the Farnese Gardens, washing down the soft, white triangles of their sandwiches with lager, solving all her parochial problems with unimpeachable theory.

'The whole parish feels like a thundercloud lowering over me, tensing me up, leaving me waiting for it to burst and dissolve me into the ground. It's not so much any one thing, it's everything together, I can't seem to get on top of it, but I don't see what I can do. You can't refuse to see someone who's just been bereaved, or bring in a stranger to do a funeral. I can't work to rule, it's not that sort of job. I knew that when I came into it.'

'It serves no one if you collapse, though. I'm not saying you should be nine-to-five, but you surely need some constraints on it? You need somebody to take responsibility for helping you to handle it. You're only a trainee when all's said and done.'

'I know, but it's not that simple. If I say I can't cope, they'll think it's because I'm a woman, or there's something inadequate about me.'

'That depends how you approach them. Let me make a few suggestions, and if it helps, use them, if not, ignore me. The service is free.'

For half an hour, she listened, and considered, and made some notes in the small notebook she fished from her rucksack. His acuity was invaluable.

'I feel better already,' she said at the end. 'I can almost see from one end of the dragon to the other. Here, stay there. I want to take a photo of you, then every time I look at it, I'll remember your advice.'

He laughed, at ease with his blue shirt open at the neck, a navy jumper draped loosely round his shoulders, glasses barely tinted in the hazy light, and his last sandwich in his hand. That was how her camera captured him, a picture she could revisit in the future, a memory for the times ahead when they had to be apart.

Iain got up, and held out his hand. Together, they left the garden, and travelled on down the Palatine hill towards the ruins that lay in wait.

Alison arrived home late on Saturday night. The hall had been festooned with a large banner welcoming her home. Josh's handiwork, immaculate printing that must have taken hours: Welcome Home Mum! Illustrated, judging by the cheerful smudges of colour alongside it, by Luke.

Her mother was watching a film, with Josh asleep with his head on her lap. She zapped the television off as soon as she saw Alison.

'Hello, darling. You look a lot brighter. Did it all go well? Did you have a good journey? Josh wanted to stay up, but he's tired, poor thing.'

Alison sat down and loosened her boots. 'Fantastic. It was the best holiday I've ever had, and Iain ...' She shook her head. 'This is it, Mum. True love at last. I'm crazy about him, and he adores me.'

'I shall look forward to meeting him. I am glad you've found someone nice.'

'So am I. I'd better not say any more or I shall cry. It was awful having to leave him at the airport.' She blinked rapidly. 'Rome was fascinating, we walked miles every day ...'

Josh woke up as she began to relive the Colosseum, and threw himself into her arms, full of every event of the last week.

A few minutes later, James appeared, still dressed. 'Have a good time?'

'Brilliant. Bring my case in, would you? I've got some things for you.'

James exerted himself to heave her luggage in from the hall, and Alison disentangled herself from Josh's embrace in order to open it up. It hurt to be confronted by the clothes she'd packed that morning in Iain's presence, knowing she wasn't going to see him for weeks. The parcels lay on top: football shirts for the boys that had cost an arm and a leg, a silk scarf for her mother, bought from the same shop as the one she wore herself.

'I got this too,' Alison added, touching the gold brooch that kept the scarf in place. A present from Iain. A souvenir. Something that would last for ever. She wondered if he was missing her as much as she was already missing him.

Iain made coffee, and carried it through into his living room, where he set one cup in front of the faded, fair woman currently absorbed in the film on television. He sat in the other armchair with his cup clasped between his hands, sipping occasionally, thinking about Allie, and the obstacles that lay ahead of them. The film wound to a weepy end, and the woman switched off the set.

'So were you OK in the end?' he asked. 'No problems?'

'No, we managed. Jean came and stopped the night. Did you enjoy yourself?'

'Yes, I did. You see things afresh when you're introducing somebody to them for the first time. I wish we'd had longer.'

'Did your friend enjoy herself too?'

'Oh yes.' His brow furrowed, and he rubbed his lips with a dry hand before speaking again. 'Carol, it's really serious this time. I love Allie. I want to be with her. I want a divorce.'

Seventeen

'I won't agree to it,' Carol said calmly, regarding him from the security of her armchair. 'You promised you'd look after us. I let you have relationships when you want to, I keep the house for you, I've kept my part of the bargain, you can't wriggle out of it that easily. Give it a few more weeks, and you'll be getting bored anyway, you know you will. Besides, what about Hetty?'

'I'd make sure you didn't want for anything. Please, Carol, at least talk about it ...'

But Carol had risen from her chair, and left the room.

Iain leant back and closed his eyes, drowning in impossibilities. The click of the door behind him made him turn round. A small figure stood in the doorway, a skinny brown-eyed little girl of nine, in a long white nightdress, brown hair straggling onto her shoulders.

'What are you doing up?'

She came into the room. 'Mummy woke me up. She said you want to send us away. Please don't. I can't look after mummy by myself.'

Swearing at Carol under his breath, Iain opened his arms, and Hetty crawled onto his lap. 'I know you can't, poppet. I wouldn't let you. Mummy didn't understand, I'm not sending either of you anywhere.'

He held her close to him, her bony limbs jabbing into his chest and thigh as she tried to tuck her toes under her nightie. Not his child by blood, but he'd been the only father she'd known in the six years since her real father sent her back from Cyprus. With Carol confined to the house by panic attacks, and periodically needing psychiatric care, he had provided stability and normality in Hetty's life. Carol had gone to the heart of it when she sent Hetty down to plead their cause. He might be able to escape for the short spells that preserved his sanity, relying on a network of neighbours to deal with emergencies, but he couldn't walk out on them permanently, lest it tip Carol over the edge, and cause Hetty fresh agonies of separation.

He had married Carol too quickly, moved by her plight, wanting to protect her and Hetty, flattered by her grateful dependence. Needing, if he were honest, to restore his reputation, for Heads were not generally supposed to have affairs with their pupils' mothers. And however bitterly he regretted it now, unless Carol agreed to his leaving, he regarded himself as bound by the promises he'd made her. He could swear undying love to Allie all he liked, but in the end, duty would keep him chained, and she would be lost to him.

He murmured stories of Rome to Hetty until her eyelids closed, then carried her upstairs to tuck her into her bed, and went to his room. When he saw Carol again in the morning, she wouldn't refer to his request. She would see Hetty cheerful over breakfast, and know she'd won.

'My cousin went to your mum's church last week.' Sarah Day said, sitting down next to James on one of the benches placed sporadically around the edges of the playing field, in anticipation of the crowds who might watch school sports. 'She's getting religious. She went at Christmas as well.'

James scowled at the reference to his mother. Sarah herself was OK. Nice hair, long and blonde, but tits like table-tennis balls, a freckled face and goofy teeth despite the brace she'd worn last year. Not a girl to get off with, but she passed for a friend in the absence of anyone else.

'It must be weird, having a vicar for a mum,' Sarah continued. 'Do you have to go to church all the time?'

'Nah. It's just her job. Don't make no difference to me.' James fished in his pocket and took out a packet of cigarettes and a lighter. He extracted a cigarette, put it in his mouth and lit it.

'Don't, you'll get caught!'

'So what? Here - you have one.'

'You must be joking! Disgusting habit!'

Privately James agreed, but he needed the confidence it gave him. Even Danny and Matt had looked at him with something akin to respect when he'd been excluded back in January. He inhaled now, fighting off the nausea it still induced in him.

'You'll get suspended again.'

He shrugged. 'So?' He flicked ash onto the grass. 'I don't care.'

'Please, James, I hate it when you're in trouble.'

Her pestering gave him an excuse for giving in to his qualms. He stubbed the cigarette out on the bench, and put it back in the packet.

'Are you tryin' to be tough, or something? Is that why you got your head shaved?'

Now that had shocked his mum, when he'd gone off for a haircut soon after her return from Rome, and come back with nothing left of his smooth black hair but a fine stubble. He'd had to do something, once he'd seen the photos. He'd been taking a phone call in the study, and seen the twin pack of photographs, newly arrived in the post, lying on her desk. He'd flicked through them as he listened inattentively to Ellis, with a growing sense of outrage as he recognised the same white-haired, vaguely familiar man cropping up again and again, and finally captured by a third party with his arm proprietorially around his mother's shoulders. How could she? It made him want to puke.

He brushed a hand across his scalp. 'Don't you like it?'

'No. It's much better longer.' Sarah's tone was matter-of-fact, easy to ignore.

'You done your Biology homework?' he asked. 'What d'you get for number three?' Sarah pulled her book out of her bag, and they looked at it together.

Away over by the school, the bell sounded out.

'Here, have a mint,' Sarah said, fumbling in her bag as they walked back across the grass.

'Don't want one.'

'Your breath'll stink. You'll get into trouble. Go on, please.'

She was so insistent that in the end he shoved a mint in his mouth to shut her up.

With so much catching up to do after her absence from the parish, and with the onset of Lent bringing a new series of meetings and duties, it was several weeks before Alison could get away to visit Lisa and her new baby. Before her next trip to Nottling with the boys, however, she posted a note to Lisa saying that they would call.

Colin had rented a flat at the top of a three-storey block on the edge of the East End Rows, Greathampton's sprawling housing estates across the ring road from the area where Lisa had grown up.

'What a dump!' James said, kicking a broken bottle off the pavement as they made their way from the car to the entrance door.

Alison surveyed the spiritless grey concrete of the buildings beneath the neon lights, the sole shop steel-shuttered, the aggressive graffitti, and the twists of dog-dirt on the only patch of threadbare grass, and gripped Luke's hand more tightly. No wonder Lisa had sounded nostalgic for Wellesley.

Lisa showed them round the cramped rooms, pointing out her

161

improvements: the brightly coloured pegs on the nursery door, the second-hand washing machine squeezed into the kitchenette that occupied the corner of the living room:

''Cos I couldn't be goin' down the launderette every day, could I? Col complained, but tha's not 'im 'aving to do the bloody washing, is it? He's always saying I wanna spend too much.'

'He got another job, though, didn't he?'

'Yeah, but it don't pay much. He's at this restaurant the other side of town, an' I never see 'im now. He's off before lunch, an' he in't back till midnight.'

'That is tough,' Alison said.

'Not that 'e's any bloody good with Karli when 'e is 'ere.' Lisa stopped by the bright-blue carrycot that stood on its wheels beside the curtained living room window. 'She's still asleep. I thought she'd wake up soon as you lot walked in.'

Within the carrycot lay a large pink infant with a downy, bald head, and scratched cheeks. Alison and Josh made admiring noises. James grunted, then went off to slump in one of the sagging, burnt-brown armchairs, his portable stereo headphones clamped to his freshly cropped head.

'Can you see, Luke?' Alison asked, lifting him up to see inside, though he seemed more impressed by the yellow teddies that danced across the padded blue material.

'Tha's nice, in't it, Lukey?' Lisa said. 'Midge lent us a pram, but that was murder to get up an' down, so I got this off my catalogue, so's I could pay a bit each week. Col says "ooh, we can't afford it, you'll 'ave to send it back", but Karli'd already puked on it, so 'e let me keep it.' Lisa bent down, and picked Karli up. 'You mustn't stay asleep when you've got visitors,' she said gently.

Karli's eyes opened slowly, and she grimaced.

'Oh, isn't she sweet! Can I take her?' Alison asked. She went to sit in the other armchair, with the baby cradled in the crook of her arm, reflecting that she wasn't too old to have Iain's baby if he liked the idea.

Lisa arranged herself carefully on the sofa, with Luke next to her, and began an account of Karli's birth. By the time she got to the current state of her Caesarian scars, Alison was feeling a lot less broody. She was grateful when Josh interrupted from his seat on the floor:

'I got detention last week. First one,' he proclaimed to Lisa, with a certain degree of pride.

'You never! Go on, you never get in trouble. You don't wanna turn out like James.'

'I didn't do anything really. These boys were shouting at me, saying "There's another one of them, thinks he's the son of God".'

'Don't be silly, Josh,' Alison said, scarcely listening to this repeat of a garbled story she'd heard before, as she concentrated on seeing whether Karli could yet be coaxed to smile.

'That's what they say. They call James "Jesus", too, 'cos of you being a priest. Anyhow, I said, "Right, if I'm the son of God, does that mean I can walk on water?" And they said "Go on", so I went over to this deep puddle and jumped in it. I got soaked, my shoes and all up my trousers, and I had to wear my PE stuff all the rest of the day, and I got detention. I shut them up, though,' Josh grinned.

Lisa laughed. 'You're terrible, you are. What does James do? Hey, James ...'

But James was in his own world, and made no response.

'Do they tease you about me very much?' Alison asked. 'Do you want me to talk to someone about it?'

'Nah. If they say things, I make jokes about it, and after that they don't bother. James ignores them. They soon get bored.'

Luke clambered down from Lisa's sofa and came to stand by Alison, an anxious look on his face. 'Want to come up,' he whined, jealously pushing at Karli as he tried to climb onto his mother's lap.

She made room for him on her lap. 'Isn't she tiny? You were like this once. Look, if you put your finger in her hand, she'll hold on to it. She likes you, doesn't she?'

'Baby likes me,' Luke said. 'Hushabye baby.' His tuneless attempt to sing had Alison and Lisa biting back laughter.

'In't 'e sweet! You'll 'ave to come an' visit me, gorgeous, won't you? Come on, Lukey, come'n 'ave a cuddle before you go.'

Luke scrambled into Lisa's lap, making her wince. 'When're you coming home?' he asked her.

'I live here now, Lukey.' He wrapped his arms round her neck. 'How's 'e doin' with 'is new childminder?' Lisa said, through his hair.

'He's got two, different days. He's beginning to settle down, though he still misses you. He asks where you are, and I've caught him watching all forlorn from the landing window, thinking you're coming back. Josh is being very good with him, takes him to the childminder, and picks him up if I can't manage it.' She smiled at her middle son, who'd found the toys section of Lisa's catalogue, and was obliviously planning how to spend the remainder of his carefully hoarded Christmas money. 'I'm trying to keep a couple of hours free around teatime, so I get more time with Luke, but you know what it's like in a parish. People get a sixth sense that you're trying to have some time off duty, and arrive on your doorstep in flocks. At least now I can send James to answer the door, and frighten them off.'

Karli, who had been growing restless in Alison's arms, began to wail, refusing to be comforted.

Lisa sighed. 'She's 'ungry again, little sod. I won't 'ave no boobs left by the time she's finished chomping away at me. I weren't goin' to feed 'er meself, but Col's mum kept sayin' it'd get easier. You fed yours, didn't you?'

'Yes.' Alison kissed Karli, and handed her over. 'I enjoyed it. I used to take Luke everywhere with me ...' She picked him up, hugging him with nostalgia. 'I'll call again soon, Lisa. I'll try and make it when Colin's about, I'd like to see him, too. Give him my love.'

'If I ever see 'im,' Lisa said.

Alison had informed Michael that she was visiting Lisa, and he had invited her to supper after she'd delivered the boys to Steve. She arrived back in Greathampton as Michael was about to get his children ready for bed. She volunteered to help by bathing Rosie, who at six months seemed gargantuan compared to Karli.

'Now we try and keep her amused until Jen gets back,' Michael said, when she brought Rosie downstairs again, neatly encased in a fleecy sleepsuit. 'She still has a feed at bedtime, and she gets cross if she has to wait too long.'

Alison read to Lyddy, held Rosie, and occasionally exchanged sentences with Michael as he prepared supper in the kitchen.

Jenny arrived back at half past seven. The muted slam of the door, and some shuffling in the hall, announced her presence, then the sound of her footsteps ascending the stairs, presumably to see if Lyddy was still awake. Two minutes later, Jenny appeared at the door of the living room.

'Hello. Do you mind if I take my baby now?' Unsmiling, she plucked the baby from Alison's lap, and disappeared upstairs again.

'Was that Jen?' Michael asked, putting his head round the kitchen door.

'Yes. She's gone to put Rosie to bed. Are you sure it's alright for me to stay for supper? I realise Jenny must be tired by the end of the week.'

'No, that's fine.' Michael glanced anxiously at the door to the hall. 'She isn't in a very good mood today, though, so make allowances for her.'

Alison helped Michael set the table in the dining room, and when Jenny came down, they began their supper. In the past, Alison had been accustomed to being frozen out by Jenny, used to her abrupt manner and the snide remarks she shot in both Michael's and her own direction. To find the same thing happening when Michael had sworn his wife was fully recovered, puzzled and perturbed her. She found herself bringing up topic after topic in an effort to draw Jenny into the conversation: parish anecdotes, Karli, Rome ...

'Did you like my card?'

Jenny shot her a look of such contempt that Alison quailed; Jenny was surely not a closet Catholic? Fortunately, they were near the end of the meal.

'That was lovely. Thank you,' Alison said as she finished the remains of the hot apple strudel Michael had bought. 'It is kind of you to invite me,' she added, making a last attempt to win Jenny over.

'We're always happy to see you, aren't we, Jen?'

'The more the merrier as far as Michael's concerned,' Jenny said coldly, eyeing her husband. For an uncomfortable moment, the two of them stared at each other. 'Right,' Jenny said, 'I've got work to do tonight, so if we can get everything cleared out of here ...' She began to stack the dishes.

'Surely that can wait till tomorrow - Allie's here to see us both. At least have coffee with us.'

'I'm sure you can entertain her on your own.' Jenny handed the dishes to Alison. Michael picked up the remaining items, and Jenny shut the door firmly behind them as they left.

'I'll wash up, you dry,' Alison said, taking charge in the tiny kitchen.

'If you don't mind ...' Michael picked up a tea towel and stood waiting while she stacked the first of the plates in the drainer, biting his lip.

'Do you want me to pretend I haven't noticed something's wrong?' she asked.

'Jen's worried about something, that's all. You know what she's like. She takes it out on me, and anyone around me.'

'You should have told me, I could have gone straight home.'

'I wanted to see you. Don't take any notice of her, she'll snap out of it in her own time.' His voice was flat, so unlike himself that Alison stopped mid-glass and turned to him.

'She's not thinking things about me again, is she? Because that's ridiculous. She knows I've got someone else in my life now. There's no way I'm a threat.'

'It's nothing to do with you. Something I did, and she's taking her time forgiving me.'

Alison turned back to her bowl, waiting for him to ask her about how things had developed with Iain during their holiday, since he obviously wasn't going into any more detail about his own troubles.

When he next spoke, however, he was being purely practical. 'We can leave those to drain, I'll make some coffee.' He put his cloth down, and reached for a cafetière. Once the coffee was made, he carried a cup through to Jenny.

He returned a few minutes later, the cup still in his hand, looking no happier. He placed it on the coffee table, and sat down at the other end of the sofa from Alison. 'She didn't want it,' he said. Then, after a pause, 'I'm sorry, I'm not much company.'

'And you can't tell me what the problem is? We always used to tell each other everything.'

'I know, but Jenny made me swear not to. It's not anything that drastic, just something that's worrying her, and that worries me.' He smiled for the first time in hours. 'You'll probably lie awake all night trying to guess what it might be, won't you?'

'I've got other things to lie awake at night thinking about, and other people.'

'You mean Iain,' Michael said after a pause.

'I really love him, Mikey, I can't see it's so very wrong.'

'Try explaining that to your parish, or your bishop,' he said drily. 'Oh, it's none of my business. I'm glad you're happy. I'm glad you're here, otherwise I'd be having to sit here talking to myself.' He leaned forward and squeezed her hand. 'Tell you what, you put some music on, and I'll give you a game of crib before you go. Memories of all those wanton evenings on the Programme.'

He wasn't prepared to discuss Iain, Alison realised, which was a blow - there didn't seem to be anyone she could talk to properly about him. Still, in Iain's absence, other forms of entertainment were welcome.

When Jenny put her head round the door an hour later to say she was going for a bath, Alison and Michael were lying on the floor with cans of lager beside them, their heads almost touching as they laughed over the cribbage board, with Sting's music drifting plaintively through the room.

Michael laid his hand down and pegged out triumphantly.

'I don't believe it!' Alison said, looking up at Jenny. 'He's done it again, the lucky sod! I know when I'm beaten.' She stretched out a hand to him and he kissed it solemnly.

'Can I get you anything?' he asked Jenny, sitting himself up.

She shook her head hurriedly, and withdrew from the room.

Alison sat up. 'Oh, dear. We shouldn't have been enjoying ourselves, obviously.'

'I needed the distraction. The jokes, the competition, and the chance to look down your blouse all evening.'

She looked down in alarm. 'I wasn't showing anything, was I? Jenny'll think I was trying to seduce you.'

'Serve her right if you were.'

From upstairs, the sound of a door slamming reverberated through the house.

'I think it might be time I went,' she said.

Another evensong, switching off from the rush of collecting the boys, putting aside the tiredness that ached in her eyes, because she had a public role to fulfil. Experience had made her singing passable; members of the small congregation pressed her hand warmly at the door:

'Thank you, dear, lovely service.'

'It's so nice to be able to hear properly.'

'Could I have a copy of your sermon?'

Alison returned to the vestry fortified by their approval; she might be imperfect, but she had something to offer.

'You used the same sermon at evensong that we had this morning,' Bunty complained as soon as Alison walked in. 'And I can't say I got much out of it the second time round.'

The word 'either' hung in the air between them.

'It's very time-consuming producing two sermons a week, and it's mostly different people come. I had three funerals this week, and what with the funeral visits, I've not had time ...'

'That's because you're not using the Home Ministry team like you should,' Bunty interrupted. 'And the drama club are perfectly happy to put something on instead of one of your sermons. It would be nice to have something lively. You only have to ask. Now,' she continued, without letting Alison speak, 'I really wanted a word with you about the notice board. It won't take a minute.'

Alison sat down heavily. She knew all about things that didn't take a minute.

'You said you were going to get back to me about it. You *said* you'd look at it before you went away, but it's been weeks now. We have to get the order in. Shall I call tomorrow and collect it?'

'No, not tomorrow, I've got meetings all day. I'll do it when I can, a few more days won't make much difference. Now, if you'll excuse me, I ought to fill up the registers. I don't want to get in trouble with my churchwardens!'

She dragged the register off its shelf, and turned to March, wondering why such comments sounded jovial when Nigel said them, and merely pathetic in her own voice. As Bunty said her goodbyes and left for home, Alison picked up a pen to complete the details for the service she'd just done. Most peculiar, someone had already filled in this evening's slot. She was still staring, trying to make sense of it, when Brian came through from the church.

'You look all in,' he said. 'Why don't you get off home? We can't have wonderwoman breaking down on us.'

'Will you *stop* calling me that!'

'It's only a joke. I didn't know you minded.'

She could feel her eyes filling, but she wasn't going to let herself break down on Brian's shoulder, the poor man wouldn't know what to do. 'When you've heard the same joke so many times, you can begin to get fed up with it,' she told him, feeling in her pocket for a tissue to blow her nose.

'Here, are you alright? I didn't mean to upset you.'

Alison blinked rapidly before looking up. 'Of course I am. Apart from having a bit of a cold.'

'You must tell us if it's getting too much for you.'

'I told you, I'm fine. It's this register, it doesn't make sense.'

'Do you mean to be looking at last year's?'

Alison looked again at the page in front of her. 'No. That explains a lot. Where's the current one?'

Brian pointed to the book underneath her handbag. 'Would that be it?'

'Yes. Thanks.'

'Can I help?'

'No, I know where I am now. See you tomorrow.'

Brian hovered for a few seconds, then left the vestry. The door closed softly behind him.

She was alone. Through the open door, the church brooded, settling itself down after a crowded day. No sound but the pipes contracting, and, in the distance, Brian's car leaving the car park. Around her hung racks of robes, and the smell of incense still scenting the air from the morning's use. She rested her head in her hands. Despite the resolutions she'd made with Iain, once back in the parish, she had been almost immediately overwhelmed by the new set of demands that came with the season of Lent: extra services, house groups, preparing couples for Easter weddings, and the confirmation class on its home run. Her struggles to organise her diary had been hampered by the flu epidemic that ravaged Wellesley, from the school to the church to her own children, piling up the requests for house calls, and causing a glut of funerals as the illness took its toll in the nursing home on the boundaries of the parish. And now Nigel had been signed off for another three months. Oh, God, *do* something about Nigel, can't you? You owe me *some*thing.

A tear of exhaustion dripped down her face. She removed it with the tissue. It was time to go home.

She did not even have the near prospect of seeing Iain to fortify her. He had to do another inspection in March to cover for a colleague who'd had a heart attack, and she wouldn't be able to see him until after Easter. Only his frequent phone calls kept her going:

'Oh, Iain, darling, I wish you were here in bed with me. I wake up almost every night, and I need you to take the nightmares away. I miss you so much.'

'You should call me. I wouldn't mind being woken up.'

'It would make it worse, hearing your voice and not being able to hold you. Sometimes I feel like jumping in my car and simply turning up on your doorstep, just so I can touch you again.'

'Don't do that!'

'Why not? Don't you want to see me?'

'You won't solve anything by running away, Allie. And you're coming here for a few days after Easter, it's not that long now. I can't wait to have you ...'

She melted when he spoke his longings in her ear in that soothing tone. It wove itself into her dreams, relieving her loneliness and the stresses of work. She couldn't find it in herself to regret the liaison, and her commitment to him remained non-negotiable in all the prayers she uttered through Lent: I'll pray and say my office religiously. I'll give up chocolates and cakes, I'll practice tolerance with Bunty and keep all the paperwork up to date. I'll get up half an hour early each day to catch up on my theological and devotional reading. I'll be the most devoted disciple you've got, only don't take Iain away from me. It's not much to keep one vice, and I don't sleep with him very often. Not that he's a vice anyway. We love each other, and I'm not really married any more. You see my heart, and you know I couldn't survive without him. Oh Lord, make me holy, but not too much. And not yet. Not yet.

Eighteen

At last Easter Sunday was done. That was hardly a priestly way to regard things, but Alison had been suffering from a head cold all day. There she was, with the privilege of celebrating the most glorious Mass of the Church's year, and all she could think about was whether her sore throat would survive the Eucharistic prayer. She croaked her way through evensong, and went home for an early night, in the hope she'd feel better in the morning.

When she woke on the morning of the Easter bank holiday, her throat had worsened, and her head was tight. Dosed up with plenty of pills, she managed to drive the boys to Nottling, then, abandoning her plans to call on Michael and Lisa in case she passed her cold on to the babies, came back home to spend the rest of the day in bed.

Iain woke her from a feverish sleep when he rang at eleven that night.

'I feel awful,' she told him. 'I don't think I'm going to be in a fit state to travel tomorrow. I can't stand without feeling dizzy.'

'You poor thing. Perhaps it'll be a twenty-four hour business, and you'll be right by tomorrow?'

'I don't think so. I reckon I've finally got this flu bug that's been going around. Everyone else who's had it has been in bed for a week.'

'What a shame. I'd been counting the days ... here, don't cry.'

'It's only because I'm ill, and I'm all on my own, and I wanted to see you.'

'I was all set to surprise you, too. I was going to tell you to go to Heathrow, because I was taking you to Paris.'

'I am sorry. I've spoiled everything. You didn't need to go to that trouble, though. I'd have liked to see your home.'

'I was trying to be romantic for you.'

'Maybe we can do it another time. Perhaps I could still come to you for a couple of days later in the week, if I get better quickly.'

'You can't rush it, or you'll have a relapse. You can come some other time. You'd better get back to sleep. I'll ring you tomorrow.'

Alison spent Tuesday, Wednesday and most of Thursday in bed, coughing, feverish, with her head ready to explode, feeling iller than she'd ever felt in her life. Expecting her to be away, no one called or became concerned at her absence. On Friday, she had to drag herself out of bed to go and fetch the boys. She dosed herself up with everything she could find, sucking strong throat lozenges to keep her head clear, and drove slowly and carefully to Nottling through the busy Friday morning traffic.

Steve opened the door to her, eyeing her curiously. 'You OK?'

She shook her head. 'I've had flu.'

'You should've said. I'd have borrowed a car and brought them back. You'd better sit down.'

Alison went through into the living room, taken aback by what came perilously close to concern from this unexpected quarter.

Steve sank into a black leather recliner, and she lowered herself onto a matching black leather sofa, both new since her time.

'James told me about being excluded,' he said. 'Why didn't you tell me?'

'You'd have gone up the wall.'

'I should think so, too. I'm not having a son of mine screwing his life up getting chucked out of school every other week. He's got GCSEs coming up. I want to know if he's in trouble. I've told him if there's any problems this term, I won't take him to the States in the summer. I'll take one of Josh's friends instead.'

'The States? You're going to take them all to States? That's ambitious. And expensive. The condition you keep telling me your finances are in, I'm surprised you can afford it.' Her voice faded as she spoke, unaccustomed to exercise.

'Been doing a lot of overtime.' He was watching her with a faintly pleased expression that would have annoyed her if she'd had the energy for emotions. 'I can't take Luke, obviously.'

'But you agreed you'd have them for two weeks in the summer.'

'You'll have got rid of the others for three weeks, that makes up for it. I've hired a camper van, and he'd be a pain cooped up in it for hours on hours of driving.'

'But it's Josh and James who help look after him while I'm at work. What am I supposed to do with him when I'm busy?'

'You might try looking after him yourself. You were keen enough to have another kid, now you can't wait to get rid of him.'

'That's hardly fair,' she began. A fit of coughing shook her, grating her throat. She couldn't think clearly enough to argue. 'Could I have some water?'

As Steve came back with a glass, Luke arrived from the hall to throw himself onto her lap, chattering excitedly about what he'd had for breakfast. When Josh and James came in with their bags, she nodded a goodbye to Steve, and took them out to the car.

The sips of water she'd had eased her throat, but not her dizziness. 'Tell me if you see any traffic lights or junctions coming up, I'm not very alert,' she told James. He made no reply.

'You can go back to bed when you get home,' Josh called from the back seat. 'I'll look after you.'

'Thanks, love, but I've got Bunty and Ella coming to see me, expecting me to be revived from my Easter break,' Alison said, braking sharply as the car ahead slowed down without the prolonged warning she needed in her current state.

'Anfea buyed me a Easter Egg with Smarties!' Luke piped up.

'Shut up!' James and Josh said simultaneously.

'She *did*. An' she give me a pound.'

'Who's Anthea?' Alison asked.

James and Josh fell silent.

'Dad's fwend,' Luke announced.

'Dad said not to say anything, you little twat,' James said.

'Don't call him that,' Alison said sharply. 'He's only two, you can't expect him to keep secrets.'

'Dad didn't want us to tell you, 'cos you might be upset,' said Josh.

'How very thoughtful of him. Who is she?'

'She works with him,' Josh said seriously. 'She's quite pretty, and not as old as you.'

'How long's that been going on?' Alison was managing to keep her voice even, despite the temptation to scream. It shouldn't have upset her to think of Steve shacking up with another woman, after all, she had got Iain, but it did. It meant his failure to love and care for her was a deliberate choice, rather than genetic.

'She moved to Leathwell in October. She was on that skiing trip he did at Christmas,' James told her. 'It was her idea for us all to go to America.'

Buying up her boyfriend's children. Alison hated her already. 'Well, fancy dad stringing enough sentences together to chat someone up.' She began to cough, rubbing her throat raw again, and setting her head thumping. Sod Steve. Sod Anthea. No wonder he'd seemed more amenable.

173

'Do keep still, Josh! You're distracting me.'

'Sorry!' Puzzlement in Josh's voice. She shouldn't take it out on them.

'Oh, God, I don't think I can face Bunty Ranger tonight, even diluted by Ella. Perhaps I will go to bed when I get back. Could you fend them off with tales of how poorly I am, death's door and all that?'

Home, bed, rest until woken by the evening sun low and bright through the bedroom window, and Josh standing there helping Luke hold a tray with her supper and a sprig of blossom from the cherry tree. A couple of hours downstairs with them, then back to bed, and Iain ringing to see how she was.

'Oh, Iain, I want you ... Josh is being sweet, only he's not you ...'

On Saturday she had two weddings to take, and on Sunday Bishop Ronald came to confirm her seven confirmation candidates and to both preach and preside at the morning Eucharist. It was a pleasant relief to be doing the service in tandem with him, and a source of pride to have these two teenagers and five adults to present to him, after all her hard work with them.

'And how are you getting on?' Bishop Ronald asked, leaning over her earnestly as they disrobed in the vestry afterwards.

'Oh, managing,' she heard herself saying.

'Things are always hectic around Holy Week. You must make sure you have a break.'

'I've had my break. I had flu for most of it.'

'What rotten luck.' The bishop stooped to peer in the mirror as he smoothed his remaining strands of grey hair over a shining scalp.

'I don't suppose there's any chance of getting someone attached here to help me while Father Nigel's off sick?' Alison asked brightly.

The bishop stood up and smiled benevolently. 'Oh, my dear, would that there were! I'm afraid we've long since lost the days when parish churches could have a cohort of clergymen.'

'One would do me,' Alison said, 'I'm supposed to be a curate in training, not an incumbent.'

He laughed. 'No one ever said ministry would be easy.' He patted her shoulder. 'You women are keen enough to break down these all-male barriers. You mustn't complain when you find it's hard work!'

Alison was about to take issue with him, but was prevented, perhaps fortunately in terms of her future career in the church, by a fit of coughing.

'Nice to be here again, anyway. Now, I must go and find the wife, and make our little presentation to the confirmation candidates. I always like to give them a token to show I'm remembering them in my prayers. As indeed I remember you.' He bowed slightly, and made for the door.

Alison made a face at his retreating back as she followed him over to the hall.

'Good to see you're on your feet again,' Bunty said, gripping her hand firmly after the service that evening. 'A shame you weren't well enough to see me on Friday, after your day out. I wanted to collect the order form for the notice board. You have dealt with it now, haven't you?'

'No, I haven't had time, and I've been in bed most of the week.'

'What time will you be free tomorrow? It's important we get the notice board up and running. I cringe every time I see that old wooden affair. I know this new design I've come up with is a little more than we planned, but Benny says we've got the funds, what with saving on Father Nigel's travelling expenses. And yours, of course - you're not claiming much with all these holidays you're gadding about on. Still, it's a good thing you're taking time off, we don't want you to collapse on us as well. People will begin to wonder what we do to our clergy!'

Alison took time out to cough, wincing as the effort seared her throat. Her voice had barely survived evensong, with Terry gone deliberately andante, she was sure, so difficult had it been for her already-strained voice to hold onto her notes.

'How about nine o'clock tomorrow morning?'

'No. Bunty, my desk's an absolute mass of papers, it'll take me a while to dig the notice board forms out. I'm going to be trying to clear my desk this week, so let me ring you when I've found everything.'

'In other words you've lost them. I rather thought there was a reason for your prevarication. I can always phone up for another order form.'

'I haven't lost it. I'll get round to it this week. Excuse me, there are other people waiting ...' Alison extended her hand to an elderly man, who had been standing patiently behind Bunty until he could take his leave of her.

'You want Fisherman's Friend,' he told her, pressing her hand earnestly.

Bunty tossed her head, and set off down the path, stalking quickly past the gravestones towards the lychgate, pausing only to glance at that square object of her desire, the as yet unreconstructed church notice-board.

Alison forced herself back into harness. Another week of meetings to attend, visits to the school, sermons to prepare and services to take. Illness had finally put paid to the plans she'd formed with Iain in Rome. Demands rained down on her whichever way she turned, all the dimensions of her life severally spiralling out of control, as Nigel's absence was prolonged. She visited, to find him recumbent and pale: yes, Nigel, I'm managing. No, I won't bother Sandra, I know she's snowed under. People who had been waiting hopefully for Nigel to be fit after Easter, turned impatiently to her, adding their individual requests to her usual procession of duties. Correspondence piled up: concerns about the fabric of the building, diocesan forms to be completed, her own mail about parish and school piling up haphazardly on her desk alongside whatever of Nigel's Janet could not cope with in the church office:

... Dear Father Sanderson, Ivan is a Christian in Albania who is studying for the ministry. He needs books, and I am writing to ask you whether you could spare a few pounds ... Bin.

... Dear Brothers and Sisters in Christ, As your bishop, I know how busy we all get ... Too right. Too busy to read three pages of purple prose. File, in case he proved to have said something important.

... Dear Ms Thompson, the annual meeting of Chairs of Governors will be held ... oh God, that'd make five nights out in a row.

... Dear Revd. Tompson, I am doing marriage for my GCSE project. Please would you fill in the enclosed questionaire. 1. Do you agree with living together? 2. Do you remarry if someone's divorced? 3. What is the policy of the church of england on homosexual marriage? Please reply by the end of the week ... More difficult to ignore that one, with some wretched child showing initiative by approaching the Chair of Governors.

... Dear Revd. Sanderson, I am doing marriage for my GCSE project. Please would you fill in the enclosed questionaire ...

On the other hand ... She lowered her head to her desk, and banged it gently on the papers in front of her. I do not have time for this. I do not have any wish to do this. I want Iain ... Her spirit tiptoed away on a journey as she shuffled her papers, out into the hall, out to the car, onto the highway, and away to Rome, to Paris, to Iain wherever he was, oh, anywhere but here.

On the Wednesday evening after her return to work, Alison took the midweek Eucharist, and then set out to meet Iain, buoyed up with the anticipation of seeing him for the first time in two months. Though not completely recovered, the ibuprofen she'd taken had left her feeling more or less adequate, and careful make-up masked her lack of colour. Iain was doing some consultancy work at a school twenty miles away, having staked a claim to any of his organisation's contracts that were in striking distance of Wellesley. He was waiting in the lobby of a brightly lit, purpose-built, modern hotel, sitting behind a copy of the *Guardian*, and glancing up every now and then to scan the people coming and going, until he saw her and rose to meet her. They hugged for a full minute without speaking, like travellers relieved to feel firm ground after a turbulent flight. They laughed as they released each other.

'I am sorry about last week,' Alison said. 'It doesn't seem fair that these things always strike the first chance of holiday you get in weeks.'

'I remember that from teaching. You survived all term, but the first day of the holidays, wham.'

She coughed, a rattling croak that shook her body. 'Sorry to sound disgusting. It's gone to my chest. I don't think I'm infectious.'

'I don't seem to pick things up these days. Do you want to eat now or later?'

Bed now or later was what he meant, and while she wanted above everything to be in his arms, she suspected once she got near a bed she wouldn't feel like moving again; and the long drive home didn't bear thinking about.

'I'm not very hungry. Could we get a snack in the bar?'

'Whatever you'd like.'

They ordered toasted cheese and tomato sandwiches with their drinks, and found a corner of the bar. She produced her photographs, and they relived their holiday as they waited for their food.

By the time they had finished eating, Alison's head was beginning to feel hot and light. The wall-lights and pictures behind Iain's head showed an alarming tendency to recede, making her lose the thread of his conversation. It was a relief to be escorted to his room, where she could lie down on one of the twin beds neatly laid out, one against each side wall. She removed her jacket; it left her shivering despite the long-sleeved top she wore with her trousers, so she got under the quilt and waited for him to join her. And at last they were together, exchanging a long and passionate kiss. She sighed with pleasure, shut her eyes and buried her hot face in his neck. Nice to be in Rome again, strange, she couldn't hear the traffic any more ...

177

She resurfaced with a start. Despite the quilt, and Iain's arms around her, she was shivering again.

'I'm sorry. I crashed. How long have I been asleep?'

'Half an hour or so.' He'd taken off his glasses, and was watching her tenderly, concern in his eyes. 'You're really not at all well yet, are you? There's hardly any of you there, it's like holding a child.'

'I've not eaten much lately. I am sorry, falling asleep on you. It's not exactly what you invited me over for ...'

He stroked her hair. 'I'm with you, that's all that matters. I've been lying here looking at you, wishing I was at home with you to tuck you up in bed and look after you.' He kissed her forehead. 'By, but you're a silly woman. What on earth did you come out for in this state? How am I going to get you home?'

'I'll drive. I'll be alright.' Alison tried to sit up, wishing her head hadn't taken a day trip to Alton Towers.

'You can't drive. You might pass out. You're not safe. I'll run you back, and then I'll bring your car over some time tomorrow. I expect I can get a bus back here.'

'I'm alright,' she insisted, blowing the statement almost immediately with a fit of coughing. 'I can't have you going to all that trouble.'

'You're not driving in that state. I couldn't bear it if anything happened to you.'

Alison gave in, not altogether displeased to be directed.

It required an increasingly difficult effort of will to remain upright during the journey. Her head continued to spin and throb, despite the additional pills she'd taken. She could barely recall the route through Wellesley to her home, and she was grateful for Iain's support between his car and the house. As they came into the hall, the faint sound of a television could be heard behind the living room door. James still up, awaiting her return.

'I'll be OK now,' she said, fumbling at the buttons of her coat.

'You mind you go straight to bed. I'll bring your car back tomorrow, probably around lunchtime. If you're not up to answering the door, I'll put the keys through the letter box.'

'Don't do that. Come and find me. I'll leave the door unlocked.'

The door of the living room opened, and James appeared, looking suspiciously at the stranger whose hands were easing his mother's coat from her.

'Ah, James,' Iain said easily. 'Your mother's feeling poorly, so I gave her a lift back. You make sure she goes to bed and stays there till she's better this time.' He turned to Alison. 'I'll be back tomorrow. Take care.' He kissed her cheek lightly, and let himself out. A few seconds later, they heard his car scrape on the gravel, and fade out of the gate.

'I'd better get upstairs. You couldn't make me a hot-water bottle, could you?' she asked James.

He stayed where he was. 'Who's that?'

'Iain Sutherland. You might remember he did the inspection at school last year. He's been a kind of work consultant for me, helping me sort out how I cope with my job.'

'He kissed you.'

'He's a friend as well. I am entitled to have friends,' she added, detecting the beginnings of a sneer on his face. The hall was beginning to sway. 'I must get to bed,' she said, and escaped.

She lay under the covers at last, relieved to be horizontal, cradled by pillow and mattress.

'D'you still want this?'

James's voice made her start. She opened her eyes to find him standing by the bed, the hot-water bottle in his hands. He made no attempt to pass it to her.

'You went to Rome with him,' he said. 'I saw him in your photos. He's who you've been meeting all those times you've been dressing up and going out. How could you? A bloody inspector! Everyone'll laugh at me.'

'What's it got to do with you? I don't have to answer to you for what I do.'

'He's not coming to live with us.'

Alison gazed up at her son, debating honesty. 'It's possible. Oh, James, I didn't mean to get involved with someone else before dad and I were divorced, but Iain's been a good friend to me. I need someone to care for me. Dad hasn't wanted me for years.' There was a tearful catch in her voice; she was going about this in entirely the wrong way.

James's expression was surly as his hands wrestled with the bottle. 'Why d'you both have to get off with other people?'

'I'm sorry you've been in the middle of it all.'

'One of those things, innit?' He dropped the bottle on the bed, facing her down with the tight lines of his mouth an uncanny likeness of his father's.

Alison held her hand out to him. 'Don't begrudge me a chance of happiness,' she whispered.

James turned abruptly away and headed for the door.

Defeated, Alison reached out to extinguish her light. Darkness enveloped her, and she slept.

The rustle of someone moving about her bedroom tossed Alison back into consciousness. She opened her eyes, and looked round. A few feet away at the window, a square figure was silhouetted against the light.

'Iain?'

He turned round and came over to sit on the bed, his weight tightening the quilt over her. 'Sorry, did I wake you? I was trying to think whether to wait. The front door was open, you said to come in.'

'What time is it?'

'Two.'

Alison put a hand out of her cocoon to push her hair back from her face. 'I've been asleep most of the day. Still, I feel a lot better.' She raised herself a little on her pillows.

'I brought you these,' he said, indicating a large bouquet laid on the chair under the window.

She stretched out her arms and kissed him lovingly. 'I am sorry about last night. I didn't realise what a state I was in. I've had the doctor round this morning, and she gave me antibiotics for my chest, and told me to stay off work till Monday. Ella's been here too, and she's sorting out getting a priest for Sunday. She should be calling back some time to see if I need anything.'

'And do you need anything? Can I help, or do you want me out of your bedroom before anyone sees me?'

'I just want you with me,' she said. 'I'd love a cup of tea. And if you really wanted to be kind, you could do me an egg.'

'I'm not much good at cooking.'

'Surely you can boil an egg! You live on your own, what on earth do you eat?'

He had the grace to look embarrassed. 'I eat out a lot. I'll see what I can do.'

She dozed off again, registering a couple of rings at the doorbell, but content to leave him to cope. Iain returned bearing a tray supporting two cups of tea, a boiled egg in a Snoopy egg cup, a plate of buttered bread, and his flowers neatly arranged in a large jug. He cleared a space on her bedside table, and set it down.

'You had two callers. One said she was your churchwarden - Ella was it? - and one was an old man who thought I was the vicar, and ought to give him the train fare to Birmingham. What a rich life you lead.'

Alison propped herself up on her pillows. 'Did Ella look shocked to find you at the door?'

'I explained I was an old family friend who was seeing to your every need, and who's well-accustomed to seeing you in your nightwear.'

'I hope not, rumours take root very quickly in parish life.'

'No, I don't think I compromised you. I let her arrange your flowers and do your egg, and said I'd pop it up to you when I said goodbye, and she left perfectly happy. So I made another cup for myself, and here I am.'

Ten minutes later, Iain placed his crockery on the tray and consulted his watch. 'I suppose I ought to be off. Am I right in thinking I can get a bus at the end of the road?'

'Yes. Thanks for bringing the car back.'

He leaned forward to kiss her. Alison put her arms round his neck. 'Do you have to go straight away? I'm feeling a lot better than last night, especially when I'm lying down.' She interspersed her words with kisses. She had thought of him often enough, lying here; now she wanted the memory of him in her bed, beneath her covers, beneath her skin.

'Join me?' she whispered recklessly.

He needed no second invitation.

Nineteen

Alison had barely moved in the half hour since Iain had left. Her body lay in the hollow into which he had pressed her, her nightdress pushed around her waist, her arms hugged around her as she recalled his embrace, lived without for far too long. Deep contentment pervaded her; she moved a hand to her breast beneath the quilt, and smiled to herself. A slight sound brought her to her senses. She opened her eyes to find Bunty within a foot of her bed, hand stretched out towards the flowers and the tiny card Iain had stuck among them.

'What the hell are you doing here?' Alison exploded.

'The door was open, I came in to see how you were.'

'You can't simply walk into my house!' Alison dragged herself upright. 'How dare you?' Her indignation fed off her sense of horror. Thirty minutes earlier, and Bunty would have walked in to find her writhing beneath a man whose presence no amount of imaginative falsehood would have been able to explain away.

'I needed to get hold of the papers about the notice board. They were down near the bottom of your In-tray, and I thought you could sign now, and I could get the order sent off,' Bunty said, waving a wad of paper at her.

'You've been going through my papers? Who the bloody hell do you think you are? What right can you possibly have to walk into my house, mess around with my private papers, and walk into my bedroom! You're an interfering old busybody. I don't care about the bloody notice board, do whatever you like, sign the order yourself, but don't ever, *ever*, intrude into my bedroom again!'

Bunty fixed her with an offended eye. 'Very well. I hope you recover your manners along with your health.'

Bunty stalked from the room, and a few seconds later, Alison heard the front door close.

She breathed a sigh of relief. Be discreet, Michael had told her, and she'd let herself come infinitely close to disaster. God, the flowers! Had she intercepted Bunty before the old bat had read his card? Hopefully Iain's handwriting would have rendered the words illegible for anyone but the closest reader, which was just as well. The lines he'd penned gave away almost as much as his presence in her bed would have done. She reached out for it, reread it, and slipped it into the drawer beside her bed. She *must* be more careful. Must.

Though she had pronounced herself cured after a further few days recuperating, Alison was conscious of picking up her work with depleted levels of energy. It was reassuring to find her mind intelligent again after a fortnight of inability to concentrate or even to spell the word creative, but she could sense herself wobbling before situations she would once have taken in her stride, and there was still no prospect of Nigel's return.

On Tuesday evening, she was back in church to take evensong for the three people who braved the rain. Since she had a duty to say this evening office for herself every day, it should not have mattered that so few came, but it made for a dispiriting service.

Afterwards, Alison exchanged a few words with them, and returned to her stall to straighten her books.

'Oh, Bunty?' she called, seeing the churchwarden approaching down the aisle. 'Do you know whether we've had all the tenders for the roof repairs yet?'

Bunty continued walking. She drew level with Alison, turned her head to stare coldly at her, withdrew her gaze, and carried on walking.

'Bunty! I asked you a question.'

There was no response. Bunty disappeared into the vestry.

Alison stood where she was, fighting the temptation to storm after her and to force a response from her. Ella, calling on Sunday afternoon, had mentioned how upset Bunty had been by Alison's outburst, and reported that Bunty was not going to be speaking to her, but Alison had taken this as a figure of speech. Bloody woman! The last thing she or St Peter's needed was to have Bunty playing childish games. She frowned, and wondered how to limit the damage.

'Bunty, I'm sorry I lost my temper,' she said, following her into the vestry. 'But you really had no business walking into my house, and going through my things. I had a right to be angry.'

The set of Bunty's head showed what she thought of the apology. She picked up her bag, headed for the door, and Alison was left alone and defeated in the church.

Though she tried to take it in her stride, the breakdown of relations between herself and Bunty haunted Alison. Despite Ella's best efforts, Bunty refused to communicate directly with her, and instead wrote notes, or used intermediaries to pass on messages. It might have been a relief not to have Bunty nagging at her all the time, except that Bunty had communicated her outrage to her cronies, and the shadow of discord hung over the congregation. However wholeheartedly Alison threw herself into her preaching and her pastoral encounters, however open and generous she tried to be with those who judged her, she could not escape the sense that she had failed.

'But what more can I do?' Alison asked Ella. 'I've said sorry, which is more than she's ever done.'

'She says she was trying to be kind and helpful, and she thinks you owe her a public apology for branding her a busybody.'

'What else do you call someone who goes through your papers?'

Not that Alison had much leisure to brood on Bunty's behaviour as she rushed around from church to school, from home to meeting, from shops to dry cleaners, one eye on the Wellesley Festival, another on the flower festival, and none to spare for Luke turning three at the end of the month and a party to organise, God help her.

'You must bring Lyddy over for Luke's party,' she told Michael, ringing him for solace in the middle of the afternoon, since Iain was unavailable during social hours. 'You could come with Lisa, she said she'd like to drive over for it last time she rang.'

'I'd like to, but I don't think I can,' Michael had replied awkwardly. 'Jenny's still being peculiar, and she's taken against me seeing you again.'

'What on earth for? She must know I've got someone else.'

'She's not exactly being rational. Thing is, she's pregnant again - I'm allowed to talk about it now it's getting obvious. Due in September. She's really upset. She says it's all my fault, and she's barely speaking to me, let alone anything else, so she's worried that means I might start making passes at you. And me being so much more wonderful than any other men you might happen to have in your life, she thinks we probably will run off together this time. I know it's silly, so does she, but there we are.'

'Poor Jenny, just when things were going so well.'

'I know. I guess she hates this feeling of not being in control, especially when she'd only just got back to work full-time. She felt awful telling them at the surgery. The receptionists say they wouldn't say no to me either, and her partners crack little jokes about getting me in for minor surgery, or leave booklets about contraception on her desk with post-its saying "Have you tried this? It really works".'

'Oh, God, that's why she looked daggers at me when I asked if you'd liked my postcard from Rome. I am sorry, I'd no idea.'

'I laughed, but that made it worse. She can't see the funny side of any of it.'

An alarming thought struck Alison. 'You're not dropping out of the festival, are you?'

'No, but it might be as well if you leave me alone till then. It's not as if you'll miss me. You've got Iain.'

'I could do with having you as well. I was going to ask if you wanted to stay the night afterwards. The boys will be away, and I'm inviting Becky to stay as well, and Iain.'

'We'll see nearer the time,' Michael said.

Luke's birthday celebration consisted of a trip to the swimming pool with five friends, two mothers, and a father, followed by a special lunch and a birthday cake back at Alison's house. Lisa rang the day before to confirm that she and Karli would be coming back to Wellesley for the occasion, but she had not arrived by the time Alison and Luke left for the pool. She had still not arrived as the last of Luke's friends toddled out of the front door clutching his party bag, and Alison was feeling decidedly anxious. When the doorbell rang at three, and she opened it to see Lisa on the step with Karli asleep in her buggy, Alison threw her arms round her in relief.

'Where's the car? Has something happened?'

'Tha's bust, innit? I 'ad the man from the garage, an' he said it'd 'ave to go in, and it'd be 'undreds to fix it. But I thought, I can't miss Lukey's birthday, so I went down into town to get the bus. An' I tried to ring you, only you'd gone, an then the bus took two hours, an' Karli screamed all the way, an' I'm knackered!'

'Oh, Lisa, you poor thing. Do come in! The others have gone, but there's some food and cake left, and Luke'll be really happy you're here.'

She helped Lisa get the buggy into the house, and wheeled it through into the living room. Lisa collapsed onto the sofa.

Alison took Luke to collect a plate of food while she made coffee.

'That's my cake. I'm three,' Luke told Lisa proudly, pressing the plate onto her lap.

'Clever boy!' she said. 'God, I dunno what we're gonna do about the car. We can't afford to get it fixed. Tha's one thing after another.' She sighed, and rubbed her face, before picking up a sausage roll. 'That'd be better if Col'd let Midge an' Bernie 'elp out, but no, 'e's far too bloody proud for that.'

'You mustn't worry about the money I lent you for the car,' Alison said. 'It's hardly fair if you're having to keep paying back the loan when the car's not even on the road. Leave it until things get easier.'

'Oh, really? Oh, thank you! Allie, you're a saint! That'd really help with payin' off the buggy, if we don't 'ave to pay you. ... Careful, Luke, you'll 'ave my coffee over.'

Luke, who had been getting frustrated at Lisa's lack of attention, began to cry. Alison called him over, and wrapped him in her arms.

'The washing machine's buggered, an' all. I knew we should never 'ave got it second-hand. Col says we can get another one through the local paper, but wha's the point? That'll only break down, an' there's no guarantee, is there? I told 'im, I'll get a job. I got this friend from school, Gemma, looking for someone to 'ave her boy Ryan, an' that would've been ideal. But no, Col won't let me. He is such a bloody prick, I'd've been better off staying 'ere with you.'

'It's always difficult with a new baby,' Alison said. 'I expect you're both tired, and it's doubly difficult when money's tight.'

'I've a good mind to 'ave Ryan anyhow. Tha's not as though Col would know. That'd pay for a new washer.'

'It's not a good idea to go behind his back.'

Alison had been rocking Luke gently; now she looked down, and found him asleep, tired out by the swimming and the excitement. She could cheerfully have closed her own eyes; instead, she was bound by duty and friendship to listen to Lisa's endless cycle of complaint. There were moments in the afternoon when Lisa could be distracted by other topics, and by Karli and then Luke when they both woke, but she was unable to prevent herself returning to her preoccupations:

'You couldn't lend me some money to get a new washing machine, could you?' she asked suddenly, breaking into Alison's account of Bunty's campaign. 'I mean, if you don't think I should 'ave Ryan ...'

'I can't do that, Lisa. You have to sort this out with Colin. I'm sure he'll be reasonable if you approach him the right way.'

Lisa looked sulky. 'I told you, 'e's never bloody reasonable! I didn't think *you'd* be mean as well.'

'I have suspended your car loan payments. That ought to help,' Alison pointed out. 'But I can't do anything that's going to make things worse between you and Colin.'

'Yeah. Well, I'd better be going. Gotta get a bus down into town.'

Alison stood up, and began helping Lisa to collect her things. She began to wonder whether it was the need for money, rather than the desire to celebrate Luke's birthday, that was Lisa's real reason for making the long trek on the bus. But perhaps that was unfair. 'I could run you back to Greathampton if you like,' she said. 'Save you having to cope with Karli on the bus again.'

'Nah, don't bother. I wouldn't want to put you out.'

'You mustn't be offended, just because I won't lend you more money. It doesn't mean I don't care about you.'

But Lisa was offended. She would not let Alison take her to the bus stop, and stalked off down the road with Karli without even a wave to Luke.

Alison shut the front door behind her, and sighed. 'I don't seem to be doing very well, do I Lukey?' she said to her son.

He held up his arms, whining the complaint with which he'd started the day, too many hours before: 'Where's Dad? I want Dad.'

She picked him up. 'And I want Iain, but there's nothing I can do about it. I just subsist, and count the days till Whitsun. And you'll see Dad then too, it's not long.'

Not long, thank God, not long.

'Allie, I am sorry to do this to you. You're not going to be able to come after all.'

Alison had been about to put out her bedside light to snuggle down on her pillow for an intimate Saturday night conversation, but Iain's words left her where she was, sitting up in bed with a book open on the cover in front of her, her lifeline yanked from her. She had already taken the boys to Nottling, and on Monday, she had been expecting to begin a restful few days with Iain in his home.

'Why not?' she managed.

'I've been stupid. I agreed ages ago to speak at a conference in Southampton, and for some reason I forgot to put the dates in my diary. I'm speaking first thing on Thursday morning, so I'll have to travel on Wednesday, and I'll need the next few days to prepare my paper.'

'Can't I come anyway? You won't be able to work all the time. We'd at least have the nights. I've got everything arranged so I can be off for a few days.'

'It wouldn't work, Allie, I wouldn't be able to give you any attention, and you'd distract me. We'll have to fix something up another time.'

'No, I've got to see you this week. I need you.' Panic shook her voice. 'I'd keep out of your way.'

'You couldn't, I'd know you were there, and I'd not be able to work.'

'You're talking to me now, why should it be difficult if I'm there? You don't love me any more ...'

'Allie, you're being unreasonable. I love you very much, I'd love to be with you, that's why I can't see you - I wouldn't be able to think about anything else if you were here. You can't come over, you'll have to accept it.'

He wasn't to be persuaded. When she finally turned out her light, Alison turned her face into her pillow and spent a restless night sobbing out her disappointment.

Iain arrived unannounced on her doorstep on Thursday afternoon, summoning her to the door during a pain-filled interview in her study.

'That's a relief, you're in,' he said, smiling. 'I was on my way back from Southampton, and I thought, it's not far off my route.'

'You should have rung. I've got someone with me,' Alison replied, struggling to surface from the immediacies of the problems she had been listening to. 'I can't send her away, it's important.'

Iain was looking at her oddly. 'Would you rather I left?'

'No, of course not. Come in, get yourself a drink. There's a paper somewhere, if you haven't read it.'

He came into the lobby. 'Am I allowed to kiss you when you're in uniform?'

'Oh, yes.' Alison gave him a perfunctory embrace. His expression was explained. He'd never seen her as she was this afternoon, a short-sleeved black shirt with her clerical collar, and a straight knee-length black skirt. A cream jacket had lightened the effect earlier in the day, but it was warm in her study with the sun shining in, and she'd removed it.

Back in her study, Maggie Brundall was dabbing at her eyes with a sodden handkerchief. 'You've got another visitor. I'll go,' she said.

'He doesn't matter.' Alison sat down, leaning forward in her chair. 'You were saying ...'

She opened herself up to Maggie's grief, striving to push away the inexcusable darts of impatience that wished her friend's uncontainable needs taken far from her.

The doorbell rang again, Iain could be heard answering the door, and, several thuds later, closing it behind whoever had called.

Maggie had not noticed. Alison took her hand and struggled on. Beyond her visitor's back, she could see Iain through the window of her study, wandering in her garden in the sunshine, with a glass of juice in his hand.

Nearly an hour after his arrival, she was at last able to join him on the wooden patio seat where he was resting with a paper on his lap.

She sat down and sighed heavily. 'I'm drained.'

'Someone being difficult?'

'With justification. She lost both her children in a road accident a year ago.'

'Was that the accident that happened when I was here for the inspection? Weren't they old pupils at the school?'

'Yes. Twenty and eighteen they were. I had to go out to the hospital in the middle of the night and be with her. Imagine having your whole family wiped out like that. I can't think of anything worse. How do you survive? Not that she really wants to survive. She keeps their rooms as they were, cleans them every week, she can't bring herself to throw anything out, because that would be to admit they're not coming back ... '

Tears came to her eyes, just as they had fallen as she held Maggie's hand. 'I feel so bloody useless. I've sat with her so often over the last year, and there's nothing I can offer but to listen. There's nothing I can say, and I'm left feeling as if I've had a ton of lead dumped on me. Do I even want to believe in a God who shatters people's lives like that for no apparent reason?' She turned to him. 'Not much point in expecting support from you on that, though, is there? You'd simply agree.'

'I hope I'd be more sensitive than that. I'd be concerned that you had someone to support you when you have this kind of thing to deal with. It can't be easy.'

She looked across at him, relaxed in his shirtsleeves, with a discreetly patterned dark-red tie awry at his neck where he'd undone a button. His arm rested across the back of the bench as if he owned it.

'You always say the right things, don't you? That's not what you'd really be thinking.'

'I don't want to argue with you, Allie.'

'But I do. I want to argue. I want to fall out with you, and get back together again the next day. I want to have a normal relationship instead of having to be polite and kind all the time because I'm not going to see you

189

for six weeks. Damn. There goes the phone.' She got up and went to her study to deal with it.

Iain met her in the living room on her return, and put his arms round her. 'You can be angry with me if it helps. Or you could let me take your mind off everything ...'

He tried to kiss her, but she pulled away. 'I can't. I'm too churned up. I can't suddenly switch off.' She sat down on the arm of the sofa. 'Who was at the door?'

'Someone delivering your new notice board. It's in the hall.'

Alison got up again, and went to look at the ominously large object wrapped in heavy polythene, that had bypassed her attention on her previous journeys through the hall. She fetched scissors from the kitchen and proceeded to strip away the packaging.

'Oh my God! Oh, Iain, what's she done!' she exclaimed, and burst into tears.

Iain stood behind her with his arms around her, while the new board gleamed maliciously back at them. St Peter's Wellesley emblazoned across the top of three panels in solid oak, with glazed doors and provision for lighting. Provision for just about bloody everything.

'It's going to cost a fortune. I never authorised this - what am I going to do? It's the design she wanted the first time round, she knew I'd vetoed it. It's my fault, I told her to go away and get on with it, but that was only because she came bursting into my bedroom when I was ill. Oh, God, what will Nigel say?'

'You can always send it back,' Iain pointed out reasonably.

'What if they insist we pay for it? Then we'll have to have it, and it'll look awful, it's all wrong ...'

He moved his hands to her shoulders, his fingers biting into the tension of her muscles. 'Calm down. It's not like you to panic. All you have to do is to ring the company and explain some wires got crossed. I'm sure they'll be helpful.'

'I can't face it.'

'Then why don't you go and make yourself a cup of tea, and I'll ring them for you.'

'I didn't mean you to get involved.'

'Go on, I'll get it sorted out, then there's one less thing on your mind.'

He pointed her in the direction of the kitchen and went into her study holding the form that had accompanied the delivery.

Alison had made them both tea by the time Iain returned.

He sat across the corner of the table from her and smiled. 'No problem. There'll be a small charge, but otherwise, you send it back, let them know what you do want, and they'll rig it up for you. They'll even collect this one next week, because they've got another local delivery to make.'

A smile came to her lips for the first time since his arrival. 'Thank you. I'm sorry to be so helpless. You've caught me at a bad moment.' She took a swig from her mug, wincing as the liquid scalded her mouth. 'But then, you're the only one I don't mind seeing me in my bad moments. There's no one else knows what a wreck I am really. It's funny, the worse I feel, the more confident I hear myself sounding in public. The more I can't seem to stop myself telling everyone I'm absolutely fine. But what else can I do? I'm letting everyone down if I go to pieces on them. I just save it all up for you.' She tried some more tea. 'Why did you come, anyway?'

'Why do you think? I wanted to see you, and to apologise for messing you about this week.'

'It's not like you to forget about meetings. I was wondering if you did it deliberately because you're getting tired of me.'

Iain reached across and took her hand. 'I wouldn't have made a long detour to see you if I was tired of you. I wanted to make it up to you. Is there any chance you could come to a wedding with me? Some very close friends of mine from university days have got a daughter getting married, and they've invited me to stay with them for the weekend. They'd love to meet you if you could get away.'

'I'm probably doing a wedding myself if it's a Saturday - it's a picturesque church, we're usually booked solid. When is it?'

She laughed when he told her. 'That's even worse. It's the weekend of the church fete and flower festival. I can't possibly miss that. I'm in enough people's bad books at church as it is.'

'That's a shame. Do you have to do anything for it?'

'There's a big service on the Sunday. Saturday I'm supposed to show up, spend a few pounds here and there, guess the weight of the cake, that sort of thing.'

'But if your friend was getting married that day, surely folk would understand you not being there. You could come for Friday night and Saturday, and get back for Sunday morning.'

191

'What would I do with the boys? Steve won't have them again so soon.'

'Have they not got friends they could stay with?'

'I don't know ... Maybe I *could* ask Steve, he owes me one for not taking Luke on holiday with them.'

'Can you try him? It's important to me, Allie,' he added, sensing her hesitation. 'I'd like to do something public with you, show I'm serious about you.'

'I shouldn't really be away ...' she said, in the voice of one who is going to do it anyway.

'It's time we spent a night together again.'

'You could stay tonight,' she said recklessly. 'The boys aren't here, and if you left early, before there's anyone about, it should be safe. I've got a service to do later, and a meeting here, but you could wait for me in my bedroom. You could stick your car in the garage, and no one would know.' She stood up and bent over him, fastening her arms around his neck and rubbing her cheek against his hair. 'I'm sorry I was sharp with you earlier.'

'It doesn't matter.'

He shifted in his seat so that he could embrace her, and she shut her eyes as she rested against him, a warm rock to shelter by on a blowy day, an anchor in a frantic world.

Sex isn't what matters, it's only a part of it, she thought. Nevertheless, she raced through her activities to reach the time when she could join him in her bedroom, and it was the interweaving of their bodies that gave her back her equilibrium, laughing with him as they wrecked her bed with the night ahead of them. Almost as good as being at his home, to have him in her bed; waking not to the endless recycling of tasks undone and conversations mishandled, but to the friendly solidity of another human presence. To be able to butt him like a cat with her head until he turned, half-asleep, and contained her in his arms, so that she could sleep.

Only he still had to leave at dawn; she would never sleep in peace again if anyone got to know.

Twenty

Voices called after James as he walked across the playing field towards the wild garden. He liked to think he ignored the taunts as successfully as his brother did, but something about the way he walked away from his tormentors must have told them their comments went home. They'd had History just before lunch, and he always hated sitting through Howells' lessons, on edge lest he be singled out for some mild offence. He couldn't stand another lunch-hour listening to his classmates' jibes; he needed to get away. He set out across the playing fields. Past two separate football games being played to an accompaniment of cursing and calling. Past pairs of girls wandering the grass, intent on their incomprehensible conversations. Then at last slipping down beside the sports hall on the opposite side from the entrance to the garden, where a narrow corridor ran between the building and the thick hawthorn hedge that marked the boundary of the school grounds. Nettles waved knee-high as he passed, and newly shooting brambles clutched at his clothes, but he persevered. At the far end, the wooden fence panels that protected the wild garden were loose on their posts, and he'd discovered a few weeks ago that it was possible to squeeze inside.

Every so often since - though not too much in case he aroused suspicion - he had made his way here, and begun the task of clearing away the undergrowth and overgrowth which choked the more delicate vegetation that had sprung to life since spring. He reached to the bottom of his backpack to bring out the carrier bag in which he brought a small fork and a pair of secateurs to school, and spent a satisfying quarter of an hour cutting back the rambler roses that were shutting off the pathway to the gate, swearing to himself as the thorns drew blood from his hands. That done, he sat himself down on the sawn log that lay near the pond, and got out his lunch.

The solitude was comforting. When a voice interrupted his reverie, he turned angrily, ready to erupt, until he saw that it was only Sarah Day, her hair tousled and her clothes awry after negotiating the gap by the hedge.

'Look at me, I'm stung all over,' she said, holding out an arm and indicating a leg mottled by white weals. 'I saw you go down by the sports hall. I never knew you could get in here. Ow, this really stings.'

'You want to put a dock leaf on it,' James told her. 'Hold on.' He jumped up and fetched a broad green leaf from a patch near the compost heap and began to rub it over her leg.

Sarah was strangely still; he looked up to find her gazing at him, and became self-conscious.

'You do it,' he said quickly, thrusting the leaf into her hand and sitting back down on the log to reunite himself with his cheese roll.

Sarah finished treating her arm, and threw the leaf down. 'I say, James, you don't want to go to the pictures on Saturday night, do you? There's a whole crowd of us going.'

'I can't. I gotta go to my dad's again. My mum's away.'

'Oh, well. Some other time?'

'What?'

'The pictures.'

'Oh, yeah.' He finished his roll, and took a swig from his Coke can. 'Here, can I tell you something - promise not to tell? Not anyone at all?'

'Course. Promise.'

'My mum's got a boyfriend, and that's who she's going off with this weekend. It really pisses me off. How could she do all that stuff, at her age? I can't get my head round it.'

'She's not that old, and she's really pretty - not a fat lump like mine. Why shouldn't she have a boyfriend? I thought you said your dad had got someone else.'

He'd forgotten he'd told her that, one rainy Saturday afternoon when they'd caught the same bus back from town. 'That's different,' he said. 'You expect men to, you know ...'

'To have sex? Whereas nice women don't do that sort of thing? What age are you living in?' Sarah tossed her head, messing her long hair still further.

'He's horrible, though. Really old. D'you remember that white-haired old git who did our inspection last year? That's who she's going with. I don't know how she could.' He bit his thumbnail viciously.

'Oh, him, I remember him. Me and Krystal had to talk to him, and Krystal was so nervous she was practically wetting herself, so he got these chocolate biscuits out of his briefcase for us, and told us we hadn't to tell anyone. I liked him. He made us laugh. So is he going to be your stepdad?'

'Better not be! I'm not staying if he is.' James stood up, kicking at the ground with his toe. 'I'm going back to live with my dad anyhow, soon as I can.'

'You can't leave Wellesley!'

'Why not? It's a dump.'

'What about your friends? You wouldn't want to leave them, would you?'

'There's no one here I give a damn about.'

He heard her catch her breath, and looked down at her. Her jaw had fallen, and her eyes were bright, like Luke about to spout his horizontal tears.

'What's up?'

'I thought *I* was your friend!' Sarah sobbed, standing up.

'You're a girl,' he said cruelly.

She stared at him for a few seconds, then turned on her heels, and stumbled back towards their unauthorized exit.

James rolled his eyes, and dropped down onto the log again, the peace he'd sought in the garden shattered. Why the bloody hell did everything have to be so complicated?

'Hey, Jesus!'

James, newly arrived in the jumble of students waiting outside the door for the bell to go for afternoon school, attempted to look unconcerned.

Matt and Danny took a few steps closer to him.

'Jesus Christ! I forgot my bloody homework,' Danny said, smirking.

'You could say your prayers, ask Jesus to kill Mrs Giddings, then it wouldn't matter,' Matt advised.

'I'll ask 'im. Jesus ...' he whined the name, pushing his face within a few centimetres of James.

Anger engulfed James and he snapped. 'Fuck off!' he shouted.

'James!'

Oh God, there would have to be a bloody teacher materialising. He turned, praying it wouldn't be Mrs Giddings, who treated the new discipline policy like her personal mission statement. Mrs Tarbuck, thank Christ for that. Short grey hair and a red face like some army sergeant, but well known for her lenience. One of his beloved mother's parishioners, and his Head of Year, who'd always had a soft spot for him.

Close behind her, Sarah Day watched with large, pink eyes.

'You know not to use that sort of language on school premises,' Mrs Tarbuck said, coming up to him. 'Shouting it at full volume is particularly stupid. I expected more from you, with your mother being a vicar.'

Fuck you fuck you fuck you. He couldn't say it to her face, but he spat it out inside his head. She must have read his expression. 'Come over here.'

She separated him from the group, and he waited for his sentence.

'I'm sorry. I shouldn't have said that about your mother. You must get it all the time.'

Her sympathetic tone surprised him. 'Yeah. I do.'

'They were teasing him, Mrs Tarbuck,' Sarah said, coming up to them. 'They call him Jesus, 'cos of his mum. Making out like he's a creep.'

'How very amusing of them. Does it bother you, James? Would you like me to have a word with them?'

'No! Don't bother me. I mean, I get annoyed sometimes because it's so childish.'

'Well, unfortunately I have to do something about the bad language. We all have to stick to the rules these days.' She fished in her pocket for a slip to complete. 'Actually, I really ought to send you straight to Mr Cowley ...'

'Don't do that,' Sarah pleaded. 'It's not fair, they started it. I saw them.'

Mrs Tarbuck frowned. 'Well ...'

'And he only said "Bog off".'

Mrs Tarbuck smiled conspiratorially. 'Oh, was that all? In that case you'd better get off to your class. But don't do it again, James, my hearing might have got better another day.'

'Thanks,' James said to Sarah as they headed back into school. 'My dad's not going to take me to America if I get into trouble.'

'I had to say something. It wasn't your fault.'

'Sorry about in there,' he muttered, nodding in the direction of the garden. 'You're a mate. You're alright.'

Colour rose to Sarah's face; James walked quickly away, in case she got the wrong idea.

Three year old Ryan wasn't the easiest of children to look after, unable to sit still for more than a minute at a time, and into everything. Lisa was glad that she only had him a few hours a day. A packet of crisps and the television had temporarily halted his hyperactivity, and she was sitting at the other end of the sofa playing with Karli, when the door to the flat clattered open. She jumped at the unexpected noise, and Karli, startled, began to cry. Footsteps came through into the living room.

'Col? What are you doing back?'

'I cut my hand on a broken glass.' He raised his left hand, thickly bandaged around the palm. 'I've been up at the hospital having stitches, and I've got the rest of the day off. I ... who's this?' His eye had alighted on the cropped head of Ryan, who had given up on the crisps and was heading for the kitchen area.

'Tha's Ryan, Gemma's kid. She was goin' to the shops, an' she dropped 'im off. She'll be back for 'im in a bit.'

Colin pulled off his jacket. 'Hey, you, leave that alone!'

Ryan didn't even pause at the raised voice, but continued to stamp on the pedal of the bin he'd discovered, threatening to upend its contents on the floor.

Lisa, with Karli pinioned in the crook of her left arm, used her right to haul Ryan from the kitchenette. 'Remember what I told you, Ryan? If you don't stop goin' in the kitchen, no choccy biscuits for lunch. Why don't you get your cars? Let's 'ave a game.'

She found a dummy, settled Karli in her buggy, and helped Ryan start to fit a track together for his cars.

Colin watched suspiciously for a few minutes. 'How often does he come here?'

'Hardly never. Only when Gemma needs to shop. That in't easy with him wrecking everything 'e touches.'

'You wouldn't have been minding him behind my back, would you?'

Guilt made her aggressive. 'Don't be so bloody stupid.'

'You are, aren't you? How dare you! When I expressly forbade you!'

'Yeah, an' what are you gonna do about it? Put me over your knee?'

'I'd like to. I can't trust you an inch ...'

'What am I s'posed to do, when you treat me like a bleedin' kid? I wouldn't need to go behind your back if you weren't so mean. You don't earn enough, so I 'ave to help out. Tha's only sense.'

'If it was sensible, I'd agree to it. You don't lie to me.'

A wail interrupted them. Ryan had taken advantage of their argument to jam one of his cars into Karli's face.

'Look what he's doing!' Colin shouted, white with anger, thrusting Ryan roughly away from the baby. 'You get this kid out of our flat, now! He's a thug. You can tell your friend you're never having him here again.'

'I can't do nothin' with 'im till Gemma clocks off. An' I can't let 'er down suddenly. Don't be so bloody silly. An' stop tryin' to boss me around.'

'I'll boss you around all I like. You're my wife, and you do as I say,' Colin spat. 'You are *not* having a job. You are *not* child-minding. You are not doing *anything* without my say-so. And get that bloody kid off my furniture!' He left the room, slamming the door behind him.

With Karli howling and Ryan on the rampage, Lisa suppressed her desire to follow Colin and commit murder, and turned her attention to the children. She grabbed Ryan, smacked his bottom with a satisfying thwack that threw two years of child-care lectures out of the window, and forcibly plonked him on the armchair.

'Don't you dare move!' she hissed at him, as she freed Karli from her buggy, and began to calm her down.

Gemma arrived an hour later, and they held a hasty conference in muted voices.

'Fuck it, Lisa, you can't stop havin' him just like that. I'll lose me job. Can't you come round my place tomorrow at least, till I get something else sorted?'

'Depends if Col's still off work. I will if I can. Otherwise you'll 'ave to phone in sick. I'm sorry.'

'If you're not having 'im, how're you gonna pay off the washing machine? There's still a couple of hundred to go.'

'Oh, Christ!' Lisa sank down onto the sofa, and put her hand to her temple.

It had seemed a good idea. Put the sixty quid Colin had supplied for a second-hand machine towards a new one, scratched here and there to make it look used. Gemma got the machine on her credit card, and she was keeping back the child-minding money to pay off the debt when it became due. But if Lisa couldn't have Ryan any more ...

'You gotta pay it, Lisa.'

'I know,' Lisa said. 'I will. I'll get it from somewhere. I'll ask Colin's mum. She's alright - not like 'im.' She gestured towards the hall. Colin had not reappeared, but as soon as Gemma was gone, Lisa intended to make him pay for humiliating her.

Five minutes later, she entered their bedroom, to find him lying on his front on the bed, reading a book. He didn't look up when she came in.

'Don't you never talk to me like that again,' she said coldly. 'You in't my bloody boss.' He ignored her, stirring her resentment into a desire to hurt him. 'You talk about bein' my husband, but you in't no husband, you can't get it up, can you? Like bein' tickled with a bloody chipolata, that is.'

He still didn't move, but she had seen his shoulders stiffen. They'd barely touched each other since Karli's birth, what with their tiredness, and the tenderness of Lisa's scars.

'Christ, I was stupid to marry you,' she continued. 'I'd've been a lot better off staying with Allie. I'd have had a job, and money, and someone to talk to who in't laying the law down all the time. But no, you thought you wanted to be a daddy, didn't you? Dear little Karli's gotta have a daddy. But you're no good with her neither, are you? Can't hold 'er for more'n two minutes without 'er screamin' 'er 'ead off.'

'That's not fair,' he said, turning on his side, finally stung into a response. His face was pale and drawn. She hoped his hand hurt like hell.

'No, course it's not. You're always changin' nappies an' feedin' 'er, an' gettin' up in the night. I'm so bloody lucky. My kid's got a great dad, I got a great lover, blowin' my mind every night. An' as for your job, we're bleedin' millionaires, in't we, with your talents.'

He stared at her, undone by her taunts. Once, his obvious misery would have moved her, now she merely uttered a satisfied laugh, and left him.

Colin turned back onto his front and buried his face in the quilt. His hand was throbbing; he wished the glass had slashed his wrists rather than his palm. It was the only way he could see out of the nightmare in which he was inextricably caught.

On a Friday afternoon early in June, Alison packed the new outfit she'd bought for the wedding, changed into her colourful cotton sundress, and set out, via Nottling, to meet Iain. Steve had grumbled about having the boys, but she'd offered to keep Luke behind when they were due to stay over the weekend of the Wellesley Festival, and he'd accepted the deal. Behind her at St Peter's she left a muttering of ill-feeling at her absence from the fete, but they'd have to lump it.

She had underestimated the amount of traffic she would encounter, and her announcement that she'd be there by seven took the form of fantasy long before she negotiated the narrow private road that terminated in front of Iain's friends' imposing residence in a village on the outskirts of Leicester.

Encouraged by the fact that Iain's car was one of the group in front of the twin garages, Alison parked her car, and got out. He moved in affluent circles if his pals lived somewhere like this. Ahead of her, whitewashed walls stretched upwards and outwards in ad hoc fashion, a room jutting out to the left, a wing to the right, attics distorting the line of the roof, and over it all, vegetation vying for space: honeysuckle, clematis, roses and virginia creeper. As Alison rang the doorbell, she could clearly hear its chimes echoing through the house behind the polished front door.

A fair-haired, pink-faced young man opened the door, a stained wooden spoon waving in his hand. 'Hi, another one for the bean-feast? They're all in the garden, do you want to come through? At least,' he added, as she followed him into the hall, 'I invite you in, you might be here to deliver the flowers for all I know.'

'I'm with Iain Sutherland,' Alison said.

'Oh, you're Iain's ...' his voice tailed away, unable to find a suitable word. 'Yeah, he's out there.' He led her into an elegantly furnished sitting room, and out through french windows to the garden. 'Visitor Alert!' he called, and left her standing on the step.

The ten or so people who stood on the grass or rested on the green cast iron garden furniture, all turned towards her. She looked round for Iain to rescue her.

'Allie!' He detached himself from a small group of men, and came smiling to welcome her, still formal in shirt and tie after a day at work. His right hand held a glass of wine, his left slipped round her as he kissed her and steered her over the lawn.

'Come and meet Moira and Seb.'

'So you're the infamous Allie,' Seb said, taking her hand and holding on to it. A tall man, with a baggy face and shaggy grey hair, and alcohol fumes on his breath. 'No wonder Iain goes on about you all the time, lucky old dog.'

'Don't mind him, he's been at the sherry for the last three hours,' said a sophisticated blonde woman with a narrow, lined face, rising up out of a sun lounger, bracelets jangling. Another Scot, though with a harsher accent than Iain's. She held out a ringed hand. 'Nice to meet you. Get her a drink, Iain, and fetch a chair, I expect you're tired after the journey. My sons are supposed to be doing food. Heaven knows when it'll be ready!'

'So what do you do?' Moira asked, when Alison had finally been settled next to her with a drink.

Alison took a quick sip while she debated what kind of reply to give. 'I work for the church,' she temporized.

Iain leant over to Moira confidentially. 'She's a vicar, didn't I tell you?'

'Och, stop pulling my leg! I can just see you getting off with a vicar!'

Moira shrieked with laughter.

'What do you really do?' Seb asked.

Alison looked at Iain for help, but he merely smiled. 'I'm a priest,' she admitted uncomfortably.

'I don't believe it!' Moira said.

'Really? Well, well, it's enough to make me start going to church again, if they're all like you,' Seb said, leering a little.

'Now, Seb! Och, we're being thoroughly horrible, aren't we? It's just that Iain's the most hardened atheist we know, and it's such a surprise to find him taking up with someone religious, let alone a clergyperson, or however you describe yourself. How on earth did you meet?'

'He inspected the school where I'm Chair of Governors.'

'Gave you a mark for outstanding performance, I dare say,' Seb chipped in.

'He's not usually this bad,' Moira said, 'he's worrying about losing a daughter and giving a speech tomorrow. Go and get yourself some strong coffee, Seb, and sober up. So what made you want to be a priest?'

'Don't harangue the poor woman,' Iain said. 'She's off duty.'

'She doesn't mind talking to me, do you, Alison?' Moira pushed at Iain with her foot. 'Go and find out when that food's coming, and let us have our little gossip.'

'I put you and Iain in the same room,' Moira said when he'd gone. 'Is that what you were expecting? Iain said so, but he might have been making assumptions. I hadn't realised you were in the church, and perhaps clergy don't, you know ... Not that it bothers me at all, but I wouldn'a want to put you in a difficult position. I'm sorry, I didna' mean to embarrass you.'

Alison cheeks had begun to burn as Moira spoke. She bit her lip. 'I was expecting to be with him. I know I shouldn't, but I'm afraid I'm not very orthodox when it comes to that. I did mean to be, only Iain rather swept me off my feet.'

'He's very fond of you, we can all see that.' Moira glanced around her, checking that her other guests were occupied with their own conversations. 'Forgive my bluntness, but have you made plans for the future?'

'Not formally. I'm not divorced yet.' She saw Iain appear at the french windows and pause to exchange conversation with a couple who were on their way in. 'But that should go through next year, and hopefully we can get married, though I'm not sure how we'll manage with Iain's job.'

Moira was smiling at her, almost sadly, but the light was fading, and it was difficult to read expressions.

'Twenty minutes,' Iain said, rejoining them. He put a hand on Alison's shoulder. 'What's she been saying about me?'

'Oh, that you're a bigamist with sixteen children,' Alison laughed. 'I said I didn't care.'

'There's hope for me yet,' he said lightly. 'You always used to say you'd run a mile from married men.'

'Did I? Well, bitter experience, and all that.' She smiled up at him, then turned to Moira. 'Could I use your bathroom?'

When she came out again several minutes later, Iain had taken her seat, and was engaged in an animated argument with Moira. He jumped up abruptly as she approached.

'Am I interrupting something?' she asked.

'No, no,' Iain said. 'We're always having arguments.'

'Are you?' Alison made herself comfortable on the seat. 'You never argue with me, you're always very reasonable, on your best behaviour. You must tell me all about him,' she said to Moira. 'All the guilty secrets he's keeping from me.'

She held out her hand to him, but he didn't take it. She looked up to find Iain and Moira staring warily at one another. She sensed their unease, but lulled by wine, and intoxicated by the delight of being in Iain's company, she did not let it worry her. Iain noticed her hand, took it, and smiled down at her. Moira shifted in her seat, and began to tell a story about Iain's hot-headed involvement in student politics. The evening raced towards nightfall, and once she was in bed with him, the incident, along with everything else, passed from her mind.

Twenty-one

The weddings Alison conducted at St Peter's were seldom grand affairs, so she enjoyed the more lavish scale of the nuptials laid on by Moira and Seb. She liked the chance to dress up, with a hat, no less, navy to match the linen suit she wore. Walking on Iain's arm through the village to church on a fine August afternoon, she felt desirable and full of life.

'I never thought I'd be going to church with you,' she said, squeezing his arm.

'I make exceptions for weddings and funerals. Besides, the church is architecturally very interesting.'

Sitting hand in hand beside him in a pew, with the warmth pouring in through the windows, and the solid curves of the stone arching over her, Alison was filled with a rare sense of contentment. Even the parish felt manageable at this distance, and at last she was feeling a part of Iain's life.

'That's my ex-wife,' he whispered, indicating the short, rotund woman in a voluminous red hat who had taken a seat across the aisle from them. Ros's eyes alighted on Iain, and took in Alison with raised eyebrows. She gave him a little wave which he returned with a nod of his head.

Alison got to speak to her in the Ladies halfway through the reception. Ros emerged from the toilet while Alison was touching up her make-up before the onset of an evening's Scottish country dancing.

'Rumour says you're a priest,' Ros said as she washed her hands. 'That stretches credulity, I must say.'

'Clergy do have relationships. We are human. I'm not sure why everyone seems to find it such a joke.'

'It's Iain. He's always been anti-religion. Moira and Seb wanted him to be Sophie's godfather, but he wasn't having it. He wouldn't stand there and say words he didn't believe in, even for a friend.'

'I admire his integrity,' Alison said.

'That's one word for it.' Ros passed a paper towel over her hands, and dropped it in the bin. 'Well, nice to meet you.' And she was gone.

Alison applied more lipstick as the door closed behind Ros, wishing

Iain hadn't felt it necessary to tell absolutely everyone about the profession she shamed. She was putting everything in her bag prior to leaving the cloakroom, when a cubicle door opened, and an elderly woman in a lilac suit emerged tight-lipped and frowning.

'Did I hear you say you're a priest? I've got no time for clergy myself. My husband went to church all his life, and then at his funeral, the priest didn't even mention his name ...'

Alison put her bag down as the saga continued, and prepared to be pastoral.

When she finally got back to their table five minutes later, she found Iain looking worried.

'I saw Ros come out, and I wondered if she might have said something to upset you,' he said.

'No, it was an old lady wanting to complain about the priest at her husband's funeral. I felt I ought to listen. You'll have to learn to live with that kind of thing if you're going to be a vicar's husband.' She looked across at him. The worry remained etched on his face. 'But perhaps you don't want to be.'

His eyes rested on her. 'I don't know how keen you are on dancing, but I wonder if perhaps we could slip away early, and go for a drink. I'd like to talk to you. About us.'

With a few reels under their belts to show willingness, Iain and Alison left the reception to walk to a pub set beside the nearby river. Beyond them, the sky glowed orange as the sun slipped behind the trees that shaded the water. In the shadows on the far bank, ducks and geese grumbled among themselves as they settled for the night. Alison and Iain sat side by side at a table in the crowded garden, speaking in low voices as they sipped their drinks.

'I've been wanting to talk about us as well,' she told him. 'People keep wanting to know whether you've asked me to marry you, and I don't quite know what to say. I've assumed it's what you want, it's what I want, but you've never actually said. Perhaps you don't believe in marriage.'

'Oh, I believe in it. Almost too much.' He was silent for a long time, looking out over the moving mirror of water to the banks beyond. 'If you couldn't marry me, would that be the end?'

'It would have to be. I can't carry on like this for ever. And I want to live with you. I can't do that unless we're married.' The grimness of his expression alarmed her. 'You're not keen, are you? You don't want to commit yourself to anything.'

'It's not that. I am committed to you, only there seem to be some logistical problems.'

'I could try and get a post near you, if you can't move. I could do with a reason to escape from St Peter's.'

'It's not only that.' He was silent again.

'What is it, then?'

'There's what you said about being a vicar's husband, I don't see myself being able to do it. I'd resent the demands it made on you, and I wouldn't be the kind of support you need.'

'But you've been wonderful so far. And there's lots of female clergy whose husbands don't go to church.'

'And there's your family, too. They wouldn't take kindly to me moving in.'

Alison sat with her chin on her hands, a finger toying with her lips. 'It sounds as if you're looking for excuses.'

Iain leaned forward, his head bowed and almost touching hers. He drew her hand into his. 'No, I'm only saying marrying you and living with you might not be easy for a while.'

'Don't tell me you want to call it off,' she whispered, conscious of the tears collecting in her eyes. 'I think I'd die if you did. I can't cope without you.'

'Bear with me, Allie. I'm not looking for excuses. I do want to be with you, I want to marry you, I don't know how, that's all.'

'But I shall need to have things settled one day. When I'm free, when I'm looking for my next post ...'

'I know. I'll work something out.' He looked up. 'Don't set me any ultimatums, I couldn't bear to lose you.'

Alison left at six the following morning, to allow herself plenty of time to get back to Wellesley for the eight o'clock service. For the first half of her journey on the virtually empty motorway, she thought only of Iain. She could not quite understand his reluctance to marry her the second he could, but she had no doubts about his love for her. The proof was in the tenderness with which he had made love to her last night, and again this morning, holding her to him a last time before she crept from the house. Proof, too, in the pride with which he'd introduced her to his friends, and the immediate rapport she'd had with them.

As she neared Wellesley, she tore her thoughts from her lover, and refocused on the day ahead of her: three more services to take, the mayor there for the flowers, the boys to collect from Nottling. At least she could approach it all with more inspiration as a result of her time away.

She arrived at the church earlier than she expected, and the building was empty. She put on her cassock, and walked through into the chancel. The scent of flowers suffused the air, their colours gleamed from every surface, radiant in the early morning sun. Alison made her way to Nigel's stall, and knelt down. Opposite her, the empty stall that she had not occupied since just after her priesting. Her ministry then had held so much promise. Collaboration with Nigel, as he trained her slowly to take charge of a parish. Iain's friendship a treasure yet to be fully unearthed. And now here she was, acting as an incumbent, acting as a virtuous priest, and nothing was anything like the way it had been meant to be.

But you mustn't judge me for it! she cried quickly in her head. It's not that wrong, I wouldn't survive without him, there's nothing wrong with sex if you truly love each other, and we'll be married soon ...

Something stopped her before she could recite the usual cycle of blustering justification with which she warded off any divine denunciation; an infinite kindness, washing over her. A kindness that said nothing of rights and wrongs, but understood her struggles and sympathized with her isolation: you were meant to be whole. This relationship is not making you whole. For an instant, she allowed herself to recognise how far she and Iain had fallen from the mature, equal friendship to which they had both aspired. She saw the unreasoning dependence that kept her from seeking the help she really needed, the leaching away of her integrity in a thousand dissimulations. Maybe she *could* step back, put the relationship on hold until she was free to court him without deceit ...

No! Impossible! I cannot lose him! The cost is too high. Ask me anything but that.

... No, don't go, don't go! I will do anything else ...!

But the moment had passed. She was alone. She opened her eyes, shaken by a profound sense of loss.

Bunty arrived as she stood up, stalking down the aisle as if Alison wasn't there.

'How did it go yesterday?' Alison asked, expecting no reply, but feeling she ought to keep trying.

Bunty tightened her lips, averted her eyes, and carried on past her.

Thoughtfully, Alison watched her disappear into the vestry.

'You could always give in,' Iain had suggested as they'd walked beside

206

the river on Saturday morning, discussing Bunty's impossibility. 'It takes two to fight. Give her her public apology, and you take the wind right out of her sails.'

Alison had dismissed the idea at first: what did Iain know of handling church politics? But things couldn't go on like this, and maybe it needed a grand gesture. A few choice words, woven into the end of her sermon, perhaps? The thought of Bunty's reaction to such a volte-face brought a furtive smile to Alison's lips as she began to prepare her service books.

Half an hour for the eight o'clock service, home for a quick breakfast, and then she was back for the ten o'clock, with the mayor in the front row and a full congregation here to round off the festival. A sermon about building up community in the church easily lent itself to her purposes.

'I've hardly been a good model myself over the last few weeks,' she said as she ended, looking down the ranks of pews, making sure she engaged their attention. 'Regulars here will know I forgot myself, and lost my temper with Bunty, one of our invaluable churchwardens. So I'd like to take this opportunity of apologising unreservedly to her. Her intentions were kind, and I shouldn't have made the accusations I did. Bunty does a tremendous amount here, and I do appreciate that. I hope she'll be generous and forgive me.'

So saying, she stepped down from the lectern and walked along the aisle to where Bunty sat, startled, in her seat. Alison offered her hand. 'Bunty, I'm sorry.'

For a second, Bunty stared at her with antagonism, but the whole congregation was watching, and what could she do? Outflanked, she stretched out a grudging hand, and muttered, 'Accepted.'

'It's despicable!' Moira said.

'I know.'

'You're despicable, treating that poor woman like that!'

'I know,' Iain said again.

'You promised you'd tell her last night.'

'I tried. I couldn't do it.'

Moira sighed loudly as she heaped coffee into a large cafetière. She filled it with boiling water, and sat down at the breakfast table next to Iain.

They had all risen late, and it was several hours since Allie had left, though the memory of their love-making still hung about him.

'How long are you going to deceive her? It's not fair. She's bound to find out some time, and the longer you're together, the more it's going to hurt.'

'Or it might be that the longer we're together, the more impossible she'll find it to walk out on me. That's what I'm hoping. She needs me, especially now, with her job being difficult.'

Moira had placed a basket of bread rolls and croissants on the table. Iain broke one with his fingers, and nibbled it half-heartedly. He was afraid, sometimes, that he encouraged Allie's dependence on him, because it bound her to him more tightly.

'She won't have a job if it gets known she's having an affair with you. She's taking an enormous risk. You should never have started it. You must have known it could never go anywhere.'

'It can. I'm going to marry her as soon as I've got Carol to agree to a divorce. It'll be easier telling Allie once I can say I've started proceedings.'

'And if Carol doesn't agree?'

'She has to.'

'But why should she? I know it's no kind of marriage, but you're all she's got. She can't cope on her own, and what happens to Hetty?'

'I know, I know. Do you not think I've been over it a thousand times?' Iain ran his hand through his hair. 'The thing is, Carol thinks I'll get fed up with Allie. She says that's what's happened with other women. Once she realises this is different, that I genuinely love Allie, I'm sure she'll not want to cling onto me. Not if I can find some other way of making sure she and Hetty are looked after properly.'

'I think you're being thoroughly selfish and irresponsible about the whole thing. I'd never have agreed to your bringing Allie here if I'd realised. I thought she'd be like the other dalliances you've had. I'd no idea you'd both be so serious about each other. I'd no idea I'd like the poor woman so much.'

'I know it's a mess,' Iain said. 'I know that. But I'm in it now, and I love her beyond anything I've ever felt, and I don't know what I can do except wait, and hope something will work out.'

Moira pushed the plunger into the cafetière with unnecessary force. She poured herself coffee, looked at Iain and shook her head. 'I'm taking this back up to bed,' she said. 'You help yourself.'

Twenty-two

Bindweed had curled its way around the sweet pea that climbed the trellis near the entrance to the garden. James uncoiled it strand by strand, taking care not to damage the frail stems of its host. He had come to the wild garden so often without discovery, that it failed to enter his head that the white of his shirt seen through the barricaded archway would give him away. He was standing with a handful of bindweed in one hand, together with one or two flowers that had torn away despite his efforts, when he was startled by a voice bellowing his name.

'James Thompson!'

James jumped.

Terry Howells stood on the other side of the gate, glaring at him. 'What *do* you think you're doing in here?' Howells asked, unfastening the padlock, and pushing the gate aside. 'What's that in your hand?'

James tossed the collection of weeds he'd been holding onto the ground behind him.

Howells peered past him. 'Ripping up the plants, are you? I thought I told you not to come in here. How dare you destroy something that's taken years to set up?'

'I wasn't destroying anything, I was helping. I've been here sometimes to do some gardening, so it wouldn't get overgrown. Those flowers coming off was an accident.'

'But you had no right to be in here at all. You know perfectly well it's out of bounds. How did you get in'

'You can move the fence panels at the back by the sports hall.'

'Wrecking the fencing too now, are we? This is a very serious matter. I wouldn't be surprised if this warrants an exclusion. You'd better come along with me to Mr Cowley.'

'That's not fair! I haven't done anything, I was helping! I won't do it any more, only don't send me to Mr Cowley ...'

Howells smiled nastily, and James began to panic. He had calculated that being discovered in the garden would earn him a reprimand at the most. Surely they couldn't exclude him for it, prevent him going to America when he'd striven all term to do exactly what they fucking well demanded of him?

'Your mother *will* be pleased, dragged along to school yet again to be embarrassed by you. We expected a lot more of you, with your mother being a ...'

The phrase snapped what was left of James's control. 'Yes, I know, with my mum being a fucking priest!' he yelled. 'Why can't you leave off for one minute? You've always had it in for me, you've bullied me ever since I arrived, just 'cos of my bloody mum! I hate you!'

He knew what he'd done as soon as he heard the words leave his mouth. Cowley, exclusion, and three weeks kicking his heels at home with his bloody baby brother while Josh toured America. He stared helplessly at the teacher, seeing the beads of sweat on Howell's forehead, the quivering of his moustache as he prepared to pronounce judgment, and was filled with a desperate urge to escape. Only Howells stood between him and the entrance. James grabbed his bag and ran forward, pushing the teacher aside, ignoring the oaths as Howells stumbled and fell, ignoring the commands to come back. He raced out from under the archway, across the playing field to the bike sheds, his bag thudding against legs, his breathing rasping loudly in his ears. With fumbling fingers, he unlocked his bike, looped his bag around his neck, and rode away.

When the phone rang to unleash this new element of chaos, Alison was sitting at her desk with a sandwich, following up the actions demanded of her by the previous evening's PCC. Though she had approached the meeting feeling relatively in control after the time she had spent with Iain, it had been an extremely difficult evening to navigate. Bunty had been anxious to offload the accumulated grievances she'd been unable to air during the previous two months, from disapproval of the curate's absence from the church fete, to the appalling way in which Alison had unilaterally sent the notice board back despite having given Bunty full responsibility for it. Alison had tried to be conciliatory, explaining again her absence from the fete and flower festival, and pointing out that she'd ordered a new board which should arrive in August, but she had not slept easily that night. She was not feeling strong as she took Alex's phone call.

'Ah, Alison, sorry to disturb you. Has James returned home?'

'No. Why?'

'He got into trouble at lunchtime, and went off on his bike.'

'Oh God! What's he done this time?'

'He'd got into the wild garden, and Terry found him pulling plants up. I'm afraid he lost his temper, and swore and knocked Terry down.'

'What, hit him?'

'Pushed him. It's going to mean another exclusion. I'm sorry. Will you be able to come to school tomorrow to talk about it?'

'Oh, God, he was doing well this term, he was really trying hard. Why does he have to be so stupid? Where do you think he's gone? Do you think I should go and look for him?'

'I expect he'll turn up.'

Alison rang off, and sat for a few minutes at her desk, taking deep breaths to calm herself down. It was no use, she had no concentration left for parish business. Instead, she got out her car and drove slowly around Wellesley, looking unsuccessfully for signs of James. Her tour brought her to the park, and she stopped. James came here occasionally to play tennis, there was a chance he'd sought refuge somewhere among the trees.

She locked the car, and walked along the tarmacked path that ran around the grass and on into the gardens, past large signs prohibiting cycling, unleashed or incontinent dogs, and rollerblading. Ahead of her, a bike had been slung onto the grass, and a boy sprawled on the wooden bench beside it, staring up at the swaying boughs of a line of poplar trees. James, his school bag and jacket flung down next to the bike; a lonely figure, and for far too long, beyond her reach. She sat down on the bench next to him.

He glanced at her once and looked away.

'What happened?' she asked.

James brooded for a while, then blurted out, 'They're kicking me out. I'll never go to America. Dad'll never let me go back to Nottling. It's not fair.'

'Why don't you tell me about it, then I'll know whether it's not fair or not?'

'You wouldn't believe me. You always say I'm making it up.'

'Making what up?'

Again, James was silent, his chin raised defiantly heavenwards.

'James, when you're facing something as serious as this, I need to know. I'll do everything I can to help, but I can't do that unless I know the facts.'

He bent forwards, scraped at a mud-stain on the leg of his trousers, and began to talk. 'I've been getting into the garden sometimes, to cut it

211

back, pull out weeds, you know ... Michael said why didn't I, and Howells said no, but I wasn't doing any harm. Then Howells turns up, and makes out I've been wrecking the place - as if I would. And then he starts going on about how I should behave better because my mum's a priest, gloating, like he's finally got me where he wants. I couldn't help it, I swore at him, and tried to get past him. I didn't hardly touch him, it wasn't my fault he fell over, but he's probably saying I assaulted him, and that's it, isn't it? I'll never get to America, and dad'll kill me, but it wasn't my fault. He's been bullying me for over a year.' James's voice shook with indignation as he finished his speech.

'You can't say things like that,' Alison said, with some exasperation. 'What possible reason could Terry Howells have for bullying you? He might not be the best teacher at the school, but he's a professional, he's on the PCC for heaven's sake! You'll have to do better than that.'

'You never listen, that's the trouble,' James exclaimed. 'Right back last year, you know, when the Brundalls were killed, and I got into trouble for going to sleep in his lesson, he said if I did anything else wrong, he'd tell everyone about you being a priest. And every time I did do something, he'd threaten me again. Then last November, I forgot my homework, and he pulls out some church paper with a picture of you on the front, all dressed up, and waves it around the class so everyone'd know. And don't tell me that wasn't deliberate, because the picture was months old, and he'd been carrying it round in his briefcase waiting to do it.'

Alison's instinct, as James rattled through his story, was that he had simply misinterpreted Terry's behaviour. The incident with the photograph was less explicable.

James carried on. 'And after that, everyone called me names, said I was Jesus or the son of God, and I tried to ignore them but it really pissed me off. I wanted to smash their faces in! I thought when I got into trouble, they'd shut up, but they kept going on ... "ooh, Jesus, you didn't oughter do that".' He reproduced the whining tones of his classmates.

'So the smoking, and the haircut earlier this year - was that trying to show how hard you were?'

He shrugged, and she took it for agreement.

'But if the teasing was that bad, you should have told someone - me, or the school. They shouldn't have been allowed to get away with it.'

'I did try to tell you, you didn't take any notice. And I said to Mrs Tarbuck once, but she didn't do anything. I mean, what can they do, when it was Howells started it, and him encouraging them? When we came back to school after Christmas, he practically got everyone to sing happy birthday, because he said it wasn't much fun for me having a birthday on Christmas Day. I'm not making that up, you can ask anyone.'

She considered James's story, acknowledging to herself that he had given hints of what was going on during the past year, had she chosen to hear. 'Oh, James, I am sorry. I should have listened. Everything's been so ...'

He glanced at her.

'No, that's no excuse, I know that. But I do understand now, and I'll make sure I take it up with the school. If this has been going on for months, there's no way I'll let them exclude you. The trouble is, I don't see how you can prove it if Mr Howells threatened you. It's your word against his.'

'No it isn't. That Inspector of yours was there when Howells threatened me. He must've heard. He could back me up.'

'Iain was there? That is a help. Even if he doesn't remember, he'll have kept notes. I'll ring him tonight.'

'So you've got to tell me,' she said to Iain later that evening as she sat up in bed with the phone to her ear. 'If you back James up, he won't be in nearly as much trouble.'

There was a silence, then Iain said in a clipped voice, 'I thought I'd made it clear, I'm not discussing anything about your inspection with you.'

'But it's ages ago, what possible harm can it do? All you have to do is tell me if you remember Terry either threatening James, or saying something that James might have taken the wrong way. I know you wouldn't usually remember details like that, but it was out of the ordinary, and you'd have taken an interest because it was my son. Even if you can't remember exactly, you must have notes. Please, Iain, it's James's future, I need your help.'

'Alison, I am not going to discuss anything from the inspection with you. It wouldn't be correct.'

His obstinacy dumbfounded her. 'That's all you care about, being correct! James gets expelled, and his life'll be ruined, and Steve will crucify me, all because you won't answer yes or no to a simple question!'

'You're exaggerating. Look, Allie, I'm your lover, for God's sake, that complicates things. I cannot do with anyone drawing attention to how I may or may not have reported anything relating to your son at the inspection. There's people would be asking whether I had an interest in you at the time, and whether I was as impartial as I should have been. I

213

cannot afford to have my integrity questioned. It could ruin my career.'

'I can't see why there's a problem - we weren't lovers then. And I've got far more to lose than you if people get to know about us. I don't understand why you have to be so difficult about it.'

'Right, so you don't understand,' Iain snapped, 'but I'm not discussing it, and that's final.'

'Oh, go to hell! I don't love you at all!' Alison answered, and slammed the phone down.

'What did he say?' James asked the following morning when Alison returned from taking the eight o'clock service.

'He doesn't feel he can take your side publicly,' she said.

James's mouth twisted. He didn't say, 'you've let me down again', but she felt it. Between them, he and Iain had left her no choice.

'James, can you remember Mr Howells' exact words?'

'He told me off, and said I shouldn't use your job as an excuse. Then he said, I mustn't get into trouble again, because "you don't want your classmates to get to know your mum's a priest".'

'And you swear that's the truth? I've got to know, because I may have to go out on a limb for you, and if you're wrong ...'

He met her gaze frankly. 'I am telling the truth.'

An hour later, Alison was sitting with Alex, Terry and Mrs Tarbuck, listening to her son make his accusations in a flat, faltering voice that was far less persuasive than his impassioned outburst to her. When he came to a halt, all of them tried to speak.

Alex held up his hands for silence. 'There seem to be a number of issues here,' he said. 'If we take the lesser one first, James admits to having entered the wild garden, knowing it was out of bounds. At the most, we might consider a detention for that. Mr Howells reports that James was causing damage, James says quite the reverse, and that he had been doing some gardening to keep the place tidy. We can easily check out the truth of that.'

'Sarah Day came in once, she saw me,' James said. 'You can ask her.'

'We will. There's also the matter of whether you deliberately knocked Mr Howells down, or whether, as you claim, it was an accident as you were trying to get past. Either way, of course, you had no business laying hands on a teacher. However, if you have, as you claim, been subject to a long period of name-calling and bullying, and if it were true that you thought

Mr Howells had been associated with that, it does put things in a different light.'

'I had nothing at all to do with it!' Terry stated loudly. 'You can't let him get away with saying that kind of thing!'

'I'll come on to that in a moment if I may,' Alex told him. 'I would first like to ask Mrs Tarbuck to do some further investigation into James's general allegations about bullying.'

'I hardly need to,' Mrs Tarbuck said. 'I've heard them at it myself. But James told me it didn't bother him. You should have come and told me, James, not suffered in silence ...'

'It would still help if you could gather some evidence for us,' Alex said. 'Now, as to the accusations about Mr Howells ...'

'Utter claptrap!' Terry proclaimed. 'I apologised at the time over the business with the newspaper - I simply wasn't thinking. But you couldn't possibly have expected to go through school without someone finding out. It was the other pupils who asked me to say something about your birthday, I wasn't to know they were teasing you. And as for this business of me threatening you, it's hardly worth me wasting my breath disputing it. I deny it categorically.'

'You must have said something, even if James misinterpreted it,' Alison said.

'How can I possibly remember any detail of an incident over a year ago? I do remember James explaining about the Brundalls, but I can't imagine saying anything that might have made him think I was threatening him.' He laughed dismissively. 'I'm afraid that's a story he's made up to avoid getting into trouble for assaulting me.'

Alison took a deep breath. 'No, it isn't. We've got evidence,' she said. 'The Registered Inspector was there - Iain Sutherland. I've spoken to him.'

Terry froze in his chair, and sat staring at her.

'As Alex knows, I've been in touch with Mr Sutherland to invite him to be on a panel for the churches' festival here in a couple of weeks, so I rang him to ask for his recollections. He's checked in his notes, and confirmed that Mr Howells did suggest he'd tell the class about me being a priest if James didn't behave himself. He said it was unusual, so he'd made a note.'

Alison watched Terry as she spoke, trying to ignore the cold flush of shame that washed over her as she heard herself embark on the lie. He pursed his lips and folded his arms as he listened. She held her breath, praying her bluff would work.

'Maybe I did make a remark to that effect,' Terry said at last. 'But I certainly wasn't intending James to take me seriously. It's the kind of thing you do say when you've got someone playing silly buggers in your lesson, especially when they've been doing it right under the nose of an inspector. It was a joke. How was I to know he'd brood about it for months, and then think everything I said or did anywhere near him was somehow fulfilling this non-existent threat?'

He spoke with self-righteous indignation, but he had made his admission. Relief swept through Alison; James was going to be safe.

'That's helpful, Mr Howells,' Alex said. 'You've been admirably frank with us. I'm sure there was no malice or threat intended, but I can see why James might have thought there was, and might have lost his control when you made your unwitting remark about Alison. I can't let the pushing and swearing and general rule-breaking go unchallenged, but given the circumstances, I don't believe excluding James is the appropriate course in this case. Perhaps detention would be more in order.'

'I agree,' Mrs Tarbuck put in. 'I think he's learned his lesson, haven't you James?' She smiled fondly at him.

'If there's any chance of keeping it out of his report ...?' Alison said, looking imploringly at Alex. 'James promised his dad he'd be good this term, and we'll both be in hot water if he finds out. He has tried, you have to admit that.'

Alex gave a little smile. 'I was going to suggest community service. Two nights a week from now until the end of term, during which time he works in the garden under Mr Howells' supervision. How does that sound?'

Terry puffed out his lips. 'Three nights a week.'

'That's too much,' James exclaimed.

'It's supposed to hurt,' the Head said. 'I wouldn't argue, you should count yourself lucky. It's just as well your mother kept in touch with the Inspector.'

'Helpful to have a mother who's Chair of Governors too,' Terry muttered next to her.

Alison didn't challenge him. She was still trying to persuade a less than elastic conscience that her deliberate lie on James's behalf was excusable in a just cause. She rather doubted that the Almighty saw it like that - but He probably had others of her misdemeanours in his sights at the moment; she knew for certain that Iain wasn't going to see it like that.

Twenty-three

Though Alison had rung Iain to apologize for provoking an argument, and to explain that James's situation had resolved itself, she had avoided giving details. She thus came to their next meeting a week before the festival knowing she would have to confess her duplicity, since Alex was bound to mention it when he and Iain met there. She joined him at a country hotel thirty-five miles from Wellesley, in a town where he had yet again landed work with a local school, and for the first part of the evening, simply tried to relax and enjoy his company. The hotel, an old red-brick coaching house, formed a mellow backdrop as they sat out on the terrace outside the dining room eating Tally-Ho Trout and Stable Lad's Steak with the sun reddening the sky over undulant hills away to the west.

Alison had decided to leave her confession until she had ensured Iain was at his most amenable. The warm evening gave her an excuse to bare her flesh and look sexy. When she suggested they forgo dessert and go for something more appetising, Iain responded readily. Behind the locked door of his bedroom, she suppressed her qualms about her motivation, and deliberately employed all the artifices she had learned would most arouse him. Undress to almost nothing, a slinky body-shaper tight around her hips and breasts; slowly remove his clothes, taking time between each garment to explore his skin with her mouth, to articulate in precise detail her passion for every part of his body. Then down onto the bed, to move astride him until he could sustain himself no longer and fell back against the pillows, his chest rising and falling in rapid gasps as he recovered his breathing.

She laughed, and lay down beside him.

'You're pretty amazing,' he murmured, propping himself on one elbow beside her, while his other hand stroked her breast. 'I must have arguments with you more often if you're like this when you make up.'

The tenderness in his eyes accused her, making her laughter hollow. 'Are you feeling forgiving?'

'Definitely. Why, what have you done?'

She took a deep breath. 'I let Terry think you'd confirmed James's story. I had to ...' she carried on, seeing the cloud descending on Iain's face, 'He'd have got excluded otherwise.'

He pulled his hand away and sat upright. 'How do you mean, you let him think?'

Alison could see she was going to have to be honest. 'I told him I'd spoken to you, and you'd checked in your notes, and confirmed what James said.'

'That was a lie!'

'Yes.'

'I thought I told you I wasn't prepared to talk about it. I explained how damaging it could be if you dragged me into this. What the hell were you playing at?'

'There's no harm done. Terry admitted it, no one's dragged you into anything. I only told you in case Alex mentioned it at the festival.'

Iain's lips tightened. 'So that's what tonight's been in aid of. You thought you'd put me in a good mood before you confessed. Well, I don't appreciate being used.' He got up off the bed, and pulled on his underpants and trousers. 'I'd rather not sleep with you at all if you're going to play games with me.'

Alison sat up with a sheet pulled around her to protect her from his judgemental gaze. 'You don't have to be so touchy. I still don't see there's a problem.'

Iain zipped his trousers cautiously, and stood looking down at her. 'Obviously not.'

He turned his back on her and wandered to the window. Drawing the curtain to one side, he stood gazing out, a pale outline of flesh and head against the darkening sky.

Alison reached for her underwear, and began to dress.

'I don't see how I can come to your festival now,' Iain said, turning back to face her. 'What do I say if Alex asks me something? What if Terry Howells is there and complains about me breaching confidentiality? What am I supposed to say? I refuse to compromise myself by going along with your lies, and I don't suppose you want me to tell them you lied about it to get your son out of a tight spot?'

'You don't need to say anything. He's admitted he did threaten James, but he says it wasn't intentional, he's not in trouble for it. He's not going to challenge you.'

Iain advanced towards the bedside table to retrieve his glasses.

'You won't really drop out of the festival, will you?' she pleaded, holding out her hand to him. 'I need you there.'

'You should have thought of that before you started being so inventive.' He reached down to the floor to pick up her dress, and tossed it onto the bed. 'And particularly before you put me through all this rigmarole, letting me think you meant it.'

'I did. I love you. I don't think Alex will make an issue of it, and I'll see if I can keep Terry away from the festival. I'll tell his wife to take him out of the way for the day in case he's disruptive about the inspection. Please, Iain, don't let me down. It'll be alright.'

Iain pursed his lips. 'I'll think about it. Come on, get your clothes on, I'll see you to your car.'

Now that he had proof that Lisa was not to be trusted, Colin felt justified in asserting his authority over her. He could not watch her all the time, but he could make sure she accounted for every penny she received and spent. He could discourage his parents from visiting unless he himself was there to correct any false impressions she might give. When, as today, they did turn up for lunch, he tried to behave as if life was the rewarding enterprise it ought to be, and fought off their probing concern.

'You mean you're cycling four miles each end of your shift, and at that time of night! No wonder you're looking worn out, Colin, darling,' Midge said. 'You must let us get your car back on the road for you. We can do that, can't we, Bernie?'

'Oh, that'd be brilliant,' Lisa said. 'It's terrible havin' to do all the shopping round 'ere, and it in't good for Col being out all hours.'

Her spurious concern annoyed Colin. She was always like this with his parents, cheerful and talkative, making him seem dour and mean-spirited when he objected, as he was bound to do.

'We'll manage,' he said, without looking up from the plate of roast chicken Lisa had set in front of him.

'Don't be silly, that'd make it much better for you,' Lisa said.

'We'll manage on our own,' Colin said, his lips tight. 'It's my responsibility to provide for my family, and that's what I'll do.'

He looked up in time to see Lisa and Midge exchanging a surreptitious glance across the table, as if they understood one another and his inadequacies perfectly well. He returned to his food in silent fury, hating them for their conspiracy against him, determined not to give Lisa any time alone with his mother.

Lisa was too crafty for him. She waited until near the end of the visit, when Colin was in the middle of an involved discussion with his father about developments at St John's, and took her chance to lead Midge off to the nursery to watch her change Karli's nappy. Colin could not excuse himself for several minutes, and when he did finally get out into the hall, it was to hear Lisa saying,

'That'd just be a loan.'

'What *are* you doing?' Colin asked, pushing the nursery door open.

Midge was standing with Karli draped over her shoulder. At Colin's entrance, she ceased patting Karli's back, and glanced uncertainly at Lisa.

'I've told you before,' he said, grabbing Lisa's arm. 'You're not to touch my parents for money all the time.'

'Get off! I only wanted a loan - you never give me nothing.'

'We're perfectly happy to lend you money, I know things are tight for you,' Midge said. 'You mustn't be proud, Colin, we want to help you out.'

'We don't need help. Thanks for offering, but as long as Lisa doesn't spend money like water, we can manage perfectly well. How much has she touched you for so far?'

'Nothing,' Midge said. 'I've bought a couple of presents for Karli, but she is my grandchild, I like to do it.'

'Come off it, Col ...' Lisa started.

'We'll discuss it later.'

His mother looked at her watch. 'It's about time we went,' she said.

Colin walked his parents to their car. When he returned, he found Lisa in their bedroom, rapidly applying make-up before the mirror. She'd changed into a short skirt and a pale velour tee-shirt that had been tight enough even before Karli, and she had appropriated Colin's black leather jacket. Her hair lay loose on her shoulders. She picked up her handbag from the dressing-table, and turned round.

'Where d'you think you're going?' he demanded.

'Out.'

'Where?'

Lisa shrugged. 'The pub.'

'You can't. What about Karli?'

'There's a bottle in the kitchen.'

'You can't simply walk out. And what are you doing in my jacket? Take it off.'

'No.'

'You're not to go. I forbid it.'

Lisa laughed. 'Yeah, I'm so scared!'

She headed for the door, leaving Colin standing in the middle of the floor with Karli, powerless to do anything other than call ineffectually after her:

'Lisa!'

The door shut. He looked down at the baby, wondering what on earth he was supposed to do with her now. Karli was gazing solemnly at him. All of a sudden her face broke into a beaming smile, the one she had learnt normally brought rich rewards. Colin stared blankly at her. Bewildered by the absence of response, the baby's face crumpled, her lip quivered pathetically, and she began to cry.

The last time Lisa had been out on her own had been before Karli was born, and it felt odd to be unencumbered. A faint sense that she was being ridiculous visited her, but she fought it off. She was twenty years old, and out for some fun, and Colin could bloody well lump it.

Her first call was at the pub on the corner by the shops, smoky and loud after hours of use. An hour or so there, but it was too early to go home when she wanted Colin to shit himself worrying about her, so she wandered to the bus stop and rode into Greathampton. She couldn't spend anything, but it was nice to window-shop without Karli yelling her head off because the buggy had stopped.

An hour of that was enough, and she was starting to feel tired. At the far end of the street, the spire of St Martin's poked up above the shops. Seeing it like that five years ago when she'd run away from Nottling, she'd been reminded of Michael and Jenny, and had gone to throw herself on their mercy. Maybe she could do that now. Maybe *they* could lend her some money. She hadn't seen Michael for weeks, not to speak to, only in the distance on the few occasions she'd managed to get to St Martin's, but he wouldn't let her down.

An unfamiliar car was parked outside the Turners' house. A metallic blue sports job that had cost somebody a packet. Michael opened the door to her.

'Hiya. Won the lottery, did you?' Lisa asked, smiling and gesturing at the car behind her. For the first time in their acquaintance Michael did not greet her with immediate warmth.

'Lisa. This is a surprise. You're looking dolled up - are you on the way somewhere?'

'I just bin out for a drink. Col's minding Karli - about time he did something for her. Thought I'd call an' see how you were - I in't seen you for ages. I'll go if you're busy,' she added, sensing his awkwardness.

'No, come in. It's only that I've already got a visitor, and you might not want to meet him.'

There was only one common acquaintance Michael would have said that about.

'Not Ty ...' she said.

'Yep. He had to be in Leathwell for something, and he stopped by. You're welcome to join us if you don't mind ...'

'No, course not,' Lisa said. In her present mood, catching up with an old boyfriend and showing him what he'd thrown away, had its attractions. 'I don't s'pose we'd even recognise each other now.'

She was right, she hardly did recognise him. He looked much smarter with his hair, and the small beard that sat around his mouth, neatly trimmed. The leather jacket he wore was expensive, making Colin's cut-price affair look shabby.

Lisa came in and sat down, aware that her skirt was showing a lot of thigh, and that Ty's appraisal of her had taken in the fact. He said hello briefly, giving most of his attention to the continuation of a conversation about his car with Michael, but his eyes kept returning to her.

Lyddy clambered into her lap almost immediately with a picture book, while Rosie crawled over and stood clutching her knee for balance. She settled them both in the chair with her, and read the story in a low voice. It felt peculiar to be in the same room as Tyrone, after the way he'd treated her. To think she'd once been desperate to get him back.

'Lisa's married to Colin Blatherwycke,' Michael was explaining.

'Oh, yeah? I think I met him in Wellesley when he came to do that show for Allie Thompson.' Ty looked across at Lisa. 'Weren't you working for her?'

'Yeah. Wish I still was.'

She glanced at Michael, hoping he'd ask why, but before he could respond, they were interrupted by the preliminary note of the telephone in the hall.

'Excuse me a minute,' he said, leaping up. 'That might be Jenny.'

Lyddy followed him out of the room, complaining. 'Want to talk to mummy! Let me!'

Left to themselves, Tyrone and Lisa eyed one another self-consciously.

'You doing alright?' he asked.

'Brilliant.' She paused to turn another page for Rosie. 'I gotta kid now, you know.'

'How old?'

'Four months.'

'Congratulations.' Tyrone was regarding her speculatively. 'When did Michael say you got married?'

'January.'

'And that was to the same bloke who spent last summer going round the country explaining what a righteous virgin he was, but you must've been pregnant all the while.' He laughed. 'I like it! Now that would make an entertaining story for the tabloids.'

'I think I might go to 'em myself. That'd serve 'im right. E's so bloody self-righteous, 'e needs takin' down a peg or two.'

'Well you let me know. I can be your agent. Should clear a few thousand for an exclusive like that.'

Lisa grinned. 'I s'pose I shouldn't be so 'ard on 'im. He does 'is best.'

Michael came back into the room, frowning. 'Jen won't be back till late - there's something come up. You're welcome to hang on if you want, Ty.'

Ty consulted his watch. 'No, I'd better be getting back. Which way do you go, Lisa? Can I give you a lift anywhere?'

Lisa looked across at Michael, waiting for him to urge her to stay and talk to him about whatever it was she wanted.

'You might as well, Lisa,' he said. 'Save you a bus fare. I've got the kids to get to bed.'

'I'll give you a hand if you like ...' she offered.

'No, I'll manage. I'm used to it.'

He took Rosie from her, leaving her no alternative but to pick up her bag and follow Ty out.

Lisa consoled herself with the prospect of riding in a car many degrees of luxury above anything she'd experienced before. She stretched back in the leather seat as Ty accelerated loudly away from the house, extending her legs and not sorry that her skirt rode further up as she did so.

She looked across at Ty and laughed. 'You've come up in the world,

I should've stuck with you.'

He kept his eyes on the road; his hand crept down to push the gearstick into second as he approached the junction. 'I'm sorry about walking out on you like that. You didn't deserve it. I should have ended it properly.'

'Have you got a girlfriend now?'

'Yeah. I'm living with Becky Patten.'

'Wow!'

'Only you'd better not tell her mum that, or Ridgefield. They don't like me much, and she wants to break it to them gently.'

He talked to her as he drove, more kindly than he'd ever been in the past. When the car eventually came to a halt in the road at the foot of her block, Lisa leaned across and kissed Ty's cheek swiftly, before manipulating herself out of the low seat.

'Cheers. Thanks a lot. See you.'

She heard the car roar off as she entered the building, and began to climb the stairs. She was preparing herself to forgive Colin, so long as he had been sufficiently worried, and was properly apologetic, until she got closer, and heard Karli's wails piercing the flaking walls.

Anger rose in her again as she went into the nursery to find Karli screaming alone in her cot, her dummy lost on the carpet.

'Baby! Sshh. Hush.' Lisa picked her daughter up, recovered the dummy, wiped it with her tongue and plugged Karli's grateful mouth. As the baby began to settle in her arms, Lisa walked through into the living room.

At the far end, Colin stood gazing out of the window.

'What the hell d'you think you're doing, leaving 'er screaming like that?'

'She'd have cried herself to sleep soon enough.'

'She'd lost 'er dummy, poor pet, didn't you think to check?'

'That's your job.' Colin turned round, his face white. 'Don't you ever walk out on me like that again. I slog my guts out as it is, I'm not being left to look after some squealing baby because you fancy tarting yourself up and disappearing. Was that a bloke you came back with? Did he give you money? Here, let me look in your bag.'

He came towards her, reaching out for the strap that still sat on her shoulder. His fingers closed round it, dragging it from her.

'Get off!' With her free hand she held on to the bag, her movements hampered by Karli, complaining on her other arm. 'You've no right to go through my stuff!'

'Yes, I have.' Colin's breath came in jerks as he fought her for her bag. 'Let go. I want to see ...'

Lisa let go suddenly, afraid she'd drop the baby if she carried on. Karli began to cry again, spitting her dummy out onto the floor.

Colin finished his examination of her bag and purse, and tossed them onto the floor. 'I know what you've been up to, you little tart - you'll do anything for money! Where have you hidden it?'

The crescendo issuing from Karli demanded Lisa's attention, but she couldn't allow Colin's accusations to pass. She stepped forward and slapped his face as hard as she could.

The shock of it knocked him backwards. He cried out and clutched his cheek with both his hands.

She met his eyes, conveying as best she might her complete contempt for him. Then she took Karli back into the nursery, and sat on the floor with her back to the door, tearfully rocking her baby into sleep.

Twenty-four

The Wellesley Festival got under way with a couple of hundred people turning up for the day's talks and workshops. Rod Little, as Chairman of the festival committee, was ostensibly in charge, and got to introduce the day, but Alison felt herself to be the only one who had a full grasp of all that needed to be done for the event to run smoothly. The responsibility hung over her during the week beforehand, a night-churning catalogue of tasks to be done and points to remember. Early on the day itself, she dressed smartly in a knee-length black skirt suit, and short-sleeved, pale-blue, clerical blouse, and set out for the school. Within a few minutes she was rushing around sorting out minor crises and averting major ones, until at last the time came for her to push Rod Little up front to kick the whole thing off.

The morning passed, and as packed lunches were being consumed in the school hall, Alison hastened around the building checking that all was in place for the afternoon workshops. As she did so, she kept a constant eye out for Iain's arrival. He wasn't pleased with her, and there had been a certain stiltedness in his phone calls, but at least he had phoned, and he was coming. Afterwards, both Michael and Becky had agreed to stay the night, which meant she could invite Iain too, without any suspicion attaching, and she was sure she could restore their friendship.

She was arranging chairs with Alex in his office when Iain arrived. The Head had been hovering protectively around the school much of the afternoon, and was now supervising the transformation of his office into a hospitality room where the panellists would be given a light buffet supper before the Any Questions panel at six-thirty.

A gentle tap on the half-open door made her look up to see Iain standing there in a pale grey suit and what looked suspiciously like his blue Nessie tie.

'Ah, Iain, hello,' Alex said, striding to the door to shake him firmly by the hand. 'Remembered your way, did you?'

'Indeed. You're very forgiving to have me back again, though I can't say I remember much about the inspection here by now.'

'It was helpful that you'd kept enough notes to help us sort out the incident with James,' Alex said.

Iain glanced at Alison thoughtfully before replying. 'We do keep notes for a specified period.'

Alex had followed his gaze. 'You remember Alison,' he said, gesturing with his arm to include her in their conversation. 'You've spoken to her on the phone, I understand.'

'Oh, aye. I'd not forget Alison. One of the more memorable Chairs of Governors I've had to deal with in my career.' He held out his hand, amusement crinkling his eyes as he shook her hand with an added pressure that suggested she was already forgiven.

'Good to see you again,' she said. 'Have you had lunch? There's food laid on for workshop leaders in the hall, and I'll take you along if you like.'

'I'll look after him, Alison,' Alex said helpfully. 'You've got enough on your plate. Where are you for your workshop?'

'The small hall. Thanks.' She smiled more generously than she felt, annoyed to be deprived of a few minutes with Iain, but not liking to argue.

Alex ushered him out of the door, and she returned to her task.

Running the workshop alongside her lover created greater strains than Alison had anticipated, for their familiarity with each other was hard to disguise. She was acutely conscious of just how shocked these friends and parishioners would be, should they discover the truth about the relationship. Ella and Mrs Stubbings, attending because it was Alison, and they liked her. Megan, here despite her awful experience during Iain's inspection, 'laying a ghost', she told Alison. But thank God no sign of Terry. Vee had done her work, heeding Alison's plea to keep her husband away lest he embarrass them all by laying into Iain about the inspection.

With the workshop at an end, Alison and Iain disentangled themselves from continued discussion with several of the keener participants, and moved out into the corridor.

They had gone only a few steps when Alison spied Becky Patten, eye-catching in shiny trousers, satin shirt top, sleek hair and bright lipstick, wandering towards them. She greeted Alison with an extrovert embrace, and shook hands with Iain.

'I've been looking for you. God, I'm shattered! I was up talking to Ty half the night, and I've been filming all morning. I hope I'm not putting

227

you out, but I won't be able to stop tonight. I need to get over to Great-hampton to see mum.' She dropped her voice and made a face. 'Ty says I have to tell her about us. Christopher's going to be out tonight, I thought it'd be a good opportunity.'

Alison extracted from Becky's words the one point that mattered to her. 'You aren't stopping? Oh, but surely you can go to Greathampton tomorrow. I was expecting you. Michael's staying.'

'I know. Sorry, but Ty says if I don't tell mum about him soon, that's it, he's off. So I've decided to get it over with tonight.'

'In that case, good luck,' Alison said, concealing her annoyance. 'Come and have some tea.'

Inside the Head's office, she found Beverley from the festival committee setting cups of tea, and plates of cakes and sandwiches, in front of Alex, Michael and Christopher Ridgefield. Michael, unusually smart in decent trousers instead of jeans, and a white polo shirt that emphasised his summer tan, stood up and embraced both her and Becky with enthusiasm. Christopher, formal in his dark-grey suit and light-grey clerical shirt - 'positively Hawaiian for him', Nan would have said - shook hands politely. Alison had found him formidable while she'd been on the Programme, his grey hair neatly ordered around an austere face, looking down his long nose at anything female. Years of Nan's informality had had their effect, though Alison still felt she had to choose her words carefully in his company.

'I'm very interested to be here,' Christopher said. 'I'm spiritual director for Father Mark, your predecessor, so I feel I already know Wellesley. Have you ever met him?'

'No,' she said shortly. 'Did you and Michael arrive together?'

'I gave him a lift,' Christopher replied.

'There's been a slight change of plan,' Michael added. 'I need to get back tonight.'

'But I'm expecting you to stay.' She glanced with consternation at Iain. His face remained carefully blank.

'Jen wants me back. I thought I'd better agree. She was kicking up enough fuss about me coming here at all.'

'But ...' Alison frowned at him, but she couldn't take it further with Christopher looking on. 'Oh well, never mind. Let me introduce you all.' She went around the group, filling in the names, until, with one eye on Michael, she could announce, '... and this is Iain Sutherland.'

She was aware of Michael and Iain scrutinizing each other as they shook hands, each conscious of the other's significance in her life. Before long, however, all five of her guests were talking easily with one another while she and Beverley waited on them. Iain was good at this, she realised. He spent his life lubricating social interactions, able to be confident and agreeable whatever the circle. A definite asset for parish ministry.

'Come and have a walk round the school,' Alison said to Michael as they finished eating. 'We've got half an hour before the panel.'

She led him out of the front door, past people arriving for the last event of the day, and stopped in the middle of the car park to make a last attempt to persuade him to stay the night.

'Becky's pulled out as well, and I was relying on you both being here so I could have Iain to stay over. I can hardly have him on his own, and I need to see him. We had an argument last time we met, and I want to make up. Please, Michael. You know Jenny's being unreasonable. You shouldn't let her dictate to you.'

'*She* knows she's being unreasonable, but it doesn't make it any less real. I've promised I'll be home tonight, I can't go back on it.'

'That's not fair, you promised me!'

He jammed his hands into his back pockets and turned away from her. 'Don't you start on me. I'm depressed enough as it is. I know I'm letting people down, but what can I do? I was nasty to Lisa the other day. She obviously wanted to come and tell me why she and Colin are barely speaking to each other, but I couldn't face it.'

'Are they still having problems? I wonder if I should try calling ... only she wasn't too friendly last time we met, and I'm always so rushed when I take the boys to Nottling. She's got Colin's family, though, she sees Midge once or twice a week, doesn't she?'

'I suppose so. Look, Allie, I am sorry I can't stop. I would like to.'

'Maybe I could let Iain stay anyway,' Alison mused. 'He's done it before, and no one's known.'

'Sounds risky to me. It's bad enough you having him here for this. People aren't stupid, you can't hope to hide the fact there's something between you.'

'I don't mind people realising we like each other. Once I'm divorced, they'll all know I'm seeing him. What did you think of him?'

'He seems pleasant enough, but that's not the point. I don't think you should be involved with him the way you are, not yet.' Michael ran his hand through his hair. 'God, Allie, what if people in the parish find out? You're crazy.'

'I know what I'm doing.'

'But you're a priest. You can't go round having affairs!'

'What I do in my private life is my own business, and we're going to get married as soon as I'm divorced. I don't see what's so wrong about sleeping with him when we love each other. You've done the same thing yourself, and so did Nan and Christopher, come to that.'

'Stop trying to justify yourself.'

'I thought you'd be more understanding. Don't tell me you're jealous.'

He made a face. 'I'm jealous of anyone who's getting it up, frankly.'

'Don't be crude. Well, I'll know not to rely on you in future. I must go and find Iain and make arrangements for tonight.' She began to walk back into the school.

'Allie ...' Michael caught up with her and took her arm. 'Please, this is stupid. You're obsessed, you're not thinking straight. It's like you were with me. Haven't you thought what happens when you're found out? You lose your job, your house ... think of the embarrassment for James and Josh. Be sensible, cool off for a while - if he really loves you, he'll accept it.'

She shook him off, angrily. 'I don't have to take this crap from you. It's none of your bloody business.'

She walked unhappily away from him, scarcely believing that she had managed to argue with Michael, of all people. What had come over her? She struggled to compose her feelings and her face into the smiling mode appropriate for a priest on duty, and went to gather the rest of her panellists.

Sitting at the back of the hall as the question time got under way, Alison decided she had chosen her guests well. They responded intelligently to questions from the floor, and argued good-humouredly with one another. Michael sat beside Iain seemingly unaffected by his argument with her, Becky flirted with Alex and Iain, as well as with Michael, and Christopher steered the discussion with the confident authority of one who believes that his next visit to the locality will be in episcopal purple.

Alison was busy working out how she was going to convey her house key to Iain without anyone noticing, when she became conscious that two people had slipped into the empty seats beside her. Glancing across, she was annoyed to find Terry Howells removing his jacket in the heat of the hall with Vee making an apologetic face beside him.

'Hello,' he whispered. 'How's it going?'

'I thought you and Vee had gone to Leathwell today.'

'We did. We're back, fortunately. I've got a bone to pick with Sutherland.'

A man in the row in front turned to glare at them, and they fell silent. For the next half hour, Alison sat biting her lip, wondering how she was going to keep Terry from accosting Iain.

As Christopher brought proceedings to a close, she turned to engage Terry in conversation, but she was too late. Directly the last of the applause died away he was out of his seat and advancing down the hall towards Iain.

'He insisted on coming back, I couldn't stop him,' Vee said. 'He's decided this business with Mr Sutherland talking about what he said to James was a breach of confidentiality, and he wants to ask him.'

'Hell! Can't we stop him? I can't let him hassle my speakers ...'

The two of them fought their way through the tortuously slow groups vacating their seats, and finally made it to the front where Terry was jabbing his finger in the air in front of Iain's face:

'... "respect the confidentiality of information received during the inspection",' Terry was saying. 'It's there in your instructions. I don't believe you had any right to pass that information on.'

'I'd prefer not to discuss it,' Iain replied, directing an infuriated glare at Alison as she and Vee arrived.

'Vee!' Alison pleaded in her ear.

Vee sailed in to interrupt her husband with Buntyesque efficiency. 'That was interesting,' she told Iain. 'I do love your accent. Where are you from?'

'Scotland,' Iain answered shortly.

'I meant more precisely than that. Do you go back much?' Vee persisted as Terry opened his mouth to speak again.

'Glasgow. I've a sister lives near Dumbarton, and I go there for Christmas and a couple of weeks each summer. In fact I'm there next month. Fortunately it's not far from Glasgow, so I go in and see what's new in the galleries and museums.' Iain was being more forthcoming, as if he understood that he was being protected from further inquisition.

'One doesn't expect Glasgow to have things like that.'

'It's a very civilised place. It's been European City of Culture, you know.'

Observing Terry looking restless at the development of this travelogue, Alison intervened. 'I need to give you your expenses,' she told Iain. 'I've got an envelope for you in Alex's office. Do you want to come and collect it?'

She led him away, leaving Terry frustrated.

'I'm sorry,' she said as they weaved their way back out of the hall and down the corridor. 'Vee couldn't keep him away any longer. You managed, didn't you? Actually, I've got your expenses in my bag, but I wanted to arrange about tonight. I thought, as Michael and Becky aren't going to be there, I could give you my key now, and you could park in the road and let yourself in when there's no one looking.'

Iain shook his head. 'I'm not coming on my own. It's far too risky.'

'No it's not. You've done it before and no one saw.'

'Have you not thought, there'll be far more people who might recognise me after I've been here all day? It's too dangerous with Terry Howells sniffing around.'

'He's not going to know. I'm the one taking the risks. If I don't mind, I don't see why you should.'

'Didn't you hear him? He knows I shouldn't have passed on details from my inspection the way you said I did, he regards it as a breach of confidentiality. Maybe there's some doubt about whether everyone would see it like that, and in other circumstances, I might be less circumspect myself. But what if he starts making a fuss? What if he asks why I should risk speaking out of turn for your sake? Imagine if he finds out we're lovers, and starts asking whether I was biassed in some way at the inspection because I liked you? I can defend myself to a large extent, but it would be immensely damaging to my reputation if it was thought I'd allowed my relationship with you to influence my conduct in any way. Inspectors have to be seen to be absolutely impartial. Professionalism. Integrity. Objectivity.' He waved his hand to emphasise the words. 'I cannot afford to have that questioned, I've sailed too close to the wind as it is.'

'You're overreacting. You said it didn't matter having a relationship with me once the inspection was over. Now you're behaving as if it was the worst sin in the book.'

'I'm not overreacting. There wouldn't be a problem if it wasn't for Terry Howells still feeling hard done by about the inspection, and if there'd not been this focus on your son to stir him up. It should all have been well over and done with. You've really landed me in it, Alison.'

They had reached Alex's office. Alison fished a key from her pocket and unlocked the door. Beverley had been in during the question time; the extra table and chairs and all traces of food had vanished. The room was once again a working study.

She shut the door behind them, and looked anxiously into his face. 'But Terry can't know there's anything between us, and even if he did - which everyone's going to know some time - all we need to say is that it started after we met at the festival.'

Iain regarded her soberly. 'We still have to be careful. No visits to your house for a while.'

'But I need to see you.'

'Next week. I'll ring you when I get home, and we'll talk about it then. We mustn't be alone in here too long.' He took a step towards the door.

'Do I not even get to kiss you?' she asked, her eyes beginning to fill at the realisation that he was leaving.

Iain hesitated, listening for a few seconds. Outside, all was silent in this part of the school. He opened his arms, and they kissed hungrily. His hand slid up her skirt, and between her thighs, stroking her, whispering, 'I've been wanting to do that all afternoon.'

'We could ... here ...' she breathed, excited. 'I could lock the door ...'

'No. I don't think so,' he said, smiling as he removed her fingers from the button of his trousers. 'I must go. We'll speak later.' He kissed her gently, stroked her chin once with his finger, and was gone.

Alison watched the door sweep gently shut behind him, and closed her eyes. My God, what was I wanting to do? I must be crazy. Obsessed. Damn Michael for refusing to stay and give her the time with Iain that she needed. She smoothed her skirt back down, and headed back to the hall. There would still be a good hour's work clearing the hall and checking the classrooms, thanking the helpers and reviewing the day with the other committee members; and all without her anticipated solace of a house full of friends and a night spent with her lover. Her only consolations now were the knowledge that her indiscretion had not altered his desire for her, and his promise that she would hear his voice again before she collapsed into sleep.

'You're back early,' Carol said as Iain walked into the living room later that night. 'Did you have a row?'

'No.' He sat down. 'No. It seemed safer not to stay with her. There's one of the teachers from her school starting to ask questions about the inspection I did there. I cannot afford to have people thinking I might have been biassed.

Carol carried on with her knitting, her fingers rattling along the rows of yet another jumper for Hetty. 'Perhaps you should stop seeing her. It can't be worth risking your job over a casual affair.'

'Allie is not a casual affair, Carol. I've told you that. I want to marry her. I want you to divorce me.'

'That's out of the question.' Carol put her knitting down and stood up. 'Would you like a cup of tea?' Without waiting for his reply, she was out of the room, on her way to the kitchen.

The tea was an inordinate time in coming. Eventually Iain got up and went to investigate.

Carol was standing in the middle of the kitchen, visibly shaking, her eyes shut, her hands knotted whitely together at her breast, her breath coming in gasps.

Iain watched her for a few seconds. Suppressing a sigh he went over to her and put his arms around her. 'Oh, Carol. I'd not abandon you. I'd make sure you were cared for, you and Hetty.'

She clung to him, 'No! I can't cope. You can't leave me. You promised.'

He held her until she was calm, longing and longing for this to be Allie with her hair against his cheek and her hands clutching his jacket. 'What would you have me do?' his spirit called to her across the miles. 'You'd not have me desert her.' He ached to share the wretchedness of his predicament with Alison, but could no longer envisage daring to do so. Her loss would be unendurable; he had to continue to fend it off by whatever means lay in his power.

Twenty-five

'You missed a very good workshop yesterday,' Ella told Terry, stopping by the organ after the Sunday morning Eucharist as he was packing his music away. 'Alison led it with that friend of hers - the Inspector.'

'So I hear.'

'They took turns saying little bits, and then got us to say what we thought, and they did it ever so nicely together. I expect that's because they know each other so well, with him being an old friend of her family. I hadn't realised he'd been the one who did your inspection.'

'What did you say?' Up to that point, Terry had not thought it worthwhile concentrating on Ella's softly-spoken dissertation. 'Sutherland an old friend?'

'That's right, they've known each other for years. I met him when she was ill after Easter. He'd come to see her, and he bought her a lovely bunch of flowers. I put them in water, and helped him make sandwiches for her, and he said he'd take a tray up to her. Well, I was a little shocked, because she was in bed, and you don't expect to have a man go into your bedroom, not unless he's a doctor or a priest. Then he said no, it was perfectly alright, because he was an old friend.'

'He couldn't have been that old a friend, or he wouldn't have been allowed to do the inspection,' Terry told her.

'I don't know about that. That's what he said. "We go back years." Now, do excuse me, I must get on.'

Terry swung round on his bench as Ella disappeared into the vestry. Alison was coming back up the aisle, her robes rustling against the sides of the pews.

'Alison?'

She came over to the organ. Her face, close up, was drawn, and her eyes tired. He might have had some sympathy for her after all the work the festival must have entailed, had he not had his own agenda to pursue.

'Ella tells me Sutherland is an old friend of your family.'

A look of alarm appeared in her eyes. Good God, Ella's right, he thought. Which is most odd, because that means he ought to have declared an interest in the school, and left the inspection team forthwith. I wonder how OFSTED would react to being told that?

'It's not true,' Alison said. 'Of course it's not. I never met him in my life till he came to Wellesley for his meeting with governors. I don't know what Ella's talking about.'

'She was merely repeating what Sutherland told her himself. She met him at your house, bringing you flowers, and visiting you in your bedroom. Not that anything you choose to do in that side of your life is my business, but him leading that inspection when he knew you so well is a very serious matter.'

'Oh. I can explain,' she said breathlessly. 'I went to meet him to discuss the workshop, but I was taken ill. Iain very kindly drove me home in his car, and then brought mine back the next day, and looked in on me. I don't remember much about it, I was far too dozy. I think he said he'd been worried about whether I'd be compromised by Ella finding him in the house alone with me, so he said he was an old friend. There was no call for it, but he wasn't to know. I hadn't realised she'd remember it.' She swallowed, suspiciously nervous. 'But he's hardly a friend, more an acquaintance, and certainly not an old one. I contacted him again at the beginning of the year about the festival, and that's it. I only met him the once till yesterday.'

Terry observed her heightened colour and the dampness of her forehead, and was not convinced. 'Then how come you were able to get him to breach confidentiality so readily over that incident with James?'

Alison bit her lip. 'He didn't,' she said.

'But you said ...'

'I know. I rang him about it and he wouldn't say anything. But James was so sure about it, I called your bluff.'

'Good God! Some priest you are!'

'I know it was wrong, but I was worried about James. I couldn't have him being excluded when it wasn't his fault. And it was true, you admitted you did say something. Iain was furious with me.'

'I'm not surprised! It could have been a highly serious matter if I'd been vindictive enough to lodge a formal complaint.'

'I had to tell him, too, in case you mentioned it, and he very nearly pulled out of the festival, he was so angry. He had another go at me yesterday after you'd asked him questions about it. He was horrible, I'm getting in a sweat thinking about it. I am sorry, Terry. There's been so much going on with the parish, and the school, and the festival, James getting into trouble was the last straw, and I didn't handle it as I should. Forgive me?' She held out her hand to him, beseeching.

He took it reluctantly. What she said made sense, and an admission of guilt from a woman who liked to appear perfection itself, added weight to her explanations. Nevertheless he left her with a faint sense of disappointment that he had seen his legitimate grounds for complaint against Sutherland come to nothing.

Two days before the end of term, Alison was in school again for a final inquest on James's conduct since his brush with exclusion. Wellesley High was winding down for the summer holidays. With GCSEs out of the way, the school leavers had deserted, leaving the buildings the quieter for their absence.

James was waiting for her outside the Head's room, slouched against the wall, hands in pockets. Every time she saw him these days, he seemed to have grown. Any second now, and he'd have overtaken her in height, his voice would have completed its drop to adulthood, and she'd be dressing to the regular sound of shaving in the bathroom. He was still hardly forthcoming with her, but he had been considerably less tense and miserable since the school had taken steps to deal with the name-calling he'd been subjected to. He even seemed to have gained a couple of friends. Given his hard work in the garden three times a week, and the fact that he'd been relatively conscientious in his school work, she anticipated a good report. At her approach, he unpeeled himself from the paintwork and gave her what almost amounted to a smile.

She smiled back. 'It'll be alright. You've done really well. I'm proud of you. You'll be in the States this time next week, don't worry.'

This time he smiled with genuine enthusiasm. Alison patted his back, and they went into Alex's office together.

With the meeting over, and James cleared to make a fresh start in the autumn term, Alison took herself to a staffroom at its fullest midway through the morning break. She got herself coffee and joined Megan and Lil in their usual seat under the window.

'Seen anything more of your Inspector?' Megan asked, when they had rejoiced all they could over the imminent end of term. 'I reckon he fancies you - he laughed at all your jokes in that workshop, which is more than any of us ever do. And I swear I saw him ogling your legs when you bent over your bag.'

'Oh, shut up! You're making it up,' Alison said, colouring as she recalled the hotel room a few nights before, where Iain had given an exhilaratingly practical demonstration of exactly what had been going through his mind at the time. If only Terry Howells was out of earshot rather than on a nearby chair pretending to be immersed in the *Times Educational Supplement*. She'd nearly died when he'd started his sceptical questioning of her after the festival, and frightened her into confessing her lie. She couldn't afford to have his suspicions engaged again so soon.

'Megan, please!' Lil Giddings responded with spurious horror. 'Show some respect for the woman. Can you imagine anything worse than getting off with an OFSTED inspector? He'd stand over you with a clipboard saying things like "seven out of ten acts of intimacy are good or better", or "her grasp of carnal knowledge is not secure".'

Megan shrieked with laughter. 'Yes, and then he'd declare it to be a Failing Relationship with Serious Weaknesses and order in a hit squad of counsellors!'

'Iain's not a bit like that when you get to know him,' Alison couldn't help saying.

'You mean *you* fancy *him* as well?' Megan said. 'We'd better start collecting for the wedding presents. Hey, Terry, are you any good at the Wedding March?'

Terry's nose emerged from his paper. 'You what? Weddings? Who's getting married?'

'Alison's eyeing up our former Registered Inspector.'

'I'm not. All I said was that he's alright when you get to know him. I know for a fact he doesn't think much of me.' Her blushes intensified; she could only hope it would pass unnoticed under the tinted moisturiser she'd smeared on her face that morning. When she saw the way Terry was regarding her, however, she was all too afraid she was giving herself away.

Another week gone by. Another midweek lottery winner who wasn't her. Lisa stood in the growing gloom of her living room, staring out of the window, knowing that her debt to Gemma remained as immovable as it had been since she'd had to give up minding Ryan. She'd no one left to try, now that Allie, and Midge, and Michael, too, contacted again by phone, had all refused to help behind Colin's back. Her own mum hadn't the money, and wouldn't have cared, even if she had. Lisa couldn't get a loan from anywhere else, not unless she agreed to extortionate interest, so what was left?

On the pavement below, two men were conversing. There was one quick way of making money, of course. A few seconds on your knees round the back of the flats, a few minutes of revulsion in the back of some punter's car. No different from what had passed for relationships when she was younger, except that she'd have a few tenners to bring home, along with her contempt for them, and disgust with herself. It couldn't be much worse than what she'd let Ty do to her in the old days, and if that's what Colin thought she was like anyway ... ? Her thoughts turned to Ty, with his flash car and gold watch, and his friendliness when they'd joked about being her agent when she took Colin's story to the papers.

'Bloody hell, of course!' She shouted the words aloud in her excitement. That was it! Raise some money easy, and revenge herself on Col's pig-headedness at the same time. Ty had said the tabloids loved stories about sex and religion; they'd happily part with a couple of hundred quid for a story like the one she could tell them. Ty would know exactly how to go about it. Now what had he said his company was called?

Ty had taken surprisingly little persuasion to pay her a visit; he came on the first Saturday afternoon after her call. Lisa waited until Colin had gone to work, and took a long bath with Karli, to prepare herself. The radio played from its perch on the sink, and Lisa sang along as she scooped bubbles over her skin. By the time the buzzer heralded Ty's arrival, she had done her hair, put on make-up, and pulled a tight-fitting summer dress over the baby-bulges of her figure. In the pause while her visitor made his way up the stairs, she allowed Karli her dummy, and placed her in her cot. Although she was teething, the fact that Lisa had kept her up all morning ought to mean she went off for a few hours.

'Hello Ty,' she said, opening the door. 'Nice to see you again.'

He stood there, leather jacket slung over his shoulder, a designer tee-shirt belted into his jeans, scanning her up and down. 'And you.'

He followed her into the living room, and wandered towards the window to consider the view. 'Where's your kid?'

'I've just put 'er down for a sleep. Can I get you anything? Coffee? Tea? Squash? Can't afford nothing alcoholic, I'm afraid.'

Ty shook his head. 'Nah. Just had lunch.' He directed his attention to Colin's books shelved at the side of the room, nosy as ever.

Lisa sat down on the sofa.

Eventually Ty turned, put his head on one side, and said, 'So, what d'you want to see me for?'

'Do you remember saying about how the papers would be interested in hearing about Col gettin' me pregnant while 'e was doing all his church

239

stuff about being a virgin? Well, could you fix it to sell the story? I could do with some cash, an' 'e's being such a bastard at the moment, it'd serve 'im right.'

Ty came over to sit beside her. 'You don't want to do that, Lisa. They'd crucify him.'

'I don't care. I hate 'im.'

'It's not worth it, it always backfires. They might start with him, but you'd be dragged in, and there'd be plenty of people ready to slate you if they were offered enough money. And what about your kid? You might hate Colin, but he's still her dad. Do you really want her mixed up in it?'

'But I need the money,' Lisa wailed.

'What's the problem?'

There seemed to be genuine concern in his voice, more than he'd ever shown in all the months of their relationship. She explained about the washing machine, and how this was the last thing she could think of, and Colin would kill her when she told him, but what else could she do?

'How much do you owe?'

'About two 'undred quid.'

'I could loan it to you - give it to you, if you like. I'm pretty well off. I don't have anyone else to spend my money on.'

Lisa lifted her eyes to his. 'You don't wanna do that.'

'I don't see why not. I don't mind helping a friend out. We are friends, aren't we?'

He put his hand on her bare knee as he spoke, extending his fingers up across her thigh. It was a long time since anyone had touched her like that, and it sent goose pimples pricking all over her body.

'I thought you had a girlfriend,' she said.

'Huh! We've split up.' He removed his hand. 'She has a serious problem with commitment, that woman. Can't even bring herself to tell her bloody mother about me. She was supposed to do it the other week, but Nan and Ridgefield had fallen out over whether she gives up her job if he gets to be Bishop of Wellesley. I've moved out until Beck gets herself sorted, and I'm sticking to my old friends. You are my friend, aren't you Lisa?' He moved closer and attached his hand once more to her thigh. 'And I'm your friend, I can help you out.'

Lisa licked the dryness from her lips. Ty was watching her through narrowed eyes, and all she had to do was to follow her instincts, and her debt would be paid. He began to kiss her, the bristles of his beard grating against her mouth and his fingers twisting her hair on the edge of pain.

Their sexual relationship had always been crude and stormy, exhilarating in a way that her encounters with Colin had never been.

Ty had gained experience in the years since they parted. Afterwards, her guilt was compounded by the fact that this encounter on the sofa, through the hall, and finally in the bedroom, was the best sex of her life.

He left her, promising to return with the cash the following afternoon. Lisa lay on the bed for a quarter of an hour after he'd gone. There were marks on her breast where he'd bitten her, but it wasn't as though Col was going to notice. On the whole, she decided, as she got up to wash away the traces of her infidelity, this private vengeance had its own satisfactions, and providing Ty didn't go back on his word, all her problems were solved.

Lisa prepared carefully for Ty's return, dumping Karli on the bathroom floor with a few toys, and ignoring the baby's loud complaints while she showered and made up her face. No point in getting dressed, so she wrapped herself in a bathrobe, and took Karli through to the living room to feed her lunch. Once the baby was stoked up with food and Calpol, she should sleep for an hour, even though her new teeth were still troubling her.

Ty came to the flat soon after Karli had fallen asleep. Lisa laughed a welcome, and threw herself into his arms. He pushed the robe roughly from her shoulders, and tried to take her there and then against the wall.

'Hey, take your time, we got all afternoon,' she said, struggling free and dragging him towards the bedroom.

So intent was she on making the most of their time, that she pushed Karli's intermittent wailing to the back of her mind. 'Ignore it, she'll go off again,' she'd whisper to Ty, and then she'd forget again as he rolled her around the bed once more. Two hours went by. They had slept briefly, draped across one another in the light from the afternoon sun, when Ty stirred, and pulled his watch towards him from the bedside cabinet.

'I must go. I'd better give you that cash.' He pulled on his clothes, and fished his wallet out from his jacket pocket to extract a series of notes.

'I'll pay you back,' Lisa said, taking them from him.

'Don't worry about it.'

She stood up and put her arms around his neck. 'When can I see you again?'

'I'm not likely to be round this way again, not for months.'

'I could come to London and see you.'

Ty removed her arms from him. 'This doesn't mean anything, Lise, I thought you knew that. You're married.'

'I thought you cared about me. You said we was friends. You seemed to enjoy it.'

He laughed sourly. 'I should think so too. I have to get my money's worth. Hundred quid a go's pretty steep, even for a talented tart like you.'

He lifted a hand in farewell, and was gone, leaving her standing naked by the bed staring after him, clutching her handful of twenty-pound notes. He hadn't really changed, he was still a shit. But then, so was she if you looked at it that way. A shitty little whore.

Twenty-six

Alison laid a piece of paper down on the coffee table in front of her latest babysitter.

'Here's the number if there's an emergency, and make sure his light's out by eight.'

With all Luke's regular keepers away for most of the month, and James and Josh with Steve, she was tonight relying on Cindy, a grand-daughter of a friend of Ella. The girl had put the television on as soon as Alison went upstairs to finish changing, and showed no signs of having detached herself sufficiently from it to register the instructions she was being given. Alison left a little uneasily, but this was her last chance to see Iain for weeks, and she dared not let anything detain her; not with an hour's drive still ahead before she reached his hotel.

Their meetings had fallen into a pattern by now. She would progress along roads that grew steadily more unfamiliar, into a town she had heard of but never visited, following his careful instructions with more or less success to some three-star hotel in a quiet area, where Iain awaited her arrival. A relationship played out in restaurants and hotel bedrooms; venues whose distinctiveness passed her by. In years to come, she would be able to pass through these towns, knowing she had met him there, but not recognising which facade had protected them from the gaze of the world. Red Lion or Armstrong Arms, Stakis or Forte; all she required of them was that they should seat her at a table with her lover, feed her while she realigned herself in his physical presence, and provide a room where she could lock the pressures of her life outside and abandon herself to the passion that claimed her more completely every time they met.

Iain was waiting for her outside on the hotel forecourt this time, hands in the trouser pockets of a light linen suit, smiling broadly as she emerged from her car. He embraced her, and led her upstairs to the hotel bar where he bought her a drink and they studied the menu before placing their orders for the restaurant next door.

'I mustn't have too much - I had Sandra round for lunch, and she brought a pavlova with her, and what with Luke's help, we polished off the lot. I couldn't tell her I was going out for dinner with you.' Couldn't tell her anything very much, if truth were told, because she dared not be honest about any of her feelings; dared not admit to the chasm that opened up within her when she contemplated beginning another parish season without Nigel to share the load, for all Sandra asserted that her husband was definitely getting better.

'She's taking him away on holiday for a month, and then he's going to try and come back part-time in September,' she told Iain.

'That's good. You shouldn't be having to soldier on on your own.'

'It doesn't bear thinking about.'

A waiter arrived to escort them to their table at the side of the restaurant, beside a window overlooking a small park with a knot of youths gathered around its entrance. From above their heads, speakers amplified string arrangements of film themes, too loud for comfort, though it served to mask their conversation from the occupants of the adjacent tables.

'You should be having some time off,' Iain said as they began their meal. 'Why don't you take a proper holiday? You'll make yourself ill again.'

'What's the point, if I can't be with you? I'd come to your summer school if I'd not got Luke.' She sighed, and poked at a prawn. 'I wish you'd let me come to your sister's with you.'

'There's not enough room, I told you. There's all Fiona's family, as well as my mother, it's hard enough for her fitting me in.'

'I wouldn't take up much room, I'd share with you. And Luke could share with the other children.'

'They wouldn't have it, they're teenagers. Besides, Fiona would never allow me to have a woman I wasn't married to sharing my bed. She'd think it was a bad example for the children.'

'Then why don't I come and stay in a bed and breakfast nearby, even if it's only for a few days? Couldn't you recommend somewhere? Luke would love to think we were going on holiday.'

'We couldn't do very much if you've a child with you.'

'He sleeps at night, we'd manage something.' She rubbed her foot gently against his leg. 'One of your nieces or nephews could babysit, and we could find a private spot. The back of your car would do, I'm not proud ...'

'No! I don't want you to come.' He had almost shouted the words, and Alison recoiled.

Their neighbours glanced once at them, and pretended not to have heard.

Iain dropped his voice again. 'It would cause far too many ructions with my family if I installed my mistress down the road.'

Alison winced at his choice of word. 'Don't make it sound ugly. I'm not your mistress. I thought I was the woman you're going to marry. Surely you want to introduce me to them sometime?'

'Of course I do, but not yet. They're very high-minded. There's no way they'd approve of me seeing a woman who's still married to someone else.'

'You mean I'm not good enough for them! Great, that's all I need. A bunch of atheists excluding me for being immoral.'

'They're not atheists. That's the trouble. They're much more obedient to your God than you are.'

'You don't need to rub it in.' Alison put her hand to her temple and took a deep breath to control the upsurge of tears that was threatening to break out.

'I'm sorry.' He reached for her hand across the table. 'I didn't mean it like that. I much prefer your brand of religion to theirs, but I have to accept that's what they're like. Come on, Allie, don't get upset. You know I won't enjoy being away from you, but I'd made these arrangements a long time ago. I'll be back before you know it, and we can fix a few days together. I could take you to Paris. I owe you a trip there.'

'I don't want to go away, I want to go home with you. I'm tired of making love in hotel rooms, or having you visit me, and being scared stiff in case someone finds out.'

He released her hand and occupied himself poking at his teeth for a minute before he replied. 'Very well,' he said. 'You come and stay with me for a few days in September. The only thing is, I might be moving. I've some friends who want to move into my road because of schools, and they're talking of making me an extremely good offer if they can get the mortgage. So since it's a wee bit big for me these days, I thought I might take advantage of it, and get myself a flat instead.'

Alison frowned. 'You've never said ...'

'I've not had much chance, there's been a lot you've needed to talk about. This has only arisen in the last few days, in any case.'

'What about hanging on a few more months till we can get married, then you can move straight in with me?'

'We've yet to work that out - we don't know when that'll be. Meanwhile who knows if house prices will start falling? You're dealing with a canny Scotsman here, I want to do a good deal while I can.' His lips smiled; his eyes were wary.

'You never sound keen to marry me. It makes me feel as if I'm trying to nag you into it.'

'I *do* want to marry you. Of course I do. Only I don't see we have to rush at it the second your divorce is through. We've got years ahead of us. Decades. We've got time to do it properly.' He took her hand again, smiling that same tight-lipped smile.

'I can't cope with hardly ever seeing you.' Alison's voice shook; she pushed her plate away.

'We'll make sure we meet more often. It'll be easier when I've got my own place, a smaller place, somewhere nearer. I could find somewhere a wee bit nearer you, and you could come and stay over once a week.'

'How? I've got children, and the parish ... I need to live with you.'

'You will do. Have you finished?'

She nodded.

'Let's go up to my room.'

It helped, as it always did, to thresh, flesh welded to flesh upon the tangling sheets. But it wasn't enough to still her growing foreboding.

She reached home shortly before midnight to find Cindy still watching television. The only evidence the girl had moved was the presence on the coffee table of two empty crisp packets and three abandoned cans of coke. Going upstairs to check on Luke, Alison found her son lying fast asleep face down on the landing, fully clothed, and with his dragon under his arm. As she picked him up, she discovered a large damp puddle on the carpet beneath him. She held on to her anger while she cleaned him up and got him into bed, then went downstairs to upbraid a sullen Cindy for completely forgetting to put her charge to bed.

Luke would recover, so would the carpet. It should have been a minor complication to be laughed over with her friends in the future, except that there didn't seem to be anyone left she could ask to babysit, and God knew how she would manage now.

'Oh, dear, this is a mess,' said the health visitor. 'How did it get like this?'

'She got a dirty nappy while she was asleep, an' it went all red an' blistered, and I've put loads of cream on, but tha's getting worse.' Lisa bit her lip, tired after three nights of Karli refusing to settle, and guilty at having caused the suffering for which she was now being judged.

'Some of the blisters have got infected. What you really need to do is to leave her nappy off as much as possible. Get her out in the fresh air in the garden, and I'll give you something to clear up the infection.'

'I in't got a garden. An' I can't leave 'er nappy off in the flat, 'cos she wees all over the carpets.'

'Take her to the park, then, or a friend's house. Or put some towels down if you're worried about your floor. I'm sure you'll think of something. Have you had her weighed lately?'

'I in't been able to get 'ere very often.'

'Let's get her on the scales. Here we are, Karli, there's a good girl. ... She's a good size, what are you feeding her on?'

Lisa went through the list, accused. My baby's too fat, and that's my fault too. 'She's got big bones,' she said, 'like me. My dad was a sumo wrestler.'

'Was he?' The health visitor looked interested.

'I dunno. Even me mum don't know who me dad was. I do give her the right things. I was a nanny, I do know.'

'Glad to hear it. You make sure you change her regularly from now on, and I'm sure she'll be fine. If not, pop back here, and we'll get the doctor to see her.'

The health visitor had not been unfriendly, but Lisa walked home slowly, consumed with guilt, while Karli wriggled uneasily in the buggy. She couldn't even offer air and light and grass to crawl on, while her baby's wounds healed. Gemma had been distinctly cool when Lisa had handed over the cash two days after the deadline, so she couldn't go there. Michael was busy with his own problems, and anyway, Lisa couldn't let Jenny see the baby - she'd probably report her to social services. Midge had a garden, but Colin wouldn't let her go and see Midge. Midge would never have let one of her babies get in this state.

That night, she lay wakeful in bed on the edge of tears, while beside her the lump that was Colin grunted in his sleep. As if there was any point in trying to sleep, with Karli wailing for comfort on the hour.

'Not again! What's the matter with her?' Colin groaned as the baby's scream pierced the air for a fourth time that night.

Lisa dragged herself out of sleep. 'I told you, she's got a sore bum. That hurts 'er every time she wees.'

'You should look after her better. You've got nothing else to do all day. You ought to be able to spot when her nappy needs changing.'

Lisa suppressed the tears of exhaustion and misery, and went to lift Karli from her covers. She sat in the low chair between the cot and the window, rocking the baby in her arms. One of her extravagances had been expensive black-out linings for the nursery curtains, designed to buy a few more minutes of sleep on light mornings. She lifted the corner of the curtain. Out beyond the rise of the estate, dawn was lightening the sky, tinging the clouds with the pale pink of a baby's skin.

Karli stared up at her mother, sucking on her dummy with a puzzled expression, as if she could not understand why her discomfort was not being instantly relieved. Above the faint sounds of her sucking came the distant roar of a train taking excessively early commuters to London. It would be easy to lay Karli in her cot, to dress in yesterday's clothes from the bin in the bathroom, to raid the housekeeping, and to follow their example away out of this mess to London, or beyond. Then what would Colin do, waking in the morning to find her gone and Karli wailing? Or waking and leaving the house for work, ignorant that Karli slept on in her cot, leaving her to howl hours and hours on end, until her heart broke. God, no!

Lisa clutched the baby to her, and began to cry. She couldn't stay, she wasn't fit to stay, but she had to lay her plans carefully so that Karli didn't suffer.

Today Iain leaves for Scotland. Monitor the travel news for accidents, consult teletext for hold-ups, watch what the weather's doing on his route. Alison was conscious of the geographical distance stretching between them, for all she reminded herself that it made little difference where he telephoned her from, as long as he rang.

Only he didn't ring.

He'd got through his summer school, a highly sociable occasion, from the sound of it. He'd confessed once to having a brief affair during a similar event two years before, but '... since then, there's only been you. There only ever will be you,' he'd told her.

But Alison, missing him all the more in her August isolation, struggled with the first tentacles of jealous unease. She had rung him several times at odd hours of the evening, in case he had temporarily forgotten her in the face of temptation, and found him surrounded by the clatter of strangers and unable to talk. His failure to ring on his arrival in Dumbarton, as promised, alarmed her. Supposing he'd had an accident, and no one had thought to tell her? What if he'd got fed up with her helpless keening, her inability to exist without his constant reassurance? If she continued to harry him, his patience might finally crack, so she forced herself to hold out for at least one more day and fitful night.

When her alarm roused her at seven the following morning, she was ill-prepared for the day ahead. Breakfast. She didn't want breakfast. Strong coffee and out to a virtually empty church to celebrate Mass with Luke shut in the vestry on pain of death, with a box of toys and a cereal bar. The threats didn't work. He came trotting up the aisle towards the altar halfway through the prayer of humble access, and she had to complete the rest of the service with him sitting at her feet.

'Do you have to bring him? He was most distracting,' Bunty pointed out, cornering her in the vestry afterwards.

Alison suspected she came to these services to ensure that they happened, rather than for any spiritual sustenance. 'I can hardly leave him on his own,' she snapped as she pulled off her robes.

'I thought Ella had found you a babysitter.'

'It didn't work out.'

Bunty sniffed, leaving no doubt where she herself would lay the blame.

Alison began to gather up Luke's toys.

'I see there's still no sign of our new notice board,' Bunty said.

'I did order it. I keep meaning to phone up and see what's happened, but I haven't got round to it.'

'It's not as though you've got anything else much to do this month. We ought to have it in place before all the meetings start up again.'

'I know. I think the file's in the church office, I'll go across now and give them a ring.' She looked at her watch. Not yet nine, but they might be open, and it would get Bunty off her back.

'Come on Luke, we have to go over to mummy's office.'

She grabbed him by the arm, and dragged him over to the hall and into the office. She plucked the notice board file from the drawer marked N-R, and opened it on a desk containing, besides the telephone and computer, only three items in an In-tray and an empty basket marked Filing. Having extracted a pink delivery note with the telephone number at its top, she tried dialling. Engaged. She read through the items in the In-tray, and decided she could leave them to Janet. Luke began to get restless. She tried the phone again; this time it rang. Luke began to whine and tug at her skirt. She hissed at him crossly to shut up, and turned her back on him while she endeavoured to explain the nature of her problem to the secretary at the other end of the phone. Assured that the board was almost ready, and would be delivered in the next week or two, Alison rang off, and whirled round to shout at him.

'You must be quiet when mummy's on the phone! How the bloody hell am I supposed to sound as if I know what I'm doing when I've got you whining away like that?'

His eyes and mouth opened wide, and he began to howl.

'Oh, don't *start!*' She gathered the file up and crammed it back into the filing cabinet, picked Luke up more roughly than he deserved, and transported him out of the hall and across to her car.

Iain rang within an hour of her return. A brief call to explain there was something wrong with his mobile phone, and since his sister's telephone was in her living room, he'd had trouble getting private access to it.

'I told her I needed to talk to you, but she doesn't approve. I shall have to sneak down in the middle of the night, or take my chance when they're all out, like they are now. I'll give you her number, in case of emairgencies.'

Alison put the phone down, and went to find Luke in his sandpit outside the kitchen door. He came over immediately to be cuddled, tumbling sand from his clothing onto hers.

She hugged him. 'I'm sorry for shouting at you,' she told him. 'Why don't we take a picnic to the park?'

Back in the office, the delivery note lay on the floor under the desk where Luke had dropped it while her back was turned, waiting to be tidied away by whoever might next arrive.

Twenty-seven

Midnight. The night air was cool on Colin's face after the dry heat of the restaurant as he rode his bicycle through the town centre. The journey only added to his exhaustion, but it beat trying to catch a last bus that might or might not come, or cadging unreliable lifts from his workmates. He loathed his work intensely, but could envisage no way of escaping. He had no time to apply for other jobs, even if he were qualified for anything, and he couldn't resign, for they barely survived on a wage that bore little correspondence to the hours he actually spent there.

He always had to concentrate exceptionally hard on his journey home, lest fatigue send him careering into kerb or parked car. It was a relief when he finally saw the lights of the flats rising ahead of him. He dismounted, and carried his bike up the two flights of stairs, to let himself into the flat as quietly as he could. Lisa would be in their bed, asleep. He had to share it with her, for there was nowhere else for him, but they lay apart. He dared not touch her, dared not expose himself to failure and her ridicule. During the brief hours in which they were both awake and together, he withdrew into himself, steeled to receive her rage, her defiance or her mockery. He had no desire left for her or for anything. All he could do was to fulfil his responsibilities to provide for his family, and order their lives, whether they took any notice of him or not.

Lisa had forgotten to leave the light in the hall on for him, and when he pressed the switch, he immediately noticed that Karli's buggy wasn't there. Lisa must have left it through in the living room. He visited the bathroom, then slipped into the bedroom to undress by the light from the hall. As he fastened his pyjamas, he noticed that the familiar bulge of Lisa's presence was missing. He prodded the quilt, then activated the bedside lamp. She must still be up, watching television or asleep in front of it. He was tempted simply to get into bed, rather than provoke confrontation at this time of night, but forced himself to check. The door to Karli's room was ajar, the curtains undrawn, the cot empty. Probably she'd been restless with her teeth, and Lisa was keeping her up, spoiling

251

her. He put his head round the living room door. The room was dark.

'Lisa?' he whispered. He swung the door wider, and could see no shape on the chairs.

'Lisa?' he called more loudly, switching on the light.

She wasn't there. No buggy, no baby, only a square room with its hired furniture, and a sheet of paper, handwritten, on the table, weighed down by a gold ring and a silver locket - cheap both of them, but he'd cared for her when he had given them. He sank onto the sofa, and pulled the note towards him.

Dear Colin,

If you'd never come after me that time at St Johns it would have been much better. I've done nothing but harm to you ever since we went out. You should'nt have married me. I'm no good. I can't live up to what you want. I don't blame you for hating me. I've done bad things, I'm worse than you know. I'm not even any good with Karli any more, so its best if I go. I've left Karli with your mum. You should go back and live with them too, get a decent job and perhaps you'll meet someone else whose better for you. You can get a divorce easy when your wifes comitted adultary. I'd like to see Karli sometimes, but I know I'd better not.

I'm sorry for everything.

Lisa

Colin sat rigidly on the edge of the chair for several minutes, with the note in his left hand and his right clasping the back of his neck, while he stared at the paper. I've left Karli. Your wife's committed adultery. You should have known it, said the voice from his shoulder. She's a slut and always has been. What kind of a mother leaves a little baby? She seduced you, and she's been at it with who knows how many other men while you've been slaving your guts out for her. How do you even know Karli's yours? You're much better off without her. You can start again while she amuses herself with whoever her current fancy is. Your mother will bring Karli up properly, and thank God for it.

He put the letter back on the table, picking up the ring and the locket to restore them to their place on top of it. For richer for poorer, for better for worse ... she'd liked him then ... Lisa lying in their bed struggling to breastfeed Karli, swearing tenderly, and apologising to him with a smile when he brought her breakfast tray to set it beside her, and sat to watch her open the small parcel he'd bought to celebrate the birth. It hadn't all been hell ...

What kind of a mother leaves a little baby? One who's been driven to it by months of cold rejection. I'm no good. You hate me.

Oh, Jesus, what have I done? He bowed his head onto his knees, and wept.

Terry Howells whistled as he let himself into the church office on Saturday morning to photocopy the schedule for choir rehearsals in September. He'd enjoyed his holiday, and the start of term was still two long weeks away, a state of affairs undoubtedly to be celebrated. He switched the photocopier on and checked it for paper while it warmed up. Then, having pressed the start button, he sat down on Janet's chair to wait for the job to be done. His foot rustled against something, and he stooped to recover a thin sheet of pink paper from beneath his right shoe.

Curious as anyone would be with an idle moment to fill, he examined it. The logo at the top indicated the company from whom they'd ordered the notice board, and he realised this document related to the fiasco when the wrong board had been delivered back in May. He was laying it down on the desk when he noticed the signature in the space marked with a faint cross at the bottom of the page. Surely I. S. Sutherland? Not terribly legible, but whichever way he looked at it, that was the only name that fitted. But how on earth did Sutherland come to be accepting delivery of the parish notice board? Terry checked the address, and the date.

'I saw him once between the inspection and now,' Alison had sworn, but that one time had been in April. This was May. And how many more times were there? Perhaps Megan was more right than she knew, and there'd been something going on between the two of them for months. Good God, supposing Sutherland's story to Ella had been correct, and he was an old friend ... an old lover ... doing her inspection! Calm yourself, Terry, Vee would say. You're getting carried away. All you know is that he was in her house one more time than she said. Don't jump to conclusions. Ask her about it. Oh, shut up Vee, he told her image, I could be onto something here.

'Hello, I'm glad you've not gone,' Alison told Terry. 'I'd meant to ask whether you'd got a copy of the hymns for September for me.'

She was sitting at the table in the vestry completing the register after the Sunday morning service, and had spared only a glance to establish who had come in. The silence that greeted her comment made her look again. Terry stood with his back to the door, lips tightly aligned beneath his moustache, waving a sheet of pink paper in his hand.

'You told me you'd only met Sutherland once between the inspection and the festival, but you were lying. I've got evidence.'

God, help, now what? 'What are you talking about?'

'This.' He brandished the paper again. 'Sutherland signed for the notice board first time round. He was there, in your house, in May, and you lied about it!'

She reached for the paper to buy herself time. 'Let's see.' He was right, Iain's signature spread across the bottom of the sheet, all too decipherable. 'I'd forgotten about that,' she said with some truth. 'So he was. I don't see why it's an issue.'

'Because you lied to me.'

'Not deliberately. I forgot.' She assumed an air of puzzlement. 'I know what it was. It was around the first anniversary of Tanya and Ben dying, and Maggie came to see me. She was there for hours ... You know what it's like when people need to talk ...'

His face remained guarded, but she sensed that he did.

'Iain was on his way back from somewhere, and dropped in on the off-chance to see if I had time to discuss our workshop. I couldn't leave Maggie, so he waited a while, and that was when the board arrived. In the end he had to go before we got a chance to talk properly, so I expect that's why I forgot he'd called.' She handed the paper back. 'I'm sorry if I misled you, but it's not a big deal.'

'Maybe not to you, but his inspection report ruined my career, and if there's been any irregularity, I'm going to make sure he pays for it!'

'What irregularity could there possibly be? What does it matter how many times I talked to him about the festival? The inspection was way over by the time I approached him about it.'

'And why *did* you approach him? Why should you think of him, unless he really was an old friend of yours, or there was something going on between you?'

'Come off it, Terry. I asked lots of people. The festival committee wanted someone with an educational overview, and someone mentioned inspections, and I remembered Iain spoke at conferences.'

Terry considered her, still dubious. Alison held his eyes, knowing that if this was all his evidence, she was safe.

'I suppose I have to believe you,' he said at length.

'Why should I lie?'

He tossed the paper back down on the table in front of her. 'You'd better put that back where it belongs,' he said, and left the vestry.

When she was sure he had gone, Alison closed her eyes and sat on where she was, heart thumping, deeply ashamed of the deceits in which she was enmeshing herself. She longed desperately to share it all with somebody. If Nigel had walked in now, or Sandra, or by some miracle, Nan, or even Christopher, she would have broken down and confessed everything. But she had lost any ability to take the initiative and seek them out, and she could think only of turning again to Iain.

'No Lisa this morning?' Michael asked as Colin approached him after church with Karli asleep in her buggy. 'And aren't you usually at work?'

'I've resigned,' Colin said. 'And ... can we talk somewhere private?'

'Sure, let's go outside. I'll just tell Jen.'

He located his wife. Colin saw her respond to his words with a squeeze of his hand, and Michael returned looking inordinately cheerful.

Colin wheeled the buggy out through the swing doors and parked it on the grass while he and Michael sat on the wall a few metres from the church entrance. A thin covering of cloud concealed the sun, but the air was warm. Colin removed his jacket and laid it over the handle of the buggy.

'Lisa's gone. She went on Friday. Left Karli at my mum's, said she was going to the shops, and never came back. She just left a couple of notes. One for me, one for my mum. Sounds like she's gone off with some man. I wondered if you might know anything. She talked to you.'

Michael shifted uncomfortably. 'Not lately.'

'There was this bloke gave her a lift home a few weeks ago. I couldn't see him properly, but he had a posh car.'

'Oh, that'd be Ty Nixon. He was with me when Lisa came round. Only he's with Becky Patten these days. Or, to be fair, they're in the middle of a bloody great argument, but he's staying at his mum's, so he can't be with Lisa.' He scratched his head. 'Have you got the notes?'

Colin reached inside his jacket pocket and handed two scribbled pages over for Michael to peruse. The one to himself, and the details of Karli's routine Lisa had carefully spelt out for his mother. While Michael read, Colin watched his daughter, still peacefully asleep in her buggy. He had never been particularly close to her, but now that he was all she had left, the bonds that had always eluded him were slowly locking themselves around him. He found himself wanting her to wake up, so that he could hold her.

'It's my fault,' Michael said, passing them back. 'I could see you weren't happy, but I was snowed under with things at home, and I didn't say anything. I thought she saw your mum a lot, so she'd got other people looking out for her.'

'Yeah, except that I wouldn't let her see my mum. Lisa kept trying to get money off them, so I put my foot down, and she didn't like that. She wanted to do child-minding, and I said no. We argued all the time. I've been slogging my guts out all hours for her, and all she did was nag at me, and defy me. And then she goes off with another man.' Colin rubbed his fingers over the rough brickwork on which he sat, scouring his skin. A minute dragged by. 'I want it to be all her fault,' he said slowly. 'I want to say, everyone was right when they called her a slut, and I was stupid to marry her. But I can't.' He raised his eyes to Michael's face. 'She tried to make it work. I just took everything out on her. It's no wonder she got angry. I'm no better than any of the other men she's had, am I? I never gave her a chance.' He looked along the pavement to check it was clear. 'We never had sex. I mean, never, not properly. There's only been the once, starting Karli off. What with her being sore, and my job killing me, and not being able to stand each other ... I've made such a mess of everything.'

'Do you want her back?'

'She won't come back, will she? Not after the way I've been.'

'She's not going to leave Karli for long. And it doesn't sound like she's very happy about it, even if she is with someone else. I'd guess there'd be a chance of her coming back if you wanted it enough. Did you say you'd resigned?'

'Yes. My mum said she'd have Karli, so I could look round. I never had time before. I can't believe how much better I feel, knowing I'll never have to go to that bloody restaurant again.' He looked at Michael. 'I don't say "bloody".'

Michael grinned. 'Lisa's done more for you than you know. Look, you don't want to be leaving Karli in Leathwell. Why don't I have her till you get sorted out? She knows me, and I'm here with my kids anyway. Don't worry about paying, I'd be happy to help.'

'I can't let you do that.'

'Why the hell not? I'm going to have three kids to deal with soon, so it'll be good practice. Come on, Colin, don't be a complete wanker, let people help you if they want to. Tell you what, come back for lunch now, Jen won't mind.'

He sprang off the wall before Colin could refuse, and went off, whistling.

Colin waited where he was. It came to him that, painful though Lisa's desertion was to his pride, her action had somehow earthed the terrible tension with which he'd lived for the last few months. An unfamiliar feeling had taken up lodgings within him. By the time Michael returned he had identified it. It was hope.

With a late lunch consumed, and Luke planted in front of a video, Alison went through to her study to call Iain. Emergencies only, he'd said. Please God he'd realise this was one. Fiona answered the telephone, identifying herself in a gentle accent that echoed Iain's.

'I wonder if I could speak to Iain Sutherland?'

There was a pause. 'Who is that, please?'

'It's Alison Thompson.'

A further pause, more extensive this time, and the sound of an indrawn breath, as if the speaker were gathering herself to pour opprobrium down the line.

'Please,' Alison said. 'It's important.'

The silence in her ear became more intense. A few seconds later she heard Iain's name being called. A few more seconds, and his voice asking in the distance, 'Who is it?'

'That woman!' Fiona hissed, making no effort to muffle the earpiece. 'How dare you give her my phone number!'

'I hope you weren't unpleasant to my friend.'

A door banged shut.

'Allie, darling. I'm sorry if she was rude to you.'

'I thought she wasn't going to let me speak to you. Why is she like that? I'm not a bad person.'

'I know you're not. It's her. Are you OK? Is there a problem?'

'It's Terry, he was battering away at me again this morning ...' She revisited the conversation, finding herself becoming unexpectedly weepy as she did so. 'He's bound to find out everything, and I'll get thrown out, and you'll lose your job ...' Tears began to run down her cheeks. 'I feel as if this whole relationship's disintegrating round me, and I can't stop it. I can't cope, Iain, I'm cracking up. I need to see you.'

'Are you sure there's not somebody who could have Luke? If you could get away, I could meet you in Glasgow. I'd gladly pay for an air ticket for you.'

'And what would your sister say?'

'She'll have to lump it.'

'But there isn't anyone to have Luke, so it doesn't arise.'

Salvation arrived twenty-four hours later, when Alison opened her front door at five o'clock on Monday evening to find Lisa standing on the doorstep with a bulging sportsbag. She had known Lisa was missing, for Colin had telephoned two days before to see if Alison had any news of her whereabouts. Her first impulse on seeing Lisa was to shut the door in her face, because she had no energy left over for dealing with anyone else's crises. One couldn't do that, of course. She brought Lisa into the hall, and uttered soothing words as Lisa explained that she'd left Colin.

'I didn't know where to go, so I've come back. You won't tell no one, will you? I don't want Col to know where I am. I in't never goin' back. I tried one of them hostels in London, but that were terrible. So I thought maybe I could stop 'ere for a couple of days while I think what to do? I could 'elp out, do things.'

A thought took shape in Alison's mind. 'Could you? Would you? Could you look after Luke for a night or two? I have to see Iain, only he's in Scotland.'

'Is that your Inspector bloke? You're still seeing 'im?'

'Yes.'

'You're havin' an affair with 'im, I s'pose,' Lisa said listlessly. 'I didn't know priests were supposed to do that stuff.'

'It's hardly for you to lecture me on what's right and what's wrong.' She spoke sharply, and regretted it immediately as Lisa's face fell. 'I'm sorry. Oh, please, Lisa, I've got to see him, say you can help ...?'

'Oh, it don't matter to me. You do what you want. I've done a lot worse. You go, I'll look after Lukey for yer.'

Another twenty hours later, with a series of phone calls behind her to make arrangements with Iain and to inform Ella that services were cancelled for the next two days, Alison was waiting at the airport to board her flight to Glasgow. Above the fields and towns of middle England, the silver cities of the north glimpsed through patchy cloud, on over Scotland, her geography too hazy to know what lay below until the plane descended to glide past the grey estates and tenements and the wide stretch of the Clyde. The bump of landing, taxiing to a halt, through the door and out along passages to the concourse. And there he was, an insubstantial figure in light brown trousers and shirtsleeves, hands in his pockets, scanning the file of passengers heading for the exit. Alison fought through them to fling herself into his arms and to kiss him with undisguised passion, oblivious to the audience around them.

'I think we should get straight to our hotel,' Iain said, as soon as she let him speak.

'Is there a Do Not Disturb sign for the door?'

'First thing I looked for.'

He led her out to the car park, and a minute later they had joined the traffic hurtling down the motorway towards the city centre. Down straight streets dominated by towering buildings, until he turned aside to park in the narrow courtyard behind the weathered grey stone of their hotel. Sign the register, take the keys, journey upwards in a complaining lift, up to the third floor. Unlock the door, and lock it securely behind. Take in nothing of the well-proportioned room under its arched ceiling with its carved cornices thick with cream paint, the neatly covered bed, the pale print curtains fluttering against the nets at an opened window, with the sound of the street rising beyond it. Shut away from everything with everything that mattered. Connect again with this human body, this person who was life itself. Hold me, Iain. Remove all trace of clothing and let me lie with the bristling of your chest pressing my skin, your mouth covering mine so that I can forget about speech and all the misunderstandings which twist us apart. Lie above me, anointing my eyes, my cheeks, my lips, my breasts with your kisses, let your hands move across me, knowing every part of me, my scars and imperfections, where I stand and sit, go in and come out, my breathing and my heartbeat. Let us rise and fall in the rhythm of lovers, and make each other whole.

No need to whisper such words to her lover. He knew. He knew.

Twenty-eight

At half past eight the following night, as Alison, restored to sanity, sat with Iain over dinner in their hotel, Terry Howells was ringing her doorbell. Beside the door, leaning against the brickwork, was a large object shrouded in plastic. He poked at it as he waited for an answer, examining the labels on it and peering through the plastic until he had established that this was the replacement notice board, unceremoniously dumped by the delivery van. His mother-in-law would not be impressed. From what he could see, this board was little different from the existing one: larger, perhaps, but without the glazed panels and strip lighting that Bunty had favoured. He was ready to point this out to Alison, but instead the door was answered by a sulky young woman who looked vaguely familiar.

'Yes?'

'Is Alison in? She wanted me to drop this hymn list off for her.' He held up an A4 envelope.

'Naah, she in't here.'

'She said she'd be in. I needed to go through it with her.'

'She's gone to Glasgow for a couple of days. With a friend. I'm lookin' after Luke. I used to be 'er nanny.'

Glasgow. Now who had he been talking to recently about going to Glasgow this summer? he wondered, as he offered his hand. 'Terry Howells,' he said, while his memory processed the problem. 'I'm organist at St Peter's. She must have forgotten I was coming.' The answer came to him before he'd finished speaking. Sutherland! And surely too much of a coincidence to think that Alison should independently decide to take a break in such a dour city as Glasgow? She was meeting him, she must be; and what did that say about her recent protestations that there was nothing between them? He needed an excuse to question Lisa further.

'Have you seen this?' he asked her, indicating the notice board. 'It shouldn't be left outside all night. Would you like me to give you a hand getting it in?'

Lisa unfolded herself from the doorpost on which she'd been leaning and peered round. 'Oh yeah! Dunno when that come.'

Between them, they managed to manipulate the heavy board inside.

'Gawd, that weighs a ton,' Lisa complained as they let it fall back with a thud against the hall wall. 'Here, are you alright?'

Terry assumed an expression of suffering. 'My back. I think I've pulled something.' He massaged the small of his back. 'Would you mind if I sat down for a couple of minutes, till it wears off?'

'Sure. You don't need a doctor or nothing, do yer?'

'No, no, if I can rest a moment ...' He walked with what he hoped was the correct degree of disablement into the living room, and sat down on the nearest armchair. 'So, Alison's gone to Glasgow,' he essayed. 'That would be to see Iain Sutherland, I imagine. That's where he comes from, isn't it?'

Lisa stared at him. For a few moments she said nothing, then, belatedly, defiantly, said, 'How would I know?'

Terry needed no more. There had been too many other connections between Alison and Sutherland for this trip of hers to Glasgow to be mere coincidence. She'd been suspiciously pally with him from the start. An image returned to his mind of the two of them in the wild garden, 'just showing the Inspector', she'd said, but he'd already seen it. And she'd looked flustered. Egotistically, he'd leapt to the conclusion they'd been discussing him, but perhaps there had been something more dangerous going on. Perhaps she'd even known him before the inspection began. Hadn't he seen them chatting in the car park the moment Sutherland arrived at the school, good God, agreeing to pretend they'd never met before! Terry had no need to press Lisa, he knew.

He stayed another five minutes, to disarm any suspicions Lisa might have had about his questioning, then he left, clutching his new knowledge to him like a fragile treasure. This would ruin Alison, she'd have to leave the parish tomorrow once her behaviour got out, and serve her right. Fancy a Chair of Governors being linked to the Registered Inspector in that way! It hardly seemed credible. It must surely invalidate the whole process. As he drove home, images from the inspection continued to crowd his mind. Alison coming to the school every day, quite unnecessarily. Her defence of the Inspector, when everyone could see the man had the observational capacities of a blindworm. And yes, Sutherland commenting on how often James saw his father, a comment Terry had thought odd at the time. How could he have been that unobservant! This put a whole new complexion on Sutherland's assessment of his own teaching. No question but that the

Inspector had judged that incident with James far more harshly than he should because he was having an affair with the boy's mother. Once let that fact be known, and Sutherland would be finished.

'Shall I put the light out?'

'Mmm.' Alison tightened her hold so that she wouldn't fall away from her resting place on Iain's chest when he stretched out for the switch.

Passion had been satisfied long since, but they had stayed curled in each other's arms talking, while the day moved into tomorrow.

'I don't want to go home,' she said as the darkness dropped around them.

'Stay another night.'

'I can't. I've got to go and collect James and Josh on Friday. Anyway, it's not fair leaving Lisa any longer. Poor girl, I didn't even have time to find out her problems, I simply rushed off here to you.'

'I'm glad you did. I was worried about you down there on your own. I'm not sure you'd have lasted until September.'

'I'm looking forward to staying with you.'

Iain began to nuzzle her ear and her neck. 'I'm looking forward to having you. As many times as possible ...'

Alison laughed and wrapped her leg more tightly around his thigh, certain of her future with him now, and utterly content.

'So what happened with Colin?' Alison asked Lisa as they sat round the kitchen table over a late supper the evening of her return.

Lisa swished the remains of her coffee around a chipped Dennis the Menace mug. 'He hates me. I can't do nothing right. He thinks I'm a lousy mother, 'e complains about me spending money, 'e never touches me, 'e never speaks to me. I couldn't stay with 'im.'

'And what about Karli? How could you leave her?'

Lisa's lip trembled. ''Cos I bloody well am a lousy mother. The health visitor said so, said I neglected 'er.'

'I can't believe you'd do that, Lisa, you're wonderful with children. You are with Luke, or I'd never have employed you.'

'P'raps you don't know me.' Lisa sat biting her lip. Eventually she turned to Alison, and blurted the whole of her story out. The deception with the washing machine, the debt, Colin's discovery of Ryan; then her discussions with Ty, his settlement of her debt in return for proof of her friendship, Karli's infection, and Lisa's final decision to leave.

'I can't look after 'er, not when I done things like that. I can't sleep nights for thinking about her, but I can't go back, I couldn't face him, I'm shit ...' Tears began to course down her face.

Alison put an arm round her. 'No, you're not.' God, where to start in untangling that lot? 'Oh, Lisa, you should have rung me, if it was that bad.'

'You said you wouldn't 'elp. You were on Colin's side.'

'No, I wasn't. I wanted you to be honest with him, that's all.'

'And you never called again, like you said you would.'

'I thought you were still offended because of the money.'

But that was no excuse; she should have got back in touch. In truth, she'd been too preoccupied with the parish and with Iain to have time to spare for Lisa's concerns as well. At least now that things were right with Iain, she could give Lisa her full attention, do what she could to make restitution.

'What's Colin been like with Karli?' she asked, knowing that a long night lay ahead.

Terry had avoided sharing his knowledge with anyone. He wasn't going to listen to Vee making excuses for Alison, or trying to talk him out of the only principled course of action. Out of respect for the parishioners at St Peter's, he had decided to deal with their curate's misconduct by having a quiet word with Father Nigel on his return, rather than exposing her publicly. People would have to know eventually, but it needed careful handling. On Sunday, therefore, Terry sat through both Eucharist and evensong, keeping to himself his deep offence at Alison's hypocrisy. Had he not known the truth, he might have agreed with Ella that it was good to have their priest cheerful and energetic again after her peakiness of the previous few weeks, might have drawn fragments of inspiration from her well-crafted sermons. As it was, he could not bring himself to receive communion from her, and he left as soon as he could after the services, without giving her a chance to speak to him.

Sutherland, however, was another matter. Terry could not resist the opportunity to confront the man with what he knew, to rub his self-righteous face in the shit before it exploded against the fan, to hear him wriggle and squirm in a futile attempt to save his career.

Terry waited until the August Bank Holiday was past, tracked down the phone number of Sutherland's office from school records, and dialled the number.

'Iain Sutherland?' said a polite female voice. 'I can't see him. I thought

I saw his car this morning, so I assume he's here. I'm only just back from holiday, so I haven't caught up with everything yet. Hold on ...'

Terry held on. A clattering indicated the phone being picked up from a desk top.

'Hello? I'm afraid Iain's working on a report at home this week. I can give you his mobile number, only he doesn't always have it switched on, and it might be a while before he sees if there's any messages. If it's urgent, I can give you his home number. If he's busy, his wife will take a message and get him to ring you back.'

'His *wife*?' The words were startled out of him. 'I didn't know he was married.'

'Oh, yes. Has been for years. Second marriage, I think it is. Have you got a pen handy?'

Terry wrote the number down, though he was too shocked to be capable of using it immediately. No wonder they'd been so furtive. If Sutherland was married, the scandal was lifted to another dimension. Even Vee wouldn't be able to excuse Alison when that was what she'd been up to. His only problem now was to get through the next three days until Father Nigel was back, and he could impart his cataclysmic news.

And to work out how he was going to face Alison at their meeting tomorrow night ...

On the first Thursday evening in September, Alison crammed a circle of chairs into her study for the PCC standing committee meeting, and waited as the members arrived: Bunty, still fuming over the fact that the notice board which now gleamed primly by St Peter's lychgate bore so little relation to her visionary designs; Benny Barnes, his bald patch shining pinkly after a summer of exposure; Ella, an early arrival to help set out the chairs, and to check what Alison might want her to say in the meeting; Brian, depositing a bottle of Spanish Rioja on her desk, a present from his holidays. And Terry Howells, who dismissed her friendly comment about the imminent start of term with a monosyllabic grunt.

He sat down on the chair next to her desk and asked, 'Did you enjoy your visit to Glasgow?'

Fear surged through her. Oh God, he knows! Look at his expression! All those dubious explanations and deliberate lies, he knows there's not a word of truth in them. Horror threatened to paralyse her; she struck back at it. How could he know who she'd been to Glasgow with? Or what they'd done there? She had to play cool, face him down.

'Yes, thank you. Did you enjoy your holiday?'

There it was again, the sneer on his face, he must know! She thought her days with Iain had restored her confidence; in an instant it evaporated again, leaving her balancing precariously on the brink of chaos.

She forced herself to look away from Terry as they began the meeting. 'Father Nigel will be back from holiday on Friday,' she said. 'He's hoping to make a start by doing the eight o'clocks.'

'I'm glad to hear it. Every time I turn up for Mass, I find a notice on the church door saying it's been cancelled,' Bunty said.

'It's not happened that often,' Alison said, smoothing her hair back over her head.

'Last Wednesday?'

'I had to go away at the last minute.'

Bunty continued, her voice sharp. 'You're always away. I don't know what you do with yourself. And when you are here, you don't do anything very much as far as I can see. Look at this notice board you made such a palaver about celebrating on Sunday. It's taken you a year and a half to organise something that's virtually a straight replacement for the original one. And there's several people have said to me they've needed to talk to you after a service, and you've been too much in a rush to speak to them. Father Nigel and Father Mark always had time for people.'

'I *do* have time for people. I spend my life listening to people bending my ear about God knows what. How can you possibly say I don't do anything?' She knew she shouldn't rise to the woman's barbs, should let it flow over her like water off a duck's back, only she had lost her water-proofing.

'You do a fine job, now can't we get on?' Brian said.

'Forgive me for not being bloody Father Mark!' Alison carried on, her voice high and brittle as her control lapsed. 'I don't know why I bother. Nothing I do is good enough for you. Well, forgive me for not being perfect! It's only my first curacy, I'm only trying to do two full-time bloody jobs on my own, I realise there's no excuse for making mistakes. I work fourteen hours a day, I neglect my family, I never have any time off, and all you do is complain!' She swallowed hard, she wasn't going to cry.

'We're not complaining,' Ella said, leaning towards her to pat her arm. 'We know you work hard. You do a wonderful job.'

'I happen to dispute that,' Terry came in nastily. 'I do not call cancelling services in order to romp off to Glasgow with Iain Sutherland "doing a wonderful job".'

'Why *shouldn't* I see Iain?' Alison blazed back. 'He's the only person who's cared how I am. You lot don't. You seem to think I can simply take on everything Father Nigel was doing in my stride, but I can't, not without help. Iain's been the only bloody person in my life who's been willing to support me, who's cared ...'

'But Alison, we've all tried to help. You haven't let us. You've always said you were coping.' Ella's bewilderment was genuine.

'Could we adjourn this meeting ...?' Brian's request was lost.

Alison ploughed on, unable to prevent herself. 'You can't blame me for falling in love with him.'

'Oh yes we can,' Terry came in again. 'You had no right to fall in love with a married man.'

'He's not married, not now, he's divorced.'

'He is married. I was trying to get hold of him at his office, and they told me about it.'

'You must have misunderstood. I've been to his house. I've stayed with him ...' No you haven't, said a little voice in her head. You've never got there, he's always put you off. Just like he's always talked about how difficult it would be to marry you. She fought the knowledge away, panicking as she felt herself falling apart. 'Of course he's not married, I wouldn't have an affair with a *married* man ...'

They were staring at her, their collective shock at her admission freezing their expressions, then severally they began to look away, awkward, wishing to be anywhere else. She'd blown everything now, betrayed their trust, let down herself, the church, her entire vocation. Their disappointment in her was tangible.

'It's not what it sounds like ...' she faltered.

'How could it be anything other than what it sounds like?' Bunty asked. 'You've admitted to adultery.'

'We shall have to go to the bishop about this,' Brian said flatly.

Alison's hand went to her mouth. Oh God, what had she done? They wouldn't understand, all they saw was her failure, her betrayal. 'I ... would you excuse me ... I ...' She stood, her papers slipping from her lap unnoticed to the floor. 'I need the toilet.'

She picked up her bag, her heart pounding, and pushed past them to the door, to the hall, to freedom from the humiliation of the things she was going to discover she had said. For a few seconds she paused in the hall. From the living room came the sound of the television in front of which James and Josh were no doubt stretched. Upstairs, Lisa would be weeping into her pillows, refusing to go home, distraught to be away. Alison couldn't face any of them, couldn't go back in her study, couldn't do anything except pull open the front door and head towards the garage.

Into her car, start the engine. Her visitors had parked across the driveway, but it wouldn't stop her. Putting her foot down, she drove across the dry soil of one of James's flower beds, crushing his handiwork as she headed out onto the road.

She scarcely saw Ella and Brian on the doorstep, waving at her to stop; she cared nothing for them now. There was only one place she could go. On to see Iain, to hear him give the lie to the malicious allegations. It wasn't true. It couldn't be true. Impossible. God, please, impossible. The little voice in her head pointed out his reluctance to have her visit his home and his family. She beat it down into silence. Wasn't she going to stay in a couple of weeks? (And hasn't he spun you a story to explain why he's in a rented flat? No!) Hadn't he introduced her to his oldest friends as the woman he was going to marry? He could hardly have done that if he'd got a wife tucked away somewhere. He came and went as he pleased, she could speak to him on his mobile at any hour of the day or night. As to Terry's impression from the office - he'd misunderstood, or no, perhaps Iain had been away with *her* when Terry had rung, and he'd told the office she was his wife, because it sounded better.

It was quarter to eleven by the time Alison arrived in the suburb where Iain lived. She found a late garage and pulled in to ask for exact directions. In a few minutes, she'd be able to lay all the anxiety to rest. She turned down his road with relief, searching for the well-hidden numbers of the large houses with their double driveways and screened gardens. She'd expected something humbler, a semi, where a neighbour's noise penetrated the walls. Her destination, revealed by the white of the street lights, showed her a double-fronted, whitewashed facade standing at the end of a sweep of gravel, with a double garage adjoining it. There were lights on behind the curtains. He'd be thinking about finishing work, about phoning her. He'd be thrilled to find her here on his doorstep instead. Security lights switched into action as she locked her car, and approached the porch.

So successfully had she convinced herself that Terry was mistaken, that when the door opened on a chain, and a faded, fair woman peered round the thick ribbed glass, Alison assumed that he'd moved more quickly than he'd expected.

'Yes?'

'I'm sorry to disturb you. I was looking for Iain Sutherland. Have you got his new address?'

'What new address? He's not moving anywhere that I know of. He's here.'

The woman had a soft, flat voice that suited the expression on the worn face that looked through the chink of the door. She had probably been pretty once, blue-eyed, and blonde, but now her hair was beginning to coarsen to grey, and it was tied back in a pony tail that exposed the worried lines on her face. She wore a grey jogging suit, covered by a nylon tabard. Late though it was, she had to be his housekeeper. Had to be.

'Could I see him?'

'You're Alison, aren't you.' It was a statement, not a question. 'I thought you might turn up one day. He's working. You can go through if you like, but don't think he's ever going to leave me. He's promised. He knows it would kill me.'

She spoke matter-of-factly, an unassuming stream of words that dried Alison's lips and shook her body. Alison could scarcely bring herself to frame her question:

'Who are you?'

'I'm Carol. I'm his wife.'

Twenty-nine

Alison stared at her, gasping for breath, fighting to stay on her feet.

'I don't believe you,' she whispered in a voice withered almost to silence.

'He doesn't like to tell them he's married, not till he wants to get rid of them. You'd better come in.'

Alison followed the pale shape of the overall along the nightmare dark of the passage until Carol stopped and knocked gently on the door at the end, and opened it. 'Visitor for you.'

Iain's voice muttered back, tetchy and all too recognisable. 'You know not to distairb me.'

Carol stepped back, and ushered Alison into the room. 'I'll leave you to it,' she said, shutting the door as she left.

The room fell away from Alison towards distant walls and a high ceiling. A central light, three bulbs concealed by frosted glass bells, illuminated its furthest corners. She stood, paralysed, her hands grimly gripping the doorpost behind her for support as she gazed across the expanse of grey carpet at the man she had thought her own.

Iain had turned to identify his visitor as he spoke, and she saw the shock hit him as he recognised her. He froze where he sat, right hand resting on the keyboard of the laptop propped on the desk in front of him, left arm across the back of his chair, white shirtsleeves rolled up, the eyes that met hers full of foreboding.

She found her voice at last, a thin, flat sound that soughed towards him. 'You're married.'

He moved at last, turning his chair back round to his desk to drop his head in his hands.

'I can't believe you'd deceive me like that. All those lies. You must have known I'd find out. Oh, Iain ...' The tears were beginning to rise to her eyes; she bit her lip hard in a vain effort to hold them back.

'I couldn't face losing you,' he said through his hands. A minute went by, then he turned to face her again. 'Could you come and sit down.'

His head indicated a large leather armchair next to his desk. He saw her hesitation. 'There are things I need to say.'

Alison let go of the doorpost, and made her way unsteadily towards him. The seat was cold and smooth beneath her legs as she sat, arms wrapped around herself in a bewilderment of misery. 'How could you?'

'I fell in love with you. There never seemed to be a time when I could say.'

'Didn't you think it might be important?'

'Of course I did. I tried to tell you several times. In Rome - do you remember when the flower seller came? I was on the edge of telling you. Then you said you'd never get involved with a married man, and I couldn't bring myself to risk it.'

The picture was fresh in her memory: Iain sitting across the table, being cynical about the enduring power of love, and stoical about duty. She'd been upset and he'd comforted her, bound her ever more closely to him. What would she have done had he made his confession alone with her, so far from home?

'And at Moira's, she was very cross with me on the Friday evening, and I meant to, but you were under enough strain in your parish and I couldn't bring myself to make things worse for you. I know I should have persisted, but it was always easier not to. To have a few more hours and days without you knowing. I'm sorry.'

'God, I've been stupid. All those things I should have picked up. Why you were so strange about the inspection, and Terry; why your sister didn't want me in the house. No wonder you never let me come here. You were always going to find a way round it, weren't you? Forgetting conferences, arranging for us to go away together ... and pretending you were selling up, so you had an excuse for inviting me to a rented flat! I can't believe you could be this underhand. I trusted you. I never thought ... you of all people! Banging on about how important your integrity was.'

Iain looked away. 'I'm sorry,' he said again.

'Sorry! What good is that? You've been deceiving me deliberately for ... ever since you met me. You've persuaded your friends to lie to me!' She thought again of Moira, and Ros, and the undercurrents that she had noticed, and failed to take seriously. 'They must have thought me so naive. Is it a habit, like Carol said? You have affairs, and then when you're fed up, you say, "oh, by the way, I'm married", and it's all over?'

He shook his head. 'It's not like that. It's nothing like that.' He met her eyes again. 'I told you there'd been one or two others. I told you about

Carol, everything except that I'd married her. I knew it was a mistake almost immediately, but then Carol wasn't well, she got very depressed after she lost her boys, and there was Hetty.'

'Your "neighbour's daughter". It was so bloody obvious! Why didn't I even think she might be yours?'

'She's only my stepdaughter, but I am very fond of her. I'm still fond of Carol, in my way, I just don't want to be married to her. It was the biggest mistake of my life, but I thought I was in love with her. And she needed me. Her ex would never have left her Hetty, if she'd been on her own. I saw myself taking care of her, and helping her to get well, only she hasn't. She lost interest in sleeping with me after a few months, and to be honest, it was mutual. I've not shared a room with her, or slept with her, for years. But she wasn't going to cope on her own, so I promised I'd stay and look after her and Hetty, and she agreed I could have other relationships if I wanted. It's like I told you, Allie, there've been a few brief relationships, and then there's been you. And you bowled me over. I wanted you more than any woman I've ever met, right from the start.'

'But you're still married to her,' she said dully, 'and you don't seem to be trying to leave.'

He had been sitting hunched forward in his chair, his hands clasped together. Now he reached out to take her hand, pulling it towards him. Alison let it lie there, encased by his fingers.

'I want to,' he said. 'The first thing I did when I got back from Rome was to ask her for a divorce, and I've been trying ever since, but she says she can't cope.' Iain shook his head. 'I know it's emotional blackmail, but it works. If I try and leave, Carol gets more and more depressed, mebbe ends up in hospital again. Mebbe you say I could take Hetty to live with you, but I couldn't live with myself if I forced her to lose her daughter, not when she's lost her sons already. She's my responsibility, and I don't see how I can escape unless she agrees to let me go.'

'But what about *me*? Don't you care about how *I* feel? You've let me fall in love with you, and risk my whole career, and rely on you, because you've been the only bloody friend I've got, and all the time, it's been a lie.' A huge sob escaped her.

Iain was on his knees immediately, taking her in his arms. 'I'm sorry, Allie. I know I should have been honest at the start, but I couldn't bear the thought of losing you.'

She let herself rest on his shoulder for a moment. 'But you have lost

271

me now, and it's far, far worse, because we've come to mean so much to each other.'

'I can't have lost you. You need me.'

The door opened. They turned, startled.

'I thought you might like a cup of tea,' Carol said, pushing the door aside with her shoulder and coming in with a tray.

Alison dropped her head.

'Please, Carol, we're trying to talk,' Iain said, getting back onto his chair.

'What is there to talk about?' Carol said, putting mugs down on the corner of his desk. 'This has happened before, Alison. He's thought he was in love with someone, and started talking about divorce, but it hasn't lasted. This will go the same way. I know you think it won't, but I've known Iain a long time. I wouldn't force him to stay with us if he hated us, but we're fond of each other, and Hetty thinks of him as her father. I can't throw that away. I'm sorry he's treated you badly, but that's the way he is.' Her footsteps susurrated across the carpet, there was a small click as she gripped the door handle.

'Does he sleep with you?' Alison asked suddenly, looking up.

Carol turned round, and looked first at Iain and then back at her.

'Please be honest. I need to know.'

'Not for several years,' Carol said. 'I don't much care for that sort of thing.'

'She wouldn't lie about that, would she?' Iain said as Carol left them. 'I've never even thought about being unfaithful to you, that I can promise you.' He reached out for her hand again. 'She's wrong about it happening before. I've never felt this way about anyone else.'

Alison shook her head. 'I don't believe we're talking about it like this. It's not real. It's not true. It can't be.' She reached out for the tea she didn't want, as if like some magic potion it could restore normality.

'The only truth is that I can't marry you as yet. I still love you, you love me, that hasn't changed. What's wrong with carrying on as we are?'

'I'm a priest, Iain. I shouldn't have slept with you in the first place. I've got by because I could tell myself this was the real thing, and that we'd be getting married as soon as my divorce was through. I can't be the mistress of a married man.'

'Then give up being a priest. You could come and get a job here, go back to teaching, and I could see you practically every day. If you really loved me, you would.'

'If you really loved me, you'd have been honest with me from the start. I can no more abandon my vocation than you can give up your duty to your family.'

They stared at each other until Alison could bear it no longer and dropped her eyes. On her lap, his hand clutched hers, the skin with its tufts of hair and familiar markings, the narrow folds of flesh around his knuckles; fingers that had brushed her breasts and parted her thighs and never would again. A tear welled in her, and fell on his wrist.

Immediately he seized her in his arms again. 'I will divorce her. I've got grounds, I must have. I can fix something up for her, and we can get married and be together. And in the meantime, we can still meet, even if you don't want to be lovers. I can live with that.'

'I can't! How could I live with myself if I'd dragged you away from your family, when they need you? And I'd never be allowed to marry you if I was the one who broke your marriage up.'

'But if Carol agrees ...'

'It doesn't make any difference. The church doesn't approve of divorce very much at the best of times. If I was implicated, it'd be out of the question.'

'Then let's not meet for a while. Give ourselves a couple of years while I sort things out, and then we meet up again, and it wouldn't look as if it was anything to do with you.'

'Of course it would. People know about us, Iain, they'd know you'd left your wife because of me, however long we left it without seeing each other.'

'I can't accept that. There must be something we can do. Just give it time, Allie. Promise you'll wait for me.'

'And how long am I supposed to give you? Five years? Ten? Twenty? God, Iain, aren't you content with wrecking everything? Am I supposed to hang around waiting for you the rest of my life, without being able to see you, or even talk to you, just on the off chance Carol forgets what a good deal she's got, or goes under a bus? She can't even do that, can she? She doesn't go out. It's over. I can't ever see you again. There's no way round it.'

'Never?' He was crying too now, quiet tears glistening on his cheeks.

'Ever, never, what are words? How can I say? I only know what I have to do now.'

Iain stood up and walked towards the window. The curtains remained undrawn. He leaned his forehead against the dark glass. It was a while

273

before he spoke, his voice back under control:

'Why did you come?'

'I went to pieces at our standing committee. Bunty was going on at me about how I'd done everything wrong, and I couldn't take it. I started saying things about you, and then Terry accused me of having an affair with you - I don't know how he found out, but he knew I'd gone to Glasgow with you. Then he said you were married, he'd tried to ring your office and they'd mentioned your wife. I didn't believe it. I couldn't, but I had to see you, to make it alright. Only you haven't, you can't. I don't know what I'm going to do. I've disgraced myself, I can't go back, I can't stay with you ...' She began to cry again.

He came back and crouched at her feet, putting his hands on her shoulders. 'If you've walked out anyway, it's alright. You can come here, we can be together.'

'I haven't stopped being a priest. They'll give me another chance somewhere as long as I'm repentant. And I am. I wish I'd never met you.' She blew her nose, careless of the way her make-up must by now be smeared over her face.

'Don't say that.'

'It's true.'

Round in circles, no way out. It's over, no, there's some way round it. Wait for me, I can't. They were clinging on to this last encounter, prolonging it, stretching the pain as if by so doing they could render it manageable. One o'clock. Two o'clock. I must go. Home. Somewhere. Anywhere. Two forty-five. Three-fifteen. Finally she stood up, pushing Iain's hands away from her. They stood in the middle of the room, looking at each other.

'So this is it.' She gave a little shrug. Tears filled her eyes again, dripping over her face, hot, tight, sore.

Iain stepped forward and held her. It tore her heart to see the tears that brimmed over in his eyes. He had removed his glasses hours ago, tired of wiping them continually. His hand cradled her head, easing it back so that he could find her lips with his own. A last kiss, a passionate exchange with salty lips and wet faces sliding against each other in inconsolable longing.

'Allie, stay with me. Even if you still say you have to go, we could have one last night together ...' He kissed her ear, his breath warm in her hair. 'Please. You can't go in this state. It's too late.'

He kissed her again. For a few seconds she let herself think of giving way, of letting him carry her to his room, of surrendering her senses to him again ... only there would still be a final goodbye to be said.

'It'll only make things worse. Let me go.'

He dropped his hands empty to his sides.

'Goodbye,' she whispered, and, with a final effort of will, she was free to falter towards the door, to lurch out of the room, down the passage, and out through the front door to her car.

She drove vaguely back in the direction from which she had come a few hours before, before the ending of the world. Out of the town, out onto the wide dual-carriageway going beyond to anywhere. She couldn't face going home, had nowhere else to turn. Seeing a parking sign, she pulled up, switched off the engine, and collapsed over her steering wheel beside the silent road, to give herself up to her agony, despairing and alone.

Thirty

Karli slipped from Lisa's reach again, floating up and away from her towards the sun, while she stretched frantically, blinded by the light, striving to bring her back. A second later, and Lisa was awake, with the living room light shining brightly onto her face, and Karli long gone. Her own misery absorbed her, and it was some minutes before she registered what she was doing, sleeping uncomfortably on Alison's sofa with the clock showing a quarter past four. She got up, wincing as her stiffened joints took her weight. No sign that Alison had returned, but Lisa dragged herself upstairs to check. The empty bedroom smelled faintly of Alison's usual perfume, but the bed was flat and unoccupied.

'I'm afraid she got upset, and walked out,' Ella had said, having summoned Lisa to a tense study the previous evening to offer an explanation for Alison's absence, and the raised voices of the last half hour. 'Then Terry told her her friend Iain was married, so we think she's probably gone to him, I don't know what she'll do next.'

'Mum?'

Lisa turned to see Josh, pale-faced with blinking eyes, gazing in through the door of the bedroom. 'You should be in bed,' she said.

'Where is she? Why isn't she back? Do you think something's happened to her? Perhaps we should call the police.'

'She's prob'ly gone to see 'er friend, only I 'aven't got the number, so I can't check. She's just upset after that row at the meeting, she'll be back tomorrow, don't worry.'

'What if she has an accident? What if she never comes back?'

'Sshhh.' Lisa hugged him. 'Course she'll be back. She'd never leave you on your own.'

'You left your baby.'

'Yeah, but that was different. Go on, Josh, you go off to bed, I'm sure she'll be back by morning.'

She pushed him towards his bedroom, his shoulders bent with misery. How dare Alison disappear and worry them like that? 'You left your baby

...' Yeah, but Colin would have been glad to see the back of her, and Karli would have forgotten her by now. Only one person hurt in all that, and she bloody well deserved it. Lisa headed slowly for the stairs, and went down to continue her vigil.

An hour weeping, now where? Alison started her engine and pulled out onto the road with no destination in mind. She was parched, the swallow of tea she'd had at Iain's long since cried out of her. She slowed down as a garage appeared ahead of her, all green and yellow, neon lights fading as the first glimmers of sun rose in the east. Twenty-four hour service. Alison pulled in, visited the toilet, and bought herself black coffee in a plastic cup from the machine on the forecourt.

The woman hidden behind the security grille watched her. 'You alright, love?'

Alison forced her lips into a smile. 'No.'

'Can I help?'

'No,' she said again. 'Thanks.'

'You lost someone?' The woman had a lonely job, she must rely on her infrequent customers for conversation.

'I've just broken up with ... with the man I thought I was going to marry.'

'Aw, I'm sorry. Men, I dunno, they can't see a good thing when it's under their noses. I 'ad one like that ...'

Alison was saved from hearing a life history by the arrival of a lorry. While the driver paid, she walked back to her car, sat until she had drained the coffee, and got back on the road. A lorry sweeping past her shook her car, and she nearly lost control. I'm not fit to drive, she thought. But then, what does it matter? What have I got to live for? If I can't have Iain, why should I carry on? It would be very easy, a touch of the steering wheel, and she and her car would be flattened by a juggernaut of those dimensions. The boys might miss her at first, but they'd got their dad and their beloved Anthea. Luke was too young to remember her. And Iain would no doubt find consolation in his wife, or some other idiot who was too desperate to have a man to be capable of sense.

She crested the brow of a rise in the landscape. Another large lorry was approaching. Why not do it? Imagination swerved her into the front of it, tossed her car up and aside in a clamour of metal to lie crushed yards from the road, while the lorry came to a halt and the driver clambered unhurt from his cab to find what he'd done. The curate of St Peter's, mother

277

of three, unrecognisable, she died instantly. Fell asleep with exhaustion ... chose it as a way out, abandoning her children, her babies, all because she couldn't have the one thing she wanted.

The lorry disappeared in her rear view mirror. She wouldn't do it, couldn't. Not after seeing the devastation wrought by sudden death in the families whose funerals she took. And besides, if she was going to do anything dramatic, if she really couldn't bear it, all she had to do was to turn right round and go back to Iain. No one's loss then but her own.

The road was quiet. She stopped at the entrance to a field, and bowed her head. Oh God. I'm sorry. I've done it again, fallen in love with someone I can't have, only this is far, far worse than Michael, and at least I could still keep him as a friend ... Michael's smile rose before her; their argument inconsequential in the face of her tragedy. On what other doorstep could she turn up at dawn, with the first glow of daylight bringing the trees out of shadow, and know she would be accepted? She started her engine and pulled away in the direction of Greathampton.

Michael answered her ring himself, tousle-haired in faded shorts, shivering as the outside air caught his bare chest.

'Allie! What on earth? What's the matter? Not the children ...?'

The concern on his face brought tears to her eyes again.

'Come in.' He put an arm round her and drew her inside. 'Come through.' He eased her down onto the sofa and sat next to her with his arm around her while she sought words to convey the disaster that had overtaken her.

'It's Iain,' she managed to say eventually. 'He's married. He never told me ... Oh, Michael.'

'The bastard! God, I could kill him.'

'He's not a bastard. He loves me, he only did it 'cos he loves me, and I'm never going to see him again! I want to die. I nearly drove into a lorry ... help me ...'

Michael's arms tightened around her as sobs shook her body again, and he rocked her as if she were Lyddy after a fall, murmuring comfort into her ear.

The door clicked. Michael's embrace stiffened. Alison lifted her head. Jenny stood in the doorway, her stomach ballooning under a red cotton nightshirt, staring at their embrace as at a nightmare become reality.

Michael detached Alison gently, and stood up, leaving her to collapse doubled up onto the cushions, like a scarecrow removed from its post.

'What the hell are you doing?' Jenny asked, her voice shaking. 'What's she here for?'

'She's found out that Iain's married, and that he never had any intention of leaving his wife.'

'So she thought she'd come round and try and persuade my husband to leave me?'

'So she thought she'd try to kill herself, only fortunately she didn't quite have the nerve. So she came here as the one place she thought she could turn up feeling suicidal at six in the morning and find a welcome.'

Silence ensued as Michael and Jenny regarded each other. Years of suspicion and mishandled friendship concentrated in this single moment.

'I'm sorry. I was wrong. I'll go,' Alison said, trying to gather her resources to rise and leave them, God knew for where.

'No, you're not wrong,' Jenny said at last. 'Michael will help. Go on, Michael, she needs you. I'll be in the kitchen if you want me. I'll make some tea.'

As she passed, she reached out and touched Alison's shoulder lightly. 'I'm sorry,' she said.

Shortly after half-six, the phone woke Lisa from another fitful sleep on the corner of the sofa. She stumbled through to Alison's study to take the call.

'Yeah?'

'Oh, Lisa, it's Michael here. We've got Allie with us.'

'Thank God for that! Everyone's doin' their nut over 'ere, thinkin' she's 'ad an accident.'

'She went to see Iain, and found out it's true, he is married, so she came here. She's very upset, so Jenny's put her to bed with a few sleeping pills, and we'll see what to do when she wakes up.'

A movement caught Lisa's eye as Josh appeared in the doorway.

'Is that mum?' he whispered.

Lisa put her hand over the phone. 'No, but she's at Michael's. She's OK.'

'And what about you, Lisa?' Michael asked. 'You've had people pretty worried about you this end. We'd no idea where you'd gone till Allie turned up here and told us. Colin's been trying to trace you.'

'I bet!'

'He has. He's got himself a new job, and I've been having Karli.'

'But I left 'er with Midge.'

279

'Colin thought he ought to have her himself. You need to talk to him, Lisa, now he's not so tired, he's realised how badly he was treating you. Give him a chance.'

'Tha's not that simple,' Lisa said. 'But I was thinking of comin' over sometime. I wanna know how Karli is. Soon as Allie's back.'

Lisa finished the call, and turned to find James had joined Josh in the doorway, one on each door jamb. 'She's havin' a rest at Michael's,' she told them. 'She'll let us know when she'll be back. So go on, back to bed, you look like death. Tha's where I'm goin', soon as the bloody phone stops,' she added as the instrument summoned her again.

'Allie?' said a breathless voice.

'Nah, she in't 'ere. It's Lisa.'

'Is she there? I don't have to speak to her, I only want to know she's alright. She wasn't in a fit state to drive when she left here, and ...'

Though Lisa had never spoken to Iain, the caller could be no one else.

'How dare you ring here? Haven't you bloody well done enough?'

'Just tell me she's alright.'

'Of course she's not, now piss off!'

Lisa slammed the phone down. The boys were watching her. 'Well, he deserves it, the bastard,' she told them.

As an afterthought, she activated the answerphone, and followed the boys upstairs and back to bed.

'It's her own fault,' Terry insisted again, as he had done ever since he came and broke the news of Alison's flight to his wife.

'But if she didn't know he was married, if she thought he was going to marry her - you can't judge her for that. We did it before we were married.'

'Yes, but she's got a husband already. And it's different if you're a priest.'

He mopped his moustache to remove the milk that had escaped from his mouthfuls of cereal. He'd had a bad night, wakefully rerunning the confrontation in Alison's house, and its aftermath. He had pursued the truth about Alison and the Inspector with righteous zeal, felt the glow of triumph when his suspicions were confirmed, but now he had the uncomfortable feeling that he had only been playing games. Reality was watching Alison crumple, first under Bunty's attack and then his own cruel revelation. Wanting to gloat, he had instead felt a measure of sympathy.

'Ring and see how she is,' Vee had urged before they began breakfast. 'Say you're sorry you sprung it on her like that.'

Terry had obliged, only to hear from Lisa that Alison had not come home but, having found out the truth from Sutherland's own lips, was now in a state of collapse with friends in Greathampton. Luke had been roaring in the background, Lisa irritable, Alison's home in as much turmoil as she herself. And all definitely her own fault.

'She wasn't to know Sutherland would turn out to be a cheat,' Vee continued. 'He seemed so nice.'

Terry snorted. 'Inspectors have to be callous and unprincipled to do their job, she should have known not to trust him.'

'What are you going to do about him? You'll have to report him. He deserves everything that's coming to him after treating her like that.'

'I don't know. I don't feel like it.'

'Come on, Terry, you can't let him get away with it.'

He phoned Sutherland reluctantly, to escape her nagging. From the first few seconds, the call failed to go to plan.

'This is Terry Howells,' he'd announced when Sutherland answered.

'Something's happened to Allie! Tell me she's alright! I knew I should never have let her drive off in that state ...'

'It's not Alison,' Terry broke in. 'She's alright. Or as right as she can be after what you did to her.'

'Are you sure?'

'Yes. She's with friends in Greathampton.'

'Thank God for that. I've been worried sick about her, but Lisa wouldn't tell me anything.' Sutherland seemed to collect himself. 'What did you want? Allie said you rang my office the other day.'

'I know all about your relationship with her during the inspection. I'm going to get the school to file an official complaint.' Terry proceeded to detail his allegations, wishing he could recover the fervid indignation with which he had first reacted to them.

Sutherland listened without comment. When Terry finished, there was a pause. 'You've not got your facts right,' he said, 'but I cannot say I much care at the moment. I've been working my way through a bottle of whisky ever since Allie left, and I don't much care about anything.' He could be heard blowing his nose; a period of silence followed that Terry could find no words to break. 'I was wrong not to tell Allie I was married, but I've always done my job correctly,' Sutherland continued. 'I didn't meet her until after the inspection, the worst I did was to ask her right at the end whether I might ring her once my report was in. That's not a sackable offence. I always treated her exactly as I always treat Chairs of governing bodies.'

'But I saw you talking to her in the car park.'

'What of it? I talked to everybody. I noticed Allie when I came to the school, of course I did, but it made no difference to anything. I didn't meet her until the July, then I saw her three or four more times that year, and we became lovers last January. We haven't even met that often. Not often enough.' His voice shook on the last phrase. Terry heard the indrawn breath that suggested Sutherland was fighting for control.

'But you approached her during the inspection. That means you were biassed. That's why you misreported my spat with James.'

'I did no such thing,' Sutherland said wearily. 'I take the integrity of my job very seriously. There were others observing you, you know that. An inspection report always represents the considered view of the whole team, and there was no complaint from your school. And I seem to remember Allie saying your History results this summer were way improved over last year's, so you can't argue your Head made the wrong choice for Head of Department. Of course you can make trouble for me if you persist with these accusations, but I don't know why you should want to. I don't know why you've been dead set on pursuing me, I was only doing my job, as well as I could.'

'You broke confidentiality about James,' Terry tried.

'I thought Allie explained she lied about that. I'd not have said anything. I've always refused to discuss any aspect of your inspection with her, just to protect myself.'

Terry began to feel foolish. Sutherland's answers had the ring of truth, with no trace of the guilty defensiveness Terry had expected. Not innocent, but hardly indictable.

'I don't know what you're planning to do, but please don't make things worse for Allie. She's been hurt enough already. I've hurt her enough already.'

'Oh, forget it,' Terry replied, detecting the maudlin note distorting Sutherland's voice. 'Just don't do it again.'

He put the phone down and turned to find Vee staring incredulously at him: '"Don't do it again!" What a stupid thing to say! You're not going to let him get away with it?'

Terry avoided her eyes. His talk with Sutherland had left him unaccountably depressed. 'He's not got away with anything.'

Thirty-one

Alison lay back on the sun-lounger halfway down Nan's garden, A light breeze fluttered across her face, easing the soreness of skin given only rudimentary cleansing with cold water and soap after she'd woken in Michael and Jenny's bed an hour before. Her eyes felt gritty with yesterday morning's make-up, and her senses had not fully thrown off the sleeping pills Jenny had given her, which had mercifully knocked her out for most of the day. Her hair was unbrushed and pulled roughly back into its clip. A mess, but who cared?

Nan was sitting beside her on a plastic chair, leaning forward, waiting for her to finish the story.

'I didn't mean to sleep with him,' Alison said, 'not until I was divorced, and I could see him legitimately. I hated having to be underhand, but things were so awful in the parish that I needed someone to escape to, someone to rely on. I'd have cracked up months ago if it hadn't been for Iain ringing me practically every night, and helping me get things in perspective. I tried so hard, Nan, I really did, I kept going however tired I was, and I never complained - well, only to Iain. That's one of the things that got to me last night, Bunty saying I was lazy and couldn't be bothered with people.'

'Everyone's let you down pretty badly, in my opinion,' Nan said. 'I include you letting yourself down. You shouldn't have been getting involved in a serious relationship, let alone a sexual one, not before you were divorced, though I do know how easily one falls into temptation, believe me. But no one should have had to bear all the responsibility you have, without anyone at all looking out for you. I think I ought to go and make a few phone calls, see what your churchwardens are saying - it's Ella I should talk to, presumably, rather than Bunty? And I'll have a word with your rural dean. Did you say Nigel is back from holiday today?'

'Tonight, I think. You can't land this on his plate, he'll have a relapse.'

'He needs to be involved. I won't be long.'

Nan went inside to phone, leaving Alison to rest her head against the cushions, her eyes shut. Birds argued in the tall trees in the dell beyond

Nan's back fence. Long ago - six years, was it? - she'd sat here and dared to say: 'I've been wondering about ordination'. God, what a mess she'd made of everything. Michael had appeared to encourage her, virtual strangers though they were, just as he'd encouraged her to come here to Nan to make a clean breast of the last eighteen months, and let her decide what should happen next. What did it matter, if her future no longer held Iain? In idle moments, her thoughts had become accustomed to turning towards him. I have a lover. I am loved. A secure foundation on which she'd built and grown these last months while all around her crumbled. Hot tears seeped out from under her eyelids.

As she reached into her bag for a fresh tissue, her fingers encountered a small plastic wallet. Knowing she shouldn't, she nevertheless took it out and opened it up. There he sat with the buildings of the Forum rising behind him, his jumper knotted loosely round his neck. He held a sandwich in his hands, and he was laughing at her. 'I'm no taking a bite with that trained on me ...' His face was open, with no trace of the strain he'd said he felt in deceiving her. His smile crinkled his eyes behind his glasses, lit his face. Why didn't you tell me? she called to him. Right at the start? I'd have found an excuse to meet you sometimes, I might have fallen in love with you, but I'd not have centred my life round you. I'd not have slept with you, damn you, let you come to mean everything to me ...

'That was fun,' Nan said, reappearing a quarter of an hour later.

Alison opened her eyes. A squirrel, startled by Nan's appearance, halted its investigation of her stone bird bath, and darted across the grass, to disappear over the fence.

Nan sat down. 'I should have been a bishop, the way I've been throwing my weight around. I hope your rural dean wasn't a favourite of yours, because I've been giving him a good rollicking for not looking after you better. I told him a lesser woman or man would have cracked much sooner than you did. Then I spoke to Ella. She feels very badly about what's happened. Shocked you should have been having an affair with this gentleman whom she rather liked, and upset that you should have been in such a state and not told her. It sounds as if they're all feeling devastated by what happened last night, and they'd like you to come back so you can explain things to them, help them to make sense of it. My impression is that even Bunty and Terry might be prepared to forgive you so long as you're really repentant.'

'I can't believe that.'

'You've just been telling me how much effort you've put in; people do notice, you know, even if they don't say anything.'

'But no one's going to respect me now, however sorry I am. I suppose it's all round the church by now. All round the town, probably, and the school, and ... Oh, God, what will Alex say?'

'It's only the standing committee knows about Iain. Your rural dean knows there was someone, but not the name, and obviously Nigel will have to be told, but the committee decided it would be bad publicity for St Peter's to have a scandal get out. They've just given out you've had a bit of a breakdown through overwork.'

'The one thing I was trying to avoid,' Alison said. And all Iain's advice come to nothing. Her eyes fell on the picture, still lying in her lap.

'Is that him?' Nan asked.

Alison handed her the photograph. 'He doesn't look like a lying bastard, does he?'

'No.' Nan studied it, and passed it back. 'Rather nice, actually.'

'I ought to tear it up and throw it away, but I can't quite ...'

'You won't feel up to anything at the moment, I don't imagine,' Nan said. 'You've been through a lot in the last twenty-four hours. You stay the night here, and we'll talk about it again in the morning. You can have supper with us. We've got Becky bringing Ty Nixon, of all the boyfriends she could have chosen, and she's going to show us what a reformed character he is. Christopher can't stand the idea. He's in black from head to toe, which is always a worrying sign.'

'Ty's not that bad now. He came to the Wellesley Festival last year, and he was OK.'

'Well, you're doubly welcome if you get on with him. Michael and Jenny are coming to help keep the peace as well, I expect they said.' She considered Alison for a moment. 'Could I say something to you? You won't take offence?'

Alison shook her head.

'I can understand you turning to Michael this morning. I know you've been close, and I know there's no question of the two of you overstepping the mark again, so you wouldn't think there was any harm in it. You'll be thinking you need all the friends you can get, and knowing Michael, he'll have said he wants to help. It's just that I think you'd make life an awful lot easier for Jenny - well, for both of them - if you left them alone.'

'I'm no threat,' Alison said. 'Jenny knows that now. She's been really kind to me.'

'She would be. She tries very hard to be generous, and she doesn't like to be possessive about Michael. But the fact remains, the time they were happiest in their marriage was the time you left them alone.'

Alison put her hands to her face, and shut her eyes for a moment, contemplating a future bare of comfort and encouragement from Michael.

'Use other people for your support,' said Nan. 'Use me.' She reached out a hand, and laid it on Alison's shoulder. 'I'm not quite as lovely as Michael, but I can offer you spiritual counselling. Or gin, of course, if you think getting quietly paralytic would be more helpful.'

Alison smiled. 'That sounds tempting.'

'It does, doesn't it? You know, if tonight goes badly, I might even join you.'

Once Colin had found out where Lisa was, he decided to take Karli with him, and go straightaway to have things out with her. He collected their car from the garage where it had been repaired, thanks to his parents' loan, and arrived at Alison's house in the early evening. Leaving Karli asleep in the car, he crossed the gravel, and rang the doorbell.

No one answered. He tried again, and knocked loudly, surely they couldn't all be out? Perhaps they'd got fed up with answering the door to inquisitive parishioners. He walked along the front of the house, opened the side gate into the back garden, and tried the handle of the back door. It swung gently open, and he stepped inside.

He called, 'Hello?'

Light footsteps sounded in the hall, the kitchen door burst open, and a small boy with a huge smile on his face rushed in calling 'Mummy!' in a delighted voice. He took one look at Colin and burst into tears, standing rigidly while tears sprayed horizontally from his eyes.

Two seconds later, Lisa was there, her arms round the child as he howled his disappointment. She looked up at Colin as if she were afraid.

'I'm sorry,' he said. 'No one answered the door and this one was open, so I came in.'

'He thought you was 'is mum. Hush, Lukey, you know she said she was coming back tomorrow.'

She stroked the child's hair, and at last he relaxed enough to put his arms round her neck, pressing his distraught face against her cheek. 'You'd think 'e was used to 'er being away, but 'e's picked up there's things wrong.' She stood up, still cradling Luke in her arms. 'Where's Karli? Did you leave her with Michael?'

'No, she's in the car. She's asleep.'

Lisa bit her lip and moved to the window. 'You got it mended.'

'My parents lent us some money. I've left the restaurant. I've got a job at that new bookshop in the High Street, starting next week. Oh, Lise, I feel completely different now I've left the restaurant. I'm sorry about how I've treated you. You can do childminding if you want, we'll get a better flat. Let's try again?'

She pulled a face. 'You wouldn't say that if you knew everything.'

He watched her as she spoke, the swing of her hair, the outline of her breast against Luke's body. A wife that any man in his senses would desire, yet he'd rebuffed her repeatedly, and who could blame her for turning to other men?

'I don't want to know,' he said. 'Whatever you've done, it was my fault too. I want to start again. Let me stop with you tonight?'

Her eyes rested on his face. 'I need to tell you, Col. Then if you still wanna have another go, we could. See 'ow it goes, anyhow.' She grinned suddenly. 'Tha's not like you, sayin' you was wrong, sayin' I can do what I like. Wha's changed you?'

Colin smiled back. 'Michael said I was a complete wanker. I realised he was right.'

'Well, tha's something we got in common. There's hope for us yet.'

Becky arrived with Ty a few minutes earlier than expected. Alison remained where she was, chopping salad vegetables in Nan's kitchen, but she could hear Becky in the living room, on edge, over-loud and laughing too much. Ty too seemed nervous, greeting Christopher and Nan with an inappropriate heartiness which he didn't seem to be able to shake off. Things got slightly easier when Michael and Jenny arrived. Michael could always be relied on to oil social functions, and once the alcohol was flowing, they all started to relax.

The table was laid neatly with shining silverware and damask mats on the white of the tablecloth. Candles flickered, barely visible as the rays of the evening sun overpowered them. Alison sat safely between Michael and Nan, following Christopher's polite attempts to converse with Tyrone with the surface of her mind, while she tried to dull everything else going on inside her with the wine that kept appearing in her glass. Ty was talking with a touch of arrogance about the importance of his work, but Becky was gradually settling down as if she had decided that they were going to get through the evening after all. Conversation turned to the Wellesley

Festival; one of the few neutral experiences Ty and Christopher had shared.

'Becky was most entertaining on the panel, and Michael. Then we had a Headteacher, and who was it ...?' Christopher ploughed on, failing to register the quelling glance Michael was trying to send him. 'The Inspector. Iain Sutherland, that's right. Do you ever see anything of him, Alison? I said I'd send him an article he might be interested in ... Have I said the wrong thing?'

With the exception of Ty, who was pouring yet more wine for himself, they were all looking at Christopher, speechless in the face of his solecism.

Alison shook her head, and felt the tears rising to her eyes again. To avoid losing control, she downed the contents of her glass and stretched out her hand for the bottle to refill it.

'There's obviously something I don't know. I beg your pardon,' Christopher said. 'Could you pass me some more salad, Nan?'

'I was seeing him, and now I'm not,' Alison said, feeling the need to explain, and taking refuge in the anaesthetic properties of her glass once more.

'Sorry for putting my foot in it. Let's change the subject.'

'Have you got everything ready for the baby?' Nan asked Jenny. 'I don't envy you having three little ones to look after.'

'I've been getting in some practice with Karli Blatherwycke,' Michael said. 'It's a doddle until they all want carrying at once.'

'I don't know what Colin will do when you can't have her any longer,' Jenny said.

'With any luck he'll have made things up with Lisa.' Michael turned to Alison. 'He's over there now, paying her a visit, so let's hope she's feeling forgiving.'

'It's more a question of whether he'll forgive her, once he finds out,' Alison said, her words unaccountably slurred. 'Though it's hardly her fault if certain men treat her like shit and take advantage of her.' She glared at Tyrone.

'Colin was under a lot of pressure at work,' Michael said. 'He knows he deserved a lot of what she said.'

'I wasn't thinking of Colin,' Alison said, continuing to stare at Tyrone.

Becky followed the direction of her gaze and accosted Ty. 'Have you got something to do with this?'

'Me? Don't be stupid! That was over years ago.'

'Then why couldn't you leave her alone?' Alison inquired.

'What's been going on, Ty?' Becky asked.

'She asked me round, if you want to know.' Ty said, pausing to drain his glass. 'She had this idea about selling some nasty story about her husband to the tabloids, and she thought I'd be able to help, being a specialist as I am. I wouldn't do it. She needed some cash, so I gave it to her.' He shrugged. 'That's it.'

'In return for services rendered,' Alison said.

'Keep your mouth shut!' Ty blared.

Becky turned to face him. 'You slept with her!'

'Could we leave the recriminations for another time, do you think?' Christopher asked. 'It's hardly fair to have all this arguing with Jenny in her condition.'

'Wha's up with you?' Ty jeered. 'Afraid we might start mentioning all that crap you've got up to in your time? Everyone knows you screwed around when you were a curate!'

Nan turned on him. 'Tyrone! Stop it! Leave him alone.'

'If you'll excuse me,' Christopher said, getting up, white-faced, 'I think I should like some fresh air.'

'Chris!' Nan clutched at his sleeve as he passed her. 'Take no notice, he's drunk.'

He ignored her. A few seconds later, the front door slammed.

'It takes more than a couple of glasses of cheap plonk to get me plastered,' Ty said.

'You're forgetting the couple of shorts you had on the way here,' Becky said.

'Calm down, Ty,' Jenny said. 'There's no need to be obnoxious.'

'Thanks, Jen, nice to know you're on my side.' During Christopher's exit, he had finished his third glass of wine, and was reaching out for the bottle to pour a fourth.

Michael stretched across the table and seized the bottle first. 'Stop buggering around,' he said. 'Why should anyone be on your side when you're going on like this? I thought you were trying to make a good impression. For God's sake go and stick your head under a cold tap, and come back and start trying to behave yourself.'

Nan stood up and tried to speak lightly. 'I'd better go and see to the dessert. I'm afraid I forgot to defrost the gateau with Alison coming round, so I thought I'd do some banana fritters - you've always liked them, haven't you, Becky? I've got the oil heating.'

Becky, sitting twisting her paper napkin to shreds in her fingers, seemed not to have heard.

Jenny collected the plates from either side of her, and passed them to Nan's place. Then she sat back tiredly in her chair, and took a deep breath.

Michael put an arm round her, and whispered, 'You OK?'

Jenny eased her hands around the taut skin of her belly and nodded.

Becky finished dismembering her napkin, and brushed the pieces into a neat pile. 'Did you really sleep with Lisa?' she asked Ty.

Ty shrugged. 'She wanted it, little tart.'

'When?'

'I dunno. A few weeks ago. We'd split up at the time, I don't see why you should get uptight about it.'

'Silly me! I was only under the impression we were supposed to be in love, and you were waiting for me to demonstrate my commitment by telling mum and Christopher about us. But no, you were feeling free to fuck around. And then you lie to me about it. I don't think I like you very much. I certainly don't trust you!'

'Fair enough. I'll go.' He stood up unsteadily.

'Don't be stupid. You can't drive like that,' Becky said, trying to grab his arm.

He threw her back in her seat, and lurched towards the door that led from the dining room into the adjoining kitchen.

Nan had been standing at the cooker beside the door. As the argument between Becky and Tyrone developed, she moved into the doorway, one hand still on the handle of the pan of oil gradually coming up to temperature on the hob. Ty pushed rudely past her, and as he jogged her arm, the pan lurched. Oil leapt from it to land over the bare skin of Nan's right hand and arm.

'Fucking hell!' Nan shrieked, jumping backwards to avoid further injury as the pan bounced to the floor and spread its tide of oil across the vinyl.

Ty did not pause to see what had happened. They heard the front door slam behind him.

Jenny was up in an instant, ignoring the bulk of her pregnancy as she went to Nan's aid. 'Cold water,' she said. 'There's no room in the sink, come on, into the bathroom,'

By the time the others caught up with her, she had got Nan's arm submerged in the sink.

'I think you ought to go up to the hospital,' she was saying to Nan. 'It's looking quite nasty.'

'I'll be alright,' Nan began.

'Michael, see if you can find Christopher. He can't have gone far.'
Michael left the house.

'You're shivering. Shall I get you a cardigan?' Becky asked her mother.

'I wouldn't mind.'

Jenny put a hand on Nan's shoulder. A grimace passed across her face.

'Are you OK?' Alison asked.

Jenny nodded. 'Do you think you could find some frozen peas, and a towel, to keep her arm cool while she's in the car?'

Christopher arrived as Jenny was arranging the towels and packs of peas against Nan's arm. He came into the bathroom, and went straight to Nan.

'What's happened? Darling ...?' He hugged his wife gently as Jenny explained.

'I'm well organised, aren't I?' Nan said in a shaky voice. 'If I'm going to have an accident, I make sure I've got a doctor handy.'

Christopher began to lead her towards the front door.

'I'll come, too,' Becky said.

'Did you not see Michael?' Jenny asked Christopher.

'No. I just saw Tyrone leave, and thought I'd come back. Perhaps Michael went the other way. I expect he'll be back soon.'

And then the three of them were gone, and Alison and Jenny were alone.

'I'd better see if I can clear up in the kitchen,' Alison said.

'I'll do the bathroom,' said Jenny. She took a few steps down the hall, and stopped, leaning one hand against the wall for support.

'Are you sure you're alright? ... Jenny?'

Several seconds passed before Jenny replied. 'I think I probably need to get to the hospital, too.'

'The baby?'

'I've been getting a few contractions on and off today, anyway,' Jenny said calmly, 'but they're getting closer together.' She gave a quick smile. 'It's alright, not that close. You won't have to do an emergency delivery.'

'Shall I phone for an ambulance?'

Jenny shook her head. 'Michael should be back any minute.'

An awkward silence fell between them. Alison broke into it: 'I'm sorry about this morning. I shouldn't have burst in on you like that. I wasn't thinking.'

'That's alright. Michael likes to help people. I shouldn't have accused you. It's just this.' She rubbed her belly. 'I didn't really want another one.'

'You'll get used to it. I expect Lyddy will want to help, and Michael's wonderful ...' She caught the glimmer of unease in Jenny's eyes, as if Nan was right, and Jenny could not help but see her as a threat. 'I don't want Michael like that any more, Jenny,' she said. 'I put all that behind me a long time ago. I'd never break anyone's marriage up. And if I was going to, I can assure you it wouldn't be yours. I won't contact Michael again. I won't visit. Not unless *you* ask me to.'

But Jenny looked to have stopped listening. She turned to the wall, and pressed her hands and forehead against it, her eyes shut as she breathed deeply through the pain that tightened her womb.

Above the whish of her breathing, Alison heard the front door open. 'Oh, Michael! Thank God you're back!'

'I went all the way down the hill, but I couldn't ...' Then he saw Jenny, and went to her immediately. 'Is it getting serious? It's all that effort with Nan.'

Jenny straightened up and smiled. 'It's all that effort with you before we came. I warned you.'

Michael put his arm round his wife, and kissed her. 'Come on, I'll take you in.' He began to guide her towards the front door. 'Will you be alright?' he asked Alison, looking back.

'Yes. There's lots of clearing up to do. Let me know when there's any news.'

The door shut behind them.

Alison made her way to the kitchen, and began to restore order. Slowly, she blotted up the pools of oil on the cooker and on the floor, and mopped the surfaces with detergent. Her head and limbs still felt heavy from the wine.

With the kitchen passable, she moved on into the dining room. The silence of the house intensified as she gazed on the abandoned table and the empty chairs askance at the angles at which they had been left when their occupants had risen. Two empty wine bottles, and another two-thirds full, stood alongside a small arrangement of flowers and two tall candles in marbled pottery holders, still burning. The pile of plates Jenny had stacked, the two half-empty serving dishes cluttered with salad, and the scattered cutlery and glasses, formed a stark and understated still life. And nobody left here but herself. She had come for help, and they had all gone.

She sank onto one of the chairs, and leant on the table, head on her hand, staring into the candle flame. No one to comfort her now, no one to ease her way back into St Peter's, only the empty evening hours and an intolerable yearning for her lover. What was he doing now? What was he thinking? She imagined him as she had seen him last night, seated at his desk, trying to lose himself in the participles and paragraphs that might get him through another small space of time, making manageable the hours and days, the weeks and lonely years ahead. Oh, Iain! How could you? I can't bear it.

And you don't have to, whispered his voice inside her. You could give up being a priest, and come to me. Two hours, that's all it would take, and we could be together ... There's no one here to keep you, come back to me, Allie, come back!

Oh, God, she couldn't stand it. She wasn't strong enough any more, not on her own. She leaned forward and blew out the candles, and stood up.

Thirty-two

Alison got as far as the hall, then stopped, assailed by practicalities. Did Nan or Christopher or Becky have keys with them? Should she lock up? Ought she to leave a note, and what could she say? Only this afternoon, she had been telling Nan that even if she gave up her priesthood, she couldn't stay with Iain, and nothing had really changed. There would still be the strains of being a mistress, and always second best, the difficulties if she wanted children with him. What, too, of her own family? Poor little Lukey, and James and Josh: how could she inflict a second major upheaval on them so soon? She'd forced through the first on the grounds that her vocation could not be denied; unfair from their point of view to give that vocation up as precipitately as this.

And impossible for her to live with herself if she did. That was in the end what held her back. She might be a traitor to her faith, her reserves drained until scarcely a mustard seed remained, but it was nonetheless the centre of who she was.

The telephone rang as she retraced her steps to the living room.

'Yes?'

'Only me,' said Michael's excited voice. 'We have a son, perfectly healthy and absolutely beautiful. Edward to the registrar, and Tad to all the rest of us. Jenny sailed through it, and she's feeling fine. You must come and see him tomorrow, before you go. We should be back by mid-morning.'

Alison mumbled a reply, unable to engage with his enthusiasm as much as she ought. 'Do you know how Nan is?'

'Yeah, I saw her just now. She's dopey from having painkillers, and they're keeping her in overnight, but it's not as bad as it could have been, thanks to Jenny. Christopher's staying with her, but Becky's coming back. She's got a key, so you don't need to wait up. I imagine you're staying there, or you can go back to our place if you like - the babysitter's staying the night, but she's probably still up. I'm sorry everything happened at once, just when you needed us.'

294

'That's alright. Thanks for ringing, Michael. Give Jenny my con-gratulations.'

She disentangled herself from the conversation and rang off. The hall was beginning to sway around her, but she dared not go to bed for dread of the dreams that would flood into her mind as soon as she relaxed her guard. She poured herself a glass of wine, switched on the television for company, and lowered herself into Nan's wicker rocking chair. She nodded to and fro with her wine swilling round the glass, trying not to think.

She must have dozed, for she came back to consciousness with a start when Becky came into the living room at midnight.

'Hello, you still up?' Becky said, throwing herself down onto the sofa.

'I didn't feel like bed,' Alison said. She stared bleary-eyed at her glass, still a quarter full, and drained the contents.

'I feel awful,' Becky said. 'Like it's all my fault for bringing Ty. I had no idea he'd get that aggressive.'

'It was an accident.'

'He could have stopped to find out whether she was hurt. And fucking Lisa too! How would he feel if I'd gone with someone else the minute he walked out?'

'What will you do? Will you kick him out?'

'I don't know. Wait and see if he comes crawling back, and see how I feel. What about you?'

'I don't have a choice. Iain says he can't leave his wife unless she agrees to it, and even if he did I couldn't marry him and stay in the church, so that's the end of the story. Yet again Alison Thompson falls for a married man with a crazy wife in his bloody attic.' She blinked back tears. 'I'm a mess. I think I'd better find a bed.'

The nightmare of loss woke Alison with the sky still dark beyond the curtains. She'd given birth to Luke all over again, and stretched to take him in her arms, but Nan and Christopher had appeared and plucked him from her to pass him to Jenny. 'He's not yours ... not yours ...' She was crying when she woke, and it took her some minutes to realise it was only a dream. A nightmare, like the one in which Iain refused to leave his wife, or the oil seared Nan's skin. She reached out to feel for her watch beside the bed, but met only the surface of an unfamiliar wall. Slowly the world came into focus. She was in the bed that had been made up for Ty, while

Becky appropriated her mother's bed across the landing. There had been a birth, there had been an accident, and Iain's deception was unbearably real.

'No!' The word was torn from her to echo round the darkened room. Tears flooded from her as she howled with abandon into her pillows, ceasing only when she was exhausted. But nothing had changed, and there were still three hours left until morning.

The next morning, Becky appeared at eight to set a mug of tea on the floor beside Alison before departing for London. Alison, her head pounding, dragged herself out of bed to search for some pills to swallow with her tea, and went back to lean against her pillows while the drug did its work. Alone in Nan's house again, this time with the day ahead of her. She showered and dressed. Her own clothes had been worn since Thursday, so she was grateful that Becky had thoughtfully left some clean underwear and a black ribbed top for her in the bathroom. She dried her hair, clipped it back, and made up her face, but nothing disguised the redness of her eyes and the lines she'd gained. Breakfast next: a piece of toast and a mug of coffee, and then she must decide what to do.

Pausing in the hall, she noticed that the door to Christopher's study stood ajar. She put her head inside, and her attention was caught by the arrangement in the corner of the room, the candles and crucifix on a small shelf over a prie-dieux. Scarcely knowing what she did, she went in and lit the candles, then knelt down on the wooden ledge to bury her head upon her hands.

Minutes later, the sound of the front door disturbed her. Aware of a presence in the doorway, she turned. Christopher Ridgefield stood watching her, his face pale and lined, his short hair dishevelled.

'I'm sorry ...'

'Carry on,' he said.

Alison got up. 'I'd finished anyway. I've nothing more to say. I'm sorry about trespassing.' She blew the candles out.

Christopher sat down on the low chair inside the door. 'That's what it's here for.'

'How's Nan?'

'In pain, but they think her arm should heal on its own, without a skin graft. She'll be out later today.'

'Good. Well, I suppose I'd better be off.'

'Where are you going?'

She shrugged. 'I don't know. Nan was going to talk to Nigel, but now ...'

'Sit down, Alison, I'd like to talk to you.'

Summoned by the Headteacher. She wasn't sure she could cope with Christopher Ridgefield in authoritarian mode when she had so much to confess.

'You haven't got time, not now,' she said, edging nearer to the door. 'Anyway, I'm not your responsibility.'

'Ah, but you are. It's not going to be public until next week, so keep it quiet, but I'm going to be your bishop. I've accepted the Wellesley post.' He indicated the chair next to his. 'So sit down and let me see how I can help.'

'What's the point? I've completely screwed up.'

'It's not your fault that your parish situation has been difficult.'

Alison sank into the chair. 'It is my fault how I've coped with it. I didn't have to have an affair with a married man. I didn't have to let everyone down. I didn't have to snap and end up screaming and shouting at them all.'

'The affair was with Iain Sutherland?'

Alison nodded. 'Only I didn't know he was married.'

'He seemed a very pleasant man, very plausible.'

'All of that, but it's no excuse, is it? And now half the parish knows, half the PCC, anyway, and I don't see how I can ever go back.'

'I made a complete balls-up in my first curacy, you know,' said Christopher frankly. 'As Tyrone likes to remind everyone at every opportunity. Seducing a married parishioner. It was all hushed up, and I was moved rapidly on somewhere where the youngest female member of the congregation was eighty-seven.' He smiled. 'I behaved with perfect propriety for the next twenty years, until I met Nan, anyway. But you see, Alison, I find myself wondering if that was such a good idea. What would have happened if I'd stayed in my first parish, and been forced to face up to what I'd done? Perhaps having to work with people who knew all about my imperfections would have taught me some humility. Maybe I wouldn't have developed such exclusive ideas about priesthood.' He ran a hand through his hair, dishevelling it even more. 'What do you suppose we teach people, if we hush things up, and move clergy on the minute they show they're human? You're repentant, and you'll learn from it, that's what's important. Suppose you go back, and say "Sorry. I was under pressure and I was lonely. I let things go further than I should have done. The relationship's over, and I want to ask your forgiveness." I'm sure they'd respond to that. They have a very high opinion of the work you've done.'

'Hardly! They never tire of telling me I'm not a patch on Father Mark.'

'Well of course. Every vicar is always a failure compared to their predecessor. I'm quite prepared for Bishop Ronald to be seen as a saint by the time I arrive.'

Alison gave a sour smile. 'But Mark really was gifted.'

'Yes, true, but he had to leave after a couple of years, because it got too much for him.'

'They said he left because he was so wonderful he was head-hunted into a brilliant job.'

'That's how he explained it to them. Father Nigel and the other clergy in your chapter knew the truth. Mark used to have awful battles with the organist blocking everything he tried to do with the music. It's not an easy parish, we knew that when we sent you there. But we all feel you have a great many abilities, and Nigel is an excellent trainer. It would have worked well if he'd not been ill.'

Alison shook her head in weary disbelief. 'It might have helped if someone had told me.'

'They wouldn't want to scare you.'

'So it's not just me being a disaster?'

'No. You were wrong to have a relationship with Iain, and foolish not to ask for help from the right people. But then, I suspect one of your troubles is that people do think you're very able, so they assume you can manage.'

'They did ask, but I couldn't bring myself to confess I wasn't coping. It would have felt like letting the side down. It's worse now, of course. I'll have confirmed everyone's worst prejudices about female clergy.'

'Not if you go back and prove them wrong. There'll be some who'll say you're not fit to be a priest, but they're mistaken. You'll be a much better priest because you know you're fallible, yet you're prepared to put things right.'

'But you don't believe I am a priest.'

'A minister, then, I'm happy to say you're that. I do believe women like you and Nan have an enormous contribution to make.' He smiled wryly. 'That's why I'm being risked in Wellesley. And I don't want to start out by losing one of my most able curates.'

'They might throw me out. That's probably what my rural dean will recommend.'

'I'll have a word with him. And with Nigel. I'll remind them how much you've got to offer.'

'I wouldn't have too much faith in me if I were you. All I want to do at the moment is to run away.'

'But you won't. You'll be brave. You'll go back and face them, and it'll be the hardest thing you've ever done in your life, but you'll do it. You're not a quitter.'

Alison met his eyes, drawing strength from the knowledge of his unexpected support for her. She stood up.

'I might as well get it over with, if I'm going. They were going to be meeting about me this morning. I shall have to try to explain ... Oh, I've let everyone down so badly. They believed in me ...'

'They're right to. You have done a good job - look at your festival, for example. You've slipped up in one part of your life, and you're ready to put things right.' Christopher had stood when she got up. He held out his hand, and clasped hers in it. 'As long as things really are over with Iain.'

She swallowed, and nodded. 'I explained to him, even if he got divorced tomorrow, I couldn't take up with him again. Not if I was the one who'd broken his marriage up. Even if it hadn't been a real marriage for years before I appeared. Could I?'

She looked beseechingly into Christopher's face.

'No. No, I don't think so.'

'Not ever?'

He let go of her hand. 'I don't know about the future, Alison. Perhaps it isn't quite the usual case, but there'd still be a lot of hard questions to answer if he were free and you were to want to see him again. You have to accept it's over.'

Alison left Christopher making himself breakfast, and set out to walk to Michael's house to collect her car for the journey home. Home. She'd do it. Face down the betrayal in the eyes of Ella and Bunty, of Brian and Terry, Sandy, and Nigel: you should have told us if it was all getting too much; you should have told us how things were with Iain. There never seemed to be an opportunity. I was scared you'd throw me out if you knew the truth ... they weren't really valid excuses, whoever made them. Maybe they would ask her to leave, despite Christopher. Bunty and Terry might even now be leading the campaign to oust her, unworthy as she was. Or maybe they'd be magnanimous, which would be worse. Lord preserve me from the love of my enemies. No, life would probably carry on as normal, but with everyone keeping a close eye on her. There was plenty of work to do, even if Nigel was better: the parish, the school, another festival to organise. Next year, if she got that far, it would be time to think about moving on, away from the memories. She couldn't envisage that future Alison, one who would enjoy making decisions about her future, who would have enthusiastic visions about ministry, who might care how she looked, or might, post-divorce, respond to a different man taking an interest in her. She shuddered at the thought. A man watching his dog squat on the grass of the verge glanced at her curiously. Perhaps she ought to do what Josh had always wanted, and buy a dog. That would provide a distraction. Something to snuggle up to at night, a patient body to cry on. An excuse for walks, for getting away from everything.

'I think we should get a puppy,' Alison told the boys on Sunday as they sat round the kitchen table having tea before evensong.

Josh's face lit up. 'Can I choose it?'

'It'd better not shit all over the lawn,' James said.

He'd stayed around the house much more the last couple of days, being eminently helpful. They'd all clung in their different ways, sensing her frailty.

'I want a Rotten Whiler,' Luke stated firmly.

Alison laughed. 'How do you know about Rottweilers?'

The word brought Iain back again ... 'Let me tell you about this chap I came across in a school recently - I won't say where - who used to put his Rottweiler in charge of detention.'

'I don't believe you.'

'Aye, it's true. If I wanted to be indiscreet, there's all sorts of things I could tell you.'

'Be indiscreet,' she'd laughed, sliding her hand into his ...

He never was, not really, he stuck to what he thought was right in everything except the one place where it mattered. Oh God, was there any subject that wouldn't bring him to mind? Any part of her life that wouldn't have connections? They'd talked about everything, his presence clung to her home and the school. Every time the telephone rang late at night, every time she heard of OFSTED, or saw pictures of Rome ... a bereavement to be lived through, with the difference being that he was still alive somewhere, living, breathing, longing for her, just as she was consumed by longing for him. She'd see news of him, perhaps pictures of him, when she flicked through the *Times Educational Supplement* in the school common room, educational consultant Iain Sutherland putting other people's worlds to rights as he had once promised to right hers ... Tears blurred the plate in front of her.

'Mum? What's the matter? Don't cry.' Josh looked anxiously at her.

She blinked the tears away rapidly. 'You mustn't mind me.'

She pushed her half-eaten pizza aside, and picked up her mug of tea. She must pull herself together, she had evensong to lead, with Terry subdued and helpful on the organ and the congregation wary after her limited public confession before that morning's Eucharist. There would be rumours, she would have to fight to win back the trust she had broken, but she was committed to it now.

The boys had finished eating. Luke wriggled down from the table. Josh followed him out of the kitchen.

James stood up. She was aware of him hovering behind her.

'You sure you're OK?' he asked abruptly.

She turned to look up at him. 'I will be. It may take a while, but I will be. Thanks for asking.'

He gave her a quick smile. The door swung shut behind him, and she was on her own.

Carol placed a mug of coffee in front of Iain and rubbed his shoulder lightly. 'Don't work too hard, you'll make yourself ill. I know you're upset now, but you will get over it. You always do.'

He offered no response, and she crept away. In truth he'd sat at his desk for the best part of the day without doing anything very much except look at the photograph of Alison he kept there, unable to bear the thought of removing it, however much it contributed to his despair.

'Is that the lady you want instead of mummy?' Hetty had asked, visiting his study that afternoon to ask his opinion of her latest work of art.

'As well as,' he'd said, for her sake.

'She's very pretty.'

'Yes.'

'Is she coming back?'

'No. No, Hetty, she's not.'

'Don't be sad. You can have my picture. It'll cheer you up.'

There's no cure for this, little girl. No cure at all. Even had Carol not resisted his repeated requests for his freedom, Allie's profession came between them.

He picked up his telephone yet again, her number tingling on his fingers, as familiar to them as their own print: Allie, darling, I have to speak to you. Please, can't we meet? I'm missing you so much. I love you. Surely there's something we can work out? We could be friends, I could at least phone you sometimes, but I can't bear you cutting me out permanently.

There was no point. Nothing had changed. He had nothing to offer her. His own responsibilities and the requirements of her vocation loomed too large. Neither could countenance the compromises any resolution would demand of them, and so the parting had to be final.

Nevertheless he sat for a long time weighing the phone in his hand, rehearsing what he might say when he heard her voice, knowing that his words would be indecipherable through the tears that were rising to mist his glasses. Sat until he knew the call must remain unmade; whereupon he put the phone down to rock quietly on his desk, and reached down to the floor to pick up the large box that held the papers for his next inspection.

Another school. Any school. A school like any other. A ream of paper to digest. For a period of weeks he would get to know it, to name another staff, another Chair of Governors, another set of students. Then he would forget, let it slide from his memory as they all did eventually. What would he remember of Wellesley High a year from now, except perhaps the whitewashed lines of the car park in which a woman in a black coat and red gloves had sworn ineffectually at her car; except perhaps the quiet of a garden in which a woman's smile had once provoked a fall from grace?

A physical aching for her tore at him again ... Never to see her? Never to have her, warm and naked, possessing his senses?

Oh God ...

Oh Allie ...

He shook his head, turning her picture to lie face down on his desk as, ruthlessly striving to drive her from his mind, he drew the top set of papers towards him, and went back to work.

The End